The Green Muse

Also by Jessie Prichard Hunter

Blood Music
One, Two, Buckle My Shoe

The Green Muse

An Edouard Mas Novel

JESSIE PRICHARD HUNTER

WITNESS
IMPULSE

An Imprint of HarperCollins Publishers

To David
For David knows what
And David knows why

She used to place her pretty arms about my neck, draw me to her, and laying her cheek to mine, murmur with her lips near my ear, "Dearest, your little heart is wounded; think me not cruel because I obey the irresistible law of my strength and weakness; if your dear heart is wounded, my wild heart bleeds with yours. In the rapture of my enormous humiliation I live in your warm life, and you shall die—die, —sweetly die—into —mine. I cannot help it; as I draw near to you, you, in your turn, will draw near to others, and learn the rapture of that cruelty, which yet is love; so, for a while, seek to know no more of me and mine, but trust me with all your loving spirit."

J. SHERIDAN LeFANU
CARMILLA

Chapter 1

Edouard

THIS MORNING I was called upon to photograph the dead again.

The messenger boy came at five-thirty. His name is Martin. I gave him a few sous: Martin works hard for his sous, running errands all over Paris for the Prefecture of Police.

I sent the lad off and packed up my camera and plates; I took the omnibus to the rue Mazarine, in the Ninth Arrondissement. The building, number 21, proved to be a dreary four-story tenement. Police Captain Bezier was there; he led me around to the back courtyard. The morning sky with its huge racing clouds seemed far away. The windows no longer went up in straight lines but listed as though the whole building were a rocking ship. There was an empty wheelbarrow; there was a tunnel leading to the front of the building; there were two dirty awnings; there was offal on the ground.

Of course a crime scene cannot be photographed at night, but the dead can wait till morning. It is all the same to them. I change nothing, other than to cover a naked body. We must preserve the setting quite exactly as we find it but a sheet disturbs nothing, and I cannot bear that the dead be subjected to indignity.

Capt. Bezier motioned me to a patch of darkness under one of the awnings. Night had not left it yet. A woman lay there.

I checked the camera's register to see if the magazine was full: eighteen plates. It was just a habit, a necessary part of the ritual; I have never gone out on a job with an unloaded camera. The night before, I had treated cotton papers with albumen and sodium chloride, dried them, and dipped them in a solution part silver nitrate, part water, to render the paper sensitive; I had again dried the paper, then fixed it carefully against the glass plates that it might be ready for my camera when I awoke. There is always a stack of newly treated plates in my darkroom, as I never know when I may be called upon. I am naturally in need of but little sleep; sometimes I think that the city wakes me early, like a lover, because she knows that there is so much each day to be seen and experienced together. And sometimes I awaken so refreshed, so eager, that I almost feel I might indeed have been kissed awake by this city I love so much.

But now I readied myself to kneel in foul semidarkness and see the unbearable.

"Have you questioned the tenants?" I asked the captain.

"No," said Capt. Bezier. "There will be time for that. It's not likely to be someone from the building, anyway. Why leave her here to be found?"

The captain is something of an ass.

I ran my right hand up and down the pebble-grained leather of the side of my camera box, once, as I raised it to my eye: another facet of the ritual. I walked around the body, looking at the corpse through my lens. Through the round aperture, everything recedes except sight, and you are alone with the image before you.

And yet the image is made distant, merely a collection of lines and angles of light. This distance is necessary if I am not to be overwhelmed by pity, anger, and disgust. For my day-to-day existence I work part-time in a fashionable studio where tintypes are turned out as though they were loaves of bread. I also make sentimental portraits of those who die in their beds, either peacefully or after long illnesses. Sometimes I photograph them before they die, that the family might having a living subject for their memento instead of a dead one. For the police I record the scenes of murders. Sometimes, if the victim is unknown or well-known, my photographs are put up on flyers all over the city. More commonly they are filed with the police and used later, as a tool to incriminate the murderer.

I stooped to capture the image before me.

The woman was young; she was lying on her back with her hands folded over her heart, and her head was turned away from my camera. She was wearing a black bolero jacket and a sky-blue silk waist; her skirt was dove-gray. Her shoes were of leather too soft for these streets. It is difficult not to put a story to the posture, clothing, and obvious social standing of the dead: This woman did not belong here.

I took a shot; then I lifted the back of the camera and held it at the proper angle to let the exposed slide drop down from the magazine so that the next slide would be before the lens. I do not always like my job. The simple, mechanical tasks associated with it soothe me and enable me to maintain both composure and a seeming objectivity in even the most hideous of circumstances. I moved slowly around the side of the body. The woman's hair was loosed from its pins and flowed in a yellow cascade across the dirty ground. There was blood in it.

"The identity of the victim gives us the identity of the killer," Capt. Bezier said. He said that every time.

There was blood on her dress, on her folded hands. I did not want to see her face. I knelt by her side and focused my lens on her neck, which had been severed. The blood there was dull and clotted, and the wound looked like nothing more than a cut of meat.

"—not a gentlewoman," Capt. Bezier was saying. "A midinette, a shopgirl. A night of drinking, an argument with her boyfriend. It is always the same story."

My hand trembled, but I kept my silence. Her long, curved fingers were not marred by the stings of the sewing needle or the calluses of the shopkeeper. She was not as thin as the midinettes, who have only a snack instead of a full midi lunch. She was not a member of the upper classes, that much was clear by her manner of dress and by the short lavender glove I noticed beneath her left hip and pointed out to the captain. Ladies of the upper classes wear gloves that reach to the elbow and are almost always of white kid.

I prepared myself to see her face. Her dress was neither rich nor poor; perhaps she could afford a maid, and that is why her hands were unmarred; perhaps she had children at home even now.

Capt. Bezier picked up the glove and spanked it against his thigh to dust it off.

"Very fashionable," he said shortly. He brings his prejudices to his job. He does not approve of fashionable women unless they are of the upper classes; he will make assumptions about their morals from the cut of their gloves.

THE GREEN MUSE 5

I stepped around the blood that had gathered at her neck. She had not been dead when her killer brought her here. I knelt again. I moved her hair away from her face. She had been beautiful in life; she was not beautiful in death. Her features were very fine, indicating a lively temperament; her forehead high and white, a sign of firm yet maidenly intelligence; the space between her nose and mouth was somewhat large, and the dint was so faint as to be nonexistent—the —angels had not touched her there with their fingers that she forget heaven—what —visions had she had while she was alive? She did not look as though she were seeing heaven now. Her eyes were wide with evident horror, her mouth contorted with fear. But from behind my lens I was reassured. Her agony was spurious, nothing more than the effects of rigor mortis. It was death that had contorted her pretty features into a grotesque mask. There was no way to tell what had been on her face at the moment of her death—fear, —resignation, fury? In a few more hours her hands, which lay so prayerlike now, would be trying to claw their way into her heart. And within less than thirty-six hours all of these effects would soften and disappear, leaving her once again unembattled.

I stroked my beard, which is gingery and sharpens to a point in my hand. With my goatee and mustache I look like any young man of my station, although perhaps somewhat more fair. I have a photographer's eye, made more noticeable for being exceedingly pale blue: I must be careful not to appear always to stare. My features are quite regular, which would seem to indicate a moderate, even modest, temperament. There is no indication of the passion I feel for my work.

Capt. Bezier had gone over the body and found no identification, and surely a woman dressed as she was did not live in this sordid tenement.

"We will begin questioning the tenants shortly," he said.

No one will have seen or heard anything. No one ever does.

Why here? I wondered as I dropped the second-to-last slide into the tray. Perhaps the courtyard was a piece of the puzzle. Perhaps not. I stepped back to take in the entire scene: the awning, the piles of dirty clothing and human waste lying behind the body, the body itself, which seems to float in the early morning light.

"Thank you, Edouard," said the captain. "I do not know what we would do without your work. The state of the body at death is often what turns the jury toward conviction. And, of course, we will pass the photographs out among the various police precincts, to see if any of our contacts recognize the lady."

"They will not recognize her," I said, closing my camera with a satisfying click.

"And why not, Edouard?" Capt. Bezier thinks I overstep my bounds. I do although all I do is tell him what my camera shows.

"Because your contacts are all among the criminal class, and I would be surprised if this unfortunate young woman had any such connections."

"Ah, Edouard, you are such a sentimental young man! A becoming figure, an abundance of pretty hair, and you cannot believe that a woman could have contact with my criminals! It is a good thing you are not a detective, young man—you —are far too idealistic. This woman could be a whore, have you thought of that?"

"She is not dressed as well as a whore," I said shortly, then turned and busied myself with my equipment. The entire equation was there in the foul-smelling tenement courtyard on that drab spring morning, although I did not yet know the answer.

None of them can speak. I am their voice.

You will no doubt see them in the Morgue. But they do not tell their stories there, as they tell them to my camera. In the Morgue the world sees only their empty husks. The dandies of Paris who go to see the latest morsel of flesh are dupes to their own desire. The dead show their secrets to me. They show nothing to the crowds: Even most of death agonies have faded and altered by the time the bodies are transported. The slightest movement displaces the original expression of death. I wish it softened it. Sometimes I think of the one among the dandies and curiosity seekers who may sincerely be looking for a lost loved one, and both fears and hopes to find her at the Morgue. Of the one who stands waiting his turn on the queue, not wanting to see, cursing sight that it can bring him to this. It is my job to look at things no one else wants to. But I cannot not touch the bodies. I have been asked, as I pack away my photographic equipment, if I would be willing to lend a hand; and I've been curt in my refusal. I could not violate these corpses that so lately were animate souls, I cannot move limbs that have no more volition, cannot support a head or back, that the body be taken where no living person ever lies.

"Captain Bezier, this young woman was not yet dead when she was laid here. And yet there is a trail of blood, so she must have been wounded elsewhere and killed here." My voice was flat, as though I did not care. I cared. She was evidently"—I wanted to say, obviously—"brought here from another location. If I were you, I would look toward the tenements within a quarter-mile radius. Perhaps she was on her way home late, after dinner with friends. She should not have been walking alone after dark, but perhaps she felt herself emancipated, and not in need of an escort. Perhaps she found the wrong sort of escort. But I will tell you this: that she was left with her hands thus folded at her breast indicates a reverence for life or for death."

"Oh, Edouard, you are such a fool!" Capt. Bezier said complacently. "Always I have to hear your theories. It is true that you have sometimes been right in the past. But you let your poetic imagination rule your intelligence. Leave police work to the police, young man."

He would, of course, take careful heed of what I had I said. But he would take blustery credit, too, for any information he gleaned from me.

"I am done here," I said brusquely. I was not irritated by Capt. Bezier, any more than I was intimidated. But I was done with the dead. High above the listing tenement the wide sky of Paris awaited, the day awaited, and I was hungry for the day. I glanced once more toward the young woman who had not seen this day come. And turned away. Later, in the quiet of the darkroom, I would see her again.

And she would tell me her story.

Chapter 2

Charles

"LET US GO to the Morgue and see if there are any pretty corpses today," said Theo one early spring morning, handling the fire irons deftly but with some agitation. The fire, which we had started before breakfast, was almost out, giving the room an enticing chill that makes a man long for a challenge.

"Charles and I went three days ago," said Leonard, who was spooning too much compote on his bread. "There won't be any good ones today, Theo, it's only Thursday. You know the really good ones come in over the weekend."

The Paris Morgue is all the rage, listed in all the guidebooks. Tout le monde goes there.

"It is almost the dawn of a new century, Charles," Leonard sometimes says to me. Chiding, perhaps. Sardonic. I am heartily tired of this new century that had not yet even arrived. It is an age of miracles. Travel is miraculous, and communication, and medicine, and science. We sped on wheels swifter than the gods', and time annihilates space; we speak here and are heard elsewhere almost simultaneously, and once again space is leapt over, this time by thought. The body has become practically superfluous. We are in the midst of miracles, on the verge of great things. Perhaps one day we will even overcome death, and I will have nothing left to care about.

I and my two companions share rooms and attend law-school lectures. We live in the usual student dishabille: books, papers, plaster busts in the Renaissance style, an old female concierge who provides lukewarm café au lait and buttered bread for breakfast. Theo never attends lectures; he spends the money his mother sends on liquor and nights at unspeakable places. Leonard grew up on a farm in the Camargue. He worked for several years as a tailor to earn the money to come to Paris and study law. Theo smokes Turkish cigarettes for his asthma and makes insinuating remarks. Leonard has all the low cunning of a self-made man. He likes to think that he is more sophisticated than the rest of us; but he is only older.

We take our dinners on the boulevards. We take young ladies walking in the countryside. We visit the Morgue two or three times weekly. We are ordinary young men.

Theo was lighting his pipe, an intricate ritual designed purely for show.

"You can't wear that cravat today," I said to Leonard. "You wore it last time. If Theo's got to drag us to that wretched place again, at least don't disgrace yourself by your attire."

"Nor you by your attitude, Charles," he said lightly, flicking his cravat at me before tossing it on the sofa. Leonard knew me rather better than I would have liked.

"Tea, cousin?" I asked Theo, who could at least be counted on not to understand too much.

"Don't be disdainful," Leonard said. "It does not cover your desire."

But at least he didn't know what it was I desired.

For young men with education and money, there are many things to do in Paris. Pleasant things. Cheap or posh clubs where women dance, diaphanous onstage before us, plump like partridges, and gleaming white. Offered up to us to touch with our eyes. Or perhaps more intimately, for a price: like partridges.

I do not much care for what I can only touch. If one of them were mine, it would perhaps be different: if one that I possessed were to show her body to all Paris. But I have not had luck. They want roses. And trips to the country, and hats, and chocolate. From girls like that, I just want flesh.

I can strike that kind of bargain too, of course. I don't even have to see their faces. But then only they know, and what conquest is that? One can hardly say, *She is mine; she does me no credit, she is any man's.*

There are places to do other things. Eat, drink, talk politics, and play cards. Watch the shopgirls go by at lunchtime, clutching sausages from the cookshops, or radishes or shrimps; they wear paper flowers on their bosoms, wire and purple tissue paper and false green leaves that quiver slightly as they breathe.

There is liquor everywhere, and the opera, and the Louvre, and the society of young men of good character. These things do interest me, but not enough. Young men of my class are all the same. Connoisseurs and dilettantes at once, experts at opinion only. We do study. We go to our lectures at the Panthéon. We sit in drafty large rooms and listen to old men talk. What I have learned most well is what kind of old man I do not want to be. I am supposed to crave excitement—I am young—well and good. But I want to leave behind me more than words in books, words in court records. I would have another kind of canvas.

Liquor is more interesting. Or rather, absinthe. In too great quantities absinthe strangles the will; we have all seen the stupid clouded eyes of the habitual absinthe drinker. The soporific effects of the drug can be avoided, but there remains the risk of slavery: It tantalizes me to see those who have capitulated. Peace like chains around their necks, oblivion their heaven.

I drink enough to quiet my nerves. They tighten and stretch, but I will not be ruled by them. Absinthe dampens some fires while stoking others. I feel I might do anything. Nerves are primarily what keep men moral, I think; which is to say, fear. When I drink absinthe I am no longer frightening to myself. Nor to others, because it made me gentle.

Theo declined tea, and somebody brought out absinthe. A small glass for each of us, sugar and spoons. Absinthe is properly drunk with a cube of sugar balanced over the glass on a slotted spoon. First the green liquor is poured into the glass. Then ice-cold water is dripped over the sugar, dissolving it into the vivid green liquor until it acquires a yellow-ochre opalescence. Then the process is repeated twice more. The clank of the spoon and the granular sugar on the tongue are as much part of the experience as is the sudden hot calm when the fluid hits the stomach. I paid careful attention to my elaborate ritual; each man has his own way of doing things.

The one glass was sufficient. Its effects helped soothe the horrible excitement building up in my stomach.

The Morgue.

The most extraordinary pleasures are to be had there. There is a wall made of glass. The living stand on one side, staring; the other side is occupied by the dead. Thousands of people come to the Morgue in a week's time. Some of us come again and again. We recognize one another underneath the blank, artificial lights.

Leonard is in love with the Morgue. The light; the uniformed policemen directing the crowd. The crowd! Forty thousand in one day: that was when they were showing La Femme Coupée en Morceaux. The Lady Cut in Pieces. Sliced in half, cleanly, they say. She lay on a slanted wooden board, her nakedness draped discreetly from neck to foot, and nobody knew her name. We came, Leonard and Theo and I, to do our civic duty. To give a name to the charming dead. And she was charming, the Lady Cut in Pieces. After three days went by without identification, a wax mold was made of her head. It reclined for many weeks atop a sheet-draped dummy waiting for all Paris to do its civic duty.

But the lady was never identified. The newspapers never did reveal the exact manner of her death. Leonard went to see her every day for two weeks. He had dark slashes under his eyes. I believe he dreamed about her.

Perhaps the Morgue needs introduction. Since the early part of the last century the Paris Morgue has been open to the public. For a time it lay in the shadow of Nôtre Dame, with a small, meshed window through which to look, and room beyond for one corpse, which must have been lonely. (Theo leans over my shoulder to see what I am writing. Theo sees smut in the most innocent statement, and he eats too much red meat. It makes him bilious.) The corpse lay in a leather apron with a tap of cold water running over its head for as long as it took to be identified. But there was no allure to that.

Then the Morgue was moved, for a time, to the Ile St. Louis. Anyone traveling there would likely end up a guest at the very place he sought. No one came to the Morgue when it was in that slum. Bodies went unclaimed. Is there a superstition that an unclaimed body means an unclaimed soul? Absinthe makes my eyes grow dim, and I become capable of believing anything. (Leonard has just tapped my wrist with his cane: It is time to go.)

The Morgue is once again in the shadow of Our Lady, on the Quai Nôtre Dame. When a man or woman is found dead, by natural means or foul, and cannot be identified, the body is placed on display at the Morgue, and Paris is invited to come and stare.

It is an effective ploy. There are many who cloak desire in virtue, many who sleep well at night after having done their civic duty. And there are those who simply love the dead. Leonard is one of those. Theo loves spectacle. I am merely an observer, of the living as well as the dead. Because the dead, however charming, are without volition. It is the living who present a challenge. Vice is a challenge to me. I make my own rules, and I do not break them.

The streets were crowded and wet when we left our apartments. We did not call for a carriage, preferring instead the jostle of the crowd. That was one of Leonard's affectations, that he enjoyed contact with the common people. Theo merely liked variety. He was always ready for conquest. My thoughts were ahead of us, already searching the crowds for her face.

The others didn't know about her. The lines were long that day, three people deep and stretching three blocks down the river from the Morgue door. But I found her. I always found her. How beautiful she looked that morning! She wore a halo of mist outside the door. The Morgue was quite busy, for a Thursday. The weather was queer, with a low sky, and cold; the crooked streets behind the cathedral would be dusky by mid-afternoon. She stood on the line, which snaked ahead of us some five hundred feet. She carried a newspaper and wore a hat that wasn't suited to the weather. I was nine people behind her, trying to distance myself from Theo's antics: He would cry out, and read *Le Journal Illustré* aloud, interrupting himself with vulgar asides.

"The body of a fashionably dressed gentleman was found yesterday evening in the Bois de Boulogne"—indeed, was he fashionably dressed? Let us know more. "The man was attired entirely in black and adorned with a red cravat. A green carnation was found next to the body!" Why, we know what that means, don't we! Theo considered himself a member of the Green Carnation Society. His amours were of no interest to me, but he shouted his indiscretions where a whisper would more than suffice. I did not want her to see me, and if Theo did not stop his buffoonery she would turn.

I grabbed his arm.

"Shut up," I said.

Theo sulked, rubbing his arm. I looked at her. I could see only her cheek and the line of her jaw. She was excited, flushed, with stray dampened wisps of hair escaping her chignon. There would be fine white hairs at the base of her neck, fine hair on her arms. I hadn't seen these things, of course; one benefit of these long queues was that they gave me time to dream.

I resolved to speak to her that day. The newspapers spoke of regulars. I had heard gossip about the Morgue set. If it was shameful to be in her company, then I was a willing slave to shame.

She was young, she was small, she had blonde hair. How little that means, what little justice it does her. She had in her eyes the look of a trapped and wild thing; that is more to the point. Or of passion constrained. If she took off her hat the simple wind at the nape of her neck might drive her to ecstasy.

I would have liked another glass of absinthe, another wave of that heady voluptuousness that was at once familiar and unexpected. She turned around at looked at Theo, quite directly.

He was telling Leonard a story: "—entered the burial vault of his wife a year after her death, to view what remained of his great love."

She smiled; she was amused.

Quite suddenly the queue began to move. Her smile flashed and disappeared, and I turned in anger and slapped Theo on the arm, hard. When I looked again she was gone.

Leonard looked up from *Le Journal Illustré* he had taken from Theo to say, "Charles, have you—?" She had only moved to one of the vendors lining the avenue: a slice of coconut. She could have chosen oranges or cookies, she could have been stepping to the street to check the length of the queue.

"Your gentleman is here today, Theo," Leonard drawled. "The newspaper says he was unidentified."

She stood back in her place with her head turned half toward me, delicately scraping her bottom teeth against the rough skin of her coconut. I could feel her teeth. She closed her mouth on the coarse sweet, and Theo said, "Did anyone think to bring along any liquors? Charles is looking positively spectral. Charles"—with real consternation—"you've made your lip bleed."

I found I'd bought a small paper sack of orange peel. Having stepped away from the crowd to see her more easily, although I had no pretext for doing so. I did not like orange peel, but I knew, inhaling the sweet, dry smell while I look at her, that for me the smell of orange peel would always be inextricably mixed with the way the wind and her hair look. I wanted to sprinkle orange water in her hair, across her face, her mouth.

"The papers always say he looks to be of dubious reputation," Leonard said.

"Exactly how," asked Theo, having forgotten me and my bloody mouth, "does a dead countenance of a dubious gentleman differ from that of an equally dead gentleman of quality?"

She was listening, smiling, and the coconut had made her lips wet. They looked swollen.

"Is this a philosophical question, dear Theo," Leonard was asking, "or the setting up of some dreadful joke?"

Theo amused her. But she'd not yet noticed me. I had been coming to the Morgue for six months, and she was always there. She preferred coconuts to oranges. She had two cloaks, a black and a burgundy. She was always alone. Sometimes she brought a sandwich of cucumber and sliced meat and butter. I never saw her speak to anyone. Twice she had caught my stare; twice I have bowed my head in greeting; twice her brows have twitched and her eyelids swept her gaze out of sight. If she recognized me now she gave no sign.

I craved the bitter, almost unbearable taste of absinthe now, which rested unsugared in a silver flask in my inside coat pocket. But Theo was greedy, and I would have it for myself.

There was a family of six in front of us, obviously up from the country, the Morgue being a standard listing in any Cook's tour of Paris. Listed between the Tuilleries gardens and Nôtre Dame.

Only the husband seemed to be embarrassed by his surroundings. He kept stepping away from the queue and back to it, too acutely aware of its destination. The wife's eyes were shining, and the four children, two boys and two girls between the ages of six and fourteen, were wild with anticipation. The oldest boy whispered in the six-year-old's ear, making her cry. The wife wore a long white apron and a white cap, and carried a basket filled with greens. The children carried cooked shrimps and sausage in greasy paper from the cookshop on the corner. The father gulped his beer and did not wipe the foam from his mouth. The older daughter caught my eye. She simpered, as if I would even hold her gaze. She flushed and took a furious bite of her sausage.

And with a lurch the queue began to move. The women screamed coyly, and the men took the opportunity to clutch their arms, to touch their waists. But her expression did not change even as the press of the crowd grew. She was sure-footed and walked as though she were the only one there. I followed her hat. I was tempted again by the warm green in my vest pocket; Leonard caught my eye, and we both began to laugh. When she turned again it was toward my wide smile.

A flicker of amusement passed over her lips, and she walked into the Morgue smiling.

Chapter 3

Edouard

IN MY DARKROOM I stood quiet and still for a moment, as I always do before developing photographs of the dead. It is one of my rituals; I do not pray. I do not know why, really, as I pray nightly and attend church regularly at Our Lady of the Fields. I suppose the process of development itself, the careful undertaking of each step in the process, is in a way my prayer for the dead. And I suppose my moment of stillness is also a putting on of armor against what I am about to see.

My darkroom is nothing but the bathroom of my apartment. I cannot afford to rent a studio, but I am comfortable with the space I have. My needs are modest: running water, room for creating exposures, a dry place to put finished pictures, and just the right amount of darkness.

If I owned my own home I would put red-glazed glass in the

bathroom window; but since the plates and papers involved in developing an exposure react only to ultraviolet, violet, and blue light, it is sufficient to cover any sources of natural light with a warm yellow, amber, or red hue. As it is I have covered the bathroom window with several sheets of different-colored paper in reds, oranges, and yellows. But not so many layers that I cannot see; it is said, after all, that if you cannot read a newspaper in your darkroom, it is too dark. I cannot yet afford the cost of red or amber for the globe of an oil lamp, so when it was already dark outside, a simple candle suffices for my needs. And I had the requisite tray for the developing of the exposures, a wooden box lined with thin sheets of zinc. And as I have said, there is sufficient space on the counter to dry the developed prints.

I love my darkroom. It is my refuge. There I escape the everyday while doing work that I consider important and satisfying. Here in the quiet of my darkroom, as I light my candle against the setting of the sun, I am alone with both my thoughts and the poor creature whose photographs I have come here to bring to life.

I grew up wanting to be a doctor. I wanted to help my fellow man. But I dreamed over my studies; I read poetry instead of Hippocrates. I particularly loved to look at things. The way a certain drop of water hung upon a leaf, the way a certain shaft of sunlight lit the corner of the kitchen hearthstone. I didn't seem to have an aptitude for anything. But I was lucky: My mother was kind and, although my father beat me for laziness, she saw in me an artist. I was ashamed; I was no artist. But I loved her so fiercely (and do so fiercely still) that I wanted to live up to what she saw in me.

I just didn't know how. All I really remember of my school years is the games I used to play with my friends, and staring out the classroom window when I should have been paying attention to the schoolmaster. I loved clouds and birds, and all the different colors a field could turn in the course of an autumn morning. I tried drawing and had no knack for it; I tried painting, and although I loved mixing the colors and preparing canvases, I had no talent for rendering nature, or fruit, or my little sister's pretty head.

My mother, however, never despaired. She seemed to be waiting for something, so much so that when I was thirteen and suffering an excess of nerves about my future I asked her about this feeling I got from her that she was always looking for something, but without fear or weariness.

"What you are to do with your life is out there, Edouard," she'd say to me, cupping my face in her hands, which were always cool. "And when the time is right you will find it—or more likely it will find you. You do not have to be impatient, my darling. It is there, I feel it. And it is beautiful."

At fourteen I took a job helping the local portrait maker develop his plates. I fell in love with photography. I even fell in love with the word. *Writing with light.* I had been waiting all my life to discover that it was possible to write with light.

My mother was right. My destiny had found me, and it was beautiful. M. Martillon, my boss, reveled in his power. He was a force in our little town because he stood for both Progress and Art. He dressed in the Parisian style and talked a great deal about the refinement of his craft. He was a symbol of another life, and although he was fat the ladies sighed over him. His hands were always greasy, but he knew about the latest Paris fashions; he made trips to the capital several times a year and claimed the acquaintance of both Nadar and Charcot.

Although he was kind to me, I did not like him. He equated

photography with power and an entrée into society, and he had no reverence for his work. I could not pretend indifference to his connections: Nadar, the Parisian photographer who had made intimate portraits of Sarah Bernhardt in a studio that contained a cascading waterfall; who went down into the Paris sewers to take the first flash photographs. And Charcot! The man many called the Father of Neurology, which was less important to me than the fact that he was promoting the use of photography to document the symptoms of his hysterical patients in the Hôpital Salpêtrière, in Paris. But I suspected, even then, that M. Martillon had scant reverence for the great men Time and Fortune had given him the privilege of knowing. And in spite of his connections and high standing, I felt his world was small, and I looked with burning anticipation to the days when such opportunities as he had had might open up for me, that I might show my mettle by my manner of taking advantage of them.

After a year of running errands and developing portraits, I became intensely curious about the people on the other side of the camera. I knew how faithful the camera was, and yet I wanted to see these people in the flesh, to see their eyes and hands before the light captured them. I wanted to be the one in back of the lens. I was fifteen years old.

Of my own initiative I took a job with M. Bousson, the town's only other professional photographer. He did less business than M. Martillon, and so he paid me less, but I liked him better. He preferred the colloidal method of photography, which involved working with materials as diverse as mercury vapor, beer, and honey. He made portraits for those who could not afford my former master, but although he did excellent work his heart lay in two very different places: Nature, and the deathbed. On Saturdays we would go out into the woods, I without pay, and photograph the natural world in all its raw glory. M. Bousson could make a paltry tumble of water, hardly worthy to be called a fall, look like a ladder to heaven. Colloidal slides must be developed immediately, and they must be developed using water. There were photographers who carried along huge complex darkroom equipment and portable rooms that they can set up wherever and whenever they needed them.

Our needs were simpler. A large jug of water, a shallow pan, the appropriate chemicals, a collapsible tent that could be set up in a few moments anywhere we chose, While my master decided on what angle and aspect of his subject he wanted to photograph, I coated glass photographic plates with collodion, a thick liquid composed of nitrated cotton, alcohol, and ether, which had been sensitized to light with potassium iodide salts. After just the right amount was applied (my master being very particular in his needs), the plates had to be developed before the mixture dried. I would hurry the exposed plates to our makeshift darkroom and develop them using ferrous sulfate, then rinse and fix the image with a solution of potassium cyanide. The method was considered outdated by the Eighties, but the pictures produced were lovely indeed.

And the keepsake portraits he made for the parents of children who had just passed away—often free of charge—were works of great beauty and caring. I was so frightened the first time we took such a photograph! An adolescent girl had died of consumption and, although I did everything I could to hide it, I was afraid to enter the bedroom in which she lay. M. Bousson saw my fear and dismissed it—one of the many kindnesses he did me.

"Bring me my plates, Edouard," he said curtly, and walked into the room without waiting to see if I would follow.

The dead girl lay still against white sheets. She lay in a kind of swoon, her head sunk into her downy pillow, her hair in a cloud around her, her arms straight along her body atop the blanket and her palms up in supplication to something we could not see.

M. Bousson went about his business quietly and with reverence. I think I loved him that day, as a mentor and a friend. He showed me how to create a living memento. Many photographers relied on mountains of flowers and sentimental backgrounds to create the kind of feeling they think necessary to evoke memories of the dead. M. Bousson captured the loved one's essence. I heard the bereaved say it again and again: "That's our Nana exactly! Her expression! Her eyes! How did you do it?"

He never told me.

He showed me. In the room with the dead girl, I stood at the ready, slide in hand, hovering over the elements of the darkroom we had by necessity set up in one corner of the room. I readied the materials and watched my master go about his work.

First he stood and gazed at the body a long time. The girl looked to be about thirteen. M. Bousson moved to the bed and caressed her face—at least I thought he did. But when he moved away I saw that he had gentled her mouth, which had been turned down and slightly twisted. He passed his hand again over her, turning her face so that she seemed now to be looking directly above her instead of to the side. The photographer continued to move around the body, gently touching and arranging it as if he had known the girl in life, and wanted to make sure she looked in death as much like her natural self as possible. But when he was done I saw nothing strikingly different; I would not want a picture of this thing in the bed, I thought, if it had been my daughter. But the photographs, when I developed them, were exquisite: The dead girl did not look as if she were sleeping—but she looked as if she were dreaming, and might wake. It was the first time I had seen beauty in death. Suddenly I wanted to render death lovely, as my master did, to give the grieving a truth they could hold in their hands, a picture that would bring the loved person to them whole and palpable every time they looked at it, for years to come, for the rest of their lives.

So I learned to love death, because an artist cannot photograph any subject without real love and respect.

After some years with M. Bousson, it was M. Martillon, after all, who gave me the opportunity to go to Paris. There was an opening, he told me, at a tintype studio near the Tuilleries. I would be only one of many young men, but Paris was full of opportunities, and full, to my young mind, of possible dreams. I ended up one of a cadre of young men whose job it was to develop the seemingly endless series of photographs taken at the studio, mostly portraits of families, young men and women on the Grand Tour, and old generals. It was tedious work, but it made my hands careful, fast, and sure. But I found that I had learned more of human nature photographing the dead and dying than I ever would from the stiff and formal photographs taken at the studio. At least all the expressions of death are natural ones, and the expressions of the dying are true and clear. But these people, young and old, tourists or girls making their first debut, stood as frightened and frozen in front of the camera as people did fifty years ago, when they had to stand immobile fifteen minutes for the creation of a daguerreotype.

Although a single photograph took only a matter of seconds to shoot, each person looked somehow almost identical. Whether the subject stood or sat in front of the most lifelike setting of trees or waterfall, only rarely did the spark of individuality light the eyes. It is intimidating to most people to have their picture taken. I have read that the savages in Africa fear that the camera, in taking their pictures, will steal away a part of their soul, and it seems that there is some vestigial fear of such a thing even in civilized societies! The vast majority of subjects stare at the camera lens with a blankness more blank than death's.

But I can still remember one young girl because of her insistence on the breaking of this pattern. From the back room where I sat with a dozen other young men churning out portraits, I suddenly heard cries emanating from the studio proper: Renée, Renée, you must sit quietly! Renée, Renée, that is not an expression proper to a young lady! And I knew Renée when I saw her. She sat defiant on a papier-mâché rock next to a painted stream, her head tilted back, her eyes bold. This is a girl made for adventure, I thought, and I think of her still. She was not beautiful, but her eyes held such promise, such passion, such will often I have wished Renée well, when passing a midinette or other young thing on the street. Often I have wondered for what adventures Renée was fated, even where she is now. For a week I was half in love with her, I think. And perhaps I will always think of her now and again. Linked as we are by glass and image, perhaps I will always wonder, and wish her well. And that is the very magic of photography, that we can look, and wonder, and care, long after the documented moment has passed.

After perhaps six months of toil at the studio, I was moved into the front room to begin photographing subjects myself, a blessing not unmixed, as I had often to reject my natural urge to prod my subjects into life. It was not my business to do more than arrange the subject in proper relationship to whatever background was

chosen; mine was not the pleasure of a Nadar. No Sarah Bernhardt lithe and lively even in stillness, no great advancements to
my art. But I found satisfaction in the almost abject gratitude of
my subjects, as though each time I clicked the button I had performed some complex and quite amazing feat of magic.

After another six months I was granted the great good fortune
to photograph for the newspapers one of the officials of the Prefecture of Paris Police, Capt. Henri Bezier. He was as stiff as any
other who sat for a portrait, but he talked more, and loudly. He
was insistent that he needed, with the utmost urgency, to hire a
young photographer of sound physical and mental constitution
and a steady hand and eye in the face of death. I was to find out
later that the most important requirement for the job was a finely
honed sense of the absurd.

Now I settled into the work that was before me.

The first step toward developing the pictures in evidence that
I had gathered was simply to expose them to what light there was
in the darkness. I readied a solution of sodium thiosulfate, which
I would then use to fix the exposure to the paper and watched
the first image emerge out its hiding place in the glass plate. The
woman lay as I remembered her, her face turned away toward the
darkest part of the courtyard. I waited, watching as she emerged.
The bolero jacket, the pale gloves, the pretty dress. Even though
my lady's golden head was turned away, I almost flinched as it
crystallized into view. There was the trail of blood that led away
from the body, toward the street, the blood that had dripped from
my dying lady as she was carried hence. And there was something
. . . three dark drops leading away from the body in the opposite
direction. I remembered a door that lay that way, a back door to
the tenement, most probably.

Another photograph: her face. The strands of loose hair that had so pulled at my heart. And what was that dark object? I had not noticed it when I was looking at her face, her sorrowful hair.

I grabbed the magnifying glass and held it above the picture. A small, dark, rectangular shape. A box? Yes, a matchbox holder, probably of silver, some three feet from my lady's head. I gently released the other photographic papers from their glass plates even as I bathed the first in the solution I had mixed. I would add a toner, either of gold or selenium, in order to stabilize against fading. As my hands performed the familiar actions I wondered what this victim had been to her murderer. Capt. Bezier said that the identity of the victim gives us the identity of the killer every time, but it seemed to me that it was the relationship between the two that was important. I applied the gold toner—this girl deserved gold—and began cleaning up my workspace. I worked more quickly than usual. I had someplace very important to go tonight. After I had finished I opened my window and saw the last light lingering at the top of the sky. But even if it were pitch when I reached my destination, I was certain of what I would find.

I hurriedly put on my jacket and set off.

Chapter 4

From the Journal of Augustine Dechelette

MY MOTHER SAYS the new telegraph in town is causing this spring's hails, and Papa complains of the rumors that Paris time is to be imposed throughout all the country, saying that he will have himself tied to the face of the old cathedral clock rather than have anyone come and change its ancient hour. I listen to them talk as I boil the morning milk. Maman had to wake me to cook it before it turned, else we would have spoilt milk by afternoon. I could see the worry in her eyes; of late I have been hard to rouse. I have woken before the dawn since I was small. Now I cannot sleep at night, and dream with my eyes open. And in the mornings, I cannot rise.

I do not know what it means. I would like to think it means nothing. But Maman has a sad panic on her pretty face when she looks at me now, and questions. I stir the milk, I listen to them talk. I dream.

I look at myself in the windowpane as the milk cooks. When I live in Paris I will own a mirror. Yvette, the greengrocer's daughter, has one almost as big as her palm. I remember the first time I looked in it; how afraid I was! It was only two months ago, in midwinter. Maman did not like that I looked, she said it fed my vanity; but all I saw in that mirror was a girl with unruly brown hair and eyes far bluer than I thought I had. My nose was quite familiar, with its little uptilt, but my lips pinker than I expected, and my skin darker than I would like it to be. In the windowpane I am not as pretty as in the mirror, but in the mirror I am not as pretty as I would wish. I have to admit that my vanity has been fed and is hungry. I go to look at Yvette's mirror at least once a week now.

But I make faces in the mirror, too, Maman doesn't know that. And Yvette makes faces, , and we pantomime all sorts of emotions into it and pretend we are on the stage. She talks of going on the stage, but I know that she will marry Jean-Pierre, the baker's son, and have babies and grow fat. But I know that someday I really am going to Paris, and I will act upon the stage. It seems such an ordinary schoolgirl dream, but it's not. One day I will stand at the railway station, next to the clock that keeps Parisian time, with my bag and my secret, listening for the rumble of the locomotive that will come into the station quite precisely at ten after ten, and in the space of three minutes will set me free.

Louis Mouret opened a bookshop in our town eight months ago. It was a brave act, as we are still practically in the provinces and quite unsophisticated. Many of our women still wear the traditional costume of our village, the blue skirt and cornflower-blue cap, with its characteristic strings at the back, as their daily dress.

Louis' bookstore is not the only innovation. A photographer opened a studio next to the train station last year, and it has been doing a steady business. Papa was even able to persuade Maman to go there to have our family's picture done, for which we stood in front of a great façade of a forest scene complete with waterfall. There was a plaster rock for Maman to sit on; for once she forsook her wooden clogs for leather shoes, and she looked lovely with her hat high atop her hair, which she had had shaped and filled out over a horsehair mold. Her hair is still thick and dark (although not thick enough for fashion, which makes demands few women can meet), and her skin is fashionably fair because she never leaves the house. Papa tells me what a great beauty she was in her youth. In the family portrait she sits with tightened lips. She does not trust this black glass eye that is making magic in front of her. At the breakfast table that morning she asked nervously how far away from these new cameras must we stand, and was there any danger, and what if it stunted my growth? I told her a thousand times, as Papa resolutely read his paper, that cameras are not new, that they have been around longer than she has been, much longer, forty years. But she would worry about the chemicals, and whether the skin on our faces would be burned.

I barely remember standing for the photograph. I was so excited, and it took such little time! We were set up and shot in no time at all.

And when I see the girl in the picture I do not know her at all. I look like a country bumpkin, such a child, with my corset laced so loosely I hardly have a waist, and my skirt so short you can see my ankles even though I am almost fourteen. Maman had almost made me wear my hair down, and I remember how I cried and pleaded with her to put it up, not in a loose, high chignon the way a woman would wear it, but at least off my face, as befitted a young lady. I stand forever fixed in children's garb between my parents, and my father wears a peasant's hat on his head. I showed him a whole page of men's hats from the Bon Marché, the Ladies Paradise that Zola writes about. But although Papa could easily afford one, he brushed away the paper and insisted that the one he wears to church on Sunday was good enough for any portrait. I must say he cut a fine figure, though, in his Sunday suit, looking proudly at the camera, showing for generations to come the great joy and achievement of his life: his women.

I am his only surviving child. He educated me in science so that he would have another mind with which to share his ideas. Both before and after my birth my mother lost children, two to miscarriage, one stillborn, and one after three weeks in this life. She has been subject to nervous prostration since the death of that last babe, the only boy. I would like to think that my father taught me to exercise my mind as you would a muscle, to shape it as you would an arm or a thigh you needed to toughen for strong work because he had progressive ideas about the feminine sex. Nothing could be further from the truth. Papa wanted sons; he got no sons. He wanted strong minds to match his own; he is surrounded by minds naturally incapable of the intricate calculations and minute observations, the abstract reasoning and argumentative abilities to which he feels he must be exposed for his own intellectual sustenance. So he has taught my mind, since I was small, as if it were a boy's mind. He sent me to school and hired a tutor to teach me at home as well: Latin, Greek; the botanical and astronomical sciences; rhetoric and the Scholastic method of argument; the study of electricity and chemical analysis; and, of course, all of the mathematical skills necessary for such work—and this in addition to my regular round of feminine accomplishment, without which I should surely never marry: dancing, singing, piano; sketching and painting; lace-making and baking and the entire catalogue of endless household chores. I argue better than I sketch. I can look at a picture of a hat in a ladies' magazine for thirty minutes, but I love to discuss Progress with Papa more than almost anything in the world. I am utterly unsuited to be the wife of anybody in this town.

How can I tell Maman what is wrong with me? She and Father whisper; I hear the word *chlorosis*. Green disease. I am vigorous and well, but I will sigh, or stare at the intricate pattern on the dining-room wallpaper, for the longest time.

My mother says I have a greenish pallor to my skin. She plans on sending me to Dr. Ronde next week. My womanly sickness came upon me last month, and although I am neither too young nor too old, she is concerned. I laugh when she thinks I should not laugh. I cry, she thinks without reason.

But I have a reason to cry, as I have a reason to laugh. I have my dreams, but it is my reality that encompasses me, suffocates and frightens me, sustains me.

I am in love with Louis. He gives me books to read, *Madame Bovary* and *Against Nature*. I read them because he has touched them. I read them because I know that as he hands one to me, perhaps our hands will touch.

I go to the bookshop on Wednesdays. But she is becoming suspicious of my Tuesday-night face, of my sulks, as she calls them, which are not sulks at all but the effects of a kind of romantic terror.

I borrow my language from romance novels, but the feelings are real. I do not even know whether I want to see the realization of my fantasies. What I would do if Louis were actually to kiss me!

And what a cruel insistence of Fate to have Louis married! I have even thought of becoming his mistress. It would ruin me; I do not believe he would allow it. (Nor that I could actually do it.) Oh, if only I could escape this place! In Paris I would ride the omnibus and be nobody at all, a girl with a shopping basket. Perhaps I could work in the Bon Marché. I could forget that I was ever Augustine. Augustine who had dreams she could not make come true: the stage, a man. Such trite dreams, so schoolgirlish; I know it even at seventeen. The stage is perhaps an attainable dream; perhaps. My parents will never approve it, for how can they? They would rather have a whore for a daughter. I do not know why: The great ladies of the stage are widely respected, widely imitated. They are the feast of Paris; what they wear today is seen everywhere in six weeks' time; what they say is quoted in all the newspapers the next day.

But I fool myself. Think of Maman, altering her dress to resemble Sarah Bernhardt's! And although Papa reads her the paper assiduously each night, he is quite careful to leave out the ladies' pages, believing as he does that such nonsense corrupts the already fragile female morality. It is all I can do to get the horoscope! I am a Sagittarius. The Archer. The arrow that forever wants to fly.

I INSISTED LOUIS lend me *Against Nature*. He did not want to do it, but this book is the talk of Paris. I pouted, I cajoled; and he lent it to me. And when I read it! Oh, my, will he ever speak to me again? What have I done? The obscenity of such a book sickens as it excites: It seemed to the hero that a dreadful grandeur must result from a crime carried out, within the very walls of the church, by a believer who, filled with horrible delight and sadistic joy, was desperately determined to blaspheme, to commit outrages upon revered objects . . .

I cannot imagine what Maman would do if she were to discover that I had read such a book. I have heard of girls sent to the madhouse for less.

I sometimes think the madhouse is all there will be for me anyway. No man here has any dream bigger than he can see from his front doorstep. Cows, chickens, a wife, children. In that order. Last week Gérard told me that he loves me. I cannot imagine why. I sat next to him at the theater two months ago, and when I went walking with a group of young people after church three weeks ago I ended up walking next to him. What has been nothing to me, things I never thought of, words I forgot the instant I said them, glances that meant nothing to me, must have meant everything to Gérard. Of course he planned to walk next to me. Perhaps he thought about it for the whole week before: Maybe the weather on Sunday will be fine, and I shall suggest a walk. In the meadow behind Gerthe's farm, next to the river. Augustine will be there. Maybe she will wear her white dress. Her calfskin gloves. The soft boot that shows her small foot when she lifts her dress to descend the steps after church. Oh, Gérard, is that an image you live with, as I live with the image of Louis' hands on the spine of a book? I have known Gérard since I was three, he is the greatest blockhead in the village. All the girls blush to see him because he is going to inherit his father's big farm and manor house one day. He looks like a mule. He asked to speak to my father, enacting who knows what cherished fantasy? Oh, Gérard, you would not recognize my heart even if you were to see it. It is perverse, it has been corrupted by love; it is not worthy of a simpleton like you!

Of course I told Gérard he could absolutely not speak to my father. My goodness, my parents would have me married off within the week! And I would spend the rest of my life a glorified servant in the house of Gérard Theirry. Oh, I would be the lady of the house, of course. I shouldn't do a speck of work. But what would I do? I could spend my mornings giving the servants their orders, writing letters, sewing, playing the piano. I could spend my afternoons playing with my children. I could spend my evenings with the biggest blockhead in the village. I could have an easy life. I would never even have to get my hands dirty.

But I don't want an easy life. I want to wear the most elegant dress, and have the most magnificent hair, and perform on the stage, in front of all Paris. I want to suffer. In my love for Louis I suffer. Only then do I really feel that I am living, when I go stand outside the door to his shop with every nerve pulled taut, with a fever in my heart. Sometimes I cannot breathe, just for a moment, sometimes I cannot see clearly. My nerves sing a strange song, and I know that the only thing that can calm me will be the touch of Louis' hand; his skin against my skin; his eyes looking into my eyes. Why must I be a schoolgirl, and stupid, and slow? I want to burst in upon him like a sudden rain, and I stutter and blush. I want to act the coquette, and I stand there looking at the floor. But then he reaches out and his fingers touch my arm, and I am the girl I want to be.

We are wrong always when we think too much of what we think or are. I want to concentrate on the beauty of the words; I see nothing at all but his slender fingers, and I feel his cheek near mine, although I do not turn to see it; I smell something wonderful, something that reminds me of Papa but isn't anything I've ever smelled around Papa. I am suddenly frightened by the force of his masculinity. His hands look strong as well as supple, and I have a sudden urge to turn and bury my face in his neck. Sometimes a lock of his long dark hair almost brushes against my cheek. I am overwhelmed, I feel faint. It is a delicious faintness; I want to swoon into his arms, I want to be just like the girls I see in the magazines Papa doesn't want me ever to see; Louis lends me the magazines, the stories. Where maidens swoon into their lovers' arms. If I were to listen to the tracts my mother gives me to read although she cannot read herself, I would believe that even to desire such things guarantees my eternal damnation, and the damnation of the entire not-yet-born generation of French children it is my duty to help produce. Oh, I do want children. But I want other things, too. Romance, and adventure, and evening walks on the Paris boulevards, the chance to lose myself in a poet's words, and speak them so that my audience is transported. I am such a country goose that I am not even sure it is where I want to transport them: maybe just to where they can feel what I feel when Louis' cheek is close to mine: That might be enough.

Chapter 5

Edouard

AFTER I DEVELOPED the photographs of my poor murdered lady, I hurried to the courtyard, which lay now in complete darkness. I looked toward the door I had remembered and thought of the drops of blood that led toward it. The tenants had been questioned. Of course no one had seen anything. But it was not the blood I was interested in but the object I had captured with my lens. I walked across the courtyard, stepping carefully around where the body had lain, certain even in the darkness of the exact spot. And there, in the direction my lady's pretty face had seemed to look, was something small and rectangular. It proved to be a silver matchbox holder of simple design, with an etched border; the matches inside were damp. But the box, when I slid it out, read "Le Bouchon." The words formed an arc. There was a picture of a bottle just opened, a spray of liquid and a jaunty cork. A sophisticated name, implying sophisticated people seated at fine tables watching finely dressed garçons working stoppers loose from expensive bottles of wine. I recognized the street name, but did not know where it was and stood, a fool in the dark; and suddenly before me was my lady.

No, it was not she. But the hair, pale and full, the lovely figure, the black bolero jacket; no, this woman was older, coarser; she smiled, and there was no pleasure there.

She spoke, and her voice was a rasp.

"You look lost, Monsieur."

"I am," I said eagerly. I reached forward to show her the matchbox, the address, but she took my arm and pulled me toward her almost roughly.

"What shall you have this lovely evening?" she asked, too loudly. There must have been a man nearby that she was signaling.

"I ask only that you tell me the way to Le Bouchon," I said gently.

"I can show you a much better time than the girls at Le Bouchon."

"No, really, I am not looking for company. I need to speak to someone at Le Bouchon."

She looked annoyed, but tried to keep sweetness in her coarse voice as she gave me directions; I was grateful to her for that, that she would attempt even the pretense of kindness in a place like this. I found myself giving her a few silver francs for her trouble, and when we said good-bye, her smile was genuine.

I went there directly from the courtyard and found it to be a rough place featuring showgirls and a rowdy clientele.

"Excuse me," I said to the first man I saw. "I am looking for the owner of this establishment." There was smoke in the air, and a strange sweet smell I could not identify. There were women on a raised stage, dancing a routine in a desultory manner. They wore short lace petticoats, corsets, and the sheerest of chemises, but their movements were more mechanical than erotic. It was easy to ignore them except that I felt very sorry for them.

The man surprised me by simply pointing. I had expected a rough remark, a challenge, mockery. But he was drinking milky liquid from an ornate glass; I recognized the paraphernalia of absinthe on the table next to him. I looked to thank him, but he had forgotten me.

M. Desquiers was easy to spot, a big man with big gestures.

I thought I would have to go to some lengths to convince him even to speak to me. But sometimes a nonthreatening aspect can be an asset, especially in my line of work. M. Desquiers was willing to talk, and he had a lot to say. I described my lady and he said, immediately, "Lenore DuPrey. She worked here six nights a week; she held a coveted spot on Saturday nights, late, when the clientele was thoroughly drunk and the tips were good. She was a good employee, a woman who worked hard on her routines As if that really mattered!" M. Desquiers said, apparently unmoved in any way by Lenore's death. "She got more tips than most. Pretty girl. How'd you say she died?"

"I didn't," I said evenly. I heartily disliked this man. He was exactly what I had expected him to be: finely dressed, oiled and powdered and scented, with a good cigar and gold lighter and no morals whatsoever. And yet I was convinced he had not taken advantage of Lenore, or, indeed, any of the other girls. It was what he did, what he represented, that repulsed me. If I had met him anywhere else I might have taken him for a banker; here I took him for a trader in human flesh, and I was ashamed I had to shake his hand.

I asked about Lenore's whereabouts the night before: Had she been to work?

"She never missed a day, Sir. Never missed a day. And she brought in more tips than the other girls. Pity about Lenore."

I could have hit his face.

"Did she have any family?" I asked quietly.

"She has a little boy," he said absently. He was watching the girls with a professional eye, and he seemed displeased. "Excuse me, I have to see to something."

"Please," I said, but he was already turning away. "It is all right, Monsieur," I said easily. "The police will be here later, and they can continue questioning."

M. Desquiers spun around as though he were a top.

"Anything I can do to assist you, Monsieur . . ." Clearly he had forgotten my name, and had also forgotten, apparently, that I had no authority whatsoever.

"Just a few questions," I said easily; I could be whatever he now thought I was. "Was Lenore DuPrey married?"

He laughed. "None of my girls are married." Marriage and this sort of work seldom mix.

I shrugged, perhaps looking like a man of the world; I do not know. I could only hope so.

"Did you see her leave last night?"

"As a matter of fact," he said, taking out a small jade snuff bottle, "I did. She was with M. Lunier. He's a regular here, a fine fellow." The bottle was beautiful, a rich green veined with white, with intricate silver overlays featuring four climbing jaguars, one on each side of the bottle, which was only a few inches high yet so opulent. I knew it had cost quite a bit of money, and that part of the reason he had brought it out at all was to show me that.

He took the pyramid top off the bottle and held it up to smell its contents.

"Tell me about Monsieur Lunier."

"There's nothing to tell, really. He acts as patron to several of the girls; Lenore is—was his favorite."

"Patron?"

M. Desquiers laughed. "Surely I don't have to spell it out for you."

"Did he live with Mademoiselle DuPrey?"

"Oh, no. Monsieur Lunier is married, and happily at that. Lenore was more important to him than the other girls, but she was still just one of the girls. In fact, you should have seen how they argued! Lenore was foolish enough to think he would leave his wife for her." M. Desquiers chuckled while wrapping his index finger around the end of his thumb. He gently tapped snuff into the space between the thumbnail and index finger, and as he held his hand us to his nose I heard the gentle *snuff* sound as he tipped the stuff into the front of his nostril; apparently the tobacco is most effective there in its rejuvenating effects. I have heard that some put opium in with the snuff.

He closed his eyes for a moment, inhaling lightly.

"Oh, yes," he said, "they had such a fight last night! Of course, it was all because of Lenore. She did not have a right to her dreams."

I was very quiet. I wanted him to keep talking, almost as though I had disappeared. I also wanted to smash his face with my fist, I who rarely angered at all. Lenore had no right to her dreams! The worst thing was that it was true.

For a moment M. Desquiers was lost to me, and I noticed the girls scattering from the stage like little mice set free from a trap, probably to take their break. There were at least thirty men sitting watching them and drinking. *How could they do that, I thought, just sit there watching obscenity, all of a company, without shame? Everyone in the neighborhood must know what this place is, and yet they would walk in, walk out, without embarrassment, time and again.*

I waited. Finally M. Desquiers said, "They fought. He slapped her, silly woman, but she would not let him be. They were still fighting when they left. Just like any other night. M. Lunier always took Lenore home."

"Did they walk, or did he hire a conveyance, or perhaps have a carriage of his own?"

"On pleasant nights they walked. Why pay for a conveyance when the lady lives so close by?"

The men in the audience stared at the stage like empty husks awaiting reanimation. The proprietor was taking himself away with the opium in his snuff; he was not present to me or anyone else at all.

"Thank you," I said abruptly. I had what I needed, and I had to get out of there. So I turned and walked away, wanting to forget this place myself.

I knew I would send word to Capt. Bezier very early the next morning, but that would not keep Lenore from being exhibited in the Morgue. She was, technically, unidentified, and besides, she would be good for business.

Chapter 6

Charles

I HAVE BEEN to this Morgue a dozen times, no, more, and with each visit I am charmed anew. The *salle d'exposition* is large and bright, with an airy feel. The voices of the crowd strike the tall glass windows and ricochet up and around the large dome of the ceiling and become one wordless, anonymous voice that drowns all senses but sight.

But sight is all that is wanted, and the noisy, thick, sweat-soaked crowd insulates me, and I stare. Earlier this week the two corpses on display were men, one old, one young. Where the manner of death is exotic or peculiarly gruesome, the victim will be shown singly; when the victim is a woman, and young, that will most certainly be the case; when she is beautiful the hall is full for days.

The two male corpses were fresh but uninteresting. The elder had collapsed in the slums. He was extremely old and was exhibited in the rags in which he was found. He was seated at a wooden table--it is always the same table, always the same dreary chairs-- with his left arm lying stiff, with a clawed hand and his head at an unnaturally high angle.

"It isn't unnatural if you're dead," Theo said at the time. I am tired of Theo; I amuse myself by thinking of him at that table.

"You wouldn't realize when a thing is unnatural, dear boy," Leonard said to Theo. "You haven't the faculty for it."

The second man was more interesting. Not more than twenty-two or -three, my own age. He sat cattycorner to the old reprobate, who had an eye, even in death, that chilled mine. The young man had died from a bullet wound to the chest; his clothing had been changed. The corpses are as often as possible displayed wearing the clothing in which they died; at times they are shown draped merely in a sheet. This is particularly true if the subject is a woman of dubious employment, the curators being conscious of the possibilities of corruption, especially for the women and girls in the audience, in showing these corpses attired, as it were, for work.

I do not know why it was that day I chose to speak to her. I did not know her name. Did I say she was pretty? Even Theo had noticed her.

"A girl who looks like that," he said, "does not have to come here for her entertainment."

Leonard's jaundiced eye had found her: "She is too pretty to be a murderess, else I would think she came so often to see if one of her victims had shown up here. But that face is too sweet--there's no sin on it."

Then what about us? I think to myself as at last the queue reaches the huge doors, the vaulted windows that have the aspect of a church. We are here as often as she, and what do our faces show?

Whether the *plat du jour* that Thursday had the face of a gentleman or a degenerate I couldn't say. I was not concerned with the corpses. In the queue ahead of me was breathing, beautiful flesh and blood, and it was her face I studied. Her hat was fresh with silk roses, her cheeks flushed. When the intensity of my gaze drew her eye, I did not let it go.

"Are you here for moral instruction," I asked, "as is that family opposite?"

"Sir, do I know you?"

"I think you might."

"Perhaps," she conceded.

"I assure you I have no dishonorable intent. I am a student of law--"

"Not of death? You are here often."

My heart moved: I was real to her, then, I had been in her mind.

"I come to see the living, not the dead," I said, and she said, "That is a lie."

I was taken aback.

"You are right," I said. "I can see the living anywhere. It is their behavior in the presence of the dead that interests me."

She breathed a soft impatient sigh. "I am not much interested in the living, myself."

"Then why do you come here?"

She did not answer right away; she stood looking at the grotesque in front of us.

"I believe," she said finally, "that I come here to remind myself--to convince myself--that I am alive."

I laughed at that. "A charming joke," I said, "from one that of all here present is most alive!"

She turned on me, she stung.

"You asked me a question, and I answered it. That was foolish of me. I left myself open to you, sir. I will not make the same mistake again."

I grabbed her arm.

"Sir, we are in a public place. I shall call the guards."

"Please." I had to make her look at me. "I do not mean to offend." If I did not make her look at me I would not be responsible for my actions. "I would not hurt you."

When she looked at me her face was unchanged.

"I will accept your apology on one condition."

"Anything." There was something fundamental in her eye––I did not recognize it.

"That you not touch me again."

"Of course," I said. "Have an orange peel."

She burst out laughing. I was ridiculous; I would like to think I did it on purpose, to make her laugh. She actually took one.

"Is that why really are you here so often, to instruct yourself in the behavior of the living in the face of death? And do not tell me it is your friends who force you to come," she said, smiling at the corner of her mouth. "They look like odd company for a man like you." Light fell from the high, arched windows in an arc across her face. "You come several times a week. Have you no more serious occupation?"

"What could be more serious than this?" I asked, throwing my arm to include it all: the crowd, the dead, and especially her.

"Do you ever think that one day you might recognize one of the dead here?"

"And who is it," I said softly, "that you think you might recognize?"

"It is who I am behind that glass. You and I.

We will all look that way one day." She was dispassionate; she was only talking. "I come here to learn to recognize myself. Because perhaps I really will be behind that glass one day."

She frightened me. I did understand.

"Will you meet me for dinner?"

She stepped back.

"You understand nothing," she said without contempt, and stepped into a sudden vacancy ahead of us on the queue. And looked again, without any horror, at the *plat du jour*.

I wanted to kiss her. I was seized by violent emotions; I stepped forward, but my hand on her arm was too urgent.

"You will let go of me," she said. It was not a question. "You promised me, sir."

Of course I did let go, with apologies. Leonard had seen us from across the room. Theo had.

"Please," I said softly.

"No. And that is final."

And she stepped away from me, following the crowd with complete composure. For her I no longer existed.

Chapter 7

Edouard

THE NEXT DAY I informed M. Bezier of all I had discovered, and later we talked again. I was as excited as a boy who has found a speckled egg in a hard-to-reach nest, and he treated me like one.

"Captain Bezier, I am no detective," I told him. "I can only see what my camera lens shows me. I can learn only what my pictures tell me. The photographs I took of the woman we found told me, by her manner of dress, that she was not a prostitute, and that, coupled with other aspects of her appearance, it was highly unlikely that she belonged in that courtyard. The abandoned glove was too fine, and her hair was clean and well-cared-for.

"And the manner in which her body was placed—because clearly it was placed, and not simply left to fall—seemed to indicate that although she had not been killed there, she had been carefully placed after she died. There was no significant blood loss, and only in a puddle at the base of her neck." I almost said, *her pretty neck*, and was appalled at myself. Were the dead becoming so familiar to me that I would have opinions on the prettiness of a corpse? Her pictures," I hurried on, "showed me that she did not come from that tenement courtyard."

"Lenore DuPrey worked in a club of the most dubious sort, Edouard. She was a dancer; that is, she showed her body off onstage to strange men."

"But she had a child. How old is he?"

Capt. Bezier consulted his notes. "She had a small son. It seems her husband died during her pregnancy."

I was silent a moment.

"She had to survive," I said finally.

"There are plenty of widows with children who manage to survive while keeping their clothes on, Edouard," he said dryly.

"But what do we know of her circumstances? Of her emotional state following her husband's death? A woman is fragile, Captain Bezier, fragile in her emotions but a mother mountain lion in what she will do for her offspring. Perhaps Madame DuPrey honestly felt that she was doing the best she could for her child."

"And perhaps she was addicted to laudanum, have you thought of that?"

"Did she have someone to watch her child at night?"

"Yes, yes she did. A friend; she was very emotional. She said that Lenore was a wonderful mother."

"A wonderful mother would work in such a place, Captain Bezier. I know you do not think so, but someone must work in these clubs, and it cannot only be those too debilitated by drink or drugs to do anything else. I mean, they wouldn't be able to do that sort of work either, would they? I imagine it takes a rather strong physical constitution."

Capt. Bezier surprised me by starting to laugh. After he had finished he said, "Oh, Edouard, there has never been such a romantic as you. Do you really judge *no* one?"

"The killer of Lenore DuPrey. I judge him. I judge all those who take human life for their own gratification. There is now one more motherless child in the world."

"Then I have news that will please you. This Monsieur Lunier—it is more than apparent that he murdered Madame DuPrey. At his apartment we found a bloodied knife. He confessed. Frankly, this surprised me. A man of his stature—he owns a shop on the rue St. Germain. But he cried. He said he loved Lenore. But there is no poetry here, Edouard. A simple, sordid lovers' quarrel."

"But," he said, "I believe he may have taken something from the body. She was not properly protected against the elements."

"So you see that it is not that I am a detective in any sense, Captain Bezier. I merely observe the things my photographs show me."

"You seem to find a great deal more in those photographs than others would, Edouard. I think it is your poetic soul. That you are sometimes correct in your assumptions--well, there are crimes that go against the obvious. That is, they do not fit the mold. It is with these crimes that you have the most luck."

I said nothing; the part of me that was small and petty wanted to say, *The cases you cannot solve, Captain Bezier,* but of course I ignored this impulse. Capt. Bezier was, after all, considered one of the finest in his field, and he listened to my opinions on his cases.

Yet who was I? A photographer, a recorder of death. Certainly he owed me no professional courtesy. And if my view of death helped him catch even one of those responsible for death . . . well, that was an honor. To help our fellow human beings is always an honor. I had scoured my mind to see if the irritation I sometimes felt at his hardheadedness was due in part to thwarted vanity: Did I really want credit for helping solve difficult cases?

The answer was no. Recognition within my own field I hungered for. Renown as a photographer has been a sweet secret dream since youth. But I was no Daguerre; I was no Nadar. I was only Edouard Mas.

"Lenore DuPrey is in the Morgue as we speak, is she not?" I asked.

"Of course. She was unidentified until this morning."

"But she is identified now. Can she not be taken from the Morgue, Captain Bezier? Please?"

"Oh, Edouard. There you go again. You know she cannot. It will not hurt her immortal soul to have a few thousand people see her empty husk. The answer is no. But Edouard, you may not believe this, but I heartily respect your opinions. It is just that I have never met anyone with fewer prejudices."

"That does not make me better than anybody else."

"Oh, yes, it does. It does indeed. But the real beauty of you, Edouard, is that you will never see that."

Chapter 8

THE MOST HORRIBLE thing has happened. I was in my bed this morning, watching the gray light outside my window as it became suffused with blue day. I woke with a tactile image of Louis, of the feel of his lips as they grazed mine the last time we said good-bye.

I woke with a familiar feeling between my legs. Voluptuousness is the word that comes to mind. A word out of novels. A sweetness and a burning at the same time. I have felt it before.

I lay as still as I could, trying to concentrate on the color of the sky. But there was nothing but the softness of Louis' mouth. I did not try to say my prayers. I knew it would be a blasphemy to say them when I felt this way. And I knew, besides, that they could not distract me.

I rolled over onto my stomach. My mother would not be in to wake me for at least fifteen minutes; I could read the sky as though it were a clock. I slipped my hands down between my legs. I knew what I was doing. I had done it before. I knew how wrong it was, what a risk I was taking with my bodily health, and with the health of my soul. And knew too that again I would not admit this sin in the confessional, as I did not admit my feelings for Louis. There is in me a whole world rotten with sin; but it does not feel like sin. It feels like love.

I closed my eyes and forgot the world. There was nothing now but Louis' mouth—just that. The skin of his lips against the skin of my lips. There was a point of fire between my legs—I could hardly touch it. I grasped the hood with the first fingers of each hand, I pressed, that is all. I thought of Louis' mouth.

And my mother walked in.

In an instant I was crouched on the bed, my blankets around my chin. My mother stood, porcelain-white, her hand on the doorknob. She was entirely still except for her eyes, which roamed the room wildly; she did not seem to see me at all. Perhaps I was wrong, perhaps she had seen nothing.

"Augustine," she said, and I was damned then. I write this as I sit alone in my room. I look out at the sky and it is changed; everything is changed. My mother said nothing but my name, then she left the room. I can feel her talking to Papa now. Not hear: feel. Their voices are in the walls. Their voices are in the sky. My mother has said words to my father that I cannot bear even to think. My name trembles on the air in my room; I can see it. It will always be there, always; her voice was so cold. Not cold with hate—cold with fear. And now her fear will inhabit this room forever.

I got dressed shortly after Maman left the room, as soon as I realized that she was not going to come back in, that she had really been there. Usually Maman ties my corset strings for me; I did it alone. I always complain that she ties them too tight, but this time I pulled as hard as I could with my hands behind my back, yanking at the cords until I stood perfectly straight and could breathe only shallowly. In Paris the women wear their corsets a good deal tighter than we in the provinces—how could I be thinking such inanities? I pulled on my corset cover with some difficulty, but when it was on I could feel the smoothness of my silhouette along my hips. For a moment I felt as I always did when my corset is properly laced, strong and prepared for another day. But I crumbled inside when I turned and saw my unmade bed and the familiar view out the window behind it.

I put on my camisole, astonished at myself for admiring its lace as I always do. I slipped into four petticoats, marking that they were clean at the hems; when I lifted my skirt they would froth out like new cream rising in the cup of coffee. I had a black lisle stocking that needed mending rather badly. I had intended to do it this morning before chores, but my hand could not hold a needle now. I pulled them on, then went to the closet and found myself taking out my second-best dress, the pink one with the large lavender tulle bow at the neck, the two rows of lavender ruffles at the waist, and the lavender satin ruffles all in a row above the lace ruff at the hem. Maman loves the way I look in pink. I cried as I put the dress on, but I stopped swiftly enough. I have no right to cry.

As I put on my boots I noted, as I always do, that the heel is not high enough for fashion. I checked the hem and train of the dress very carefully; I do not want to be a soiled dove. I am so dirty already.

I don't know how I can ever bear to have Maman look at me again. I will never forget her eyes, which could not find a place to rest because she could not bear to look her daughter in the face.

I wish I had Yvette's mirror. I touch the skin of my face, I run my fingers along my familiar cheekbones, the long, uptilted bone of my nose. It is someone else's face. I cannot be here, in this body, anymore. I look at the sky that cannot save me. I hear birdsong that I usually love, a cow lowing, children's voices. I feel so far away that it is as though I were dead. I find myself sitting on the bed and do not know how I got there. (I was still dressing a moment ago, looking in my dresser drawer for my buttonhook. Now all eighteen buttons on each boot are neatly latched.) I can only look at the sky. I cannot cry. Inside I am screaming, but I simply sit. My arms and legs are like lead. What have I done? The walls reverberate with my secret. My parents sit in the kitchen and speak in hushed tones about Augustine, and I do not even know who she is. Even Louis is just a shadow now. My name has seeped into the floorboards and even now spreads down the hallway and out the front stairway. When the Augustine who existed half an hour ago in the first faint morning light is gone now, is dead.

And a young woman I do not know writes in an unfamiliar journal as she sits waiting to hear what sentence is to be passed on her.

Chapter 9

Charles

WHEN I WALKED out of our apartment that night, I was not looking for her. The streets were wet with rain, and clouds lay like shreds of velvet still beneath swift-running cumulus. The buildings gleamed black and slick, and rain ran in the gutters.

I'd had only a small plate of fruit stewed in butter for dinner, but I was not hungry. I had drunk absinthe from a crystal cup. My limbs were heavy, making it difficult even to walk. I was engulfed in a strange melancholy and looked at everything with the same impatient dullness. I wanted some violent escape for my feelings.

The square in front of the Panthéon was deserted. The narrow, crooked streets leading toward the river were quiet. The Seine flowed slowly, like tar. I stood on the Pont Neuf and watched it. There was nothing for me in its depths.

When I saw her I was not surprised. She stood, her face turned away from me, looking at some grotesque insignificant stone monster set high in an ancient wall, eaten by time and protecting nothing with its fierce, vacant gaze.

There was no doubt that it was she. The line of her cape, her neck exposed to the needlelike rain--I spoke. I was defenseless against her.

"You came to meet me after all," I said. She didn't seem surprised.

"No, I did not," she said. But she did not move.

Her eyes were gray. My hands had gotten cold.

"Tell me what brings you here."

"I often walk at night," she said.

"Alone?"

"I am not afraid."

She wore the burgundy cape; it was rich material, opulent with warmth. The air was cold; she had a scarlet scarf wound around her neck. She had antimony at the corners of her eyes.

"The water is heavy tonight, and slow," she said finally. "I trust that you are not here with any dramatic intention."

I smiled. I was curious.

"Your words this afternoon did not produce quite so intense an effect," I said lightly.

"You mock me," she said, but she smiled too.

"Will you meet me? Tomorrow, at the Morgue." It was stupid and unsuitable; but I could hardly control myself.

She turned her head. "Sir," she said coldly, "I do not know you."

"But you do." I took her arm, perhaps roughly.

"You will release me," she said.

"What would you drink, I wonder?" Anything, to keep her from looking away. "Brandy, cut with a syrup of currants?"

"Rum," she said abruptly, "hot, with butter." I laughed to cover my discomfort.

Why was she not frightened?

At any rate she had not moved.

"Will you dine with me?" I ventured. She was on the verge of pulling away. Her eyes went catlike as she considered me. And we stood, in the rain, and I offered my arm.

"Will you consent to have a drink with me?"

"So long as you do not attempt to take my arm again," she said without the slightest coquetry, "and you allow me to choose the bar."

I was disappointed. I'd had in mind a little bistro with a certain genteel decadence, one where a woman's fragile morals might perhaps be weakened without her reputation being besmirched. But I said only, "Of course I will accompany you wherever you please, but the wind is strong, and the cobblestones uneven."

"I have walked in the rain before," she said lightly, "and I am familiar with the cobblestones of Paris."

How sweet her voice was, how lilting! And yet how subtly insinuating that statement, *I am familiar with the cobblestones of Paris.*

"I will not touch you," I said. I knew that I was lying.

"How came you to this spot tonight?" she asked as we walked, I a clod-footed mortal to her water sprite.

"I was looking for you." And it was only then that I realized that it was, in fact, the truth.

Ah. She was silent a moment. It seemed I was capable of surprising her.

"I come to that spot on the river often," she said, "to think. To dream, really, about my day. About all that I have seen and heard. As though I cannot feel it all as it is happening but must reflect upon it, once I am to myself, to understand all that I have seen and experienced."

I did not know the neighborhood. The streets were well lit but almost empty.

"Do you experience so much during a single day?"

"Oh, yes!" How like a child she was; how wise. "There are infinite pleasures in the course of a day. I could think for an hour just on the expression on that dead girl's face at the Morgue today—and I spent an hour contemplating the rain on the surface of the river while I awaited your arrival. Shall we have our drink and some dinner now?"

I was as surprised to find ourselves in front of a small eatery as I was by her statement about awaiting me. She spoke in such a carefree manner that she seemed almost not to be the girl from the Morgue at all. And yet I knew that this was a role that she had chosen for the night. Because she had known, I was certain of it, although how I cannot say. And perhaps I had really known how to find her. Destiny drawing itself to itself, it might have been that. Love drawing love. Death drawing death.

The café was not so brightly lit as it had seemed from the outside; that had been a trick of the night and the rain. We walked down ancient stone steps through a medieval door into a low-ceilinged room whose front windows let in no outside light at all. The candles in the wall sconces were not fresh, and a few of them were guttering as though there were a wind. The café was so narrow that there was room only on the right side for booths, which were deep and a dark velvet green. The brick walls were old; the entire place had a feeling of floating somehow outside of ordinary time and space. The whole outside world fell away from me, and when I turned to my companion; she too looked changed: older, more sure of herself—there was no more little girl. She turned to smile at me and for an instant I was afraid, then she was just a woman again, a potential conquest, the most prized of any I had ever known, it is true, but merely a woman nonetheless.

"Ah, V, how are you tonight?" The voice came from behind the vast mahogany bar. I had her name. A light name, a girl's name, a charade. I was instantly furious with this man who knew her name and used it so casually.

"I am well, Etiènne," she said, also casually. She felt my jealousy, I knew. She smiled. "I would like my usual booth." She was smiling at him on purpose, not for him but for me, to make me squirm. If every other smile she had ever given him had been genuine, this one was not. I tried to hide my annoyance as we walked down the narrow aisle. All the men's top hats glinted in the candlelight, moving like waves as we passed. People at the bar had to move aside to let us by; one woman let her calf slide along my thigh as I walked by her. The thrill of excitement I felt was not for her but for V; even my annoyance had felt like arousal. When we reached the booth, it was V who stood to let me sit first; when I would not, she laughed and sat where she could see the crowd, as if she knew that every time her eyes moved past me I would wonder whether she was exchanging glances with Etiènne.

When she slipped her cape from her shoulders I almost gasped; I had not before seen just how exquisite she was. She was wearing an evening dress totally unsuited to the weather: Her gown and sleeveless overjacket were of pale yellow striped with purple; her wipe, square lapels bore intricate patterns of lavender, and her sleeves, full and round, nevertheless left her arms bare far above the elbow. Her wide silk waist was of rich purple, but the blouse beneath the overjacket was of almost sheer black lace, tightly tatted, with the lace spilling down the yellow dress in an unexpected, flowing waterfall of black. When she removed her scarf I saw she wore a delicate black choker around her neck with a small cross affixed to it; it gave her the impression of being chained.

But as my eyes grew accustomed to the dimness, I noticed something that took my mind away from V. In the last booth against the wall, the only thing that I could see, really, from my vantage point opposite V, slouched an old, ill-kempt man. His jacket sleeves were not long enough for his arms, and they were grubby at the ends; his shirtfront was shocking. His head nodded back and forth almost imperceptibly; I know that movement well, having both seen it and felt it. But this man was lost. He clearly saw nothing of the table before him, the last creamy, glinting drops in the glass, the shining slotted metal spoon. His chin was sunk almost to his chest. His eyes were almost closed. Whether he was in misery or in ecstasy I could not say. But I knew who he was.

I looked enquiringly at V, and she smiled and nodded.

"For the price of an absinthe he will recite his poetry for you," she said. I hesitated. "Go to him," she said. "I will have Etiènne bring him a glass."

I slid out of the booth and moved quietly toward the man.

"Excuse me, Monsieur," I said gently. I did not want to do this—to be just another stranger with a handout, another face appearing to dispel the great man's absinthe dream to demand a memory.

Paul Verlaine, France's greatest living poet. And among her most notorious. Lover of Arthur Rimbaud, who came to Paris at seventeen and lived in the streets until one day he appeared at Verlaine's front door—and the great poet fell in love with him in an instant and left his wife, his children, his home, to begin a life of scandal and madness. When he and Rimbaud went to the opera, the papers reported that Verlaine and Madame Verlaine had attended the opera; he and his lover fought in the streets, parted and came together, fought again; Verlaine shot Rimbaud in a jealous rage.

But that was all long over. Rimbaud, not seriously wounded, left Verlaine and France, traveling to Africa to become an adventurer. He died before he reached his thirty-seventh birthday. Verlaine was only fifty-one years old now, but he could have been seventy.

Slumped before me in this grotto bar, his bald pate catching the candlelight with pathetic comedy, his gray hair sticking straight out on the sides, he looked as though he had neither eaten nor truly slept in a long time. I do not know why he did not evoke any horror in me. He had done monstrous things.

"Excuse me, Monsieur," I said again.

He did not speak, but his eyes opened and his head lurched up and he was staring at me in a half-mad dream.

"It is all right," I said, leaning forward to touch his arm. "There is nothing here to harm you." He stared straight at me but did not see me; he whipped his head about, this way and that, as though dodging quick-striking beasts; he looked down. The sight of the absinthe glass and spoon seemed to calm him. He breathed deeply and shook himself. He looked up at me and seemed, quite suddenly, to be perfectly all right.

"Good evening, Monsieur," he said clearly. "Would you care to sit with me?

"I would be delighted," I said. "I am having the bartender bring you something to drink."

"Ah. And what would that something be, young man?"

"My personal vice is absinthe," I said, "and so I thought that perhaps—" I paused delicately, giving him a moment to abnegate his responsibility.

"Ah," he said again. "If that is what you prefer." He shrugged, ignoring the detritus in the glass in front of him, the knowledge of all Paris that he was a hopeless slave to the Green Muse. As we waited in silence, I had a chance to examine him further. It was said that for the price of a drink he would recite his own poetry for you. That he drank his way down the boulevards during the day and dozed in less reputable haunts at night. That sometimes he even spent his nights on the street.

But his eyes had a hard glint. He did not seem so far gone as I had heard. His poetry had stirred in me such passions! For romance, for danger, for passion itself. He wrote of suffering with the lyric intensity of one who has been purified by pain. He seemed created to suffer, this man before me now, once so noble and now so humbled. His love, although base, had been beautiful, and the world had seen its beauty. His suffering, although ignoble, had been graced with a purity of feeling that transcended its origins. I could not despise him; I could not even pity him. To have lived such a life as he had lived! To have drunk both the nectar and the poison of the soul and drained the cup! What did it matter if his ending was vile?

A waiter came, carrying an Oriental tray that glittered with a miniature city of glass. I saw the Absinthe Terminus label, the long neck of the bottle and the red oval seal at the curve of the neck. I felt a charge of longing almost erotic in its intensity; Verlaine's eyes were hungry; V's face, as she came and sat with us, was quite calm. She smiled at the waiter and I saw that she gave her smile to anyone, like a whore or a little child.

Verlaine had leaned forward in his seat. I mentally checked my bearing and was relieved that I had not done the same. I almost laughed. I caught V's eye, and she smiled. Was it a different smile for me? I was not sure; I was distracted by the light refracting off the glass.

V picked up the bottle and began to extract the cork. She waved away my gentle protestations; actually I wanted to see her do this, to watch her hands move. They had the hard, smooth allure of the hands of a storefront mannequin. There was nothing weak about them, as there was nothing weak about her. But her face possessed a great softness, a tenderness, belied by the deft, nearly mannish way in which her hands pulled at the corkscrew as she twisted the cork from the bottle. I knew that I was seeing something of a hidden self, and that not everyone would have been able to see it; she looked up and directly at me, and I knew that she had intended me to see it.

Then she turned to the poet, and it was as if a light had gone out.

"Here you are, Paul," she said sweetly.

"Ah, V," he said, caressing her name. Again jealousy bit, and I knew I had to possess her, to make her my own in such a way that the whole world would know, in such a way that we would never be parted.

"She is an angel," Verlaine said to me. "An angel indeed," I said. She could be no ordinary mortal. But she was looking tenderly at the poet, and my jealousy evaporated, forever, because I saw in that moment a way that she could be mine. I saw that indeed we need never part.

"Drink, Paul," she said, "and say for me my favorite poem."

"Which one is that?" I asked her. "I know them all." I did. In moments of weakness I recite poetry to myself, slaking a thirst for energy or wisdom with other men's words. Poetry is a better drink, almost, than absinthe. Almost.

"Shh," said V, because Verlaine had begun his ritual. Each absinthe drinker has his own way with the liquor, the sugar, and the spoon. The ritual is almost as important as the effects of the drink itself.

The waiter had presented the poet with a fresh glass, a new carafe of water, and a full small plate of sugar cubes. Apparently Verlaine liked to start afresh after a certain amount of time, or liquor; that is one way. The waiter also replaced the volcano-shaped plate that held upright wooden matches. Perhaps the poet must start out with a completely clear table each time, a tabula rasa of marble and glass. I was leaning over the table in anticipation; V touched my arm and I found myself looking with sadness at Verlaine's disheveled hair and dirty cravat. He had been publicly repenting his actions with the poet Rimbaud for twenty years. I couldn't imagine what it would be like to regret anything I'd done. But I was young; I had not yet reached the age of regret.

He picked up one of several slotted spoons the waiter had brought and turned it about in his hands. "Too narrow," he said dismissively. He held up the next with a mischievous look: "What do you think, my dear?" It was an odalisque, a sinuous nude form in silver.

"I think it's lovely," said V. "May I see it?" It glinted as he passed it across the table. I was acutely aware of her next to me, the faint smell of green rice powder and rosewater, the musk of her hair. She took the spoon in her fingers and it became for a moment a living thing.

"Isn't it lovely?" she asked me, and her eye flashed deep into mine, and I felt she knew every trivial and base thing I was thinking.

"Yes," I said without thinking. "It looks like you."

Verlaine burst out laughing.

She was biting her lip to keep from laughing as well. Verlaine turned to the next spoon and chose it, a simple one shaped like a slotted poplar leaf.

He placed two cubes of sugar on the spoon, after first examining them in his fingers. He lifted the carafe of water and slowly poured, a shiver of water, over the sugar and into the glass. I watched the tiny green whirlpool, and felt again the pull of my own desires. When I looked up, the poet was watching me. The liquor, the woman: He knew. He knew everything, and for a moment I was afraid. Then he looked back to his potion, and his eyes went soft, as for a lover, and I knew that I was safe, that he did not really know. The liquor, the woman: He only thought he knew.

"Too little water spoils the freshness of the taste, does it not?" he asked, and I nodded. I did often drink absinthe undiluted, out of the flask I kept in my pocket. This practice was rare because the taste was bitter indeed. Normally I used only one sugar cube at a time. But this was not the place to argue the fine points of the ritual, although I could see that Verlaine wanted to, wanted to discuss at length his love. That he had seen instantly in me another lover and known him.

The poet removed the spoon and tipped the cubes over into the glass. He then used the pointed tip of the spoon to crush the sugar; I could hear it. The liquor went paler, to a pleasing creamy green, then to an opalescent cloud. Verlaine took a long time about this, delicately seeking out and tapping down stray crystals while V and I watched.

"Surely you would like a glass," he said at length, darting a keen eye toward me. "I have enough here for two."

There was no point in denying my desire. For V, for the green drink, for Verlaine's poetry. Although she had told me she did not drink absinthe, I asked her. "That is not one of my vices," she told me lightly, and I resolved to make it one, before the night was out.

I filled the cup. As I watched the river of green I heard the poet speak: "In the old park's lonely grass two dark shadows lately passed." It was his "Sentimental Conversation." It was my favorite poem.

I put three rough cubes of sugar on the shining odalisque. I heard V's silvery laugh and Verlaine's slow, calm voice: "Do you remember our former ecstasies? Why would you have me rake up memories?"

Already, the world around me was taking on the quality of a dream, as in anticipation I separated myself from everything around me and entered into the realm of the Green Muse. I became acutely aware of the cold outside the water bottle, the way the glass fit the palm of my hand. The way the glass could have been skin.

"Does your heart still beat at my name alone? Is it always my soul you see in dreams? Ah, no."

The light fell down on the table in a sharp-edged circle that cut the darkness in an arc against the dark green tablecloth. The absinthe waited, dark in the glass. I poured the water much more slowly than Verlaine had, savoring the tiny sounds: metal, water, sugar, glass. Slowly the liquid turned milky and spun. V was watching me. "Oh the lovely days of unspeakable mystery, when our mouths met! Ah yes, maybe."

I put down the carafe and shook the spoon lightly, and the remaining sugar toppled into the green.

"How blue it was, the sky, how high our hopes! Hope fled, conquered, along the dark slopes." I stirred my drink languidly, as I always did, enjoying the moment before I drank; my mouth filled with saliva and I caught V smiling. I smiled back.

"So they walked there, among the wild herbs, and the night alone listened to their words."

I drank.

"Paul, that was beautiful!" V said, her voice fresh with admiration. It was as though she had never heard the poem, and yet I knew she must have heard it many times. The old poet looked at her with affection while the room shifted under my feet. The absinthe pulled at my ear, as Theo always said of that first rush of feeling. Verlaine was looking at me but I could not tell him what I thought of his poem; I could not speak at all. The room receded, and I receded from myself and hung suspended just above and to the right of my own head. There is nothing like that first moment: All of God's creation is clear to you. It is all yours. There is nothing you need, because there is nothing you do not have. I was Verlaine's ghosts in the moonlight garden; I possessed the light that hung in V's hair. I was no mortal thing; I would not die. Then V was looking at me catlike, and Verlaine was staring into his glass, and I was only myself, and thirsty.

"Is everything to your liking?" V asked me. It was. The night outside, cold and wet, the warm light of the table lamp, the glint of liquor in the glass, the woman next to me.

"There is nothing I lack," I said. I love the illusion of completeness that liquor gives. That the liquor and whatever immediately surrounds me is enough. The cocoon of absinthe is warm and thick, then a thousand butterflies appear and brush their wings against me. This is not prattle. I have felt it: the paper-softness of a butterfly's wing as it caressed my hair, one summer night, after a few glasses of absinthe on the grass of the Bois de Boulougne. I remembered that, and felt for a moment that softness—and it was V's hand. Like a butterfly's wing.

"You have a red hair on your neck," she said.

"I am wearing Theo's scarf." I took the hair from her fingers, long and bright. It revolted me. I burned it in the candle on the wall and it made a hideous smell.

"Your impish friend?"

Absinthe makes me feel. The softness of the velvet backing to my seat—I placed my hand upon it and could nearly have swooned, like a girl or a degenerate. Texture, flavor, sight, and sound—these things come alive, they leap out from where they hide in the objects around me and assault me with their beauty. The spoon became an object of desire, the necklace around V's neck almost as delectable as the neck itself. I was seduced by the uniqueness of that neck and the laugh that lodged in her throat.

"His name is Theo, and he is a disgrace."

"I think he is very funny," she said. "Perhaps you could introduce him to Paul."

"Good Lord no, he would become a poet!"

V laughed and laughed. Verlaine stirred himself and said, "I will have no degenerates in my society. I have paid for my sins, I have been suffering for twenty years for my sins. The Holy Mother knows how I regret my sins." He went on in a quiet voice, with the words *my sins* as the touchstone of his private rosary. V and I spoke quietly also, half-turned toward each other on the softness of the velvet seat, her hair forming a golden net that caught and transfigured everything I saw. It transformed the poet's face and made golden the liquid in the absinthe glass. I leaned my head closer.

"You are a habitué of this place, and yet you do not drink."

She cocked her head and her lovely hair fell across her eyes and they flashed.

"I do not need to drink," she said. "I take my pleasure from the people around me."

I had known many women. She was not like any of them. Woman is not capable of self-individuation; she is made to be mother; she is like the waves of the sea. Each woman thinks herself unique. I listened to their stories and they were all the same. They all had dreams that do not involve motherhood. As though the wave could escape its destiny to break against the shore! But the dreams are all the same, dull dreams of fame or altruism or art. They are as dull as men, these women who think that they can make their mark in the world. It is only that the men are right, and have the character and will to carry out their dreams. The women I pretended to listen to while appraising the whiteness of their hands and the firmness of their bosoms were destined for the nursery: the shopgirls, the gentle children of the aristocracy, the showgirls of the Moulin Rouge. Waves in a great undifferentiated ocean of femininity, beautiful and inane. This woman regarded me with a man's intelligence in her smoky eyes.

As if from a great distance, Verlaine spoke.

"Have you ever longed for that which will destroy you?" His eyes were almost biblical in their intensity. A drunken prophet, lost in the desert. "One night," he said, staring past me out of the booth and back into some other time, "a man came to me and Arthur as we sat in a bar. It was nothing like this bar. Nothing. I was nothing like the man I am now." He stopped. He seemed to talk this way habitually, in fits and starts, without any reason for stopping or starting. "It was a fine bar . . . A fine place I cannot remember, except for the light. A man came and sat down next to us and began to speak without being asked. 'I have been making an inspection,' he said, 'and nine out of ten people that I have inspected are going to hell.'"

Verlaine looked for so long into his drink that I thought he had forgotten us. I wondered what the light in that fine bar had been like.

Finally he resumed.

"Arthur laughed. I was appalled. Arthur said he would greatly prefer hell to heaven. In that voice of his, which I have never been able to forget." I looked at V, who was staring at Verlaine with something I could not understand, something that repulsed and drew me at the same time. Gentle pity lay in her light eyes, and the sharp light of predation. I felt a shiver of longing so intense I was afraid she would feel it from where she sat, and indeed she turned her head and smiled at me with the hawk light still in her eye.

"What did you say, Paul?" she asked, all gentleness, still looking at me.

"I did not dare answer, and Arthur lost respect for me that night—if indeed he ever had any," Verlaine said bitterly. "That boy who respected nothing, feared nothing. I was afraid of a man who could ask that question, even though I knew he was nothing but a drunken fool. I knew that if every soul were to be inspected, the man was right, nine out of ten would be found wanting, and would be condemned. And I knew that I would be condemned. Arthur didn't care. He never cared at all what people thought, what they said or did. You, young man," he said, turning suddenly to me when I thought he had forgotten my existence. "Do you believe in heaven? Are you afraid of hell?"

I did not laugh, although I wanted to. His intensity was nothing but green vapor. The master who had written those exquisite poems was gone now, dead perhaps in the arid reaches of a hot foreign land these many years ago.

"I do not subscribe to the idea of hell as put forth by the priests. If there is a God, he has built the world on the Darwinian model." Suddenly I looked over at V and she was trying desperately to stifle a giggle. She indicated Verlaine with her head, her hand over her mouth and her eyes merry: He was asleep over his drink. I started to laugh. I was in danger of laughing so hard I would wake the old man, so I also tried to stifle my laughter. I grabbed the lapel of V s dress and pressed it to my mouth; it smelled of musk and roses. We could not stop laughing;

I fell in love with her. We hastily left the booth where the old poet sat, oblivious now, with his memories and his absinthe, in heaven or hell under the circle of light from the candle in the wall sconce. His life was over. I left some money on the table and let V lead me from the bar.

The street was slick with water, but it was no longer raining. The moon shone intermittent and full from behind thin fragments of cloud. V's hair was gilded silver, and her face seemed lit not by the moon but from some fiery source within. Absinthe made the night air feel like a field of flowers around my legs. As we stepped into the street I had the sensation of wading through irises and poppies and long-stalked allium. I took V's arm, and she offered no objection. We walked in silence a little while, the sky spinning above us.

"What do you think of Paul?" she asked at last, very quietly.

"He is like a ruined monument," I said after a moment. "He has no dignity. But he has something—something almost like grandeur. I pity him, and I have to say that he disgusts me. Anything that I pity disgusts me. But there is a spark there, an intimation of the man he once was, the man who threw over his whole life for a beggar boy who came to his door with a sheaf of poems in his hand. I do not despise that weakness in a man, although I find it grotesque. It is religion that destroyed Verlaine, not vice. If he had been able to rise above guilt, what a life he would have lived! And now he whores himself and calls it repentance. Guilt is the real evil. The man who can conquer guilt can conquer the world!"

"I think he is exalted," V said. "I think he has finally found his heaven."

"How could you think that?"

"He has wanted nothing more for twenty years than to pay for what he perceives to be his sins. Well, he pays for them every night. He is steeped in the very degradation he abhors. He is in the very hell he has always dreaded. He is happy, Charles."

All I noticed was that she had said my name.

We had walked to the river. There was a wind, and occasionally I would smell that musk-and-roses scent from V's hair. Most women's hair smells of quinine, which they rub on it more or less frequently; many women seldom actually wash their hair. V's hair looked like a cloud around her head, as if escaping. I was unused to hair that did not stick, slicked down, to the scalp, and I found it enchanting. There was also something about her smell: Women often carry flowers to hide their ordinary bodily scent, but it seemed that what I smelled *was* V's body. It was intoxicating. It smelled primal and pure at the same time. Its raw intimacy made me think of the skin at the nape of her neck as I had seen it outside the Morgue, and I thought I would go mad. But I merely stood next to her and stared into the current.

The water of the Seine had an evil reputation. It is polluted by nearby graveyards, and offal of every description is emptied into it. But its beauty is not dimmed on a moonlit night, and the wind was blowing strong. I used it as an excuse to move closer to her.

"I must go now," she said.

"You must stay."

We were looking out at the moving current and the light on the current, not at each other. We spoke as if our lines were rehearsed and we did not mean them at all. I felt bewitched; I did not know what she felt.

"It is time," she said.

"Will I see you again?"

"Perhaps," she said, "at the Morgue."

"I would like to see you there," I said, and suddenly my hands were around her neck. I caressed her skin as I removed her scarlet silk scarf, and she let me. She looked at me with a doll's dead eyes, and yet I knew that she was not afraid. I was afraid of her.

She was looking at me steadily. My hands found their grip upon her neck. I pressed. The voluptuousness of the sensation was like the voluptuousness of walking through the field of flowers that was not there. I was not sure if I was really doing this, squeezing the life out of this woman that I knew I loved.

V leaned her head back, leaned her neck into my hands. She closed her eyes, and her mouth twitched for an instant into a smile. She wanted to know what I was capable of. Perhaps she thought me amusing. I looked beyond her to the water, which did not care whether she lived or died. The moon came out from behind a cloud and gave her a silver halo. I wanted to throw her down and possess her upon the dirty stone pavement. I wanted to release her and ask her to be my wife. I wanted to press the life out of her and leave her here, a testament to my power.

She sighed, that was all.

I GOT HOME late. My boots were muddy, and so was the hem of my coat. I had lost a glove. They say cobwebs are good for cuts; I ran my right hand through the wheel of dust at the corner of the landing on my way up to our apartments. Theo snored; something I have never mentioned to him. He would be crushed by so ignominious a betrayal on the part of his body. I was thinking very clearly, although I was exhausted; Leonard slept silently, like a plant. I fell across my bed with my clothes still on and did not wake or dream till morning.

Chapter 10

Edouard

Dearest Natalie:

  It is such a pleasure, after a long and trying day, to come back to my bachelor apartment and write my weekly letter to my most precious little sister. I have intended since you were a child that when you were grown you would be my most intimate confidant, and now that I am in Paris and you are yet home in our small town I have found in you the friend and inspiration I have long sought fruitlessly in the outer world. Oh, Natalie, this world is cold! And it is not the dead who are most cold, the dead I photograph for their loved ones or for the police. Just yesterday I was called upon to photograph the scene of a murder. I will not enumerate for you the horrors of the tenement yard where I found the body of a young woman lying amid shadows and offal.

Sometimes Paris is the saddest city in the world.

The woman was young, though not so young as you, and she was blond, and wore a black bolero jacket in the latest style. I had to move her fair hair to photograph her face. I felt that I became intimate with her then, as though I touched her spirit in the curtain of her hair. And I was moved. Today I felt a need I had never felt before, to go to the public Morgue and view the body. The young woman had been found with no identification of any kind, and, as is customary with such cases, her body was set up for display at the Morgue so that the citizenry could come and see if she could be recognized.

The Morgue is a horrible place, Natalie. I may have mentioned it before. It is vast and airy, and when I went in there were children running about as though it were a park, and a woman with a dog on a leash! But I am getting ahead of myself: First I had to wait in line for thirty-five minutes. They say ten thousand came to see her that day; somehow I am ashamed; when I saw her I wanted to protect her, to take her away from all those alien eyes. But again I have gotten ahead of my story.

I stood in line outside the Morgue at ten on a Thursday morning and felt as though I were waiting for a carnival to begin. Already there were several hundred people ahead of me, some of whom had obviously come up from the country for the day, complete with lunches in huge covered baskets that could be smelled fifteen feet away. There is something about the smell of sausage, Natalie, that will always bring back the memory of the cow in the churchyard that morning so long ago!

There was the most astonishing cross section of Parisian society on display that morning. The country bumpkins were

*directly behind a group of sophisticated men speaking quite
heatedly on the implications of the Social Darwinism, now so
popular in England, for the medical and social establishment
here on the Continent. There were shopgirls, and young men
from the lyceums, and families, Natalie, with little children. I
cannot imagine what reason a mother would have for bringing
her child to see the dead. Of course death is the fitting end
to all our aspirations; it is our rest and our reward. We all
know this. And to familiarize a child early with the outward
manifestations of death is no harmful thing; quite the contrary.
But to subject the innocent soul to the sight of a woman
brutalized by murder! The modern sensibility seems capable of
accepting almost anything, Natalie; anything at all, no matter
how grotesque. Judging from the crowd, I could almost say, the
more grotesque the better.*

*There was no loveliness left to her, sitting there at the bare
wooden table behind the glass. There had been some loveliness
left in the dawn light on the courtyard floor. Here she looked
like a clown, a harlequin who might at any moment dance.*

*As I stood there sad, I heard a familiar voice. "Edouard, my
dear man, this is not the lady's funeral!"*

*It was Robert Richet, a photographer working at the Hôpital
Salpêtrière. I had met him, as I'm sure I have told you, two
years ago at one of the lectures I attend Thursday nights at
the Lyceum: "Photography and the Modern Manifestations of
Light."*

*Richet is an educated man, sardonic, a wonderful
raconteur; he keeps himself at a distance with his humor. I
greeted him warmly. I do not have many friends in this huge,
impersonal metropolis: It is as though we each go our own way,*

cogs in some great machine the use of which we do not know.

"You look as though you knew this lady intimately, my dear Edouard," said Richet. Friends keep me from thoughts such as these.

I did, I told him, in a way. He was terribly interested; I do not believe he had ever thought about police photography. We spoke for several minutes, about technique mostly, lighting and suchlike. I had to ask Richet to move away from the window, as we were beginning to anger the crowd behind us by lingering too long, and I was ever more saddened as I stood in front of my poor unknown lady. We moved into a corner and watched the crowd as we talked. Oh, Natalie, there is nothing like talk! It freshens the soul, and mine was parched that day. Richet spoke to me about Dr. Charcot, the head of La Salpêtrière. Now, Dr. Charcot is a great man, Natalie. He is studying something you ought to learn something about, so I shall essay to teach you. You know that the members of your sex are prone to hysteria and all of its attendant horrors. You remember Adelaide Blanchot, of course, whose parents own the butcher shop in town? You were too young to be told the full details of her confinement, but I will tell you now, as it has bearing not only on what Richet and I spoke of but on all that happened after.

Adelaide, as you know, was an extremely sensitive girl. She read a great many romantic novels and kept a voluminous diary that she let no one read. She wrote poetry, and had hopes of one day being a published writer. None of these things is in itself dangerous, but the combination proved an insidious erosion to her health. She won a poetry contest, and one of her poems was printed in the women's section of a local newspaper.

She began a correspondence with a young man who claimed to have been smitten with her poetry and, hence, with her. She felt that she was at last living the exotic life her romantic novels had led her to believe was possible for young ladies of her station. She fed her imagination with unrealistic dreams, and when the time came to fulfill them her woman's nature was not strong enough to bear the weight of their reality. She grew pale, and her skin took on a greenish hue. She became temperamental. She argued with her parents.

Her parents took her to a local doctor, who diagnosed green disease. This is a very dangerous thing, Natalie, and very common in girls your age. Thank heavens you have good common sense and a natural love of the domestic arts! Books are dangerous things in the hands of women; it has been proven so time and time again. You will make some man a good wife, dear sister, as you make me a good confidant.

But back to Adelaide. (I know how often you have chided me for making a point when I should be telling a story.)

Her parents were at their wits' end. The girl spent a great deal of her day crying in her room. The correspondence with the young man was terminated, of course, as well as the poetry writing, and the diary had been confiscated. Oh, the horrors the mother found in that diary! The impieties, the ungrateful spitefulness! Apparently Adelaide and the young man had actually met! She stole out from under her mother's eye to go to him on the train. It was to have been accomplished again within the month; it is by the grace of God that the mother found out in time.

Her attitude toward her mother became more and more defiant, her moods more and more despondent. At last she *attempted suicide, using her mother's laudanum, and her parents were left with no choice. I was very friendly with her older brother, as you remember, so I was privy to the details of this sordid story.*

At any rate, it turns out that Adelaide is now confined in the very Hôpital Salpêtrière at which Richet works. He does not know this; at any rate I did not ask him. I do not know if she is still there, as this was some two years ago. She may well be; it was a difficult case.

Upon confinement Adelaide was given the water treatment; that is, she was strapped into a specialized tub and had water in varying temperatures dripped or poured over her as was deemed necessary. This cure has proven very effective in cases of green disease, which is really simple hysteria in the young woman. Of course she was kept very quiet, in complete solitude, as is best for a woman, except for her hydrotherapy treatments and daily exercise walks in the courtyard; when a man suffers from a depressed state it is appropriate for him to be kept busy, to be encouraged to spend a great deal of time outdoors, to engage in athletics. A woman, on the other hand, is to be kept as still as possible, with little stimulation from visitors and no distractions such as books or letters.

I have told you about the details of Adelaide's case because the subject has direct bearing both on my conversation with Richet and the extraordinary opportunity that has become open to me because of it.

He and I retired to a café a few blocks from the Morgue, as we had tired of the crowd. We ordered luncheon, and Richet told me of his latest work. When I first met him, he was working as a portrait photographer, mostly for young society girls. *The work paid well, but it was not stimulating enough for a man of Richet's sensibilities. He is a poet as well as a photographer, a collector of rare wines and Oriental sculpture. He was languishing in his day-to-day existence; there is only so long a man can tolerate a routine that goes against the grain of his natural proclivities.*

And then one day he attended a lecture by the great Dr. Jean-Martin Charcot. Dr. Charcot is something of a legend here in Paris, Natalie, I could almost say something of a god. La Salpêtrière, as you know, is the famous women's mental sanitarium founded by Louis XIV on the former site of a gunpowder factory. For many years it housed beggars, petty criminals, and prostitutes as well as the mentally ill. In our century it became solely an asylum for the insane. Although some real improvements were made to lessen the horrors of life there, when Dr. Charcot became its director, in 1863, it was still a sinkhole of madness, a desperate place. Women roamed the courtyards dressed in tattered clothing and received no treatment. Here was no effort to cure the insane, only to house them, albeit in better conditions than those to which they had formerly been accustomed.

Dr. Charcot changed all that. He is a neurologist, that is, a physician of the brain, and he knows more about the ills of the human spirit than anyone else on earth. His particular passion is to find and understand the physical causes of hysteria, in men as well as women. He is doing great work in the world: He is working to prove that hysteria is caused not merely by circumstance and emotional disposition but by actual physical lesions on the brain.

I have heard a great deal about Dr. Charcot's hysterics. At his Tuesday afternoon lectures women are brought forward, women who are strangers to him. He puts them into an hypnotic state, at which time he watches them perform certain acts of hysteria, certain reenactments of the hysterical story, as it were. Richet is one of the photographers who records these sessions, and the glorious news, Natalie, is that another photographer is needed, and my friend is quite willing to put forth my name to the great doctor himself! He assures me there will be no objection, that his recommendation will be enough to assure me the position. Oh, Natalie, think of the opportunity! I who have photographed the dead, the dying, and the vainly self-aware, am to have the opportunity to photograph a new subject, Life itself, as it were, as it has never been seen before. And I will be able to quit my work at the tintype studio.

I will let you know when my assignment starts. Until then, dear sister, keep up your studies, and keep sending me the lovely little things you knit. And don't forget you promised me a violet ribbon from your hair that I may carry in my wallet, close to my heart.

> *Your affectionate brother,*
> *Edouard*

Chapter 11

THE CLOCK AT the train station, which runs on Parisian time, runs a full twenty-eight minutes faster than the clock in the old church steeple. My father could not stop looking at it. I stood, my handkerchief soaked with tears, in my best dress, going to Paris at last. My father had placed us some twenty feet down the station platform from the clock, but he kept walking over to it, his hands folded behind his back, his neck thrust forward and tensed, as though the clock might in fact be alive, and strike.

My best dress: rose-colored, with an ivory overskirt. Ivory lace at the neck and sleeves that my mother had tatted for me. Wine-colored ribbons in the shape of roses hitching up the overskirt, which hung in lazy arcs that swirled gently around my legs as I walked. The same ribbons all up the front of the bodice. Just the right puff at the shoulders of the sleeves. I had been so proud of this dress. My six petticoats frothed out at the bottom like new milk. I had thought of how I would feel standing in this dress on the train platform the day I left for Paris.

I had a brand-new travel bag at my feet, calf's leather with a pocket for my journal. The pocket was empty. I write now on a journal that has been given to me, out of kindness or routine I do not know.

My mother took my diaries, and I have not seen them since. Are they burned, with the dried poppy Louis gave me in the meadow that day, the postcard of the Eiffel Tower on which he wrote those sweet words? I hope it is all burned, after my mother defiled it with her eyes. I burn with shame at the thought of her reading what was meant only for my eyes; I have some consolation in knowing that she will never know which passages of my journal I read aloud to Louis; which fragments of poetry I wrote down that he read back to me, one hand in my hair as I sat at his feet in the room behind the store. These things remain for me unsullied. Unlike paper and ink, they can never be destroyed.

My father paced, eyeing the clock, which stood on a cement pedestal. My mother stood near me, making small awkward movements with her hands. She wanted to comfort me but did not dare; I had become a stranger to her. They would not tell me why we were going to Paris. I did not care. Everything that had meant anything to me had been taken away: I held my few pitiful jewels in my hands and protested that my treasure was still intact, but my jewels only sparkle in the dark; my mother had dragged them out into her harsh drawing-room light, where they looked cheap, plaster and sequins only, with nothing precious about them, things a trollop would wear.

The train was due in at 12:10. By 11:50 my father was in a kind of hypnotic agitation. He could not keep his eyes from the station clock; my mother picked up my bag and suggested we go to him. There were other people on the platform, and I could not help but feel that they must see my shame surrounding me like a shadow. In my good dress I felt conspicuously unclean, although my mother had fussed endlessly to get every detail just right, ironing for an hour before putting the dress on me and examining it from every angle while I stood like a wooden doll.

I had had nothing to say for a week. I had had little to eat or drink. I had cried upon awakening, lay in my bed and cried through the day, and gone to bed weeping. My mother had tried to speak to me but I could not bear it, I screamed at her and threw a book.

And then two days ago she told me that today we were to go to Paris, and that I must ready myself. I did not know what to think. I had thought almost nothing for the entire week, except that my Louis was gone from me forever and that I had done nothing wrong. What I do with my body is supposed to mean so much—only what he did to my body ever meant anything. A kiss, a touch only: a heaven.

But my thoughts, my dreams! To be defiled that way was like an undressing, was like being touched with a stranger's dirty hands. The pain was physical, it still was, on the station platform, an ache in the hollow under my ribs, a pain that ran straight through my body like the trail left by a knife.

This was to be my dream, then. Waiting for a train to take my to my fairy-tale city as a captive, with no idea why or where, and no right to ask. Clearly I had forfeited my rights as a person when my mother walked into my room. I know I committed a sin, but it did not feel like a sin; it felt like the only way I could touch Louis' flesh.

My mother looked at me with fear and contempt, as she had been looking at me for a week, and the train came.

I hardly glanced out the window. I remember nothing of the scenery. Father talked about clocks until my teeth were on edge. Mother looked at me until I said something snappish, then I was sorry. That is all I remember.

And then we were there. Here. A long, long row of trees, an imposing tall façade. I did not understand. The Hôpital Salpêtrière.

I had heard of it, of course. A place for madwomen. The very finest, I heard my mother telling me. I wanted to run away, but I could not stop my feet from walking obediently beside my mother's. She held my arm and I hated her; but I knew that from now on to show anger would be to show madness. I have effaced myself in order to survive.

I felt dwarfed by my surroundings; I felt myself shrinking. Once inside, I could not adjust my eyes to the light. I could not accept the laughter I heard echoing around the great empty front lobby. Perfectly ordinary laughter, no doubt from the throat of someone insane.

Somebody came. We were ushered into a room. I looked out the window, which gave onto a back garden. It was empty. Somebody came. He asked questions of my parents and ignored me completely.

The entire time, I heard that laughter. Eventually it seemed to be coming from inside my own head; I wanted to ask if anyone else heard it, to scream. And then it was gone, as if it had never been.

Suddenly everyone was on his feet. My mother was crying. My father held me awkwardly. My mother held me fiercely and whispered something that sounded absurdly like toiletry advice in my ear, something about flesh worms; I recoiled. And then they were gone.

"I am Dr. Duret," said the man who remained. He stood up at his desk. I stood and curtsied; momentarily I did feel as though I was insane because this could not be happening to me, I could not have been abandoned here.

"Sit down," the man said. He did not say my name. I could not think of his. I sat. I was trembling, my hands, my knees. I was afraid he would see it. I knew he would see it. I looked him straight in the eye.

"You are suffering from green disease," he said authoritatively. He started to go through the symptoms quite thoroughly, noting down the ones I apparently have: Yellowish, green, or blue hue to the skin. Hmmm. I would say there is a definite green pallor; now, let me see, open your mouth, yes, it is quite visible in the gums, although not so much in the lips. Now"—quite suddenly pulling down my lower eyelid— "yes, there is a white here rather than a healthy pink tone.

"Have you lassitude? Your father says you do."

"My father? What else does he say?"

"He had not noticed any weakness in the legs; he says you walk a great deal."

"Yes." I was terrified that the doctor was just waiting to confront me with my self-abuse.

"You are somewhat slim for a farm girl," he continued.

"I am not a— "

"And you have complained of pains in the head."

"Yes." I could feel myself getting smaller in my chair. "I have a—a sound in my head sometimes."

"What sort of sound?" He seemed unsurprised.

"A wheezing sound."

"Ah."

I knew I had pleased him.

"I hear it in the silence of the night; I think it is the strangled beating of my heart."

"Have you any feelings of oppression?"

Oh, I almost laughed then. As I sat in that chair getting smaller and smaller I could feel the entire oppressive weight of the hospital on my poor aching head. Quite soon I would be the size of a mouse!

"Since my arrival here," I said.

He wrote again in his notebook, and then we sat in silence for another little while.

"Your father," he said finally, as though surfacing from some great depth, "says that your disposition for intellectual work is very good."

"Well," I said, not knowing the correct answer to this, "we like to talk in the evenings."

"It will be good for you that all such discussions will be suspended while you are here.

"Dr. Charcot has authorized me to give this to you." He pushed a small journal toward me across his desk. I had noticed it the moment I sat down: a black journal with hard cardboard for front and back. I had been eyeing it with something like lust the entire interview! I could not believe that it was now mine.

I burst out, "Why?"

"The doctor feels it will be beneficial," was all he said, and I found myself thinking, *To whom?*

"I have called for an orderly," he said. "He will familiarize you with the routines of your rehabilitation."

He turned and looked out the window. I did not know what to do. I had thought I was going to be given a chance to defend myself. Instead I heard footsteps coming. They started as a far-off rhythm, then became a tapping that turned loud as a drumbeat in my head. Somewhere the laughing started again. I wanted to throw myself on the mercy of the man in front of me, but I still could not remember his name. I felt like the condemned listening to the executioner's footsteps. Then another man was standing in the doorway, and I said to the doctor, "Is that all you have to say to me?"

"Guillaume will tell you all you need to know."

"Am I to have nothing to say for myself, then?"

When the orderly took my arm I dared not shake it off.

"Young woman," said the doctor, turning around, "I am familiar with the particulars of your case. If you follow the excellent regimen Dr. Charcot has set up for his patients, you will almost certainly make a full recovery. It is not too late for you to be made fit for your future duties as mother and wife." With that he turned back toward the window, and the orderly took a more firm grip on my arm. There was a noise in the hall. As we came out the door I saw an older woman, perhaps thirty, being walked down the hall by a male attendant. The woman was talking to the attendant; she smiled quite naturally at me as she passed. Was this the woman who had been laughing? It felt wrong to have a strange man holding my arm. He hadn't said anything but to greet the other attendant, though not, I had noticed, his patient.

The halls were an interminable labyrinth. Again it became difficult not to laugh at myself, waiting for the Minotaur.

But of course there was no monster, just empty halls, then an empty room. The orderly left me standing by a naked white bed, looking out a window without seeing a thing, and I heard a timid voice ask for some ink and a pen and realized it was I who spoke.

The orderly paused; that was all. And then I was alone, and I gave way to despair, and threw myself upon the bed and cried, feeling all the time like an actress in a bad play: The young woman threw herself upon the cold hard bed and wept disconsolately.

After a long while there were footsteps, but I did not sit up or look around. I simply did not care. Now they were going to take me somewhere else and do something to me, I knew not what; I had heard of the water cure but did not know what it was, had heard something about electric shock being applied to the insane but had not wanted to know more. I was a thing now among other things, with no more volition than the single chair that sat by my new window, the empty desk against the wall, and people I did not know were going to decide what was to be done to my body and my mind.

The footsteps stopped near the bed. A shadow fell across my face. I hardly dared look up. When I did, the same orderly Guillaume, I supposed—stood, a queer expression on his face. I could not read it: Envy? Curiosity? And something feral and almost rapacious.

"Dr. Duret says you will surely be of use to Dr. Charcot," he said without expression.

I buried my face in my pillow again, I was so frightened. After what seemed an eternity the footsteps receded. Once I could no longer hear them, I dared look up and saw an inkpot on the little table by the single chair, and a pen.

And I was weeping again, this time for joy, for the clear bright joy of seeing the pot of brown ink, the old black pen made of scarred wood. Suddenly there was something that was mine, something that Augustine knew and loved. And suddenly, for the first time in these endless blighted weeks, I was Augustine, a brown-haired girl with an upturned nose, a seventeen-year-old girl full of the romance of the theater, the country bumpkin who had somehow become the heroine in her own phantastical play. And I sat up and wiped my face and looked out the window, where there was a wall and a patch of grass and an ancient, tangled rosebush. I walked to the chair and sat in it, and it became my chair, Augustine's chair, the chair where I will sit and write about everything that happens here. This is not the end of Augustine's story. This is the beginning of Augustine's Great and Terrible Adventure.

Chapter 12

Charles

THE NEWS IN the *Journal Illustré* was in my favor, although the weather was not. The rain of last night had begun again. Last week Leonard had arranged for a carriage this morning, and a country ride—there was a lady he wished to impress. Theo was disappointed in the rain because he wanted some diversion instead of his Friday law lecture.

So we breakfasted at a tabac, and read that there was a new *plat du jour* today. *Apparent Suicide Proves Murder Victim.* A young woman, nicely dressed. Clearly not a prostitute.

"Charles, where were you last night?" Leonard asked, and I laughed. Nothing could spoil my good mood.

"I was with a lady," I told him. Rain was pouring from the gutters and down the street. The sky was black. I suggested we go to see the plat du jour, Leonard's outing being impossible, and Theo leapt to his feet and capered like a puppy. I was sick of them both. Leonard felt bound, with the failure of his plans, to attend our lecture; I believe he was just avoiding the rain. We parted at the Panthéon.

"You are morbid," said Leonard.

"And you are jealous," I said. "We will memorize every feature of the *plat du jour* and bring our portrait home to you."

"Charles is in a singularly good humor this morning," Theo had observed as I ate bread and butter and drank the bitter coffee our landlady provides.

"He came in late," said Leonard. They spoke of me as though I were insensate.

"I took a walk," I said.

"He took a walk."

"He has worn down the streets of Paris, by the look of his shoes."

"And his cape is muddy."

"I noticed that. As though it had provided––let us say––a refuge."

"A moment of safe passage for a delicate foot?"

I heard it all, dismissed it all. Like the chattering of birds. I did not care. My love. I was going to see my love. As I pulled my boots on I was certain of her: She would be there.

It took only a few minutes to walk from our apartments near the Panthéon to the Morgue. On the way Theo asked me indiscreet questions about the lady I had spoken to yesterday afternoon and of the lady I had seen last night. Were they one and the same? Were her morals as supple as her young body? I answered nothing. I told Theo that I did not even know the lady's name.

But I was thinking about her.

The crowd was tremendous, and feverish with excitement. The same country family from the day before was once again in front of me. The father now shared the shining eyes and flushed cheeks of his wife and children. The wife carried what seemed to be the same basket of greens. I bought Theo some cookies to fill his mouth, and some warm wine for my own. I craned my neck without subtlety; I knew I would not see her but that she was there, and she was waiting.

And quite suddenly the huge entry doors opened and we were all swept inside.

There was only one figure behind the beckoning glass. Voices rose in pity and admiration; I heard the broken echoes as they swept up and around the vast hall. The crush to see her was three and four deep; but I was in no hurry. Even Theo's sharp exclamation meant nothing to me. I waited my turn, I stepped up to the glass and beheld the lovely corpse.

And for an instant I possessed her, naked under the lights in view of all Paris. I heard them speaking about her: *Oh, but she has such lovely hair.*

Oh horrible pity, she is so young.

"It doesn't seem decent," the country boy said. "Shouldn't there be a crucifix on her cheek, and holy water, and a sprig of box to sprinkle it with?"

"There'll be all that when the police find out who she is."

"Do you see, Father? She looks as if she were talking to angels."

I turned my head: a little girl, no more than nine or ten; a pretty girl. She held her father's hand.

"She is smiling," said the girl. "I wonder what she was thinking when she died."

"That is morbid, Nicolette. I did not bring you here to think morbid thoughts, merely to lose your young fear of death."

"Perhaps," I said suddenly and to my own surprise, "she was thinking of this place."

The girl turned to face me. Her father put his hand on her shoulder.

"Perhaps," I said to the young girl's unafraid, wide-open eyes, "perhaps she was thinking that today would be the happiest day of her life. Because today she would be coming to the Morgue to meet her lover."

And the man hurried the little girl away.

I heard my name and turned. And it was her, with her light wild eyes. In spite of my bravado, I had been so afraid she would not be there.

She wore a suit of the type so popular at the time, with a tight-fitting bodice, a wide skirt, and exaggeratedly wide sleeves above the elbow that made a most satisfying rustling sound as she moved. The suit was of sea-foam green with turned-back ivory cuffs, revers, and vest, and the blouse that showed beneath was purest white. At the neck the blouse sported a rose-red bow that matched the silk roses on her hat, of felt decked with false sprigs of green, which, although they were certainly not even meant to be rose leaves, set off the roses to perfection. Her shoes, which barely showed beneath the dress, were black kid, as were the buttons on her suit.

"You did not expect to see me." That was true. I had told myself I was certain of her, but I was not certain.

"She is not so beautiful as you," I said, gesturing toward the figure behind the glass.

She smiled. "She is me."

"I walked all night," I said, "thinking of you." The first lie I told her; after we dined I had walked, but after two hours I had gone into an absinthe bar to still my nerves, and slept, seated in a booth with the candle guttered out. My nerves had not been stilled.

But here in the Morgue, she among the living was the most alive, and I knew that from that moment I must have her always by my side.

Chapter 13

Edouard

I AM HOME now, after my first day of work at La Salpêtrière. Richet spent hours just showing me around: The place is a city, an endless labyrinthine series of hallways all identical; I half expected a Minotaur. If this place that houses five thousand souls were a city, its patients could walk its streets freely, stopping to talk to neighbors and shopkeepers along the way. There would be blue above, or the famous pearl gray of the Paris sky. Here the halls are dim, and although the ceilings are not low they feel low: I had the impression that we were in fact underground here, and every window was a surprise.

And it seems as if one can walk for what seems like miles without seeing a window. The halls are all lit with electric light, with which I am unfamiliar; it disorients me. I was shown the rooms where hydrotherapy is performed, with their constantly working bellows assuring a steady supply of hot water; I glimpsed a young woman immersed to her neck in a steaming tub over which a tarp had been placed; she was kicking her legs, causing water to spill from beneath the tarp, and screaming in the most awful language at what she called her captors.

"You're going to have to learn to be tough," Richet said to me, "if you are to work in this place." And then, as I look hastily away from both the wailing woman and him, "But your sensitivity shows in your photographs, and that is just what is wanted for our studies here. I just do not want you to be damaged by the things you see and hear at La Salpêtrière."

"I am no delicate flower, Richet," I reminded my friend, but he ignored that and started talking about how all the methods and equipment here are state-of-the-art, the finest anywhere.

I saw the electroshock machines, black boxes with shiny knobs, and Richet explained how a jolt of electricity to the brain has been proven to activate certain dormant centers, thereby bringing a cataleptic back to life or calming the wild spirit of the madwoman out of control.

It was a city with dark places indeed, and I was relieved that there were no patients in that room when we were present.

I did not know which would be more difficult: looking death in the face day after day or observing the details of lives destroyed by insanity.

Although I was hot to see the Amphitheatre, it was closed up (tomorrow I was to photograph, for the first time, a patient from this place). Richet showed me the room behind the Amphitheatre, a large space replete with plaster casts of former hysterical patients, death masks, two skeletons, a man's and a woman's, and various tools and equipment Dr. Charcot uses in his studies and experiments. It was a most satisfying place.

There was a darkroom, off to the left, with all of the latest photographic equipment; and Richet showed it to me proudly. I envied the electric lamp, the shiny new zinc trays, the rows of bottles containing every kind of developer imaginable. Stacks of gleaming glass plates, stacks of paper ready to be treated. Long marble countertops so unlike the space I have to make do with at home. The sinks were zinc, and deep, and as Richet showed me each item it was obvious he loved this place, and I knew that I would come to love it as well; the idea that its strangeness would in time be replaced by a comfortable familiarity was a solace to me: La Salpêtrière is a cold, forbidding place, and I look forward to a not-too-distant future when I feel at home in its great hallways, no matter that today this seems an impossible goal.

I was anxious to meet with the great Dr. Charcot of whom I had heard so much. But Richet informed me that the doctor was busy, and would be busy, for several hours. His dedication to his work was common knowledge, his stamina legendary. I was not to see him today.

Everywhere I went I saw the sad inhabitants of this placed, walked or drawn along or half-dragged by burly young male attendants. There was not a single smile from either, and no words exchanged that I heard. I had to remind myself several times that I was here to help these poor souls only by documenting the phases of the illnesses, that the Father of Neurology might study these illnesses in a new and different light.

But still the obvious suffering made me uneasy.

At home that evening I looked at my darkroom with a jaundiced eye, but I was determined not to let envy eat at my spirit.

I tried to remember I was a lucky man, and I intended to live up to my possibly unrealistic expectations. "You cannot save the world," Richet said when he saw my expression as one of the unfortunates of the institution was led past us this afternoon. I knew that I could not save the world, and I did not intend to try. But what I could do was help Richet and the great Dr. Charcot improve the lives of the women housed at La Salpêtrière.

And that would be enough.

Chapter 14

I MISS MY hairbrush. I miss the hair oil Maman and I made together, rosemary and lavender oils mixed with vanilla for my brown hair. I would have preferred oil of lemon, which is suggested for blonde hair, but Maman would take a length of my ordinary brown and explain, once again, that lemon for blondes, or saffron, which is used on red hair, would only bring about damage to my own mouse-fur locks.

Every evening I daubed a bit of this mixture onto the brush, let my hair fall, and bent my head until my hair swung freely almost to the floor. Some nights Maman would brush it for me, one hundred strokes. Some nights, when I preferred to dream, I did it myself, although Maman would stand in the doorway with a worried pout on her pretty face. But I would turn away, then I would lower my head and close my eyes and it was Louis brushing my hair, Louis' hand on the brush; why can I not remember him here? The smell of his person, which was not one particular smell, no soap or cologne but only his scent, the scent of his hair and skin: It is lost to me. Sometimes after I had seen him I would let down a lock of hair on my way home and hold it across my face that I might smell his scent before it faded. And now it is entirely gone. Everything about Louis is gone, has been gone since that awful moment in my room. Oh, am I really so wicked? I must be, and losing my memories of Louis, which were both so immediate to the senses and so precious to me, must be my punishment. And my penance is to be served here, where the smell of steam pervades the halls, and a strange undeniable odor that smells like nothing I have ever known, nothing I could ever have imagined before they brought me here: the pervasive, intangible scent of fear.

They have given me a scratchy white cotton dress that barely covers my shoulders, and a blue smock. Flat leather shoes and thick white stockings; there are no petticoats at all. The stockings itch. I have no mirror to gauge my ugliness.

There is a small panel on the window to my little room; it is covered with closed curtains of indeterminate hue, and I dare not open them, lest by the noise I excite the interest of one of the male orderlies who prowl these halls. Every time I hear footsteps the globe in my throat threatens to strangle me. That had come over me, of late, even when at home, most often before or after seeing Louis. As I neared his shop my breathing would all at once begin to quicken, and my throat would seem to have an obstruction, and I would find myself stopped and standing with my hand at my throat and my heart in my mouth. I knew what it was a symptom of, but I refused to believe it. I took it as a symptom of love.

Now all of a sudden I felt my heart begin to pound. I was

afraid, suddenly, of what I did not know. The blank white walls of my room shimmered and seemed almost about to move. My heart constricted, and I could hardly breathe. What was wrong with my heart? It was beating almost out of control; my throat began to tighten, as though a great, angry hand were reaching down my throat to pull my heart out of my body. Suddenly I thought that I might actually die here, a thought I had never seriously considered before. I am young; I have always been healthy: What was happening to me now?

I walked with agitation about the room. The bed, the small table, the dirty mullioned window, all seemed designed to create a sense of oppression,

Ah. My heart had calmed. It was merely the shock of being here.

The attendants frightened me, with their white smocks and tight mouths. They were all men, and so big! As big as farm boys. And they never said a word, not one of them. There was one who smiled at me, but I was not sure I liked it. He had insinuating eyes. Other than that, he was like Gérard back home, with a face like a cow's and a clod-footed gait. But oh, I would be happy even to see Gérard in this dreary place! Anybody from home, anybody who smelt of dandelions and meadow air. It is always stuffy here; I suppose they think we should escape out the windows if they were opened up. Certainly I would run away!

The other women here are so different from any I have ever met as to seem almost another species. There is an old woman who shouts that she is Mary Magdalene; she is old enough to be Mary Magdalene . . . but I am being uncharitable. There are several women who for much of the time are kept in what are called straitjackets; the straitjacket immobilizes the arms by securing them inside long sleeves that are then wrapped around the body and fastened tightly at the back. These poor souls are piteous indeed.

There is one who woman who does not speak, but emits high-pitched screams at intermittent intervals, her face impassive all the while. She rouses my pity. I tried once to approach her, a vacant-eyed woman older than I but with the eyes and unlined face of a child, but the moment I came near she screamed and screamed, all the while seeming completely unaware of me. And a burly attendant hurried over and took her brusquely by the arm and hurried her away; he was very rough with the poor thing, and I felt responsible both for her distress and her punishment.

There are those who mumble, those who hold converse with the air and the walls. There is Marie-Renée, who talks to herself, quietly, all the time. And the woman who screams is called Lucille. She has been at La Salpêtrière almost all her life; she has been as she is almost all her life. This really is her home, although she seems to be unaware of almost everything around her. Something draws me to her; perhaps it is simply that she is clearly more helpless even than I am.

And then there are those women who do not seem the least bit insane; we eye one another warily, unsure. I have been afraid to speak to any of the other women, and even more afraid, I think, lest they speak to me. But I am intrigued by some of them. There is Lise, for example, whose husband wanted to marry another and so had her put away. And there is one in particular, a girl roughly my own age, with big brown eyes under a fringe of dark hair. She spends a great deal of time staring out of the big windows. There is nothing to see. Her doe eyes are often sad; but so are my blue ones, I suppose. Laughter is against the rules, I do think.

All I have is this journal, this bad ink, and Maman's advice to me about flesh worms. My skin is not prone to these pernicious and disgusting creatures that leave a black mark on the face and come out all yellow-white and putrid if you press at the skin around them. What would I do about them anyway? Well, I suppose the soap here, which is so abrasive, is a good preventative in itself; it practically takes the skin right off, it is so harsh.

Ah. I hear footsteps in the hall. I believe it is time for my hydrotherapy session.

Chapter 15

Charles

AFTER OUR MARRIAGE we never saw Theo or Laurence. I told her they were vulgar and morbid, but she lamented Theo. She spoke more candidly than any woman I had ever met.

We never went back to the Morgue. We had our own bodies, and each other's, and the repeated exchange of caresses consumed all desires. I learned things from her that I cannot even name. She had no family. She had no past. There were intimations––she reassured my jealousies and poured me absinthe.

We went to Italy. We made love in an old graveyard in a forgotten suburb. She liked to read aloud the names of the dead. *The dead show me how alive we are. The dead excite me.*

One Sunday after our return she persuaded me to drive into the country. I expected an inn, or a forest with a creek where we could undress and hope for prying eyes. She would have been equally at home in either. *I love the feel of dirt between my naked thighs*, she told me. *I like the way the twigs and stones bite my skin.* And yet she also loved silk sheets and firelight.

After a two-and-a-half-hour drive, our carriage pulled up at a Carmelite nunnery, a great old stone monument in the middle of empty hills. Where I was born, she told me as we waited at the door. And the sister who answered the door cried out in joy; she called my lover by a childhood name; she led us to a bare table. My lover embraced the nuns, and looked at me and smiled. The nuns turned the bare table into a table of plenty for her sake. Clearly they loved her. They told me what a lovely child she had been, how quick to learn her catechism, how diligent in her studies.

I could not see her here, although I tried. A small blonde head silhouetted against a rainy windowpane; a light fast step just around the corner in the vaulted hall. I could not see her. Yet to the sisters she was real.

"You see?" she told me afterward, her hand soft inside my pocket against my leg. "I received excellent training. Don't you think?" Pushing against the satin to reach her fingers up along my thigh.

I never asked her anything. She chose to give me the convent. She could have given me something less pleasant. On our wedding night she bled, but I have heard there are ways to assure a timely bleeding.

I could hardly bear the obligatory darkness of the wedding night. Before a week was out, I was watching her undress. I would hold her mirror as she washed. *Pissoir* was a word she liked; *baiser*. She astonished me.

I might not have minded images other than those the nuns showed me. Somehow she knew; and she arranged a scene for me.

One day I came in from the rain to absinthe on the sideboard, and a lighted candlestick at the bottom of the stairs. She made no answer to my calls.

I went up the dark steps. The door to her bedroom was locked. I went into my own room, where I found another small glass of absinthe. There was no light beneath the door that connected our rooms. That door was never closed.

I stood for a moment, frightened, with my fingers on the cold doorknob. The door opened without a sound.

The bed was hung with silk and tapestry. There were tasseled pillows all around it and satin bedsheets, with silk pillow shams; there was an antique lace throw and lace bedspreads of every description.

She lay white across the bed. I could hardly see her: a shadow, an intimation of flesh. Her languidity was desire itself. She lay silent. Absinthe made me unsure of what I saw: my love, covered with roses, roses trailing red petals down her arms, overflowing her hands, her hands dripping petals drifting to a silken pile on the floor.

She had slit her wrists. There were no flowers. She was not silent; she said my name, the one candle turned the blood all gold, and I was by her side.

I knelt, I took her hand, and blood ran silently all over my hand too. She looked at me without expression, like a cat. I bent my mouth to her hand and bloodied my lips. She had done this for me, that I might choose. The candle guttered in a sudden wind, a shutter flung itself loose and clapped against the wall. She tried to smile. Her life was mine, to recapture or destroy. If I wanted, she could be behind the glass of the Paris Morgue tomorrow. I could leave her naked along an alley, and she would be displayed that way, with only a white sheet to cover her body. For a moment I imagined her as all Paris would see her, and I was quickened by desire. Then I tore off my jacket and ripped the lining of the sleeves, that I might make a tourniquet. I lifted her arms, both cut with a knife that she had managed to lay back on its plate next to the apple she must have been eating. The blade was bloody; and the blood and the apple made me laugh. I laughed as I bound up her wounds

"A new Eden," I told her as I lifted her head. "We have made a new Eden, where there is no temptation in the apples of this Earth." I felt the soft sigh of her breath when I laid her head against my neck.

When I was certain her wounds had stopped their bleeding, I lifted a sugar cube to her mouth. I dipped my finger into the glass of absinthe I had found on the mantelpiece; I brought it to her lips and said, "Suck." And she closed her eyes and breathed in the sweetness of sugar and blood and wormwood, and that night, when I made our choice for her, our souls became one soul.

Time passed. Time made me love her more. We traveled again; we experienced every kind of passion; every act, every aspect. We lived entirely in the moment, and the moment was sweet. There was never anything we longed for: no other place, no other food or drink or company. We had no need of anyone but each other. I would do anything to please her, and she knew that. One day she decided we must return to Paris. We were in Constantinople. We had only arrived two days before; but she said we must go, and I willingly gave up Nicea and the Bosporus crossing. She wanted to go; we would go.

We arrived at the Gare Montparnasse on a rainy night, a night much like the one when I was first alone with her, albeit much warmer. As we waited in the rain for a free cab, she said, "I do not want to go to the house."

"We will go wherever you wish," I said, but when she told me I was astonished. I asked her to repeat herself.

"You heard me," she said.

The most dangerous quarter in the city. There was nothing there for a lady of quality; there was much there in the way of pleasure, if you took your pleasure coarse. I knew in an instant what she wanted there—she had bought me a large knife as a present in Rome, and I had never doubted what it was for.

When we got into the cab she threw the lap rug over us both, despite the warmth.

"Do you have your knife?" was all she said. I had carried it with me, in the large inner pocket of my coat, from the day she gave it to me. When I bought a light, long coat for late-spring wear I made sure it had a large pocket on the inside.

Beneath the throw she stroked me to hardness, and I knew I would do whatever she wanted.

When we reached the quarter the rain had stopped. The streets seemed at first to be deserted, but then I saw the women in the doorways. I became almost afraid; of her, of my love! The fear was sweet to me, a feeling almost of intoxication, with the same voluptuous disarrangement of the senses. The wet cobblestones fractured the light and sent it up in sharp little knives. The women remained. I wanted to touch the breasts of one of these women, to touch her neck.

V walked easily toward the nearest building, a dim brick tenement utterly like all the others. Watching her I became aware of how little I knew her, and I felt my love for her quicken. I followed, content to let her set the rules of this game.

The door closed behind us, and we were left in utter darkness. Then V stood smiling in a flare of candlelight. She was holding a dirty porcelain candleholder with a stub in it. I didn't recognize her, my love, my wife. We stood at the bottom of a dank, empty landing, but she was looking upward. I followed her glance: ancient wallpaper of Paris green with dirty flocking; cobwebs and small scuttling bugs. She smiled again at me and started up the steps.

I followed. I was nearly ill. My V could not be so at home in this place. She could not have known where to find that candle stub, that filthy striker. She could not now have a destination up that dark stair.

Two flights, three, four, in silence, then the turning of a key in a rusty lock. I had not seen a key—had she picked it up from the shelf in the lobby? Had she had it with her all this time, secret from me, undreamed of as this building had been undreamed of? Oh, I knew she had a past. All people do. But I had chosen to accept the convent as the image of that past. As though there had been nothing else.

We entered, and the candle illuminated a small, low-ceilinged attic room. The roof slanted to the floor, with deep-set windows showing only blackness now. There was nothing but a bed and a table. The bed was iron, and narrow, and the table was deeply scarred and thick with dust. There was no air in that room, and yet the candle was guttering, and the air was unseasonably chilly. V walked across the floor to a small hearth set in the facing wall. She reached for a tinderbox on the mantel, and I then I knew: I had to accept that she had been here many times before.

There was wood in the fireplace, so dry that when she placed tinder to it, it burst immediately into bright flame. The bright light rendered the mirror above the mantel absolutely black. V turned, and her face was changed. She was harder; she was cool as glass.

"I want you to do something for me."

I didn't recognize her.

I suddenly wanted her, violently. On that dirty bed, in this squalid place. She was smiling because she knew, and I took her with something like hate. I would obliterate every memory she had. She was a different woman in that bed, silent, passive. I knew that she would do anything I wanted. I took her like a whore.

Afterward, in the light from the dying fire, she said again, "I want you to do something for me." Her face was turned away, toward the dark wall. I had not removed her dress, and it lay crumpled around her. There were cracks in the ceiling. I knew she knew them all by heart.

"Anything," I said. How many men, here in this bed, had moved as I had moved, had seen what I had seen, had taken what I had taken?

"I want you to kill a man." She spoke softly toward the wall. I had to strain to hear her, but I knew what she wanted.

"A stranger," I said.

"I will bring him to you," she said as she turned her face toward me. I did not know what woman I would see. But it was my V, with her eyes light and shining, as innocent as a girl.

I sat on the bed while she smoothed her hair and painted her face. She took a mirror from the mantelpiece. She asked for my handkerchief to wipe the dust from its surface. She set the candle on the mantel and stood facing away from me, but I could see her eyes in the mirror.

When she was done she was the woman I had been afraid of seeing: younger, feverish, proud and powerful, and the perfect victim. I took her again, anonymously from behind, lifting her skirts out of the way. When I was finished she walked out the door without looking back, and my love for her hardened around me and I knew that I could never live without her.

On the street she motioned to me to stay back, and I dropped behind her as she moved sure-footed along the broken cobblestone. The very first man she passed gestured to her, and as she stood with him in the cavity of a doorway I wanted desperately to hear her voice setting the terms of their transaction. *How much would he be willing to pay for her and what would he ask her to do? Would she bring him back to her room (I loved the sound of those words in my mind: her room), or would a secluded doorway suffice for his needs?* I realized that I wanted her to perform whatever he asked of her, wanted to see her act her part in its entirety. But she would never allow me that. She would never be another man's whore, no matter what she had been in the past. This was just a game for her—had been a game, I suspected, before she ever met me. The rosy girl on line to enter the Morgue had been no whore. The painted woman in the doorway had never been a whore, no matter what she'd done. I was for one moment afraid: *Was our life together also a game, a part she had chosen to play?* I took my flask out of my pocket and drank. And as she walked out of the darkness with this stranger she flashed a smile toward me where I hid in the shadows, and I was soothed.

As V and the man moved away down the street I appraised him: tall but thin; older than I, perhaps even middle-aged. Not tentative; that was bad, because a man familiar with these streets would be ready for danger. But I had surprise and certainty on my side, and an almost joyful anticipation. Because of the gift she was going to give me: more power than I had ever had. On that dirty, ill-lit street, I was like God.

V and the man turned the corner. He held her arm. When I reached them I found that she had moved him into a deeply recessed doorway and that he was fumbling already with the fastenings on his pants. And oh, I wanted to wait, to make her do what he thought he was going to live to pay her for.

I did wait long enough for the man to finish unfastening his trousers and fully expose himself. And then I made as if to pass them, and the man started and grabbed at his clothes. And V moved as if to cover his body, and I knew. I walked very quickly toward them. V moved away just as I reached them. The knife was in my hand; I will never remember taking it out of my pocket, but it was ready, and it caught the fire from the streetlamp and glowed. Suddenly I was as near to him as a lover. I plunged the knife into the soft spot between the ribs, as if I had done this a hundred times, as if I had been born to do this. I twisted the knife; I pulled it up toward his heart.

He did not say a word. His eyes went wide. I could smell his skin and his fear. It was V he looked to. But she was staring at the knife. Blood was everywhere, on my hands and coat, on her neck, on her face. The man reached toward her, and his body started forward. I moved to catch it, but he was too heavy, he crumpled at my feet, then there was blood on the sidewalk too. V and I moved away at the same time, and the man's body banged headfirst onto the cobblestones and lay facedown, one arm stretched out toward nothing. I looked at her and was for the only time repulsed—an instant only, a shiver in my heart. She was smiling at the body, and I was afraid of her, and then she was my V again.

I caught her arm to take her away, but she exclaimed, "His identification!" She worked through his pockets with sharp efficiency, and it was as though I were watching an unfolding dream. I had been thrown out of ordinary experience: I had killed a man and was watching the love of my life grope the dead body for papers and money.

She took only a moment. She stood, and again I moved to take her arm. Surely we must hurry away from this place. But she motioned me toward the dead man.

"We must arrange the body, Charles."

She pulled me down next to her. "You can roll him onto his back," she said, and I did so, mystified. "And the hands go thus," she continued, pulling his fleshy arms until they crossed upon his chest. "Straighten his legs, will you?" she continued as she worked, and I arranged them as she told me to, tilting his toes neatly together when she was dissatisfied to see his feet still splayed outward.

"There," she said at last, after tidying his shirt, coat, and pants so that he lay stick-straight and orderly as a soldier, staring sightlessly at heaven.

I heard a sound, and started; but it was V: She was trying to stifle a giggle.

And then we were walking quickly away down the solitary street, and around the corner, then we were leaning against each other, gasping for breath and laughing like children.

Chapter 16

Edouard

THE STUDENT AMPHITHEATRE at La Salpêtrière was a long, narrow, sloped, rectangular room that could hold a hundred spectators, and every tiered seat was filled. The back of the Amphitheatre was decorated with a huge mural, *Pinel Freeing the Patients of the Salpêtrière*. A very famous painting: Dr. Pinel like a saint or an avenging angel, setting free the wild eyes and matted hair, the women crouched and crawling, the shifts baring their pale breasts, their thighs. The saint, the angel, the lion tamer.

The walls of the Amphitheatre were a very dark red, and there were electric lights in sconces along the walls that could be brightened or dimmed from a switch at the front of the room. Dr. Charcot used the lights to good effect during his lectures.

The crowd had a festive aspect; there was much laughter, and the sound of lunches being unwrapped. The women wore bright hats and flirted among the medical students. Dr. Charcot's Tuesday lectures were open to the public. Sometimes Toulouse-Lautrec was there, or the writer Edmund de Goncourt; once Sarah Bernhardt had been seen among the crowd. Dr. Charcot had been accused of creating a hystericulture, with his *leçons du Mardi* the focus of intense scrutiny and speculation. On Fridays he gave by-invitation-only lectures in neurology, outlining his taxonomic classifications of epilepsy and hysteria, and putting forth new postulations.

But Tuesday's lectures were by far more interesting to the lay spectator, having an almost theatrical aspect to them. At his *leçons du Mardi*, Dr. Charcot examined new patients he had not seen before, diagnosing them right in front of the crowd, discussing treatment and prognosis as he had them variously make movements with their arms and legs to see if they displayed the chronic contractions common to the hysteric.

And there I was, this Tuesday morning. Already I was to not only to see and hear one of the doctor's lectures but to help document it as well.

A hush fell on the crowd as outside the window a bird sang. Richet paused, about to slide a prepared glass plate into the camera. Dr. Charcot behaved as though the room were empty. He had walked in with two colleagues, and they were in the midst of an intense conversation.

"—the waxy plasticity of the catatonic—" I heard, and "—hysterical paralysis." I could feel anticipation's tight halo around my head.

Dr. Charcot walked over to a dark wooden podium at the center of the stage, and the men with him went and stood behind, their hands and faces respectful and expectant. The crowd shifted and rustled quietly, then there was silence again.

"Greetings, ladies and gentlemen," the doctor began. Richet motioned to me and I moved closer to the camera resting on its oak tripod. Richet bent his eye to the lens, and the first hysteric was escorted into the room, held at each arm by an attendant.

She was young, wearing a coarse, ivory-colored shift. The attendants were having some trouble getting her into the room. She did not so much resist as seem to stumble through some unseen rocky meadow of which only she was aware. Her eyes seemed fixed on something far away, her body unconscious of being pulled along through this flat, brightly lit reality.

The orderlies positioned her in the middle of the low stage. The lighting dimmed, which rendered the walls black and the atmosphere even more expectant. From where I stooped next to Richet I applied a taper with a percussive motion to a metal sheet containing flash powder, and in the sudden glare of white light Richet snapped a picture. I handed him a new plate as he passed me the old, which I slid quietly into the holding box, aware of the movements of my hands, the muscles tightening and loosening; the woman stood exactly as she had been placed, soft and immobile like rotting wood.

"Note the lack of expression in the eyes and face, the flaccid limbs," Dr. Charcot began. "An hysterical trance may last for days; I have known of some that have lasted for weeks. This girl was brought in several days ago. Since she arrived, she has refused to eat. And every night she has been heard crying herself to sleep. Two of her aides have seen her go into paroxysms, although as yet they have been of the milder form.

"Now, let me show you. Two main causes of hysteria are irregularity of the menstrual cycle, and insanity. In this particular case—" The girl began to swallow convulsively, as though she could not breathe. But the doctor continued.

"We have not yet studied the patient to determine the root cause of the problem. But the manifestation of symptoms is consistent with . . ." The girl brought a hand to her throat. She massaged her neck, bringing back her head until she could have seen the dark ceiling of the Amphitheatre had her eyes not stopped in their upward arc to stare suddenly into my face with the terror of a small, cornered animal. Her mouth moved. Dr. Charcot glanced at her, then back at his audience.

"To quote Diderot," the doctor said, "the woman bears within an organ prone to terrible spasms." The girl's cheeks flushed with blood, drained of blood. He paused to laugh. "Of course, we men of science know today that the uterus is not the actual cause of hysteria. We no longer believe, for example, that the organ of reproduction moves about the female body *in extremis*. But the womb is, in essence, the woman. It signifies her purpose, her very reason for being. And, as such, it serves as an excellent metaphor." Pens scraped paper: *Woman as womb.*

"This organ uses her and arouses ghosts of all kinds in her imagination. It is in hysterical delirium that she returns to the past, hurls herself into the future, and that all times are present to her. It is indeed a powerful metaphor, my friends, because Woman is capable of being haunted only by the spectres of the female imagination. It is always, *always* a question of the genitals."

The girl's eyes were crying, but her face had become impassive as stone.

"This girl," the doctor said, gesturing without looking in her direction, "is lost in that most fertile place in the feminine imagination: Love." A titter ran through the crowd, and suddenly I felt my own cheeks blazing. My body went rigid and the glass plate I was preparing snapped in two. Richet glanced at me.

"Everything about this girl announces the hysteric. See how she stands, her hands clasped below her waist, at once protecting and calling attention to the most private and female part of her anatomy. Her posture, too, is a dissimulation. How erect her stance, how demure and womanly. And yet is this not also, in combination with her clasped hands, a posture designed to draw attention to the breasts? Obviously there is an excess of pride, as well as a well-masked eroticism, in the very way in which she holds herself in front of a crowd of people. I myself saw this girl enter the hospital, and she was bent and crying: There was no audience present.

To me she seemed, moment to moment, to be less and less aware of the audience. Her body seemed frozen, not with fear or even defiance; she had left the stage. The brief wetness of her eyes had been the last protest: Now there was nothing but a shell to be stared at and discussed. She was not seeking attention but fleeing it.

Dr. Charcot turned to her.

He looked at her steadily for a long moment. The he said brusquely, "We shall begin."

The audience held its breath.

"Close your eyes," he said, and she did so. Without speaking the doctor walked over and lightly pressed his thumbs against her eyelids. She startled, and he placed his fingers firmly on each side of her face, her temples, as if in a vise. Slowly, softly, her face relaxed, her shoulders, her frightened arms. Her eyes fluttered half-open and remained that way. Dr. Charcot stepped away, his right arm held stiff, his fingers pointed slightly down. The girl's head dropped abruptly to the side, her face turned away, presenting him with a cheek as demure as any schoolgirl's.

"Augustine," said Dr. Charcot. "Raise your left arm." The girl,

Augustine, I thought, what a pretty name; I was holding my breath, Augustine too, made no movement, then with no change in her seemingly unconscious face, slowly started to raise her arm, and the audience breathed.

When her arm had risen to shoulder height, Dr. Charcot said, "Stop."

The doctor stood thus a long time, and I watched the placid rise and fall of her pretty breasts, and I felt ashamed of myself.

"A similar technique has been used with equal success," Dr. Charcot said, "on chickens." Another, louder titter of amusement ran through the crowd.

"With a well-practiced patient who hypnotizes quickly," Dr. Charcot continued, "it is enough to abruptly place the hand on the head, and she falls as if struck by lightning." The girl did not seem as if struck; she had merely turned away. Richet had relinquished the camera to me, and I looked at her three-quarter profile through the lens to avoid having to feel. She looked, for the first time she had set foot on the stage, at peace. She looked to be under a spell: Sleeping Beauty. The Master had worked his magic, and now she belonged to him.

Chapter 17

Charles

RECENTLY I HAD begun to feel a certain ennui. Not with V; each semi-lit encounter enslaved me anew, and she had become to me as necessary as air or absinthe. No, it was the particulars of my daytime hours that had begun to pall: subsumed each night by animal pleasures, my waking self became pallid and dull. The pearl skies of Paris began to look merely gray, and all food lost its taste. My nerves, accustomed as they were to the nightly stimulation of absinthe, V, and the removal of all ordinary moral constrictions, had left me debilitated during the daylight hours, a vampire unable to rest in the dust of his homeland, because my homeland had become nothing less than that intoxicating nightscape.

V noticed my discontent. We were seated at the dinner table one evening, the French doors open to the balmy night. The sounds of hoofbeats and carriage wheels came into the room as if from far away, the sound of voices like the hum of insects. V was gay, and leaned toward me over the table that I might see her breasts rising out of her chemise. She was not dressed; although we had made love hours before, she had remained in the slip in which I had taken her, only throwing a long garnet silk shawl over her shoulders as the air cooled. There was a faint chill that made me restless in a pleasant way; I would gladly have packed a bag and boarded a ship to India had V suggested it.

"You are not yourself, Charles," she said. "Or rather, you are yourself, for the first time in days, and I can tell that you need excitement."

"You are quite enough excitement for me, my love," I said, but I did not feel it. She was right, I was on the edge of something.

"I think I know what you need," she said, and although she started mixing a glass of absinthe I knew that was not what she meant—at least, not all she meant.

I loved to watch V mix my poison. She caressed the bottle, the spoon, she made each step almost a form of foreplay. And yet I could never get her to drink even the smallest sip; my addiction was the only thing V would not share with me. I waited, I watched her mix my drink, I felt the water dripping over the sugar cubes as if it were a taste and not a sound. She slid the glass over to me and I drank, and waited for what she was going to offer me.

I had once seen, as a child, an Anatomical Venus. She lay recumbent under glass, nude on black satin pillows. She was wax, but she was real to me. Her skin was as supple and shaded as that of a living woman. Her face was articulated down to the eyebrows, every fingernail and toenail in place. She was a woman, and she was perfect. She had long straight brown hair fanned across the satin pillow beneath her head. Her eyes were half-open. Around her neck was a string of pearls.

She lay on her back in a museum, her lips half-parted, looking vacantly toward heaven. Her right hip was flexed, her leg slightly raised, her knee bent, accentuating the perfect line of thigh and calf. One arm lay straight, the other bent at the elbow. On both hands all fingers but the index were lightly clenched, as though she were grabbing the satin sheets beneath her buttocks, as though she were threatened from above. Her head lay back, arched at the neck, demure with her half-open mouth and supplicant hands. What was poised above her, a threat or a pleasure?

She was split open from her throat to the meeting of her legs.

She was a doll used during the last century to reveal the intricate workings of Woman's body. Each organ was nestled in its proper place; there was even a little fetus in the waxen womb.

I stood in front of the glass case as if in front of a great reliquary in some ancient cathedral. There were paintings, statues, rarities from all over the world, but for me there was nothing but her. I wanted to lift the glass. I wanted to touch her face. I wanted to see if the curve of her hip would be warm. I wanted to reach inside her perfect body, to run my fingers over the recesses of her wounds, to put my hands around her organs. Diamonds in a waxy mine.

I wanted that body to be real.

V made me wait a week, the vixen. Then we dressed one day and had our lunch at a café some blocks from the Hôpital Salpêtrière. V liked to walk, even in cold and inclement weather; such small discomforts made her feel alive. I think she could have lived naked in the woods on nuts and berries, a dryad, not a woman, freezing in her tracks at the sight of a human man, who in passing would note only the gleaming white bark and graceful limbs of an extraordinary tree.

And it was indeed a cold for a spring day, and V's small hand was in my pocket as we walked, both of us warmed inside by the love we had made that morning, a satisfying lunch, and, in my case, two glasses of my green poison. We were merry, as if going to the theater. I had no idea, and would have none for quite some time, of what V really desired when she took me to La Salpêtrière.

THE HYSTERIC'S BODY was displayed so completely that she might as well have been naked before our gaze. Her body was ours, served up as it was on the dry plate of neurological analysis. *The hysterical contractures of the throat*: and the tall young country girl arched her neck and looked toward heaven, her neck muscles working as though she could not breathe. *The lesions of the cerebral cortex*: and her eyes were lidded. She gasped, it could have been for air or kisses.

She moved with the precision of an artificial thing. She was altogether charming in her dishabille, in her silence, in her desperation. Her eyes, crystal blue, might well have been marbles for all the expression they conveyed, but I could read the signs of her passion in her fingers, which were so stiff the tendons stood out in ridges; her fingers were splayed, and bent unnaturally, each one stretched and tensed as if reaching toward some unreachable escape, as though each finger knew that it could not reach, would never reach, whatever key or ledge or doorknob would bring her freedom.

And that was her charm, of course. She was trapped, and she knew it. Even her mind was not free. She was trapped by Dr. Charcot's orders, by the gaze of the crowd, the gaze of the camera, trapped within the confines of the madness that predicted and determined her actions.

She is trapped as well within her mind: What reaches her from Dr. Charcot's mouth? Raise your left arm. And with her somnambulist's eyes, she responds: She raises her arm. But we cannot know what Augustine sees. We cannot know what it is Augustine thinks she is doing: responding to her master's orders or reaching toward freedom? His voice: Is it a touch, a caress? Is it a sound at all? A roar to which she reacts in fear? If she hears words, what words are they? A mother's reassuring murmurs? A lover's imprecations? A gentle threat? Because his voice is firm but he cajoles, his voice is iron velvet, both the key and the ropes that bind. Because she is bound, Augustine, she is bound by his voice, and our eyes, by the stiff cotton shift she wears, by the silken bonds of her exquisite madness, tight against her slim wrists, her neck, her stubborn, rigid hands.

She could not have been more beautiful, and I would have had her for myself. And yet when I turned to V she was biting her lip, and her eyes were dreaming. She seemed totally absorbed in the moment, rapt with this slave of Dr. Charcot's. The girl's face had by degrees assumed a masklike aspect, hardening into the frozen immobility of fear. It happened with great delicacy; Dr. Charcot was murmuring, his hand lightly touching her shoulder, his eyes lit with expectancy. The girl's hand fluttered up in front of her face; her body did not move at all, but rather went rigid. She seemed trapped in the face of something unspeakable.

I scanned the crowd. It had become almost completely still, completely silent. Every face was suffused with delight. This girl's palpable terror was so artificial and yet so obviously truly felt that it was like being privy to a stranger's nightmare. I looked again at V's face, and she in turn smiled up at me—a smile of complicity.

She saw what I saw: a young girl's terrified expectancy at the approach of her lover.

And then my attention was caught by one of the two men engaged in taking photographs of the proceedings. He was sliding new plates into his camera. His face arrested me. He alone, out of all the voracious crowd, showed pity. Even the most sedate matron in Dr. Charcot's Amphitheatre had something of the observer's victorious glow. Because surely this girl's agony belonged, somehow, to all of them, the entire crowd had become complicit in her dejection. She belonged to all of them, she was their doll. Even the most prudish observer had become a voyeur.

But not the man behind the camera. He alone saw through the farce to the human being inside the terrified blue eyes. His hands were not gentle with the plates—I heard it when he slammed them home. His eyes held both a rage and a sorrow infinitely deep. He almost seemed ready to rush the stage. And yet I could see that he was restrained. He did not want to frighten the girl.

The doctor lectured.

"A woman's sanity, after all, depends on regular doses of sexual gratification. And yet in Woman there is no way to express these urges. Green disease is always a manifestation of the frustration of sexual desire in the female. Marrying her off to a lusty young farm boy would almost certainly have enabled her to express her womanly needs in such ways as are appropriate to its nature: not simply sexual gratification but children, a home to care for, in short. She would have no time to think about herself. Self-examination in such a patient can be pernicious: To quote the lawyer for a woman accused of the crime of murder, 'The mind becomes troubled when the senses have not been not satisfied.' And unpleasant as it may be to accept the voracious and essentially primitive nature of Woman's sexuality, we men of science must make the attempt.

"Note the fixed quality of the eye. The gaze does not falter, and yet it stares as if into some unquiet oblivion.

"Now to the lips. See how they are parted in an almost sensual abandonment. And yet this ecstasy is accompanied by the most painful respiration: The unrestrained sensualist is struggling for breath. The loss of reason in Woman is so often accompanied by this letting loose, as it were, of the unbridled nature of her sexuality."

The women looked down becomingly and discreetly blushed at their escorts.

"The second stage is marked by extreme mental agitation. Note the constriction of the forehead, the way the eyebrows contract upward, how the parting of the lips has progressed to a state where the subject seems more animal than woman, with an almost satanic countenance, as though no man could tame her. This is the soul of Woman laid bare."

The only true pleasure is the pleasure of having power over others. And the only pleasure as exquisite is being the willing victim of the woman who would give you power over others. In the drawing room, at the most fashionable tables of the most fashionable people of Paris, in our silk-sheeted bed or our dirty garret, my power over V was complete. She was the model of decorum, the most beautiful accessory, the most charming hostess, and the most accommodating whore. But for all her acquiescent compliance there was a price: I killed for her.

That my fantasies, which had taken root in my boyhood and grown in the recesses of my mind over the years, should so perfectly match her own, was the most fortuitous grace. Without her, I would have done nothing. Oh, I had pinched whores' nipples until their cries were real, had squeezed whores' necks until their eyes faded upward into their sockets, but such escapades would have remained enough. You do not long to go places on the map that do not exist, and for a young man of my station and education, the actual stalking and killing of prey could never have become more than a daydream.

But V—what could have prepared me for V? She was victim and muse, slave and master. She could have leapt from my deepest imaginings, and yet without her my imaginings would have remained unresolved, like a negative that has been left undeveloped.

Chapter 18

From the Journal of Augustine Dechelette

I COULD NOT remember half of what was done or said to my shame. (The humiliation I have just undergone has almost undone me.) The lights were very bright, and the doctor's voice very stern. He spoke, and I disappeared. It was as if I became trapped within my body: I could feel its contours, but not as I ordinarily do. I could experience my body only from the inside. A snake's skin, a carapace, not a protection but a prison of flesh. There was a young woman who moved her arms just so when bidden, who tilted her head and mummed a part as though she knew it well—but that young woman was not me. And I was not truly bidden but controlled, utterly, by a faraway peremptory voice I could not even think of disobeying.

I remembered only one other thing: blue eyes. Paler than mine, but fixed on my own like the beam of a lighthouse and seeming to blink on and off like the beam of a lighthouse. In the storm of my immobility those eyes were my guiding star; I saw them shining as if far from shore, the one steady, rhythmic point in my dissolving presence. I felt I would disappear completely without those eyes, or at least become, against my will, something not Augustine. I looked toward those eyes, and they held me fast, and I did not drown.

And then the lights were bright again, and I was ashamed, although I don't know why: My loss of control was not of my doing at all. But ashamed I was, a gawky country girl standing near-naked in front of all Paris, and my eyes did not want to rise to meet those beacons that had held me. But I had no more will against those eyes than I had had against the Master's voice. But Charcot's voice was a call toward oblivion and death, and those eyes a call toward comfort.

And there he was, a tall ginger-haired man not so much older than I, and he was blushing, and I realized that in my trance I had heard a repeated click and shush, click and shush, like waves lapping the shore, and that that had been him loading his plates and snapping his camera, his eyes hidden and revealed in a steady rhythm as he took his photographs.

And he smiled at me.

Chapter 19

Edouard

THE MESSAGE CAME to me as I was gathering my photographic equipment after my work at La Salpêtrière was done: Bezier needed me. I sent word that I would come immediately. I had worked hard and was longing for my dinner table, my coffee cup, and my cat, Goncourt.

The address was in an area that had a distinctly unsavory reputation. I took a cab, but the driver was loath to cross the bridge; his horse shied, and he explained that he could never get it to cross to that place, especially as it was after dark. I tipped him and set out on foot. It was dark indeed as I crossed the bridge, heading away from the busy square of Nôtre Dame with its portrait artists and booksellers and couples on promenade. It began to rain, and without looking back I had the sensation of leaving a place where it was not raining and there was still light.

As I walked I thought of the girl on the stage on the Amphitheatre of La Salpêtrière. I only knew her name: Augustine. I did not know her station or her background. I did not know her age. She was a patient in a mental institution; she wore a patient's uniform, and her feet were bare.

But her hair was honey, and her eyes are cornflower blue; and she was afraid. She looked to me to reassure her, and I could not. She looked away, and a light was taken from me. Something moves in my heart when I think of her. Pity? I do pity her; but not as one would pity an unfortunate soul whose miseries were of her own making. This is odd to me because whether the weakness is inborn or the result of circumstance, surely it is weakness of character that leads to madness.

And yet she didn't have the physiognomy of the insane. She did not have the bearing of the lost. She had the bearing of a child. With all our eyes on her she retained an innocent dignity.

A thin black-and-white cat skittered across the pavement before me. There was offal in the gutters. Every so often there was the faint smudged light of candles behind a windowpane.

I will pray for that girl. But it wasn't prayers I thought of, when I thought of her. It was beauty, and fear; I thought of something like love.

But can love come like that, silent and sudden and cornflower blue? Choosing me as an anchor in that Amphitheatre was surely nothing more than coincidence.

Does she even remember me?

I had not brought my umbrella, and soon my hat dripped rain onto my nose. I walked as though I knew quite well where I was going; I was not surprised when a woman, not young, approached me, unheeding of the rain.

"I have something you might like, Monsieur," she said pleasantly as she came up to me, with no coquetry and no fear. Instead of being insulted I was filled with respect for this creature who was brave enough to apprehend a strange man so matter-of-factly.

"Why are you not afraid?" I asked her.

"What have I got to be afraid of?" she asked with honest surprise. She was pulling at the stopper of a small bottle. "Laudanum," she said, and as she smiled she looked younger, and free. I had the most absurd urge to kiss her, and felt instantly repulsed; it was almost a physical thing.

"You should not be here," I said. "It is dangerous." And when she laughed again I knew I was absurd to her; I was absurd to myself.

"It's you who are the lost kitten," she said. "Have you ever tasted laudanum?"

"No," I said, and felt young and naïve.

"These are my streets, Monsieur. This is my home. You are the one in danger here."

"In danger of what? You do not seem dangerous to me." I wanted to offer her dinner in a warm place; I wanted to rescue her; and still I wanted to kiss her.

"Do you think you are too good for me?" she asked good-naturedly. "You should see the fancy men who risk coming here to find themselves a street girl. Not everybody wants a whore pretending to be a lady. There are plenty of fancy men who are just looking for a whore."

It hurt to hear her speak of herself that way.

"I am sure," I said awkwardly, "that this was not your first choice of occupation," and was aware immediately of what an ass I sounded.

"First choice of occupation!" There was no anger in her voice, and no shame; she laughed and laughed. "I was a lady's maid, and the gentleman of the house got me pregnant and had me thrown out. First choice of occupation!"

"I'm sorry," I said, and she touched my arm with gentle fingers.

"You're a real innocent, aren't you? I'll bet you have a sweetheart. Your sweetheart, she's a lucky girl." I am afraid I blushed.

"And yet here you are," she continued. "Does your sweetheart not give you what you need?" Again she tipped the laudanum bottle, and it left her lips as dark as blood. "I will be your sweetheart, Monsieur. If you kiss me now, you will taste my laudanum."

"I am not here for that," I said, and suddenly I was afraid: of her, of these streets, of myself.

"Have it your way," she said casually. "I will give other men pleasure tonight. I will ease their hearts as well as their wallets! Go home and kiss your sweetheart. Muss up her hair and her petticoats. She will love you the more for it."

I sighed. "I am looking for 31 rue de l'Eglise. And nothing else."

"Ah, that is just down the block from Madame Sylphide's place. Not one of the Big Numbers, but her girls are good. Not as good as me, but good. I know tricks they haven't even thought of." And she pointed the way with her bottle.

"Thank you, Mademoiselle. God keep you safe."

"God!" Again she laughed and laughed. "God brought me to these streets. God brought me laudanum. It is I who keep myself safe, you little lost kitten, and I suggest you not depend on God as you are walking here tonight."

"I wish I could do something for you."

"Then give me money! And then give me money, Monsieur, and kiss me. That will ensure my safety tonight."

"Why do you want me to kiss you?" I asked stupidly.

"To corrupt you, little kitten. And to taste decency with my lips. I have not tasted decency once in my entire life."

So I took a ten-franc note out of my pocket, and as I placed it in her cold hand I leaned and kissed her lips. They were sharp with the drug she took, and they were soft as petals.

And I thought of the girl from La Salpêtrière. And could not look into this woman's eyes.

"I envy you," she said, and I looked up. "You are incorruptible. You thought about your sweetheart, didn't you? Did you know you sighed? And yet you have not wiped your mouth. I thank you for that. Go on now, kitten, and find what you are looking for. I envy that sweetheart of yours."

"I'm . . ."

"Don't say you're sorry. For once a man has given me joy. Go now, and don't look back."

And as I turned I heard her quick, resolute footsteps fade away behind me.

I heard Capt. Bezier before I saw him.

"—in his pockets," he was saying loudly to a gendarme standing next to a lit carriage. "Clearly the work of a thief."

There was a dead man lying on the sidewalk, face-up with a surprised expression on his face. A vicious-looking knife was still lodged in his chest. He had been dead perhaps one hour, perhaps two.

"His watch fob is still here," I said. "May I?" I pulled the watch, heavy and gold, from his pocket. "I would not have left this behind."

"There was no time," Capt. Bezier said impatiently. "She took his wallet. Clearly there would be enough in that for a drink, or opium."

"She?"

"A prostitute, Edouard. It is obvious."

It was getting cold. An hour ago it had been warm, and not raining, too warm for a woman selling her body to be wearing a coat that could have hidden such a large knife. And no woman could have gotten such a knife out of a bag without the man's noticing, and quite clearly he had been taken by surprise. A woman to take him off-guard, a man to stab him. My camera was ready. I knelt to take the first shot.

"—an ordinary crime," Capt. Bezier was saying. And like as not this was a not a chance meeting. A man like this would ordinarily have gone to one of the Big Numbers. I was concentrating on the photographs: the angle of the knife, the shocked and yet expressionless dead face, the unmarred hands crossed piously across his chest.

"—put him in the Morgue tomorrow," Capt. Bezier said.

"Who is it that frequents the Morgue? I asked, almost to myself. The man's legs lay military-straight, and his feet could not possibly have fallen into the stiff, upward position they were in now, toes pointing toward heaven.

"The whole populace of Paris, Edouard. People come to do their civic duty by identifying the nameless dead. And of course, it is listed in the Cook's Tour."

"So, it is like a museum. A museum of the dead."

"How poetic you are, Edouard. It is a curiosity. We do have identifications, to be sure, or we would not allow these viewings. But people come to see death, that is all."

"That is what I said." I snapped the last shot. "Death distanced. Death neatly set up and framed." I stood up. I did not know, yet, what purpose this killing had served, and certainly not to whom.

But it was clearly not the work of one woman, nor robbers, for why cross the victim's arms, why set straight his feet? I said nothing to Capt. Bezier. I simply packed up my camera equipment and made ready to leave. I refused his offer of a ride back to my apartment, for I wanted to walk alone with my thoughts, which were as clouded as this moonless, windy night.

Chapter 20

From the Journal of Augustine Dechelette

YESTERDAY EVENING THE girl with the sad brown eyes approached me. "I perceive," she whispered, "that you are not among the insane." She darted looks about the room, which was the vast airless place they call the Day Hall, where patients may walk or sit without the constant attentions of the attendants. I almost wrote *guards*.

"I don't know," I said. "I feel quite sane, although oh, I do not have a word for it, but in this place I sometimes feel almost unreal. At home I was unhappy, but I never doubted my sanity. But Papa has always known what is best for me, and surely, if something were wrong with me . . . They say I am suffering from green disease." The words were hardly out of my mouth when I was mortified. What a way to talk to a stranger! And yet I was starved for conversation. How starved I had not known until that moment. I felt sudden color in my cheeks: What if this girl knew the symptoms of green disease? What if she suspected my secret vice? I could not breathe; surely I would faint.

But she smiled and reached to take my hand. I let her. "I fancy they could not control you. Am I right?" And then, seeing the surprise on my face, "That is what this so-called green disease is. And that is all it is." Her great big eyes regarded me with the utmost tenderness. We exchanged names, and then she said, "I have been here two years because of my rebelliousness. Look, the men are not paying attention now." And indeed the four attendants were huddled in the corner by the fireplace (where we were not allowed, the perceived threat being that we might be tempted to harm either our own persons or one of the other inmates).

"Would you like to hear my story? "

"I would like that very much indeed."

"I fell in love. My parents had the `perfect young man' picked out for me. Oh, they're progressive, my parents. They married for love. And they always said that I should marry for love until I actually fell in love, and then it was, 'He has no inheritance, he has no income, he's a poet, Adelaide, he will never sell his work, and what is his work, anyway? Morbid scenes of death, degradation, and sin. And look at the way he writes about women in these poems of his! He cannot possibly respect you, Adelaide, if he is capable of writing obscene words about unclothed nymphs and dryads! This is not what we want for you. There is a boy in town you have known him all your life, and he comes from a good family."

"Gérard," I said softly.

"Gérard?"

"The boy my parents wanted for me. The greatest clodfoot in the village."

"But he had 'prospects,' didn't he?"

"Prospects! He works his father's farm. Someday he will be a landed gentleman, Adelaide, heir to every cow and chicken."

"And you could not see that every happiness was laid out for you, if only you were to come to your senses and become his wife? A home of your own in which to practice the womanly arts, lots of little clodfoot children?"

"And the chickens. Do not forget the chickens."

"And the cows. What fools we are, Augustine, worse than fools, to aspire to something other, something higher, than our mothers' dreams for us! It's a sickness, this will in young women to carve their own fate!"

"It is the chief evil of our age, Adelaide. The medical men say that neurasthenia—the weakening of the nervous system of our entire society—is caused by the intolerable pace of modern life. I say it is a moral weakness! What has changed for woman? Nothing. Her kingdom is still the home. And the following of her natural inclination for domesticity, her inborn need to follow, not to lead, is completely unaffected by modern change. If anything, the conveniences of modern life foster woman's natural lassitude. A woman reads of the fashions of Paris and is seduced. Immediately she must have dresses à la mode, and makeup in the latest style. Nerves! Nerves, indeed. The inherent weakness of a woman's mind can and must be—"

"Oh, my, Augustine, but you re good!"

I had completely forgotten myself. Instantly, I felt myself go red, and felt as well a sharp pang.

"My father used to say those things. It was a kind of game for us. What spirited discussions we had! I think he so often chose the topic of a woman's place because he wanted me to exercise my mind. He knew it incensed me. And yet, I never became angry with him. It is funny, Adelaide, but I know he was proud of my resistance to his views. He will never admit it, but he wanted me to think for myself. He brought me up from infancy to have a mind as strong as a man's."

"And yet when you used it—"

"It was my will I used. My will and my heart. I do not think he expected that. Even though he was proud of my ability to argue against his views, I truly believe that he expected, once it became time for me to choose, that the male qualities he thought he had instilled in my mind would bring me to the logical conclusion that he was, in fact, right, and that I would realize that my highest good lay in acquiescing to live as the wife of a landed blockhead that my male intellect would realize that my womanly nature could not, and should not, be denied."

"You certainly don't sound as if you think like a man, Augustine!"

"I don't. I never have. I've never pretended to, either. I am deeply grateful for the education my father has given me. We have studied astronomy, botany, history, politics, Latin, religion, in addition, of course, to the things our mothers teach us: piano, singing, recitation, sewing and tatting, cooking. I am the most dreadful cook, Adelaide, whoever I do marry is going to be quite dissatisfied with me."

"Have you studied poetry, Augustine?"

"A bit."

"I have lived for poetry," said Adelaide. She seemed suddenly lit from within. "Poetry is apparently the tool of the devil, although how something so exalted, so noble—forgive me, but this is my passion, and this is what brought me here, as much as anything else. Of course there was a man—nobody ever seems to notice that there's always, always a man involved in the downfall of a young girl, nobody insists a man be sent away for loving. There was a man—a boy, really. I sent my poetry in to the weekly *L'Illustration*, and oh, Augustine, they printed it! My father was enraged, but my mother felt that perhaps this small success would diminish my need, that such an accomplishment would suffice for a woman. And it did, for a time, and although I doubt it really would have, I did not have a chance to find out because he wrote to me. François Nanet. A fine poet in his own right, and impressed that I had the courage to send my poetry in for publication, where he had not. And he loved my poetry! He understood every nuance, he traveled in the same atmosphere in which I lived. We corresponded. It was heaven. We fell in love . We exchanged photographs and arranged to meet. I felt as if my life, my true life, my intellectual, spiritual, and romantic life, was just beginning."

Her voice softened almost to a whisper. "I met him twice before my parents found out. Twice."

Everything I would never have asked was in that word twice. She was silent then, staring into the fire too far away to warm us, lost to a sweet reverie of what had brought her here. Finally she said, so quietly that I barely heard her, "It was worth it."

"I was in love, too," I said, perhaps too quickly. "Nothing would ever have come of it. He was married. I dreamed, but that was all I did. My parents found my behavior strange. I would not concentrate on my piano, I dreamed over my lace and tatted peculiar patterns, unaware of my work, then . . ." I paused, and felt myself burn red, that curse I've always had, my skin not my own and now my body is not my own, either.

I found I had spoken those last words aloud. *My body is not my own.*

But Adelaide only laughed. "That's true," she said cheerfully. "We belong to Dr. Charcot."

"I meant—"

"I know what you meant. They try to control our minds and our wills by controlling all of our actions, don't they? I understand it when we are small, but we are women now! The way I see it, if I am old enough to marry, I am old enough to love. And if I am old enough to love, oughtn't I be trusted to choose my love? And oughtn't you be free to feel? I cannot imagine, even on our short acquaintance, that you would be the sort of girl to ruin a marriage! If I ever find that my daughter is loving inappropriately, I hope that I will be able to believe in her goodness as I believe in yours, and to help her through her pain instead of condemning her to a place like this!"

I said nothing.

I had never met anyone like Adelaide. I felt that already I was a fully formed character in the adventure that was her life. That she had made up her mind about my character on such short notice, that she had shared the most intimate details of her emotional life with almost a total stranger. Well, it was a strange place we were in, and there was something endearing in her earnest need to see the best in me. I had never met such a lively intellect, such an open countenance, such an enthusiastic acceptance of the vagaries of love and life. It was why I gave her my story. Her openness invited openness and erased caution. Adelaide lived life at a pitch that few of us could ever hope to reach.

She was looking at me with kind and expectant eyes.

"The worst thing," I said slowly, "is that now that I am here, Louis is completely gone. I cannot remember anything. I have lost his eyes. I have lost the smell of his hair." These were things I did not think I would ever say to anyone. And I looked at her face and saw only gentleness and interest, things I had not experienced since I got here. I felt an urge to cry and saw with surprise that Adelaide's eyes were moist.

And I knew I had found a friend in this place.

I came here determined not to lose hope, and God has sent me a girl who does not know how to lose hope. So I will remain Augustine, and not define myself as some ill and broken creature. I will remain the hopeful girl who dreams of one day dancing on the stage in Paris, the city of her dreams.

Chapter 21

Charles

I WAS NOT surprised at what she asked of me next. "A woman," she said. Her eyes glowed in the light of the candle next to our bed. Our bed—in that dirty garret that had been a whore's office.

Her eye glowed like a cat's.

"A woman. To be found naked by the Seine." V didn't have to woo me with her body, her arts. I would have killed for her anyway. But I let her woo me. I lay exhausted in that narrow bed as rain hit the roof and the skylight, and when she asked me we both knew what I would say.

V's apartment contained no second entrance, which had rather disappointed me. But that night she surprised me by opening a cabinet that I had assumed to be meant to hold clothing. She said, "Hold my hand. It is dark," and we descended a narrow, closed stair. The air was so close and hot that I could hardly breathe. I did not like close spaces, and was distinctly relieved when we exited at the ground floor into the back courtyard of the building. We were to use that staircase many times, finding that it lent our doings an enjoyable, if somewhat immature, feeling of getting away with something. And sometimes I would go around to the back, let myself in with my key, and walk very slowly up the stairs in the dark, no matter that mounting them discomfited me: I knew that as I lingered, V was arranging something for my pleasure, something unexpected, something hotly anticipated. The little leather cat-o'-nine-tails to whip her pussy and her tits; ice water dripping onto the sugar cube on a slotted spoon; other things I try to think of seldom, to keep them fresh in my memory.

It was raining outside, and it was windy, and chilly for the season. She wore a fox-fur stole around her shoulders and hid her hands in a fox-fur muff. Her hood was edged in fur; her face was hidden. The hem of her long, light pelisse was dirtied, the hem of her silk dress. The streets were barren; it wasn't a good night for business, apparently. But V knew where to go. She led me around corners and through narrow alleys.

I held my new knife in my pocket.

Then she stopped so suddenly that I blundered into her. She moved ahead of me; she held her arm slightly out, fingers raised in warning that I be silent and follow her lead. We were almost abreast of a deeply recessed doorway. She released my arm; she nodded; that was all.

I felt a visceral horror then, a shudder through my body and my soul. In that instant it seemed that what I would find in that dark womb would be too hideous to bear. Something worse than the dead woman V and I had determined to create tonight. I hesitated; I sensed a very great danger. I was acutely aware of V at my back; I could feel her excited breathing, although I could not hear it. She had not asked me for the knife. Standing there I realized the hideousness that awaited me: I was going to have to speak to the woman in that doorway, to ask her price and name my fancy. To notice whether she was fair, young, or tall; whether she spoke with the words of an educated woman; whether she was drunk. The man had been nothing to me. He had not uttered a sound. And to my V he was just another man. It was the living woman I recoiled before, not the dead one.

She stepped out of the dark, and I swear I almost bolted. And she did the oddest thing: She smiled at me. She wasn't drunk. She was very young, and not pretty. But her smile was genuine, or at least it seemed so to me. The smile played about her lips, as if she saw something of the absurdity of her situation, here in the rain on a solitary street, about to put herself at the mercy of a stranger. She looked me straight in the eye, as if she had nothing to fear.

"Good evening," I said stiffly. I had never done this, not on the street like this, greeting each other as though we had just been introduced at a musical evening.

"Would you like to take me out for a drink?" she asked. She spoke with a British accent; she was not afraid at all.

"Here," I said. "I have this." I took out my flask of absinthe. I drank, and I passed the flask to her. I handed her a small cube of sugar, and when she did not know what to do with it I pushed it gently between her lips. She let me pour absinthe through her lips parted by sugar; she shuddered and coughed, then she laughed.

"That was our drink, then? Come with me. I live only two doors down."

I knew I had to kill her in that doorway. Her dead body would do us no good in a room that could identify her, in a place where she might not be found until she was unrecognizably foul. And although the street was empty of traffic, at any moment someone could walk or drive by; there were many men who would brave the weather for a girl like this.

"What is your name?" I asked suddenly, and I took her shoulder and pushed her gently back into the doorway.

"Tabby," she said. "Is it to be here, then?" With the same frank, unafraid humor as before.

"Here," I said, and I forced her up against the door, which was farther back than I expected and caused an awkward, half-falling embrace; and I kissed her. She started against the vehemence of my mouth, then opened hers. I was on fire. She felt nothing. I wanted to force myself on her, to take her hard against the hard glass of the door, but I did not. What was for me a monstrous conquest and betrayal both of love and of self was nothing for her but her daily bread. I stopped; I reared back so I could see her face.

"Tabby," I said.

"Yes, sir." She regarded me. She was waiting for further instructions.

"Have you ever wanted to die?"

"No," she said without hesitation. How old was she? Seventeen, eighteen? I could see her measuring: how tall I was, and how close to her; how far to the opening of this recess, how far to the street, to the corner. Her face was calm.

"Neither have I," I said, and laughed.

Her calm, watchful expression did not change.

"I won't hurt you," I said.

"No, sir," she said, and I saw the knife in her hand. "No, you won't."

I was so startled I nearly bolted. But I did not. V was waiting only a few feet away, with the same calm, watchful expression, I knew, as this girl made beautiful by her bravery.

"I am sorry," I said gently. "I seem to have given quite the wrong impression." I sounded stiff. Had I been this young girl I would not have believed me.

But apparently she did believe me. She put the knife back in the pocket of her skirt.

"My room is just two doors down," she said again. She indicated the direction with a tip of her head.

"You can do what I want right here," I said. I realized how coarse this girl's life was and felt pity for her. But I could feel V's impatience: She wanted her blood.

"No, sir," said the girl. Tabby. "It will be my room." Again, she tipped her head; she intended that I go before her. No doubt there was something or someone there that made her feel safe.

"I'm sorry," I said, and I drove my knife into her.

And she fought me. She was ready. She lunged sideways even as my knife found her flesh.

She screamed, a long, harsh cry like an animal's. My knife slipped, and my hand slipped in her blood. I grabbed her waist and felt a sharp regret: she was slender, and my hand had found the curve of flesh at her hip; I wanted to be holding her in her room, drinking absinthe and caressing her shapely waist and hip while something or someone nearby made her feel safe.

I slammed her back against the recessed door. I caught my grip upon my knife and stabbed again, and her knife cut me. I was looking into her eyes; she'd cut my left arm, deep. She was staring sightless into my chest, so deep in concentration that she didn't need to see. She didn't seem afraid now, and she had gone quiet. She was strong, and she was fighting for her life.

Her blood made her slippery as a fish. My arm was singing with pain. How could she keep fighting? My own pain was slowing my knife. She cut me again, at the shoulder this time; and she ducked and kicked me hard in the shin, and was past me.

I jerked away from the sting in my leg. The girl stopped short and screamed, high and loud. I saw arms open, and I saw the girl fall into them. I heard V's voice, low, fast, and smooth. Her arms surrounded the girl, and as those arms tightened into steel I grabbed the girl by the hair, pulled back her head, and slit her throat.

She fell, that was all. I looked at her body a long time. My shoulder and arm throbbed with a steady beat. I could feel blood flowing down and dripping from my hand. The girl's body lay as though it had never been capable of movement. Her face was turned away from me; I was glad of that. Her waist was still slender, the curve of her hip still pretty. I would stand here looking at her body forever; there would never be a moment after this one.

I lifted my head. Laughter as free as a child's. I looked up to see my beloved with her head thrown back against the sky. Her face was covered with blood that had spurted from the girl's neck as she died. Blood ran down her bosom; there was blood in her mouth and she was smiling at me.

Chapter 22

From the Journal of Augustine Dechelette

I HAVE JUST gotten back from a session with Dr. Charcot. The Great Dr. Charcot. I don't think I have ever met a more frightening human being. Nothing in my girlish existence, nothing even in the depraved works I have read by Huysmans, by Baudelaire, could have prepared me for Dr. Charcot.

An attendant appeared in my room this morning; first the door was closed and I was by myself, then the door had opened and the attendant was standing in my room, looking at me with no interest whatsoever.

"You will be going to see Dr. Charcot now," he said, with no more inflection than if he were reading from a list of sundries. I had the wild idea of screaming, of jumping about—anything to put an expression on that flaccid face.

I restrained myself. I have these very thoughts because I am mad, I know. I went, a compliant patient, pretending I wasn't afraid. But I wished there was a woman there to comfort me. I missed Maman acutely. But then I thought of how frightened Maman would be herself and almost smiled.

But I will remember the doctor's office until the day I die. It was like entering Night. Black furniture. Black walls. On the heavy, glass-topped desk, a black lamp with a black shade. Black velvet curtains drawn against the day. A black rug on black-painted floorboards. I heard the click of the door lock. I stared around the room: no books, even the flagstones in front of the hearth were black marble, and the andirons black. Nothing to relieve the darkness except the puddle of electric light from the lamp.

The doctor sat quietly in his high-topped black-leather chair behind the desk. I realized that I did not at all remember what he had looked like on the stage of the Amphitheatre. The aspect of his face was uncommonly stern, although his brow was noble. I had never before seen eyes so deep-set; they were large, and in this light seemed lost, cavernous, and almost sad. There were deep furrows beneath them, as though he thought all night instead of sleeping. His lips were rather thin and permanently turned down at the corners; again this seemed more from constant rumination than from meeting the world with disapproval. His hair was mostly gray, a little long, and swept back from his head; there was a white streak just at the center of his brow. And there was something frightening in the intensity with which he regarded me. And something—I cannot explain it. I felt that if this man were to ask anything, anything of me, I did not know if I could refuse. He was awe-inspiring in the fullest sense of the word.

"Sit down, Augustine."

"I am afraid of you," I blurted out.

"You are?" He seemed genuinely surprised.

"Terrified," I said, and sat. A small wooden chair painted black.

"Green disease," Dr. Charcot said calmly, making a steeple of his fingers in front of his mouth, "is a form of hysteria. It is why you are here."

"Am I mad?"

"You are in need of help, Augustine. The outward symptoms of green disease are unmistakable. You have been evincing them quite convincingly."

There was something in his voice I knew I could use to my betterment here. Satisfaction, that was it. He might be seeing in me a means to an end. I remembered the attendant saying to me, "Dr. Duret says you will surely be of use to Dr. Charcot." And the journal and ink. And Adelaide speaking of the lucky ones.

I looked down demurely. The great red heat of embarrassment poured over my face. I concentrated on the way breath flowed into and out of my lungs without my volition as I tried to calm my heart; I was sure he could hear it beating.

"I will see you again," he said. "You show great promise as an hysterical subject. We will meet every few days. Pay special attention to the epileptic patients on your ward."

I stared.

"That is all."

The door opened silently and an attendant appeared, although I had not seen him summoned.

Dr. Charcot was not looking at me. I stood.

"You hypnotized me. I did not recognize my own voice."

We stared at each other. I felt, just as I had in the Amphitheatre, that at any moment I might dissolve.

"Yes," he said finally.

"Yes. You are an excellent subject. I was able to accurately diagnose you within minutes. Your body responds well."

"You told me what to do!"

"My dear girl."

"Augustine."

"My dear Augustine, the only fit subjects for hypnosis are those who already contain within themselves both the cause and the means to express the cause. My ability lies in allowing you to display as physical acts the turmoil inherent in the trauma driving your hysteria. The hysteric relives her trauma through the spectacular motions of contracture, the *arc-en-ciel*, the various cries and screams and even laughter.

"You will have your treatments, of course; hydrotherapy is paramount. But it is in hysterical posturing that I expect you to excel."

I was more frightened than I ever thought I could be.

"You will hypnotize me again," I said, so softly that he had to ask me to repeat it.

"Of course," he replied smoothly. "The symptoms the hysteric evinces, from the contractures to the attitudes passionelles, are all in a sense labile. Ideally, the patient responds to minimal prompting a touch, even just a voice that induces the hypnotic state, thereby laying the ground, as it were, for the hysteric to express the details of her trauma, each more pure, even animalistic, than the—"

Then he saw my expression. For an instant there was almost something of ordinary human feeling in his masklike face. Then he looked away.

"You need only trust me," he said. "That is all."

I could not tell whether he was dismissing me again or attempting to offer comfort.

"I shall prove an apt pupil," I said stiffly.

"I want you to watch carefully the women around you. You are being housed in the wing devoted to hysterics and epileptics. My wing. You will see many things here, some of them strange to you. Yet some will seem strangely familiar, for among the hysterics there are quite a few like yourself."

I blushed again, that curse of red staining my face right down to my bosom.

"Country girls," he said, as though he did not even see my discomfiture, "who have not been given a suitable outlet for the womanly instincts." I thought of all the abandoned lace and scarves, the tatting or set of knitting needles forgotten in my lap as Papa and I argued some finer point of the political scene.

"There are distinct phases to an hysterical attack. You can learn a great deal by observation. Your father says that you are a particularly keen observer. Although he also said that what you most enjoyed observing were the latest hats in fashion in Paris."

The doctor had no notes in front of him; he had made none. He had barely looked at me, staring instead at a fixed point somewhere to the right of my left elbow. I wondered how he could really think he knew anything about me.

"Trust me, you can find real purpose here."

He looked me up and down like a prize cow. I swallowed my bristling pride.

"But it is time you go back to your room, Augustine," and this time I felt an odd lightness at hearing my name in his voice. He was still frightening, but he seemed to be offering me something; I seemed to have pleased him.

"One more thing," he said. "You will be allowed to receive visitors."

"Thank you, but I do not think my parents can come up for at least a few months."

"No, no," he said, looking intently at the puddle of light on the glass of the table. "Other visitors. I think it will prove instructional to you."

I said nothing, being nonplussed. Who would want to visit me in this place? "Do you mean other doctors?" I asked finally.

But he seemed to have truly forgotten me now, staring inward at something far more interesting. The attendant took my arm; I started, but the doctor seemed not to notice that either.

I turned to go.

"But you must remember," he said as the attendant led me from the room, "that not everything can be learned at once."

Chapter 23

Edouard

IN A DIM, recessed entryway only a few blocks away from where we had found the last body (which had turned out to be that of a M. Reventin, a mid-level banking executive with a wife and five children), was the naked body of a very young woman. She lay straight on her back on the hard cobblestones, her hands prayerful at her breasts, her legs soldier- straight, with the feet perfectly tilted together at the toes.

In the semi-darkness of my dark room I remembered how I had knelt in the damp. It was too familiar: The only difference was her nudity, which I had hastened to cover with the sheet I always carry in the event of such a need.

The girl had probably been a prostitute. The neighborhood was notoriously bad, worse even than Belleville. Of course, Mme. DuPrey had been murdered in the same neighborhood, but this girl was so young, and had been enticed or threatened into a door-way.

I was sure that pleasure, and only pleasure, had been the motive for this killing. There had been no reason, no sense to leaving her body displayed as it was. But I began to change my opinion as I developed her photographs and begin to gain at least a rudimentary understanding of this crime.

This girl had been dead so little time that I guessed her expression to be genuine: She had died both surprised and furious. There were numerous cuts to both her hands and her left arm; her right hand was unmarred, and I felt the sharp sting of tears to see a small knife lying some two feet to the right of the body. I had seen it at the scene, but I seldom let myself feel at the scene. Now I wanted to take my mind off the pain of watching that tiny knife swim into view, lying so pathetically on the cobblestones away from the body, so obviously too little, too late. She did not look older than eighteen; why was she out alone, with no one nearby to protect her? I knew this to be a sentimental question devoid of sense, but I found myself becoming angered nevertheless.

Had I eaten today? Normally I could hold myself at arm's length or longer than that, if that was what it took to get the job done. But tonight I had no screen between myself and the suffering of others; I had no skin. Sometimes I became so immersed in my work that I actually forgot to eat, and I knew that such enthusiasm was not a credit to me but only youthful exuberance and the basics of an impractical nature made manifest. Maybe Capt. Bezier was right and I was a poet at heart: Only a poet would be so foolish as not to eat! But no, I had had at least a good breakfast and a substantial dinner today. My pain was the manifestation of a sensitivity I could no more change than I could the color of my eyes or hair. In any event, I wished, for the first time in my career, that I had chosen to aim only for success as a portrait photographer. But then I resolved to redouble my efforts to understand and help to solve the murder of the poor girl in front of me.

I gently released the other photographic papers from their glass plates even as I bathed the first in the solution I had mixed. I would add a toner, either of gold or selenium, after I was finished, in order to stabilize against fading. As my hands performed the familiar actions I wondered what this victim had been to her murderer. Capt. Bezier says that the identity of the victim gives us the identity of the killer every time. This girl: What had she been to him? Because I was certain the murderer was male. My poor victim was not a small girl, she was big-boned and strong, and she had been fighting for her life. All her cuts seemed to have been delivered by someone of more than average height; it is a pity that I have seen so many knife wounds working for Capt. Bezier that I can guess at the height of the murderer from the angle of the cuts.

Certainly her belongings had been stolen, but that did not necessitate stripping the body. Perhaps she had been violated, either in life or after, but that too was unlikely, given that the traffic in the area that time of night was not so sparse as to leave time for more than killing, then stripping and positioning the body.

I applied the toner and began cleaning up my workspace.

No time to do more than kill, strip, and position: So simply murdering a woman was not the motive. Violating a woman was not the motive. The last body I had photographed had been male, and not stripped, but still positioned in exactly the same way. So was that the motive? To position bodies? No; There was one thing more the two had had in common: Neither had been found with any identification. So the motive had been to position bodies that could not immediately be identified. It did not matter whether the victim was a man or a woman, only that he or she be taken off-guard. I was more than ever convinced the crime was committed by not one but two people. Yes, the victim was almost certainly a prostitute, so a man could easily approach and kill her, he did not need help with that, but the body would have had to be stripped quickly and effectively, more effectively, I imagined, than the man who had murdered her could do without assistance, as I was convinced he had probably been hurt by my poor victim's little knife. Or perhaps I just hoped he had.

A woman. For the first victim, a woman to lure him, a man to kill him. For the second, a man to lure and kill, a woman to assist in the part that made no sense. Why position the bodies in such a way? And why remove all identification?

I took one last look at my lady's face, snuffed the candle, and turned to leave the room. As I closed the door and made ready for bed, I thought I knew the answer to at least the second question. But it likely would make no difference what I knew or thought I knew. Capt. Bezier did listen to me sometimes. But this, I feared, would be impossible for a man like him to accept.

I knew I owed it to both victims; but I knew in my heart that it was the face of the girl that would prompt whatever effort I put forth with Capt. Bezier. As she had prompted all my musings here tonight, watching her pain come alive in the darkroom.

Two bodies positioned the same way. Stripped of identification, their logical destination would be the Paris Morgue. A museum of the dead, I had said to Capt. Bezier. Where the public was invited to view the bodies, as art is viewed in a museum. Who creates material for museums? Artists. Who would create material for the Paris Morgue? Artists of death.

As I lay sleepless, looking at the full moon out the window, I thought again: artists of death. *I will not fail you,* I thought, even as my thoughts began to drift. *Life failed you many times, that much is clear, but I will not fail you.*

Chapter 24

Charles

THE GIRL WAS a sensation at the Morgue. She hadn't been beautiful in life, but she was beautiful in death. Naked, covered only in a white sheet. V and I had taken her clothing, and her cheap rings, and dropped them in the Seine, although my memory of that was vague, clouded by more than absinthe and adrenaline. I had not asked V if she had taken the knife, because I knew she thought I had; perhaps I had. My arm in its sling attracted no attention, because how could anyone know that she had cut her attacker? As I waited outside the Morgue it seemed as if my white sling were a shroud. Since I had killed the girl I had been unable to feel anything. I felt dead. Even V seemed only half-real, insubstantial as a remembered dream even as I held her in my arms.

I stood on line smelling the orange peel V was scraping delicately against her teeth, catching sugar on her tongue. I had drunk absinthe with my morning tea, and the air felt like wet flower petals against my skin. The smell of citrus was a golden halo around V's head. She really didn't seem to care about all the people on line, about what they were going to see. About what we were going to see. I could feel V's heart beating; I could feel the girl's blood sliding down my arm like flower petals. V's blood pulsed slowly, like a ticking clock. When a little girl ran up to me and said, "What's your name, Mister?" I shrieked. V put her hand on my arm, like the landing of a bird. The little girl's mother came and pulled the child away, with many apologies.

The line moved forward with a lurch, and next I knew I was standing in front of the glass wall of her tomb. She reclined, her head against the back of a slanted board, covered in white. Her eyes were closed, her mouth slightly open. How had death made her so lovely? I became aware of all the activity in that vast arena; a moment ago that girl and I had been alone. In the dark, in the recess of a dirty doorway.

The crowd moved and pulsed around me like a single creature, voracious, unconscious. I saw that V was not looking at the dead girl at all. She was watching the crowd. The dead girl was nothing to her: The crowd was her creation. It was an animal that ate with its eyes and knew nothing, a creature whose appetite V whetted with death and watched now as it stuffed and sated itself on death. The women drew closer to their men, they took their arms. Their eyes glowed, and the men took advantage of their fear, which looked like lust, to put their arms around their waists, to touch their skin through silk or cotton. As I had touched Tabby's sweet curve, even as I killed her.

My love watched with her cat's eyes and Mona Lisa smile. I knew the kind of sex that we would have at home. But I was the one who had killed. Even V did not know that I had kissed this dead body. I took V's hand; I looked at her lovely face. She was rapt, she had found her heaven. She smiled without really looking at me.

Seeing her pleasure took away everything—the blood, the thud of the dying body, the pain in my arm and shoulder. I hadn't realized until that moment how afraid I had been of that girl and her knife and her desperate determination to live. Looking at her now I loved her a little: I had loved her a little while she was trying to stop me from killing her. V turned her smile full on me, and I realized that she knew, knew it all, everything I was thinking and had thought.

"Perhaps I should have let you have her," she whispered to me now, rising on her toes to reach my ear. The crowd made a murmur like a cat's growl at my back.

"No," I said aloud. "I like it better this way." The man next to me jostled my wounded arm as a way of getting me to move. I didn't want to say good-bye to Tabby; it was like leaving a lover. V knew I'd lied, and she liked that, although I didn't know why.

"We have seen enough," she said, and we moved on into the rippling fur of the crowd.

Chapter 25

APPARENTLY ONE CAN find at least the semblance of normalcy under almost any circumstances, provided a predictable routine is established. I wake in the morning aware that I am in Paris; and then the dreary knowledge of how far I am from the reality of my dreams sets in, sudden and heavy, and for a moment I am incapacitated by grief and cannot move. But every morning a pair of mourning doves croons outside my window, and each time their crooning soothes me, and I am myself again. I am in Paris, and although it is not the Paris I imagined, my life is neither truly difficult nor even too dull. I am, after all, one of the hysterics the great Dr. Charcot has chosen to be, perhaps, a regular performer on a stage of which I know both more and less than I would like. Surely I am not to be trotted out, over and over, on the stage of the Amphitheatre as though I were a new patient each time. But I have been given a journal; I have been given ink. Rewards for a future of good behavior, I know that. And I know that Dr. Charcot favors some patients over others.

Oh, I am incorrigible! To even hope to be favored! What would Maman think? But dear Maman is not here, and even if she were she could not comprehend what my life is now, nor what it is doing to me: A subtle shift and change is occurring even now in my character, in my heart and my soul, and I do not yet know where it will lead. But I am, for better or worse, full of anticipation. I long to find out what this new life will bring.

They make you endure a great deal here in the interest of getting well. I know I ought not complain, but, oh, it is difficult to be grateful! I am suffering from green disease. I wish I could convince the great doctor that all I am suffering from is being in love. All! Does Louis even know where I am? It is doubtful, for what family would advertise their daughter's being taken to the madhouse? And so Louis must think that I just left, without a goodbye. For him it is over already, and I am trapped here knowing that. Knowing that he leaves his shop each night and goes home to his fat wife and thinks of me, I know, less and less. Because my candle always burned more brightly than his. Always. I did not know it then. I know it now.

Did Louis ever love me? Perhaps I was just one more girl awestruck by his accomplishments, his erudition, his delicate hands and poet's eyes. Perhaps I was the girl he will long for forever. I can believe anything, since I cannot know.

But there is little here to keep my mind on the present. I should like hard work now, to be waking early to milk and care for the cows, to be maintaining the vegetable garden with my mother in the afternoons after my mending, to be cleaning out the chicken coop. I would like to work my body to exhaustion, that my mind might do its healing while I was thus occupied.

But I have been told that such a sickness as I have is best treated with rest. Rest for the body as well as the mind. I am left a long time in my room. And oh, irony of ironies, the very vice the discovery of which sent me to this place, that very evil sometimes comes to torment me where I lay healing in my bed. It is as if my body, with its own wisdom, feels that self-pollution is a valid, in fact, the valid means of dispersing the humors that combine to cause my sleeplessness and despair. And oh, that no one ever sees this journal! For I have given in to this impulse more than once, and to my everlasting shame have found it to be of more help than all the hydrobaths in Paris.

But I have not written about the water cure, as I set out to do. Nor of my peculiar diet, specially chosen to suit my circumstances. Every afternoon I am taken for cool, short baths, including local effusions, which means they drip or spray water on particular parts of my body, and the water is always ice. I am dipped wearing only my shift into a chipped tub set in the middle of the room, and afterward subjected to vigorous friction, applied by two disinterested female attendants. Before I am even dry I must put on my clothing and go out, weather permitting, for my exercises. Such silly things to call being rubbed with some towels and taking a brisk walk!

Adelaide tells me that one of the major symptoms of green disease is an overly pale complexion. Her skin is perfect porcelain. I have heard that a girl can catch a good husband for herself just on the strength of such skin. I do hope they cannot cure her skin! My own is brown whatever the season; I have asked Adelaide if my face is dark and she says no quite emphatically, but my arms are still as brown as they always were at home.

I am fed a strict vegetarian diet, which at least includes yogurt and cheeses, else I would become far too thin. I am told that I have a poverty of the blood, and that iron in particular is to be avoided, and I am given a dreadful concoction to drink every morning that Adelaide swears is sheep's blood and cod liver oil.

Adelaide knows all about it. She seems to feel no shame at all at suffering from chlorosis: She has told me proudly, more than once, that green disease is caused by disappointment in love only. She has not guessed my secret vice. I even suspect she would not care! I do not know what I would do without Adelaide.

My schedule and Adelaide's coincide a great deal, as do those of all the more-favored hysterics, so we take our exercise walks at the same time in the largest courtyard.

I am told that the hospital houses almost exclusively those who cannot afford to be housed elsewhere. Adelaide says that the exceptions are those who promise well as hysterics, although what she can mean by that I really still do not know, and I will not tell her how desperately I want to know. Adelaide does not always answer my questions, having jumped so far ahead of my original thought by the time I can formulate one that she has sometimes quite lost me. Her quickness of mind is nothing short of astonishing, and it is a pity to see it wasted here.

Oh, I sound so bitter when I write about La Salpêtrière! I cannot forget that first, interminable walk to the Amphitheatre. I was barely conscious, I was so afraid. I was afraid all the time, then. Of the locked door of my room, of the attendants, of the silence. I was afraid of the view outside my window; I was particularly afraid of Rosalie, who often screams obscenities regarding the Magdalene.

I can almost laugh at Rosalie already, although of course I pity her terribly; but her imprecations no longer make me want to cry myself. Of course Adelaide thinks me silly for both fear and pity; she cries out like Rosalie but makes it about cows and chickens! The first time I was appalled, but I soon realized that although she is a skilled mimic, Adelaide is incapable of actual malice, or even of thinking truly evil thoughts of others. It is just that her natural exuberance carries her away.

And I realize that she is continually trying to calm me, seeing in me a spirit more delicate than her own, and therefore in more need of reassurance. And truly, I do become more comfortable here day by day, although that thought is not comforting in the least.

YESTERDAY I STOOD uncertain at the entrance to the courtyard. The courtyard is approximately fifty feet square. There is a high stone wall, with forget-me-nots and Johnny-jump-ups in the chinks. There are flagstones, large and unevenly placed. There are huge old rosebushes, ten feet high and full of deadwood, spanning the walls on two sides. There is a short flight of stone steps leading up to a stout oaken door that does not ever open; it looks as though no one has even tried to open it in decades. I do not know how old La Salpêtrière is: This courtyard could be a hundred years old, or as old as the fairy tale it seems to be part of; it is a place most unreal. There is even a swing, held upright by wooden posts, that sits square in the middle of the courtyard, and strange it is indeed to see grown women sitting and swinging like little children, without modesty or restraint. I sometimes wonder if I will try it myself one day; I would like to!

Women wander about in undisciplined order, standing, sitting, staring. or sometimes even spinning wherever they happen to be. Rosalie goes to the same corner every day and has the same conversation with the bees that buzz about the rosebush growing there. There is the young woman who does not speak, the one I felt so bad for frightening; her name is Lucille, and it is she who spins, sometimes for minutes and minutes and minutes, a look of vacant joy on her child's face. I am the one who stands, for the most part: I look at the sky. I look at the sky and sometimes I do not think a single thing for what seems like hours.

Yesterday I walked straight over to the small patch of pansies that grows against the wall. If I were on the lane outside my home I would have picked one and examined the stripes on the petal: seven for consistent love; nine, a changing heart. Thick lines to the right, prosperity. I stood, and the lane and the girl that stood on the lane were equally distant from me, and I knelt and picked a petal without even noting the color. And stood in the sun afraid to look at it.

Then Adelaide comes bounding out into the courtyard like the only living thing here, and I am Augustine again, and I have a friend to talk with.

"Augustine"! Adelaide never seems sad anymore when I see her. "What are you doing?" she asked, and I almost cried, I almost laughed: "What am I doing? What would you have me do, Adelaide, in this place?" I asked her, but she was not affronted in the least.

"I would learn to dance," she said. "Dr. Charcot would like for you to learn to dance. I heard him talking."

"Whatever are you saying, Adelaide?" I was frightened to think of Dr. Charcot talking about me; I was afraid to think of being so much in his mind that he would speak of me.

"I heard him talking to one of the other doctors," said Adelaide.

I felt the petal damp in my hand. What did they say? I felt my pulse quicken and the familiar globe rise in my throat.

"He said that you showed great promise. Oh, look over the wall. There's a storm coming."

"Adelaide, please tell me. At what do I show great promise?"

She turned with one arm still in the air, raised toward the lowering clouds that had not yet covered the sun.

"At performing! They did not say that, of course. But that is what they meant. 'She shows great promise in the area of hysterical posturing.'"

I had to smile at how well she captured the doctor's sententious drawl. But my palms were sweating now, and there were sudden dancing lights at the periphery of my vision.

"I do not know what you mean, Adelaide. What is this posturing he spoke of? How can I show promise at something when I do not even know what it is?" I could hear my voice rising in panic. Adelaide put her hand on my arm, and my heart, which had been beating so out of time, halted, for so long that I thought it might never start up again, then I was simply breathing, and Adelaide's hand was on my arm.

"He thinks you make a fine hysteric, that is all. I would take advantage of that if I were you. A girl could go very far in this place if she is a fine hysteric. I haven't the talent for it. I've tried, but my arms will not stay as I arrange them, and I will smile at the wrong moment. But you, he said you were 'naturally' . . . what was it? 'Naturally expressive.' What else? Hmm. 'With exemplary extension of the extremities!' That was it. Exemplary extension of the extremities."

"But Adelaide, what on earth does that mean?"

"I have no idea, my darling." And she was gone, running like a schoolgirl back inside as the clouds crept over the wall.

I looked down at my palm. The petal was bent but not broken.

And I counted five veins across its purple width: five lines radiating out from the center: hope founded on fear.

A FEW DAYS later I spoke with Adelaide about our conversation in the courtyard. I knew she had what I needed to know: She had, after all, posed for Dr. Charcot. We were sitting in the Day Hall, the courtyard being lashed by summer rain. Lucille had screamed upon being told she could not go out today, and been taken away in fetters. So I was sad, and the warmth of the fire (for it is always, always cold in here) seemed as far away as freedom. But Adelaide could never bear to see me without a smile.

"If you want to convince the Good Doctor that you are a bona fide hysteric, you must have a story, Augustine," she told me intently, grasping my hand softly and whispering, although the attendants were across the room and paying no attention whatsoever to us. "My parents may not have known the extent of my involvement with François, but I made certain the Good Doctor did! Drama is necessary if you are to succeed in this place. And I tell you, you will succeed! I will see to it. I have told you, the hysterics receive compensation—not in money, certainly, but do you think I could charm the attendants into giving me books if I could not pose? I mean, of course I could, but would the Good Doctor allow it? No, he would not. You can get your own books; you can get pudding! You can get a journal." I had not told her that I had already received a journal and been assured books, as well as visitors. I knew that Adelaide had suffered the ordeal of the Amphitheatre just as I had, and that for it she had received no books, no journal, no pudding. She had worked hard to gain Dr. Charcot's favor, and I would never hurt so dear a friend with such unnecessary knowledge.

"So," she said, leaning forward conspiratorially. "What shall it be?" She must have seen something in my face, but fortunately she did not recognize it for what it was. "I know!" she exclaimed. "A rape!"

"Adelaide!"

"Oh, all right. You were seduced by your cousin. I know he plied you with drink. You did not know what it was! Because it was absinthe. The Green Fairy. Yes, absinthe. Do you know how it is mixed and drunk?"

I did. I had read about it. So, it seemed, had Adelaide.

"He put extra sugar in it. It is so bitter without a lot of sugar, no matter how cold the water or fine the make of the liquor."

I tried, and failed, not to look shocked.

"Augustine, I promised myself long ago that I was going to *live* my life. Adventure, love, joy, even degradation of liquor. But I was not degraded, my love François was with me!" And she sounded so happy I found I could not judge her.

"What does it taste like?"

"Oh, green. It turns pearly, but it starts out green. Just tell the Good Doctor it tastes green. That will do nicely, don't you think?"

"I . . . I suppose."

"You won't be convincing if you talk like that! Have you not always wanted to act? We will write a part for you. Oh, Augustine, what fun we shall have! But we must start right away. You will be seeing the Good Doctor again very soon, and we must have our story ready."

If ever I am fortunate enough to be a mother, I already know I will be able to deny my child nothing; certainly I cannot deny Adelaide anything. And it was exciting: my first character! And Adelaide had already spoken about dancing. I am no fool—this is not the stage that Sarah Bernhardt inhabits. It is not Nadar's famous studio, where he has photographed both her and countless other famous, talented, and renowned people. People out of magazines and books. I am never going to be one of those people. But perhaps this is just what I need: an opportunity to try to do what is so near, in such an odd way, to my dreams.

And with such a friend at my side I cannot fail. She will not let me!

Chapter 26

Edouard

I SIT AFTER a dinner of chicken stew I cooked myself over my fire in an old iron pot my mother gave me when first I left home. I am a passable cook and find that I enjoy it; the repetitive motions, the mixing of ingredients, and the careful cooking are not unlike the repetitive motions involved in developing a photograph. I must be a very simple man indeed, that such a trivial thing as cooking, a woman's job, brings me pleasure!

I have before me a photo album of pictures taken at La Salpêtrière, given me by Richet to study. He assures me that his trust in me has already proven well placed, but still he wants me to study these photographs, that I may gain a better understanding of such things as lighting, positioning of the subject—a dozen seemingly innocuous things that can result in excellence or disaster in a picture.

I approached the album with a keen anticipation. Learning is a passion of mine; why did that make me think of Augustine? Alone in my bachelor apartments I almost blushed: I wanted to learn more of Augustine; I knew she was far more than the frightened thing I had seen on the stage of La Salpêtrière, more than an ignorant country girl suffering from green disease. How I knew this I could not say. Richet had told me I was a sentimental fool, no matter that the young lady in question was beautiful and helpless.

I shook off such thoughts; after all, if I were similarly swayed by every patient I photographed at La Salpêtrière, I would not last a month! I realized that Richet had given me this album to desensitize me to the patients I would be photographing for our study. A steady mind is perhaps even stronger, in my profession, than a steady hand. And surely if I could photograph the dead I could photograph the living, no matter their condition.

So I took a sip of the coffee I had brewed before my meal, and opened the album. One thing I am not good at is brewing coffee. It is always either too weak, too strong, or burnt. One day when I marry, I really do have to make sure my wife is more than proficient in this task.

As I mused I began to look. Not to study, not yet, but simply to look. That is the first task of the photographer; I think it is the first task of man, actually, but then, M. Martillon always did tell me that I reflected too much. M. Bousson, however, did not.

As I looked I was both shocked and appalled. No other patient in these pages was as Augustine; no other possessed the grace, the charm, the beauty of Augustine. Here were pathetic specimens of insanity indeed: an old woman standing screaming in front of the camera, a young girl writhing on an unmade bed, a woman so vacant of expression that I could not tell if, let alone what, she was thinking at all. The old woman was galvanized, the caption told me, by religious mania; the young woman by the ravages of green disease coupled with an unhealthy preoccupation with sex. The other was indeed incurable; the caption showed that she had not spoken in all her life, and almost all her life had been spent at La Salpêtrière. All hope of her learning to speak had been abandoned long ago, and she showed little or no interest in her surroundings or other people. I stared at her picture a long time, trying to put myself in her place. I could put myself in the place of the dead easily enough, from long exposure to its horrors and my devout belief that without death, life would have no meaning, but I could not begin to imagine what it must be to be so trapped inside oneself that there never could be any escape.

The old woman was merely repulsive. Religious mania has never made much sense to me, our faith being so clearly laid out for us that there is no need to tax the mind and spirit by overzealousness. But of course that is one of the most common paths to madness, particularly among women. So I determined to memorize the expressions on her face as she flailed through her hysterical seizure, the particular angle of the wrists held stiff at her sides, the expression of passion on her aged face as she communed with angels, the rage she expressed when she thought herself Mary Magdalene, the effects of hysteria on her limbs.

The third subject was a pretty, dark-haired girl who seemed almost to be playing at madness. There was something unconvincing in the way she pulled her skirt above her knees as she smiled lasciviously into the camera, in the hideous arch of her body in the rumpled bed. I did wonder why the bed was not more neat, the sheets more clean. But I am not here to question Dr. Charcot's methods, I am here to learn.

Then I realized that I knew this girl. This was surely Adelaide Blanchot, of my own village! She was older, but still she wore her hair in a fringe, like my little sister, and had the biggest, darkest eyes I have ever seen. What was this falseness about her photographs that was not present in the others? Did it mean she was more, or less, mad? I had to put the book down a moment and sip at my burnt coffee while I cooled my head. It was cruel indeed to see this girl I had grown up with in such a state.

But soon enough I picked up the album again, and soon enough I was lost in the pictures and stories. I did not leave the album until I felt I felt I had attained at least a little of the distance required for my work. And by that time I had had to light a second, precious candle, as the fire had reduced itself to ember; I was cold, but I was also satisfied. The pictures of Augustine had not yet been added to the book, else my task would have been an impossible one. I could not get her out of my mind; I loved her name; I could not forget her eyes. My own eyes were tired, but my heart was wide awake.

And my dreams that night were beautiful.

Chapter 27

From the Journal of Augustine Dechelette

I HAVE HAD a visitor. It is quite extraordinary. I was sitting at my window looking into the courtyard at the woman who screams. She had no attendant with her, and her arms were free. She moved about haltingly; she held her arms at a stiff, unnatural angle in front of her and flapped her hands unceasingly. I had never seen anything like it. Her hands flopped like dead things, broken wings. And she let out the same high-pitched, intermittent screams I had noticed before. But she did not seem upset as she moved about the confines of the narrow enclosure. She had an absentminded smile on her face, and as she leaned to inspect a tiny growing thing, a rose or a dandelion, her eyes lit with a child's joy.

So that when the door opened, I was smiling too. "Someone to see you," said the attendant, whom I had not heard moving in the hall. He withdrew but left the door open. And standing there was the man I had seen at Tuesday's lecture, the ginger-haired man who had been working the camera. He was holding the camera now, so tightly that his knuckles were entirely drained of color. He looked absolutely terrified, which made me like him right away. If he had been at his ease in a place like this I shouldn't have liked him at all.

I couldn't think of anything to say; I said, "Thank you," without even knowing why.

"No," he said sincerely. "It is I who must thank you." He seemed to become suddenly aware that he was holding something, and that that something was his camera; he ran one hand across the pebble grain of the leather box, and I could see it soothed him: "You are a photographer," I said.

"Yes," he said, with evident relief. "My name is Edouard Mas. If I am disturbing you—"

I almost laughed. " No," I said. "I am happy for the company." I went and sat on the edge of the bed, indicating that he might take the chair. I felt ludicrously grown-up, like a little girl with a leaf-and-grass tea set, and beetles from the garden as party guests.

"Please," I said, motioning again to the wooden chair. With plantain flowers for cakes, and hazelnuts for buns.

"I am I am doing a study," he said, lowering himself awkwardly into the chair, "of—of this place." He fell silent.

I studied his countenance. He was no blockheaded boy like the ones I'd known. Nor yet was he a city sophisticate. He was completely without artifice, and miserable there in that chair, which was too small for him (for he was a tall man, something more noticeable when he was sitting, oddly).

"You don't have to be nervous around me," I said easily, and thought, Who is this girl? Receiving a strange man in her room at the mental institution as though it were as natural and normal as a child's tea party. And yet I could not be afraid of this man, or suspect his motives. I had never seen anyone so sincere in his aspect; he had a noble brow and an honest mouth and firm chin. There was no dissolution in that face, and no arrogance either. His eyes were completely frank, without the slightest insinuation.

"Of what does your study consist?" I asked him; only later did I notice that while we spoke I only once wondered what my own aspect was like, what I might look like to him: farm girl, crazy woman, child. But it didn't matter. From the very first, nothing mattered when talking to Edouard but the light in his pale eyes.

"Do you want to take pictures of me?" I asked. I did not want to appear excited, but I was, terribly. To be photographed as part of a study ! And instantly I was crestfallen: a study of the insane. Everything changed.

But he surprised me by saying, "What are your dreams, Augustine?"

"Is this part of your study?"

"No," he said. "I just want you to know that I am not interested in you as a specimen."

I tried not to show my delight; I tried to remain demure. " I do not know that I have any dreams here. I have given up all the ordinary dreams of my sex: a husband, children, the opportunity to create a home. I would so love a home! With a little garden, and . . . but you see, there is no point in dreaming about such things. I had a friend once, she had a mirror. Do you have a mirror, Monsieur?"

"In my apartment, yes. Would you like me to bring you one?"

"I don't know. I do not know whether I want to see what I have become now. I used to look in the mirror at least once a week. And oh! Look what that did to me. Perhaps if I had not looked, I would not have dreamed. I would not have dared . . . Oh, if I had never thought, *Perhaps I am pretty enough for—*" I stopped, appalled at myself.

"Looking in a mirror cannot affect your morals, dear girl," he said, smiling. "Is that what you think? I think every woman in Paris has looked into a mirror at one time, and they are none the worse for it. Who told you that looking into a mirror was hurtful?"

"Oh, I have always known it. My mother has never looked into a mirror. Papa would never allow such a thing. He is worried enough about the clocks!"

"The clocks? Surely there is no harm in looking at a clock!"

I let out a little laugh and was alarmed to hear that it sounded like a little cry.

"Oh, no, my good Monsieur, you must not think our little village that much a backwater! But my father protests the coming day when all clocks in France are set to Paris time. He says he will tie himself to the face of the big clock on the cathedral on that day."

Edouard laughed. "I think I like this Papa of yours."

"But you do not think he is right about mirrors."

"Many people fear progress, and not just scientific or industrial progress, but everything that comes with them. There can be no harm in a pretty girl finding out just how pretty she is."

I stiffened; I became aware of myself. A blush suffused my visitor's cheeks; it was clear he was sorry at having said something so bold. And I was touched that he suffered the same as I from crimsoning of the skin. He made as if to reach out his hand but did not move.

"Aren't you afraid," I said suddenly, "of being alone with an insane woman?"

He threw back his head and laughed. It was characteristic of him, I was to find. It was almost the only time he lost his restraint.

"You are not insane, Mademoiselle," he said. He was still chuckling. "I do not know how you came to be in this place, but it was not through any infirmness of mind, of that I am certain."

"But how can you know such a thing?" I asked in surprise. "I have spoken to Dr. Charcot, and he seems to think I belong here."

"You have spoken to Dr. Charcot?" His voice lowered and took on a tone of hushed respect.

I bridled; I could not help it. "Dr. Charcot is a terrible man!" I blurted. "He sits in a black room with black furniture and makes pronouncements on people as though they were here only for his amusement!" Instantly I was chagrined; what if he were to leave? I felt a sense of loss far greater than was warranted. I do not know what showed on my face.

But his eyes remained kind. "I am certain," he said gently, "that the great doctor has a fearsome aspect. I have heard"—and here he laughed lightly—"that many of his students fear him greatly!"

Perhaps it was because I had been so isolated that Edouard immediately assumed for me the importance that he did. That I was so starved for a kind word or glance that the first man who smiled on me would be perceived almost as a savior.

But I do not think it so. There was something in his eyes approaching nobility, something in his smile approaching the sublime. His compassion was at once so immediate, so complete, that, once it had enveloped me, I would ever after fear losing it. Edouard had, in the space of a moment, become my friend.

"I have been engaged by Dr. Charcot to make a photographic study of his work here at La Salpêtrière," he said. For the first time he forgot himself; he leaned forward in his seat. "First I propose to photograph the building and the grounds; next, the inmates. Then I shall make studies of the hydrotherapy equipment, and the uses to which it is—what is it, Mademoiselle?"

I pointed out the window. I put my finger to my lips and made a motion with my other hand.

Edouard slowly turned his head to see that the woman in the courtyard was holding a dandelion with a broken head in her left hand. Her right hand had not ceased its flapping, but the left had apparently stopped long enough for her to pick the flower, where-upon it must have continued its flapping at least until the dande-lion's head broke. I could not ascertain her age; I know only that she was past young adulthood and was looking at the damaged flower with awe and something like satisfaction. She flapped her left hand a few more times, and the head broke off and fell softly to the ground.

And the woman began to scream like an infant, in great big gulping cries. I turned my head away because her face had taken on all the disconsolate anguish of a toddler, and I could not bear it.

Edouard took my hand. It was a natural gesture, almost with-out meaning. Certainly he was not taking a liberty. I leaned my head against his shoulder and cried without shame for the poor imbecile in the courtyard, and for my own desolation. And Ed-ouard let me cry, and made no further move to comfort me.

Chapter 28

Edouard

THE PHOTOGRAPHS SHONE wet; Augustine hesitated. If she were to reach out and touch that supplicant hand, would her own fingers dip, and disappear into that luminescent flesh? "It's quite all right, Augustine," I said gently.

She laughed, to cover her nervousness; she succeeded only in showing it more clearly. But then she seemed to realize something obvious and somehow grotesque. "This is Adelaide!" she cried. Frozen in a gesture of helpless rage, her face contorted in pain or ecstasy, she seemed both more and less than the Adelaide we knew. I knew that Augustine was seeing her face as a stranger might, and was ashamed, as a stranger might be ashamed who happened upon a woman in the midst of her toilette. The intimacy of the shots was shocking: Adelaide was lying on an untidy bed, dressed only in a coarse shift. Her back was arched at such an angle that only her head and feet touched the bedsheets. Her eyes were half closed, and both hands were clawed into fists bent back against the wrists at an unnatural angle. Her arms looked as if she were struggling against the air, as if the air were dirt and threatening to smother her; she seemed to be desperately digging her way out of some invisible grave. Her shift was hiked up high above the knee, and her feet were bare. Her mouth was contorted, her lips half-snarling. She looked both completely mad and completely ordinary. Mad if you did not know her.

"Why do they make her do that?" Augustine asked me.

"Well," I said slowly, "it is difficult to explain." I did not want to go on.

"But what is she doing?" She seemed almost afraid of the picture; it might move.

"She is evincing the *arc-en-ciel* aspect of an hysterical attack. It has been explained to me. You see, the hand held so is an indication of what is termed tonic immobility. This contracture is unpredictable, I am told, and may sometimes be held for so long that the condition becomes permanent."

"But that's Adelaide! She isn't the least bit ill!"

I was startled. "But of course she is, or she would not be here."

"So you think I am like that, too?" I could see by her face that she really did. "But she speaks with Dr. Charcot," she went on. "She has told me. He demonstrates for her what she should best be doing on the stage. I mean"—seeing my face—"not that he does so on purpose, but that she holds her hands this way and that, and waits to see what pleases him."

"Augustine," I said gently, "Dr. Charcot is the foremost authority on hysteria in the world. Certainly he is able to tell a true contracture from a false one indeed! Surely he would not need to coach a poor sick girl to obtain the results he desires."

"Adelaide is not ill," she said again. "Her parents could not control her. She was in love."

"Augustine, we are not talking about you. We are talking about an hysteric, a woman who is being treated here for a serious illness. Dr. Charcot's revelations have changed the face of neurology. He has opened a gateway into the mind of insanity. These subjects—"

"I was one of 'these subjects' just two weeks ago! Why do you visit me, Edouard? Is it because you feel pity for me?"

I blushed beet.

"No, Augustine. I do not feel pity for you. For your situation, but not for you. Please forgive me. I did not realize how upsetting this would be for you. I will put the pictures away."

"No. No." She seemed suddenly desperate that I not leave, as if I might never come back. "I have another appointment with Dr. Charcot this afternoon." She thought I must think her mad.

I regarded her with a smile. "But that is good, is it not, to be seen by one of the finest doctors in the world?"

"I—I don't know. Edouard, I am so afraid! I swear to you that I am not insane." She had tears on her cheeks, on her hands, and I could tell she was ashamed. "My parents say they have told the doctors here—"

"Shh. Augustine, all you have to do is trust Dr. Charcot. Surely you could not be in better hands."

"When I think about the Amphitheatre, when I think about Dr. Charcot and his black office, I see his eyes looking into my eyes, and that is enough almost to put me into a trance once more. Thought becomes image only: I have no words to describe what had been done to me, and I become once again that terrified and helpless girl; the word *prey* comes to mind.

"Dr. Charcot is the Master of Sleep. He not only induces the trance, he decides exactly what the subject will do during the trance. In the Amphitheatre, I was deprived of my own will. And I could not resist his will. I was an automaton onstage. And yet it is so strange, Edouard! There is a connection between the Master and me—he forces me to give up my will, and yet as I do so it feels as if I am the one giving to him. I have some awareness during a trance not of being controlled but of giving. Oh, you cannot understand it!"

"Augustine, you are not mad," I said fiercely. "But." I reached out to touch her hand, then checked myself. "Dr. Charcot can be of help to you even so. Surely he will see how sane you are, and surely he will intervene with your parents on your behalf. He is a great man, Augustine. You need only have faith in him."

Then I busied myself with my pictures and reached to stroke my camera, and I felt a tug at my heart.

"I think I will choose, just for now, to believe you," she said charmingly, although her cheeks were still wet with tears. "Not that I should trust Dr. Charcot! No, I will believe that you do not think me mad. Because it is bearable thus, if you believe in me. I will do my best; it is all I can do."

If only she knew what I saw when I looked into her eyes!

And I will ignore the persistent tugging at my heart, and the empty feeling it carried, after I left, all the rest of the day.

Chapter 29

From the Journal of Augustine Dechelette

I SAT IN a black wooden chair across the black desk from Dr. Charcot and found him no less frightening than I had before. I tell myself I will not be afraid, but his eyes are so deep that I can hardly see them, and yet it is as though a gleam shoots out from their depths, and I am as helpless as a deer before a gun.

"At the root of each case of hysteria there is a trauma," he said, "every time."

I said nothing. I knew what Adelaide would have me do, but I could not do it.

"Augustine, in order for me to know how to properly handle your case, I have to know what the trauma was. I know this is difficult for you, but it is necessary. It is the whole crux of the matter."

I took a deep breath and steeled myself to speak.

"I fell in love."

I dared look up; Dr. Charcot was simply regarding me. Clearly this was not going to be good enough.

"It is true. He was a married man. Nothing happened," I added hastily, and I swear I saw a look of disappointment cross the doctor's face. "But he did not love me back." And as I said it I knew it was true. I was nothing to him, and I cried a great deal at home because I think I knew it even then. I would neglect my work and dream, looking at the pattern of the paper on the dining-room wall."

The doctor waited. Clearly he did not believe I had told him all.

"I have a broken heart," I said finally. "That is what is wrong with me."

The doctor considered this. Surely a broken heart is not enough to cause green disease. And just as surely my parents had told him that I had self-polluted, and oh, did he know it even now? Were his attendants peeking through the sliding panel when I did not know it?

But his next words reassured me.

"Your mother was very circumspect. She said that you became not simply recalcitrant but obstreperous, and that that is not in your usual nature. She was concerned at the amount of time you spent with a certain friend . . ." He checked his notes. "Yvette. But I imagine that at least part of that time was spent with your lover."

"He was not my lover!" I burst out, and when I started to cry I thought I would never stop. The doctor did nothing, proving himself human after all, and I cried and cried until I could not breathe, and he handed me a black handkerchief and I started to laugh. Now he certainly thought me insane, and I had not had to resort to stories of seduction and absinthe at all!

"I'm sorry," I said, when the handkerchief was so wet I dared not cry anymore.

"You need not be," he said shortly. "We have come to the root of your trauma. Unrequited love in a young woman can lead to a great deal of damage, stopping up, as it were, the natural channels through which a woman expresses her femininity."

I really did not know what he was talking about. But I was too concerned with my appearance to notice.

"I am shallow," I said suddenly, "because I am not listening. I only care how awful I must look."

I swear he almost smiled. "You need not worry about that. We will arrange for some simple toiletries for you. I know you brought a brush, and a journal as well. The journal has been restored to you already, and the brush you brought will be restored as well. And there was a book."

Cousin Bette. "Yes," I breathed.

"That shall be returned as well, and when you feel the need to read another you need only notify one of the attendants. Certainly I cannot let you read whatever you choose. I strongly suspect that you have been reading books most unsuitable to a young girl."

I blushed to the roots of my hair.

"I thought as much. Well, after dinner you will find your belongings restored to you in your room. But you must not speak of this to any of the other girls. And we will meet again, Augustine, every few days. There are aspects of your hysterical attacks I want you to learn to understand. Thoroughly understand."

And that was all. When I left, the doctor was staring at one of the black walls. I suppose they helped him think. I prefer to dream into a meadow view, but of course Dr. Charcot does not dream. But I knew I had done something right and that Adelaide had been quite correct. I did not know exactly what I was headed for, and I was afraid, but at the same time there was an agitation in my belly that did not feel like a symptom of anything but excitement.

Chapter 30

Charles

V HAS ACQUIRED the most peculiar houseguest. I had no warning. One day Odette was simply there, like furniture. She settled herself so quickly into our home and routine that I was astonished; but then, Odette was quite simply astonishing.

She was very tall. She was as dark as V was fair, rich of breast and hip. Her eyes were dark blue, large and searching, and a great many things made her laugh. She had a hideous laugh. V said she was a childhood friend; Odette said she was the Countess Odette Alexandrovna, but that her husband had died; and she laughed.

She lounged around the apartment all day in Chinese dishabille: silk dresses in the Chinese style without so much as a corset underneath, soft Chinese slippers on her feet; and I had seen her go out dressed like this with only a shawl to cover herself. I didn't know where she went at night; often she came back as late as next morning, kohl smudged below her eyes and her hair wild, as if she'd spent time in a storm.

One afternoon when V had gone to her dressmaker's I sat and watched Odette put on her makeup as I prepared myself a glass of absinthe. She had draped V's red silk scarf over the shade of the lamp that sat on the vanity; I took secret pleasure that just days ago I had held that scarf tight around V's neck in my fist while taking my pleasure with her. Odette was applying ambergris around her eyes as she smoked one of her small Egyptian cigarettes, which she always put in a long ivory holder. She spoke with a drawl acquired, V had told me, from time spent in New Orleans. Apparently she had gone to school in Switzerland with V and traveled a great deal. Since she spoke of nothing but herself it was difficult to gauge her education.

"Charles," she said, looking at me in the mirror with smoky eyes, "you know I live for pleasure. I choose to live without restraint, giving my whole heart and soul without thought of consequences." Odette was given to such soliloquies when she had been smoking her cigarettes, which, laced with opium, left a pleasant smell in the blue smoke that lay in layers about the vanity. "I have spoken of my Drago."

And indeed she had, in exhaustive detail: I was thoroughly tired of hearing about him.

"That I love Drago in this way is proof of my superiority." She laughed. "You will not say it, and V will not say it, but I have pledges to drink to the dregs of my carnal soul."

I handled the familiar, soothing items of my ritual, the slotted odalisque spoon, my sugar tongs.

"This Italian of yours, Drago, when does he arrive?"

"Oh," she said casually, "he does as he pleases." She reached to take the silver tongs from my hand, and the ruby locket she wore dangling from her bracelet made a pretty sound against the metal. I resisted her fingers and took the sugar cubes from the pot, busying myself with the ancient, almost animal motions of preparing my drink. When I am readying a glass of absinthe I do not think of anything else.

"I do not know when he will come," she said; she was not rebuffed. "You will appreciate him, Charles. He is a man much like yourself. He has promised to send me a grand piano. He told me that as a gesture of his feelings for me, he could think of no more appropriate gesture."

I was thoroughly tired of Drago and his piano. How was he to get a grand piano from Italy to France? Before I could say anything, however, Odette laughed and said, "It will be here soon. Perhaps I will have it sent to V's apartment." The sugar tumbled into the lap of the spoon. Odette's locket swung without a sound.

She knew about the apartment.

Her eyelids had already begun to droop, the ambergris had already begun to run. She applied more with fingers made clumsy by the opium in her cigarette, and I saw dirt under the fingernails of her mannish hands. I watched the absinthe fall out of its bottle; I poured somewhat more than my usual measure. The sick-sweet smell of opium clung to her hair, as full and lustrous as the hair itself, which hung in a dark cloud around her shoulders. Her blue eyes were sunken and fevered, and the smudge of her makeup made her white skin even whiter; already it was beginning to be mapped by tiny lines: Someday she would be parchment.

Her lips were almost bloodless. She roused herself and dipped a finger into her china rouge pot, she smoothed red enamel across her bottom lip. She casually picked up a small red-leather book and opened to a well-worn page:

> *I am the wound and the knife!*
> *I am the slap and the cheek!*
> *I am the limbs and the rack,*
> *And the victim and the executioner!*
> *I am the vampire of my own heart.*

"Isn't that how you feel about V, Charles? You want to mingle your blood with hers, you want to be her."

"We are man and wife," I answered softly. "We are commingled already."

"Oh, Charles." She laughed, turning her face away and revealing her white, white throat. She put down her book and picked up a sinuous nude mirror from the table at her side. "It is by others' blood that you are linked. Tell me, have you ever tasted blood?"

So V had told her of our killings after all. But I was not discomfited; I was proud that Odette knew. Had I ever tasted blood? I thought of boyhood scratches, a cut finger put in my mouth, a sudden scratch from a wayward branch soothed with my own saliva; I thought of the rivulets of blood streaming down V's arms as she lay in our bed, and how they had seemed to be rose petals drifting from the bed to the floor.

"Yes," I said shortly. "V's blood."

"What a clever girl V is. Did she pinch the same spot on her throat she pricked for the marquis, I wonder." She laughed again.

The tiny pucker of white on V's neck, the one she said she had no memory of: *I suppose I was wounded climbing a tree as a child, or some other foolish thing.* And I remember being unable to envision V doing anything so mundane as climbing a tree, even as a child. Surely, servants would have carried her, fairies would have lifted her, preventing any injury.

"You are lying," I said coldly. I hated my hands for shaking as I mixed my drink.

Odette could not stop laughing. "You're as much a fool as any of the others," she said, and went back to admiring herself in the glass. I drank. This time the green did not soothe: It excited.

"V has loved no one but me," I said fiercely.

"V," Odette said serenely, "does not love. You're convenient, Charles, so very convenient! The lifestyle to which she has accustomed herself, sexual pleasures of the most degraded sort. Don't think she hasn't told me about those. And"—casually picking up her cigarette pipe and and fitting it carefully into its long ivory holder—"V likes to kill. Surely that is not so difficult for you to understand.

"There was a game we played at school," she went on, apparently unconcerned at how quickly I mixed my next drink, by my now-ragged breathing. "The Empress's Children. It was a silly game. One of us was chosen by lots to be the Empress. There was a hill, and a big rock, a boulder, really, sitting atop that hill. It served as the Empress's throne. And all the others had to obey the Empress for the entire afternoon. We tended her flocks, we brushed her hair and did her toilette, we gave her fantastical gifts of frankincense and cloth of gold, which we found as berries and stones and hay at the bottom of the hill.

"And then one day a girl, a shy little thing, took a twig and pretended to stab the Empress in the back and proclaimed, *Now I am the Empress.* And so we obeyed her. It went on that way for a few weeks: One day a girl served the Empress a tea of leaves and berries and declared that she had poisoned her and would take her place. The Empress died a sufficiently dramatic and horrible death, and it became our goal to kill each Empress. Quite often we were found out: I will not use this pen! one would cry out, fling-ing a twig away from her. The ink is acid! We did all sorts of silly things, of course, and it was innocent. But V had always hated the game. When she was a servant there was one girl in particular who would humiliate her with chores: Muck out the stables, she would declare, and would not be content until V had muddied her own skirt. Serve me my supper, and be quick about it! and the dish of nuts and berries would be thrown at her feet lest it be poisoned. And yet V would never have resorted to poisoning.

"And then one day this girl, this Empress, threw a brush toward V, demanding she dress her hair. It was just a twig, but it hit V on the cheek. She stood still; the twig had left an angry mark. She did not bring her hand to her face. The Empress smiled; V said, You will die for that. Immediately she was ordered out of the Empress's sight. She stood a moment longer, then walked right up to the girl and shoved her, hard, off her boulder throne ; the girl fell with a sickening sound, rolled down the hill, and lay still. V looked at her a long time, then walked over and knelt to feel her pulse. The rest of us were frozen with fear. But V simply stood up, shook out her skirts, and said, I am Empress now."

My hands had stopped shaking. The lovely, imperious child who would take her right to be Empress, that was without doubt my V.

"Do you know what happened after that, Charles?" Odette did not wait for me to answer. "After that, every day we continued to play the game. And every day V was the Empress, and we were her children."

Odette took a long drag on her pipe. I took another green drink.

"She is still the Empress," Odette said eventually. Her voice was faint, her eyes already halfway to a dream. "V is still the Empress, and we are all nothing but her children."

Chapter 31

Edouard

Dearest Natalie,

 I hope the summer weather has not caused your pretty hair to frizz; I would have far more serious hopes for you, little sister, if I did not know that this is the foremost worry of your summer season: I have in my memory the most charming picture of your lovely vexed face and the curling iron you so hate and have named what is it? —Sebastian, I believe. Yes, Sebastian the curling iron that can never quite do the job. How many times have I seen your mouth screwed up in the effort of inducing Sebastian to change what Nature has determined to be the perfect frame for your lovely countenance! Isn't it enough for a girl to have a fringe without feeling the need to crimp the thing?

 But Natalie, can you tell that I am happy today? It is a perfect evening in Paris, and before I tell you the cause of my

*happiness I will describe to you the scene out of my window,
bringing to life as best I can the ebb and flow of humanity that
passes beneath.*

*It is just before the dinner hour, so even my little side street
is busy, with young workmen taking their girls out for a night
on the town. The hats alone are almost beyond my meager
descriptive abilities! They pop with red and yellow silk roses,
they sport black ribbons, they come in velvet and straw weave
and structured silk. I can discern no particular predominating
style; even the women's sleeves seem not to know whether
to simply poof out at the top or billow out to the elbow. And
the colors! Lavender and yellow, gray and russet, green and
orange—it seems that almost any combination of colors can be
made beautiful if worn by a pretty woman.*

*And all the women are pretty today, although few, I must
say, as pretty as you. But you persist in not believing me about
your beauty, I know that, and what young girl would believe
her big brother about such things?*

*Now, the reason for my happiness. You will think me
shallow beyond measure, Natalie, when you find that a simple
invitation to a party can make a fool of me. But I have been
invited to my very first society gathering in Paris. It seems like
a major step to me, for who would ever bother about a young
photographer with no connections? I have not confided this to
you, but describing the street scenes to you, and the petty gossip
I hear about this or that great star, is as pleasurable to me as
it is to you. Now you know: Your wise big brother is as much a
nincompoop as any boy in the village. But now that I work at
La Salpêtrière, my fortunes seem to have changed.*

I will tell you the story.

I was gathering up my photographic equipment after one of
Dr. Charcot's public Tuesday lectures when I was approached
by a most curious woman. I shall try to describe her truly, and
probably fail, because she is a most improbable personage. I
heard her voice before I saw her: a deep voice, rasping.

"Pardon me," she said.

I was startled: To begin with, she was as tall as I am, and
that is a rarity among women. And her clothes! She wore a
shawl (although it was quite pleasant out) of black lace that
was tasseled at the hem; as we spoke she kept pulling at the
ends of it, twirling them nervously and releasing, then grasping
at them as though she was not sure whether she was cold or
warm. Under the tattered shawl she wore an evening gown
of the glossiest garnet silk and, mind you, this was afternoon.
The gown was obviously very expensive, with a great deal of
black lace embroidery on it that I find I cannot adequately
describe, except to say that it all seemed, at any moment, about
to start moving. Yet her feet were shod in shabby slippers of the
Oriental type. They did not suit the dress at all; she did not suit
the place.

"I am interested in photography," she said. She was carrying
a long, thin cigarette in an ornate ivory holder, and she
gestured in such a way that I knew she expected me to light it.

"I do not smoke," I said, somehow sad to disappoint her.
Her aspect, you see, was itself so . . . lost is the word that comes
to mind. Her large blue eyes were framed with a great deal of
kohl, which seemed to have been applied carelessly. Her dark
chignon looked as if she had been out in the wind instead
of attending a lecture. There was something wild about her,
something untamed. Her mouth was uncertain, like a child's.

"I do not want to smoke it here," she said, strangely. She looked around helplessly, and a very handsome couple came over. The man was very tall, and quite distinguished-looking; I must confess I envied him his purple silk cravat, his shiny top hat, and his aplomb. His wife would delight you, Natalie. She was small, as you are small, but her hair was a very pale blonde and her eyes quite gray, which is very rare, as you know. She looked entirely as though she were made of porcelain. Her cheeks were apples, her hands graceful birds. She obviously had no need for that white powder you have told me about, made by Houbigant, called Poudre Ophelia.

She smiled at me, and I was struck that two women could be so utterly different; this one wore a brown satin dress with yellow silk peeking through soft plackets decorated with black fleurs-de-lis running down the front, and peeking again through wide slits in the sides of the dress.

"I am Madame Soulavie," she said in a sweet, girlish voice, but her handshake was firm. "This is my husband." He bowed. "And this," she said, indicating the woman who had first approached me, "is Madame Alexandrovna."

"Odette," she said chidingly, but as one would chide a favored child. "Why are you bothering this gentleman when he is clearly working?"

I quickly assured them that it was quite all right, being very intrigued by the trio, and I introduced myself. The man's handshake was almost too strong, and I felt a strange disquiet when I looked into his dark eyes. Mme. Alexandrovna said, "Call me Odette," and took my hand in such a way that I half expected I was to kiss it!

Natalie, I have never before met such people as these. Their *exoticism was like an intoxicating drink, and although I know perfectly well that all people are equal in God's eyes and ought to be in ours, I am afraid that I was overwhelmed, to the extent that I did not quite gather why Mme. Alexandrovna had approached me and had to ask her to repeat herself.*

"I like photography," she said again, and I felt twice over a blockhead. "I would like to know a photographer," she went on, and I must have looked as surprised as I felt, for Mme. Soulavie interjected, "Odette is a forthright person. She means no harm by it," saving me embarrassment, as it gave me time to gather my wits.

"There is a party," Odette went on as though she had not heard her friend. " I would like you to come."

I was dumbfounded, and again Mme. Soulavie rescued me.

"The man you work with, Monsieur Richet, is an acquaintance of ours," she said to me gently. "He has spoken well of you. Odette is indeed interested in photography"—with a little indulgent laugh—"and Monsieur Richet says that you are an accomplished and entertaining man, and would be an asset to any party. So—she gestured away my protestations— "Madame Gaudet has asked me to extend an invitation. We did not have any address for you other than La Salpêtrière.

She opened the lovely clutch purse she carried, which looked like a seashell, and handed me a pure white sheet of engraved paper: an invitation.

Now, Natalie, I know you have heard of Mme. Gaudet— you have even mentioned her to me. (Do not ever say again, Natalie, that your brother does not pay proper attention to you!) You have, in fact, regaled me with the doings of her famous Paris parties for years. And now I am to attend one of those parties! Are you proud of me? I know it is just an accident of place and time that has given me this opportunity, but it is an opportunity I am most anxious to grasp.

But I should first, perhaps, usher the Soulavies and Mme. Alexandrovna offstage. Odette seemed quite content to stare at my camera equipment, although she asked no questions. M. Soulavie stood strangely still; he seems to have the aspect of always waiting for something, and he watched his wife with an uncommon interest, although she did nothing out of the ordinary at all: She was politeness itself, and made just the proper kind of smalltalk with me before telling me yet again how pleased she was to have met me and how she hoped to see me at the party.

And then they took their leave, Odette giving me her hand once more, M. Soulavie simply nodding, and his wife smiling winsomely at me as she turned to go.

As I write it to you, my dearest sister, it strikes me as an altogether peculiar encounter. But what do I know of society? We have all heard that the very rich and privileged can be quite another species, and my impression being that Mme. Alexandrovna is titled Russian nobility, it would not be so strange at all that she is odd. As for the Soulavies, I know that you would love the wife and fear the husband. But perhaps he is just protective of his wife, who is, after all, so delicate of feature and aspect that perhaps I do not find it so very odd that she incites a fierce protectiveness in her husband.

But Natalie, I find myself vexed, and sorely so, with an as-now-unanswerable question: What am I to wear? Ah, well, the party is a full two weeks hence, and I think I can count on Richet to help me with any sartorial difficulties.

And I have a feeling, Natalie, that I will be receiving both sartorial and other advice from you, who know so much better, from reading the society pages, how to behave at a fancy-dress ball than I do!

I look forward to your next letter, little sister.

Your affectionate brother,

Edouard

Chapter 32

From the Journal of Augustine Dechelette

I STOPPED, A deer before the hunter's gun. The attendant tightened his grip on my arm ever so slightly: This was familiar to him. I was staring at the figure of Dr. Charcot in his long black coat, talking to a group of young men. They seem eager and starved, eating him with their eyes as they ate his words. This was the great Dr. Charcot, and they were feasting on his presence.

"Bear well in mind," he was saying slowly, tasting his own words, "that the word *hysteria* means nothing."

The attendant gave my arm a little tug. I could not breathe. Dr. Charcot turned his head, and the heads of the young men followed. If they saw me they might descend upon me like hungry animals, and I would be devoured.

But the doctor saw nothing: another patient, a young woman being led down the hall. He did not even recognize me. I did not exist.

The attendant loosened his grip; I exhaled, and was surprised that my breath did not come out as a gasp, a cry. My awareness of myself was acute. I felt my near-silent feet on the floor, my still-constricted throat, my dingy smock. I could hear Dr. Charcot's voice murmuring. For an instant everything looked wrong. The light in the hallway was wrong. The walls themselves seemed somehow wrong, as though suddenly set not quite at right angles. The fingers of the attendant, when I looked down, were almost grotesque in their chubby paleness, like coffin worms, and then I was simply Augustine, walking down the hall to my room.

The great and famous Dr. Charcot, who has diagnosed me in front of all Paris as an hysteric, says that the word *hysteria* means nothing. Nothing. I do not know what to make of it. Perhaps I misheard him; but I know I did not.

I want a mirror. I want to know if Augustine still exists. If Augustine now means nothing. What is this green disease if not desire? What is this hysteria if not the thwarting of desire? If I could have been with Louis, would I have ever have had to come here? I know I am depraved, yet I do not feel it. Am I so in thrall to the basest aspects of my womanly nature that I cannot even see my own rottenness? I am riddled through with moral depravity, yet I feel pure. How did love riddle me with its green poison?

I cannot pray. My mother prays for me even now, I suspect. Perhaps she sits now, fingering solid wooden prayers, whispering ancient words, tears on her cheeks.

The ink in this place is of a terrible quality. (I write this so as not to think of my mother.) It is a brown that looks faded even as it dries on the page, and its thickness clogs the nib of my pen. At home I used brown (although Papa used blue for his official correspondence), but it flowed evenly and shown on the page. And

Louis once gave me a vial of the loveliest lavender ink, which I used only for my journal and kept hidden beneath the delicates in my hope chest lest Maman find it.

Perhaps she has discovered it by now. To Maman, lavender ink would surely be tangible evidence of moral depravity! That would hardly trouble me were I not certain she has read my journals by now. She and Papa would not let me take them with me. I buried them with the ink in the hope chest, and it is true that Maman is not the sort to snoop. But she is the sort to sit and go through the things in her daughter's hope chest and cry for what she feels will never be, now. And maybe she is right.

And yet I do not feel sorry for myself. There is a part of me that cannot believe, against all the logic my father taught me, against all moral teachings I have learned, against all decency, in fact, that I am truly ill. And yet this does not frighten me. I look out my little window and think: Beyond that wall, even though I cannot see it, Paris eats and breathes and sleeps. All Paris moves beyond my wall, out of my vision but seldom out of my thoughts. What should terrify me does not: Perhaps I am insane. Worse still, perhaps I am not, and yet I am trapped in this place. I may be trapped here the rest of my life. Yet as I write those words, I do not believe them. My father would never allow that. I heard him arguing with Maman: *All she needs is a change of scene.* My mother wept, of course, but resisted his will, I think for the first time in her life. My father does not think me mad, I am convinced of it.

Ah! I hear the key in the lock.

Chapter 33

Charles

"YOU KNOW WHAT this room is for," V said as I lay spent beside her. I had gotten to know this room well. We have done nothing to make it beautiful. The flowers I put on the mantel died long ago, the vase was empty of water. V's petticoats are soiled from lying on the dirty floor, which was covered with ashes from the fireplace.

The cracks in the ceiling have become my roadmap. That one there, a split in the concrete, a split in the road: when she first introduced me to the extraordinary delights of pleasing her orally. That fractured star, cracked into seven directions: when she turned to offer her beauty from behind. She knew all the secrets of lovemaking, and I was not jealous. She came to me whole and free of any past. I have accepted everything; I will accept anything. She who is so completely mine cannot have had any past outside of my imagination.

But this thought made me uneasy. I did know what this room was for. But V's childhood with the nuns, their fond recollections of the lovely blonde child, had never been real to me; nothing that ever happened before I met her can ever be made real to me.

Except for the Empress's Children.

"What do you want to tell me, V?" I asked, covering my suddenly nervous hands by getting up to gather her petticoats and stockings from the floor.

"I don't want to tell you something," she said imperturbably. "I want to give you something."

I stood bent, clutching the soft silk in my hand. There was a pale shadow on the wall that showed where a painting once hung. I wanted to know what it was a painting of.

"Will you let me give you a present?" She reached over to run one sharp nail down my back, light like the scratch of a spoiled, sleepy kitten.

"You know I will do anything you want," I told her. A boating scene, a scene of indecent love? A portrait of a little blonde girl in a parochial-school uniform?

She was preparing me a glass of absinthe, sitting up naked in bed, expertly mixing the water, the sugar, the green. The familiar clink of ice and metal soothed my ravaged nerves, but still I did not know if I could take seeing what she wanted me to see.

We went shopping for fruits and vegetables the next morning, I in my cape and she demure in gray muslin. She was dressed for the summer, which had suddenly come upon us, in gray faille shaped like a proper suit coat, but lighter; it gave the impression almost of indecency although it was very proper indeed. She wore a gray hat with dyed violet ostrich feathers laced around the brim. Her boots were dove, her stockings, petticoats, and gloves brightest white. We browsed the stalls of the rue Cloisot: cheeses and live chickens and loaves of fresh bread, ducks and eggs and heaps of red tomatoes, yellow squash, and exotic delights from far away: pomegranates and grapefruit, star fruit and mangos. V had not said anything more, last night, about what she wanted to show me. And I had not asked.

We walked slowly. V took time at almost every stall. She held the fat rock doves and asked the vendor what sauce was best with squab. She tasted a walnut, the tip of her pink tongue visible for an instant, and in that instant four men were staring at her mouth, her pearly teeth. She bit. I smiled at the man nearest us, and he turned away almost angrily.

"I used to find them here," she said, bemused "I didn't have to take them home."

I should have felt only revulsion; I should have left her in the street.

I was excited. So delicate she looked, like a china figurine. I knew what she was capable of. The men staring at her voluptuous mouth did not know, no matter what they dreamed while they looked at her.

She pulled off one glove and slipped her hand into my pocket, and I grasped her fingers, surprisingly coarse fingers for a woman of her delicate beauty. She stepped closer to me. She turned slightly and brushed her hip against me; and the men stared.

"I will whet your appetite first," she said.

FOR A WEEK we spoke no more of it. We did not go to V's room. She seemed to take extra pleasure in the luxuries of our life together: dried rose petals and lavender in the bath, hot toddies and poached fruit; frequent presents of lace for collars, and new kid gloves and silk stockings. I loved spoiling her. I bought her a pair of harem slippers covered with pearls; I bought her candied quinces. She never said thank you. She knew I did not want words. I wanted to watch her pull her new stockings on slowly, with painted toe and extended leg. She knew I wanted to watch her sink into the steam of her scented bath. To see her delicate teeth bite into crystal sugar with a barely audible crushing sound.

V took pleasure in spoiling me, too. A new spoon for my absinthe ritual, shaped like a young girl with a basket and a hat with ribbons, and the clogs of a peasant. She liked to point these girls out to me on the street, so different than she. Thicker around the waist, with heavy wrists and coarse hair. Perhaps it was because of Tabby; how had I thought she noticed so little?

"What do those farmer-girl hands feel like on a man's body?" she asked more than once. She was not jealous; her eyes were shining. I told her that I did not care for farm girls, which on the whole was true. I had wanted Tabby so desperately because I knew that she was going to die.

Once, upon awakening, I found V almost ready to go out. We slept when we wanted to, and often I did not know whether I was waking into day or nighttime. It was twilight, and the streets were full. The men's top hats created a shining sea of undulating sheen amid waves of black luster. The women's skirts flowed mauve and blue and yellow along the busy street; their feathered hats bobbed. All Paris was on the Boulevard tonight.

Every man looked at V; she was so obviously not the demure young lady she looked.

"I want to give you my gift," she said to me, clutching my arm with a girlish grip. She knew that her light touch excited me, I who knew how thoroughly woman she was.

"You wanted to take me for a walk," I said. "You know that I am yours to command."

So we walked to the Seine and along the quays, past Nôtre Dame, where a carnival atmosphere pervaded the large square, as it always did: Tumbling troupes performed their antics while pickpockets fleeced the crowd; Gypsies read cards for the credulous; young men took liberties under the guise of protecting their young ladies from the frightening faces of the gargoyles smiling placidly and obscenely out of the Middle Ages on the cathedral walls, protecting nothing.

We walked on. V had one hand in her muff and the other on my arm, but she removed it to put it into the pocket of my topcoat. Such a schoolgirl gesture. I squeezed her hand. We walked over one of the oldest bridges over the water toward the neighborhood of the apartment. I was not surprised.

There was no one at all on the bridge. V took her hand out of my pocket and slipped it down to touch my crotch.

"I will take you to a club I know," she said.

We walked for a long time holding hands, seemingly aimlessly. I wasn't thinking, particularly; walking had become kind of a dream. The streets got darker and dirtier and more deserted. The air was clouded silk against my face, my body. We did not speak until we came to a small door, scoured by age, set down a flight of worn stone steps on a no-name street.

The steps were slippery, almost mildewed, and bowed in the center from wear. I felt I was descending into an underwater cave. V seemed to float down the steps in front of me, a miasma of color and scent, and at her gentle knock the door opened immediately.

Smooth dim light, a lot of red brocade. Women in clothing so diaphanous it seemed no more than colored smoke around their breasts, their bellies. A stage. A sudden, raucous can-can performed by women wearing red corsets with black trim, black garters and red hose, and short red-silk skirts with a white froth of petticoats. They wore nothing to cover the sweet darkness between their legs: When they twirled and bent, flinging up their skirts, their white asses gleamed and made the darkness leap.

I looked at V and her eyes were glistening. Her lips were parted and her teeth pearls.

"You remember La Salpêtrière," she said finally, after she saw my face relax and knew that the green music was playing in my veins. "That girl. You remember that girl."

"The young thing with the frightened blue eyes? Yes, I remember her." I closed my own eyes. I could see the girl now, standing terrified before the crowd, and I felt myself grow hard.

V laughed. "Yes, you do remember her." I opened my eyes, but V was looking only at my face; she could not see beneath the table!

"I have an idea about that girl," she went on. "It is likely that she is all alone. That her family is far away and does not visit her. I have known girls like that one, girls who were sent to institutions simply for being girls, for speaking their minds at their fathers' tables."

I waited.

"It is called green disease," she said, and I started to laugh.

"I thought this was called green disease," indicating my glass.

V laughed too. "That is the Green Muse."

"You are the Green Muse."

"Certainly not. Green is my worst color."

"But you are inspiration and addiction both. You are as powerful as a drug, and beautiful as any angel that inspires a poet."

"And you are talking green nonsense. Listen, Charles, we can do something extraordinary here. This girl she is our opportunity."

"Opportunity?" I was high in the night sky—I was the sky itself, filled with flocks of birds fleeing southward.

"We should have taken Tabby home," I said, and knew the green had taken complete hold of me.

V laughed. "Yes," she said. "We should have. But this girl from the hospital, she will be better than Tabby. Augustine is a simple country girl. She is already cowed. She is accustomed to doing as she is told, at home as well as at La Salpêtrière. A girl like that will be easy to tame. And she will not have the slightest idea of how to save her life."

This club, this table, were far away. I was flying higher than any bird ever had, alone in the night sky with V.

Chapter 34

Edouard

"LOOK, EDOUARD. DO you see her?" Rosalie was casting aspersions at the vacant corner of the courtyard. Adelaide, sunning herself imperiously on the crumbling stoop of the ancient door? And then I did see her. It was Augustine's pitiable imbecile. She was smiling the unrestrained smile of a child while she flapped her hands in front of her at the waist. She seemed intent on something, although I couldn't say what it was. There was a bed of roses, fresh petals littering the courtyard. The only other flowers were the dents de lions, which had struggled up through uneven bricks. I looked carefully at her: Her skin was so pale, her features so immobile, she might have been entirely constructed of moonlight and wax.

Then the smile disappeared as if it had never been, and her face held no expression whatsoever. I glanced at Augustine; she was watching the poor madwoman with something like a mother's pride.

"She has the mind of a child," Augustine said. "I want to befriend her." I must have looked startled; it had not occurred to me that one would want to be friends with anyone who had spent her entire life in a mental institution.

"But what possible good can you do this poor creature? If in the past twenty-five years in the mental institution the doctors have not been able to reach her, well, my dear Augustine, it is unlikely she can be reached."

Augustine shot me the first disapproving look I had received from her. She felt that I was demeaning something that was important to her—or perhaps she felt that I was being patronizing. I realized that she lived now in a place where much of the treatment she received might indeed seem patronizing to her. I went beet-red.

But it was not because I might have hurt her that I was so suddenly shamed. It was because when I had said, "My dear Augustine," far from distancing myself from her with a paternal phrase, I had simply spoken the truth.

Augustine was dear to me. This truth was a slap in my own face, like mortality, like Fate. Something inexorable that cannot be denied. Augustine was dear to me. She was not simply a beautiful girl whose misfortune had touched my heart. She was not one of Charcot's experiments, or an example of hysteria, or even a girl who had stirred more than my pity as she stood half-naked on a stage in front of hundreds of gawking men. She was Augustine, and I cared about Augustine.

She did not understand my blush: She thought I was sorry for having patronized her. I was relieved she thought it only that.

She smiled; she forgave me.

"I am sorry if I sounded like one of your doctors," I said softly.

"*Mon dieu!*" she cried, laughing. "You could never sound like Dr. Charcot! Do you know that I heard him telling some of his students that there is no such thing"—suddenly standing and throwing her arms behind her back with a motion as though she were flipping a frock coat aside—"as hysteria!" And she turned a cold demeaning eye upon me, and was for a moment almost as formidable as the doctor himself.

Then she laughed her pretty blue-eyed laugh and sank down on the wooden swing.

"I am afraid of the old man," I found myself saying.

"Oh, everybody is," she said cheerfully. "The whole hospital. The attendants straighten their sleeves as they go by him"— tugging nervously at the hem of her own sleeve. This girl was not insane. The only oddity was her ability to laugh in a place like this.

"Why are you looking at me like that?" she asked, instantly on guard like a cat, with slitted eyes.

"I'm sorry," I said gently.

"I suppose you cannot help but pity me. I will have to resign myself to people's pity."

"Pity you? You are as sane as I am!"

"Well," she said lightly, "so are many of the women here." Then, seeing my disbelief, "It's true that there are some here who, by some fault of Nature or their own decadence, do belong here, and some of them may never leave. I was so afraid of them at first! I cannot tell you how afraid. The first time I went into the courtyard I was afraid that one of them might attack me. You have studied the painting that hangs in the Amphitheatre?"

I had indeed.

"I expected them all to be like that. Like animals. But they're not. They're just women. Girls, some of them, like me. Many of them do not know why they are here. Several of them were beaten by their husbands, their fathers, and they fought back. Some of them—" She stopped. "You must wonder what brought me here, if you do not think me insane."

I did wonder. I wondered intensely, because I had suddenly found that every thought, every feeling I had about this girl was thought and felt with an intensity I had never before felt without my eye to a lens, my hands working with the solutions that could turn a negative into a photograph.

"Why you are here is no business of mine, Augustine," I said, tasting her name on my tongue. "It matters only that you do not belong here and that I want to be your friend."

"I do not have a weak mind," she said firmly. "I would hate to have you pity me for that."

"Oh, no, Augustine, your mind is not weak. If anything, it possesses an immoderate—that is not the word I mean—a perfect firmness not usually found—"

"—in a woman?" She laughed. "That is perhaps my Papa's fault, for teaching me to reason as a man does. Certainly my poor Maman must think so. She was quiet a moment, and then, "Edouard, do you really believe that a woman should always be compliant? My Papa professes to believe so, and yet he trained me from infancy to think as rigorously as a man. And perhaps this has indeed weakened my mind. Sometimes I fear I do not know right from wrong."

I sat, awaiting her confession. But instead, "I have done nothing wrong! Oh, I know they say." And suddenly her young face suffused itself with blood, flushing her cheeks a brilliant crimson.

She looked about to cry; she looked down at the floor. "I am not a bad person," she said, so softly that I had to lean down to hear it.

Within the walls of this place we had fallen into an intimacy impossible to achieve in the outside world in so short a time. I felt I knew Augustine in a way that I had never known anyone else: She was showing me her heart, and her heart was pure.

But instantly I knew it was a charade, this intimacy. She had shown me the depths of her girl's heart, but what had I given her? Kindness, solicitation, attention, some fruit. The things any suitor might bring, the same things she had so detested from the farm boys in her little village. When suddenly I knew what I did want to give her. But I had no idea how to tell her nor even whether telling her was a good idea.

Instead I fumblingly went back to her imbecile, who was standing a short distance from us.

"Augustine," I said, as though we had been discussing nothing of very much importance. "What does it behoove you to reach out to this woman? What does it behoove her? She is a hopeless idiot, it is plain to see. I do not want you to hurt yourself trying, out of the goodness of your heart and soul, to help an imbecile who is not even aware you and I exist."

"Oh, she is aware. You just have to watch her. She is much more aware of the world around her than she seems, at first, to be. She has pleasures, Edouard, she has feelings and desires just as we do."

I was overawed then, that she could see so much in such a pathetic creature. The woman was staring at the ground, the dent de lion in forgotten shreds at her feet. She seemed intent on something, but I could not for the life of me say what.

"Watch," Augustine said softly, touching my arm, and as she moved quietly toward the woman I felt that touch electric through my whole body, and felt an accompanying jolt of sadness that she herself seemed to feel nothing but the need to show me that her idiot was sentient.

But it was a pleasure to watch her move carefully toward the woman, as though approaching a timid deer. Augustine stopped a few paces from her and simply stood until the woman glanced downward in her direction.

"Lucille," she said quietly. "Lucille." The woman did not indicate in any way that she had heard her name spoken. Augustine knelt next to her on the pavement and reached a hand to touch the moss. "Soft," she said gently, as though showing one of Nature's treasures to a child. The woman did not move, for so long that I felt a pang of sadness for Augustine: This kindness was a waste of time. And yet Augustine stroked the moss, with one finger, gently, over and over, all the time watching Lucille's face.

Augustine tried a few more times to attract the woman's attention, but she could not. But when she turned her face back to mine, it was shining still.

"Lucille is very dear," she said quietly. "She is more pure than a six-year-old child. I will reach her one day. And I think she will surprise me; I think that perhaps one day she will reach for me." And she knelt in the grass, unaware of her own loveliness, plucked a dandelion, smiled at me, then held it forth until Lucille noticed it. She did not take it at once; I did not think she even saw it. But suddenly she snatched it out of Augustine's hand and thrust it up to her nose, and breathed.

And Augustine looked as happy as a child herself, and as I smiled at her I felt that I was smiling at my destiny.

Chapter 35

From the Journal of Augustine Dechelette

"You have your admirer," Adelaide tells me on the lunch line, her eyes gleaming like a hungry cat's. "Surely you can convince the gentleman to help you."

"No," I tell her, and I cannot. Even if I wanted to I could not convince Edouard to do anything that runs counter to his principles, I know that as surely as I know him; I almost wrote, *my name*. But that is by no means certain these strange days, because Augustine Dechelette is either a young woman living in the country with her parents and her big dreams about the future; or she is a waif adrift in the halls of the Hôpital Salpêtrière, under the eye of the great Dr. Charcot, who terrifies her; or perhaps Augustine is the young woman who receives visits from that nice young photographer Adelaide thinks is courting her but who is in fact only interested in her in the most professional and impersonal way;

and Augustine is crying now, sitting in her familiar little chair at her familiar little table and feeling the familiar ache of loneliness she once felt only for a dark-haired bookseller in her familiar little hometown.

Oh, I am a fool, and a brazen one at that! My only consolation is that Edouard is a good man, a man who surely does not dream that the insignificant young insane woman he visits could ever feel such things toward him. But I do! Because he has been kind, and because of the intensity with which he speaks of his work, and because his gingery mustache simply will not grow all the way in, and leaves him looking boyish and somehow chagrined. Why can I never remain pure? Each day here I wake up and vow that this day, this day I will move through like a ship on quiet water, going calmly about what I must, with no quarreling in my head, no angry retorts on the tip of my tongue, no wayward daydreams disturbing my concentration. Because I do so want to be let out of this place. I would like to say, to be made well. If were certain I needed to be made well the goal would not seem so distant and odd, and I would have something to strive for. But all I have to strive for now is the attention of Dr. Charcot, and the increasing pleasure I derive from acting the hysteric onstage at Dr. Charcot's Friday lectures. I should not like that; it is more corrupting than anything I have ever done to myself, I am certain of that. More corrupting than my silly dreams of love, whether with Louis or with my fine and noble Edouard who will never think of me that way.

But I do like the feeling of being onstage. At first it terrified me. I was nothing but the object of every eye in the Amphitheatre. That this was exactly what I had always longed for escaped me entirely, humiliated as I was with my madwoman's status and dingy smock. But it was quite easy to see what the Great Charcot wanted of me. And it is quite easy to give it to him. "The hysteric moves her arms thus," he says, and who am I to prove him wrong? I am, after all, the hysteric he is talking about; he diagnosed me before he even saw me; I did not even have a name until he found that I could mimic hysteria as though it were a part in a play. Onstage I am not insane; I am not even a silly country girl with green disease: I am Augustine, already, in so short a time, the pride of the asylum! Oh, if I were to laugh now I would not stop until my laugh sounded like Adelaide's. Until it echoed down the corridors of this place as I now recognize that hers did the first day I was here, when I was still without a future.

I am not happy here, but I am not unhappy. I have achieved my dream! Adelaide assures me (and the Great Doctor implies) that I will soon be the toast of Paris. Of course, they will not copy my dress or hair. They will not print drawings of me in the fashion pages of the newspapers, although my photographs have already appeared in several prestigious medical magazines. They do not send journalists to take down my every utterance. They do not know that I am real, any of them, excepting Edouard. But every Friday I take to the stage and put on my performance.

Finally I am able to lose myself in my posing. It is like a dance. Each movement lies before me like a choreographed step. The hysteric experiences paralysis of the left arm: I slowly extend my arm, as if searching for something; my splayed fingers tighten and fold inward as my hand stretches forward. My elbow locks, and suddenly I make a fist, thumb held out stiff, and my wrist snaps down into an unnatural angle. I pull my forearm toward my face so swiftly it seems I will strike myself, turning my cheek downward toward my clenched knuckles before halting my fist.

Then I tilt my head upward and allow a small smile to creep

across my mouth: I flirt with heaven. My smile broadens, my eyes close, and I melt with a sigh onto the tousled bed. Lying on my side I hug my shoulders gently and think of what a lover's caress would feel like against my skin.

I raise myself from the waist, bringing my hands out as if to clap; I am still smiling, as if in response to a lover's blandishments. But there is no shame now, and no coy demeanor either. This is Augustine in ecstasy: Is it a lover or communion with a saint?

Then I widen my eyes as much as I can. I must at some point actually look insane!

I fall suddenly prone on the bed. Then, from my position on my back, I raise my body from my head to my feet, holding myself up with my arms behind my shoulders; it is called the *arc-en-ciel*, and Adelaide taught it to me. Dr. Charcot has told me of the shameless antics of hysterics, and though this is the most difficult part of my performance, I must do it. It's more humiliating than anything else I do in my performance, my entire shift sliding as it does all the way up my thighs, but I have even grasped it and pulled it toward my head to show my drawers! Once the initial, inevitable humiliation is gotten over, it hardly matters to me what follows. And by this time I have fully assimilated my character, broken as she was by love. Oddly enough, it makes me feel better about my own situation as the girl with the crush on the bookseller. It is nothing in comparison with what my poor invented hysteric has been through! And her agony, as interpreted by Dr. Charcot, and reenacted almost every Friday for the rather overeager students at his private lectures, somehow quiets my own pain as it gives life to hers, which, oddly enough, I think she deserves, for all that I made her up! Perhaps every actress interprets a role thus, making it her own.

Once I have lifted my body I try to create of it a perfect rainbow of pain. And after I have held the rainbow a full thirty seconds (which is a very long time, I must say), I simply collapse on the bed—and I am done.

Once I was given a chair to sit on instead of the usual grubby, unmade bed. After I had clenched my fingers and bent my wrist inward I was momentarily at a loss. Then I lifted my knee and crossed my legs, exposing myself up to the hip, and oh, sweet Jesus, I twisted in my chair and stretched my leg out straight to give the spectators a good side view! I did not smile, but it was only because I somehow knew that melancholy would be more seductive than flirtatiousness. Afterward, I told myself that ballerinas expose their entire legs; but really it was just that that instant of indecision had plunged me even deeper into my role, so deep that I merely did what my nameless, piteous hysteric would have done.

At the lectures I must show fear, terror, and declaiming. Declaiming is the hardest: I had to think for the longest what it is that the hysteric has to declaim. But there are truly ill women here; I do more than take lessons from Adelaide and hints from the Master. I have watched, and listened, and finally come to the conclusion that the greatest pain for the hysteric, and the greatest obstacle to her recovery, is the trauma of not being listened to. After all, if she were listened to, would she have to resort to pantomiming her fear and terror? What would she even have to declaim?

And it became easy after that. Even exposing my flesh became easier. And I no longer feel shame about feigning insanity. What if even one of my actions prompts Dr. Charcot to listen to his hysterical patients? That would be worth every seductive glance, every *arc-en-ciel*, that I could ever do here!

Chapter 36

Edouard

WITH THE EXCITEMENT of our baser instincts comes an almost insatiable curiosity. This is, I suppose, what is meant by temptation. I did not want to make love to Odette, but I wanted to find out what would transpire between us when next we met, a sensation both delicious and repugnant, of wanting to experience again the same base feelings she had elicited from me before. But along with this came the desire to conquer those feelings.

For all of this I despised myself. I did not blame Odette. She was the image of Woman as Temptress made flesh. But I am not a weak man: I make my own choices.

There was a tree, when I was a boy, that I wanted to conquer. I would stand at its foot and envision myself among the topmost branches. Each summer I would climb a little higher, and a little higher, knowing the danger and knowing the thrill. When, at twelve years old, I fell out of the tree far short of my goal and broke my ankle, I did not blame the tree. It was a beautiful challenge, a challenge irresistible to me, yet even at that young age I would never have thought to blame the tree for its beauty, for the way the sounds in its upper branches made the summer breeze become a siren song to my naïve and adventurous mind.

No, Odette could not help being Odette. She could no more control the insinuating huskiness of her voice, the fullness of her bodice, the habitually parted lips and smoky eyes, than a tree can control the sound of the wind through its foliage. We are to our natures born, I think, and society molds those natures as best (or worst) it can. Clearly Odette had received no education proper to a young lady; clearly she had never been in the care of, say, nuns! The cobra is beautiful, but only a fool would expect to put out his hand to it and not be bitten, and I am no Indian snake charmer. I had seen Odette's degraded beauty, I had heard the siren song of her shadowed eyes. And I knew that not only was I too moral a man to fall, I was also too soft. It takes a certain fearless disregard, for convention, for safety, for self, to reach toward the cobra's shining head. I had not the fortitude of the willfully dissolute. I have too mundane a heart to truly be swayed from the path of righteousness. The rules are clear, and the path strewn with enough sweet-smelling flowers, enough benign beauty, for me to prefer it to a more glamorous yet dangerous road. I thought of Odette and felt a stab of purely animal longing; I think of Augustine and I feel a melting in my heart.

It is an easy choice for me.

But I must admit I had thought sometimes of Odette. Her smoky eyes would appear to me at odd times, most often in the moments before falling asleep. Blue, blue—and I would start awake, picturing Augustine's very different blue eyes. In truth, I felt ashamed to think of Augustine when I had just been picturing Odette's exotic visage. Augustine's eyes were cornflowers in a sunny field; Odette's were midnight. Augustine's whole face was light and purity and gentleness, whereas Odette's was lit by the fires of corruption. I was astounded, frankly, that such a woman as Odette could so easily have kindled a fire in my heart, but I had never before been approached by a woman like Odette. I had never dreamed that such a creature could exist outside the pages of a romance novel—I had never even read such a novel, just glimpsed the ones Natalie kept hidden at the bottom of her wardrobe. I had heard about women whose sexuality was unbridled and corrupt—there are those who think *all* women's sexuality is unbridled and corrupt, but I don't believe such nonsense. But I have been exposed to so little in my sheltered life! The fairy princess, the damsel in distress—what do I know about women? I had begun reading what little literature exists on hysteria and had been astonished at the acceptance of the idea of Woman as a succubus unable to control her own passions. Am I so provincial that I cannot understand the threat of Woman? Of certain women, of course; every man has read or heard stories of the femme fatale, and more than half hope to meet one, even to be ill-used. But Augustine was no succubus, no threat—except perhaps to my heart. Maybe that was what was meant by these dramatic claims, that Woman has the natural capacity both to entangle the heart of man and make a fool of him while doing it. But is that not our fault as much as it is Woman's? She follows her nature, we follow our basest desires or our untried hearts. I did not blame Odette for what she was, just as I thanked God for what Augustine was.

But I felt a certain guilt in thinking about both these women so close in succession, although I knew I would be foolish indeed if I thought I could control the meanderings of my mind.

And then I faced that it was not my heart that had been kindled by Odette, but the very baseness I so deplored in other men. So I was human after all. I would be doubly careful, then, when I met her at the party. Because I knew that my very humanness would make me seek her out, make me see if I could quench this unholy thirst by conquering it before it conquered me.

Chapter 37

I WAIT FOR Edouard. All along the endless hallways the air is completely still. In the Great Goctor's office the black walls soak up all the air and light, and my voice falls straight to the floor. Even outside in the courtyard the air is as still as the sunlight, which is always pale, as though it loses something in reaching past the walls and down to where we pace or cry or stand and stare. Even the sound of crying seems flat—it is only at night that sounds take on any resonance.

And in the hydro-treatment rooms even the great gasps of steam do not disturb but only add to the heaviness of the air, which weighs, like layer upon layer of cotton blankets.

But when Edouard visits he brings the wind. His hair always looks as if he has just been running. His cheeks are always flushed with vigor and good health. He has a wonderful amount of animal spirits, and during his visits he shares them with me, as if they were an elixir, a far better elixir than even the green and yellow of my own meadows at home. Edouard's Healing Elixir, like the tonics Maman used to take for her nerves. Used to. As if my entire past were dead and gone, and I only away from home these few months!

I have alluded to Edouard in my letters; but gently, lest I frighten Maman. I see now how I have hurt her: What must it have done to her to find out that her own daughter lusted after a married man! What must it have done, in the weeks and months leading up to my commitment to La Salpêtrière, for her to see my sadness, my surliness, my constant sulks and temper? Oh, I know now that I did not have green disease; I do not even believe in green disease anymore. But I cannot blame her for thinking that something was terribly wrong with me. And something was. Immaturity, bad judgment, the need to pull away from what I loved most: my parents. Even Papa felt my moods. And, scientific-minded man that he is, it was only natural that he would find a new cause for the old malady of growing up and blame it on Progress, at that.

I hear a knock on the door, how odd; I have no treatments until three. Perhaps it is Edouard already!

I am the happiest girl in the world!

Chapter 38

Edouard

I HAVE HAD a shock. A shock, and I have sorely disappointed myself: I have never before put my feelings ahead of my work. And yet, to see her limbs performing the same contortions as those of that old woman with religious mania. Not until now have I seen that old woman as fully human. Through my lens I gave her the same careful consideration I would an interesting rock formation, or a waterfall, a delicately posed corpse. The dead woman I photographed in the dirty courtyard at dawn with Capt. Bezier was more real to me, more alive than that old woman. That I could see her as less real than a pretty corpse–I am ashamed of my nature as a man.

And then I think of Adelaide. When she is in the midst of her constrictions she says appalling things: *I could be so much more . . . entertaining . . . than your girlfriend.* I am quite certain she is mad.

I have seen her befriend Augustine, but even then there is a certain nervousness, a certain overabundance of animal spirits that sometimes accompanies things worse than green disease. I give no consideration to what Adelaide says while in delirium.

Augustine said not a word, although the sounds she made while she posed were disturbing indeed. She went through each constriction and every phase of an hysterical attack as though she had been practicing a routine.

And yet it looked so real! As real as the old woman's conniptions, as real as any of the movements I had seen depicted in Richet's albums. *How could this be the girl I know?* She said not a word, but her face became as wanton as any I have seen lost in their hysteria.

THAT MORNING I was readying the camera equipment for Dr. Charcot's Friday lecture. The Friday lectures differ greatly from their Tuesday counterparts in that the latter are held for the masses; often the entire Amphitheatre is filled. But one must receive a special invitation to attend a Friday lecture, as they are intended not for the ignorant, spectacle-hunting public but for those students with a real interest in and talent for the subject. Generally those that attend are handpicked by the doctor himself.

The Friday lecture is held in a private office into which a bed is sometimes wheeled. The hysteric, once hypnotized by Dr. Charcot, enacts the whole arc of the hysterical attack, from the initial facial spasms and characteristic opening cry through the frozen contractures of the hands and feet to the attitudes passionnelles to the lessening of symptoms, until the attack is over.

And today the girl brought in was Augustine The first thing she saw was me; I wanted to run and comfort her. But her bearing stopped and almost affronted me. She was so calm of demeanor, as though walking dressed only in her shift into a room full of strange men were commonplace to her. Only her eyes betrayed her. She stared at me terrified, and yet I was certain I was the only one who saw it. She looked haunted; she looked as if she might bolt; she looked angry with me for being there.

And then her eyes went blank, and she walked lightly over to Dr. Charcot and stood in front of him, the dutiful student, and I did not know her anymore. It was her poise that most unsettled me. After that one moment of bright blue fear, the Augustine I know simply disappeared. No more was she the frightened girl I had first seen on the Amphitheatre stage, and no more the charming woman-child who caricatured Dr. Charcot and was brought almost to tears by the plight of a voiceless insane woman.

In their place was a young woman, beautiful and unapproachable. She held herself as a dancer might, still and pale as ivory. Her eyes were like a sailor's, trained always on some distant horizon only he can see. She looked toward the wall but it was not the wall she saw; I do not know what she saw. I felt a sudden, aching desire that she look toward me as she had in the Amphitheatre, as if my face were the only life raft that could save her.

Dr. Charcot spoke briefly to her, too softly for me to hear, and she walked over to the divan and lay upon it. If I had not known this girl I would have thought her a cataleptic.

And then she began to move. As Dr. Charcot narrated the steps of the hysterical seizure, Augustine moved, always few steps ahead of him, leading him through a dance she seemed to know better than he.

I cursed myself for showing her those pictures of Adelaide. And yet Adelaide had schooled her well. Augustine cried out, a clarion call. Every student drew in a simultaneous breath. Then her face became a rictus of fear that slowly melted into a beatific, disturbing smile; her eyes were fixed on something we could not see, and that something was beautiful. And then, with startling abruptness, the smile went wanton, the eyes wild, the apparition before her both alluring and threatening; she began to entreat it with little purring growls, and her hands, which had been clenched, opened like flowers and, as if they belonged to someone else, gently stroked her collarbones, her neck, her face unaware and ecstatic.

This is not Augustine, I thought, and knew I was protecting myself. Because this was as surely Augustine as the girl I knew was Augustine, and I knew I was going to have to reconcile the two. Because I would never abandon her.

The attitudes passionelles were the most difficult to watch—worse than the face of the sensual, wholly foreign Augustine were the movements she made, rolling across the bed, kicking as if at an unseen assailant, and then suddenly arching her back until she was a dreadful rainbow against the rumpled sheets.

It was over quickly. She collapsed against the mattress, and suddenly nothing was happening at all.

The lights went up, as they would at the theater, and two attendants approached Augustine where she sat straightening her shift on the bed, suddenly demure, pulling the cloth to cover her legs, smoothing her hair: like an actress after a performance.

And I understood.

One of the attendants took her arm. "Wait," I said. Dr. Charcot turned at my voice and glared. The darkness in the depths of his eyes reached for me across the room. But I ignored him and walked toward Augustine, who was looking at me now with some of the same fear I had seen on her face when she first noticed me in the room.

"Are you all right?" I whispered. She relaxed; she shook off the attendant and he abruptly left the room, following the doctor, who surveyed us from out in the hall.

"I would like to explain it to you," she said seriously, her eyes begging forgiveness.

"You do not have to explain," I said gently, sitting next to her on the bed. She scooted away; she was so clearly Augustine again! "You are confined in this place through no fault or choice of your own, and yet you have made a place for yourself. And not only a place, my most clever girl, but art! You wanted to dance, Augustine, and who am I to judge how you have chosen to dance? What else could you have done? And it is art, what you do. I can see that. You are a born actress."

"Then you do not hate me?" she asked, still cowed, still ashamed.

"Hate you? I could almost say I respect you all the more. Augustine, your pictures are to appear in a book. You are already being studied, in England as well as France, as the quintessential hysterical patient. Your pictures have been in magazines, did you know that? I have not wanted to see them; please forgive me. You have made your name. Is that not what you wanted?"

"Not this way. Not with my shift up to my thighs!"

I found myself laughing.

"But are you Augustine when you perform? Is Sarah Bernhardt herself when she performs? An actress immerses herself in her part, and I have never seen a more thorough performance. Please do not feel ashamed. We do what we must to survive, and I think none the less of you for it."

"Attend to your work, M. Mas," a deep voice said behind my

right ear, and I got up off the bed so hastily I almost fell. I looked over, expecting to see Augustine frightened, ready to protect her. But she was smiling a small smile, as if to herself. She seemed to rouse herself to speak to me, and her eyes were blank: "Thank you, Monsieur Mas. You have been quite the gentleman."

And she let herself be led away, stumbling a little, seeming weak and faint. I turned and went back to my equipment without looking at Dr. Charcot.

Chapter 39

From the Journal of Augustine Dechelette

I HAVE ONCE again received unexpected visitors. What an odd life this is! The last thing I expected, upon being committed to the Hôpital Salpêtrière, was to become a young woman who entertained visitors!

But yesterday one of the attendants came to my room to tell me I had visitors, and would I like a few minutes to freshen up? This was odd too, because I didn't know whether it was meant as a small kindness or an observation of the habitual dishabille shared by all the patients here.

I brushed my hair and pinched my cheeks. I almost used some of the blush Adelaide had given me, but I was certain it must be Maman and Papa come to see me; if it had been Edouard, Claude would have said visitor, not visitors. And for a moment I almost laughed aloud at the thought of Maman should she come to visit her only daughter in the mental institution and find her with an artificial blush on her cheeks!

So I restrained from biting my lips as well, lest so much color in my face alarm Maman, and awaited my dear parents.

I was so happy! I had not expected to see them for some time. Papa had written that there was a great workload at home and besides, he felt it would be better for me to be away from anything that reminded me of home. I knew that meant Maman was afraid to come to Paris again. But I had missed them so!

Maman would cry, of course (and so would I), but Papa and I would have a chance for one of those spirited intellectual debates I knew we both so missed. He had already indicated, in his letters to me, that he did not hold with these modern ways of treating a young woman's distress (that is the word he used, *distress*, and I loved him the more for it).

So I was sitting, all anticipation, and the door opened and I smiled my joy into the faces of strangers.

I froze. It was a lady and a gentleman, and very fine ones at that. The first thing I noticed was the feathers: a profusion of black feathers on a sleek black hat. How I had always loved to look at the hats in the copies of the Woman's supplement of the *Journal Illustré* my father did not know I managed to acquire! I had not seen a hat like this. The first thing I thought was, *Oh, I have not kept up with the latest fashions!* Which would have made me laugh, its being such an utterly ridiculous thing to think while confined to La Salpêtrière, but I did not laugh. I had no urge. The face beneath the hat was so exquisite, and had so warm a smile, that I was more moved to cry. The woman stood timid in the doorway, holding the arm of the gentleman, whose countenance, though less warm, was nevertheless welcoming. He seemed more concerned for his wife than for me. She stood like a deer come upon suddenly in the forest, and I was so struck by her consternation at barging in on a complete stranger, indeed, by her so obvious fragility of spirit, that I found myself saying gently, "It's all right." I wanted to comfort her.

She smiled, and the warmth grew deeper as her reservations were assuaged.

"You see, V, I told you the young lady would not mind," the man said, and I fell in love with her name. So innocent a name, with a purity that matched her delicate beauty.

"Excuse me," said the man. "My name is Monsieur Soulavie, and this is my wife." Again she smiled at me, and my smile in return was eager. And then for the first time I really looked at the man, M. Soulavie. He was very tall, imposing in his good looks, and would almost have frightened me were it not for the softening of his wife's presence. I could not find a reason for my disquiet upon observing him, and it was only that, a faint unease in his presence.

"My wife saw Dr. Charcot's examination of you at the Amphitheatre," he said, and I noticed that his voice was kind, and thought, *Had it been kind a moment ago?* But I was also instantly humiliated: These people had seen my degradation.

"I felt terribly bad for you," V said. Her voice was like a lullaby. "I had a sister . . ." she said softly, and I saw her small fist clench and her lower lip suddenly quiver.

"Come in," I said to her. "You are welcome here." And she ran across the room and knelt at my feet, with a loud sigh of her petticoats, which billowed around her like fog.

"Please," she said. "You are so like her." She broke down and sobbed.

I did not know what to do. That a woman of such obviously high station should be crying at my feet alarmed me. I wanted, quite desperately, to help her. She had already, in an instant, become important to me. I looked importunately at her husband.

He was all consternation and consideration, for me as well as for his wife. He knelt beside her, he smoothed her hair. He whispered comfort and endearments, his cheek to hers.

Then he looked up at me and said, "Suicide," so quietly I almost did not catch the word.

I gasped, and Mme. Soulavie looked up. "I'm so sorry," she said. "So very sorry." She was clearly trying to compose herself.

"Charles and I were at lunch with friends last week, and they absolutely insisted we attend one of Dr. Charcot's famous Lectures du Mardi. I was hesitant . . . my nerves." She looked down, a faint blush rose to her cheeks. "But they did not know of my sister, and although my dear Charles"— indicating her husband—"tried to make excuses, our friends were quite adamant. I did not want to appear rude. So we went, and it was as if the Fates had brought me there. As if God himself had wished me to see you."

"Please," I said. "Don't kneel." Her evident distress was difficult to witness. There was something about the delicacy of her countenance, now stained with tears, that made me, ignorant bumbling country girl that I am, want to be the one to comfort her, to help her, to rescue her.

"V," said M. Soulavie. "Please get up." He lifted her gently, and she rose out of her cloud of petticoats (I noted that there were at least six, and that the lace with which they were trimmed was very fine indeed) like a naiad arising from a lake.

She smiled and reached to touch my hand. "I beg your forgiveness for two reasons. One is that it was quite wrong of me to discompose you by appearing without sending a proper introductory letter first. Charles did try to make me see reason, and I apologize for not requesting permission to visit you. "The second reason I must ask your pardon is that I am quite distressed. I am afraid, actually, that you will assume I think you insane, being in this place. But nothing could be further from the truth. You are no more insane than my dear sister." Again she broke down in tears, and again her husband touched her shoulder and shushed her with whispered tendernesses. But I had the oddest sense that he was somehow in awe of her at this moment, although I could not see why this should be.

He turned to me. "She is overwrought. Her nerves. I could not dissuade her from coming here today. But V has never had a bad intention in her life, and certainly the effects of her intentions have never brought anyone anything but joy. She is a rare flower, my V."

And my fears dissipated. It was the sternness of his aspect that had unsettled me, that was all: the strength of his features, the obvious intelligence and fortitude of his character. It is in certain men's natures to be fierce, almost to the extent of frightening womenfolk. Certainly my father ought to have shown me that!

"Let us begin again," said Mme. Soulavie, "because the truth is that I am delighted to have the opportunity to make your acquaintance." She held out her little hand, and it was like holding the bones of a baby bird. I took the gentleman's hand as well, and his grip was surprisingly gentle.

I asked them both to sit, then realized I had only one chair. Mme. Soulavie put her hand on mine and asked if she might sit beside me on the bed. I suspected it would not be the last time I would see her smooth over even the slightest awkwardness with a kind word or gesture; her graciousness was both fluid and apparent in everything she did. I was, I confess, quite in awe of her from the moment we met.

I had never before met a great lady. And that Mme. Soulavie was a great lady I did not doubt for a moment. She was exquisite in every movement she made, in every delicate, kind gesture, in her immediate girlish friendliness. From the instant I made her acquaintance I felt that it was she who needed me, she who needed protection, she who needed succor. And the way her husband fluttered around—yes, fluttered, although he was an altogether manly personage—both endeared him to me and showed just how sensitive and delicate Mme. Soulavie truly was.

She plunged into conversation as though we had long been intimate, and her voice was honey. "I know I could never understand how horrible it must have been for you to go through the ordeal of having, well, not only to be onstage, but also to be under the scrutiny of such an imposing figure as Dr. Charcot. I confess, the man frightens me."

"He does?"

"Oh, yes, terribly. I was so impressed with your composure in front of that man! I fear I would have been in tears immediately."

"It is not like that. I have no control over how he uses my body. Because that is what it is like—it is like being a puppet."

I glanced over at M. Soulavie—and I was frightened of what I saw. His face had on it a fixed look. I saw that as I spoke he was looking not at me but at his wife, with an intensity as strong as that of an entomologist studying a new specimen. For the briefest instant something shifted in his eyes. I was speaking of my body being completely under the control of the doctor, and I saw a spark of something—I do not know—something feral. Something almost inhuman, as though he wasn't the kind, concerned grandmother in a fairy tale but the ravaging wolf lying in wait.

It was only for a moment. I faltered in my speech, and he caught my eye, and all I saw there was gentleness. But somehow even that frightened me, because it seemed not so much the genuine feeling but a mask hastily slipped on.

Mme. Soulavie's gentle voice brought me back to my senses. "Charles," she said. "I think your presence is upsetting the young lady. Am I not correct?"

And I realized that it was simply the fact that I had almost forgotten her husband entirely. And when I became aware that I was speaking about my body in front of a strange gentleman! Well, it is no wonder I became overwrought.

M. Soulavie was kind; he apologized first to his wife, and then to me, and said that he had wanted to walk again the long, tree-lined avenue that led up to the hospital entrance, having found the road sinister in a beautiful way.

Again I had a flash of discomfort, but Mme. Soulavie laughed after he had gone and said, "The things he says! He is a poet, you know, with a poet's morbid sensibility. He has absolutely no idea the effect his words have on people who do not know him! Come now, let me brush your hair. I insist, Augustine." And she took from her soft velvet clutch a brush with a silver back embossed with a profusion of roses entwined on a branch. I let her take down my hair, my flyaway farm-girl hair, and was not ashamed.

She brushed my hair with swift, sure strokes; she admired its thickness and color; she lamented that her own hair was not as abundant as mine. The brushing lulled me, the susurration of her voice lulled me, and I found myself almost under a spell.

"Augustine," she said, as I listened to the soothing sound of the brush though my hair. "Is there anything you need?"

"To get out of here."

At this Mme. Soulavie laughed so heartily I was worried she might perhaps have a coughing fit although I had no idea if her health was as delicate as it seemed to be.

"Well, that is something we might be able to see about, in time.

Right now I would like to give you this brush for your beautiful hair."

"I—I cannot." I could hardly catch my breath. My own wooden brush was nothing compared to this. This was beyond anything I had thought I would ever own. And yet feminine vanity, coupled with the look in the lady's luminous eyes, won out. I accepted her gift.

As she made ready to leave, I said, "My world is so very different from yours in Paris, Madame Soulavie. And yet I would give almost anything to go beyond these walls and see that world for myself."

"And I am certain you shall. You were not made for this place. You are not mad, dear girl. I am so glad you accepted the brush. My husband provides me with anything I desire. Things mean nothing to me. If I can do anything to make your stay here less bleak, please let me." She was so like a child wanting to please, and so like a child wanting to have her way, that I could not help but relent.

I was bewitched, and knew it, but she was kind as Maman, with Maman's sincerity and simplicity of manner. Only a pure heart can act thus. I have found an angel.

What adventures I am having, and what fascinating people I am meeting here where I expected only solitude and misery. I have found friendship, and light, and life, at last, in the most unlikely and unexpected place.

Ah, the dinner bell. And I am taken once again back to the mundane realities of life as a patient in La Salpêtrière.

But I have met a fairy, and spent time in an enchanted realm.

And I have made another friend.

Chapter 40

Edouard

I WAS ALL trepidation as I walked up to the door of the address
I had been given. I was wearing my best suit, but I knew it was
inadequate to the occasion. I had borrowed a cravat, gloves, and
hat from Richet; he would have given me more, but I would not
accept a suit. I am, after all, not Richet but Edouard, and I would
have been even more uncomfortable wholly portraying myself as
something I am not. I was wearing my own unfashionable suit.
The hat, gloves, and cravat were absolute necessities, though, if I
were to appear in polite society, and I accepted them gratefully.

In spite of my reservations I found myself as excited as a school-
boy. I had never before been to a truly fashionable party. I tapped
the lion's-head door knocker as though I had a right. I doffed my
hat to the servant who answered the door; she was older than I
had expected, and quite proper and prim, and it occurred to me

that what I had expected was a debauch, and I was relieved to my core. My silly boy's fantasies! Richet had introduced me to Mme. and M. Gaudet at the next Tuesday lecture, and there was nothing even remotely sordid about them; Mme. Gaudet in particular was of obvious good breeding, with her high forehead, clear eyes, and gentle manner of speech. And the first woman I met, who in fact rushed to greet me, was Mme. Gautier, was an elderly coquette encrusted with diamonds. She seemed not in the least put out at not having any notion who I was. She quite charmed me, as did her husband, who spent the entire time of our introduction feeling about in his pockets for his monocle. And then there was Mme. Soulavie, who came to me with her dainty hand outstretched; she was all in ivory, and stood out among the crowd like those bright clouds one sometimes sees in a gray sky, separated from the rest by a light that seems to come from within. She greeted me kindly and steered me gracefully toward Richet, taking the hat, coat, and gloves I had not managed to give to the maidservant from my awkward hands.

"Ah, Edouard, there you are!" Richet exclaimed, taking me from Mme. Soulavie's arm. She smiled and disappeared into the crowd. Society is an intimidating creature to those of us brought up outside its grip. Those to the manner born are also born to a language of which I knew only phrases. Were I to travel to Italy, I would know the names of the dishes I would like to order and the destinations I should like to visit, but I would be unable to say much more in Italian than "where" and "I would like," and it is much the same in the ballrooms of the elite.

I looked around, feeling the country bumpkin. Richet, after having greeted me, strolled the room with me at his side, perfectly at ease. As we spoke casually of work, I found myself embarrassed—I should not need the protection of an escort! After he had introduced me to half a dozen attractive people whose names I instantly forgot, I decided it was time to fend for myself.

"Excuse me," I said to him and the particularly pretty young woman he was speaking with, "I believe I will go pay my respects to Mme. Gaudet now."

Bowing to his pretty companion, I made my way into the thick of the crowd.

I had found myself, while in conversation with Richet, searching the room for Odette. The moment I left him I saw her. She was the center of attention; and yet I felt that the boredom she displayed was not fashionable ennui, not simply for show. She wore what looked to be an Oriental dress, although I had never actually seen one, black silk with a pattern of golden snakes and small, bright flames, with flat black satin slippers on her feet. Even so, she was at least as tall as most of the men around her, and taller than some.

As I approached she shifted her weight from one foot to the other, and the dress shifted, too, like rippling water, a shudder of movement that went from her shoulders to her ankles, a waterfall of movement designed to reveal and hide as it went: For an instant her breasts stood out in sharp relief, then her belly, then her hips and thighs and calves. I watched, mesmerized, and looked up to her face to find her regarding me with a bemused smile.

I smiled in return, fully aware of how small I was, to stare at a woman's body in such a brazen fashion. But her smile seemed genuine, and certainly her display was disingenuous. But even as I bid her good evening I knew that a woman's disingenuousness does not excuse a man's bad behavior.

"How are you this evening, Madame Alexandrovna?" I asked as normally as I could; I felt as if I had just seen her naked.

"Edouard, I am merely Odette," she said, and she laughed, and I have never before heard such a laugh, hoarse and mocking yet sweet as a siren's.

"I want to smoke," Odette said to me, dismissing the others, and so I took her arm and led her toward the patio. Actually, she led me, because I did not know where the patio was, and I must admit that I was so overwhelmed by her presence that even had I known, I'm sure I would have walked her off into a wall. Her scent was overpowering: something musky and exotic I took at first to be incense; and the strong smell of sweat, which, far from being unpleasant, was practically an aphrodisiac. And she had jasmine oil in her hair, and also the smell of foreign tobacco.

"Are you enjoying the party?" she asked. Under her keen gaze I felt as transparent as air; she knew exactly the effect she was having on me. She must see men react this way to her all the time, I thought to myself, with no little annoyance. I wanted to be different. I knew I could never mean anything at all to this woman, knew that in my heart I did not really want to mean anything to her. What I wanted was to conquer my own desires.

We walked out to the patio. I was acutely aware of both my hand against the naked skin of her arm and the frank stares of the men we passed. I was proud to be seen with her, and ashamed of my pride. I wasn't conquering anything. I suddenly quite honestly wanted a smoke myself. I had to clear my head.

The cool night air was a welcome slap. But Odette's face was all the more alluring under the light of the moon, and I hastily removed my hand from her arm under the pretext of locating my cigarettes and lighter.

"Smoke one of mine," she said languidly., "They're Egyptian." The cigarette was thin and long and oddly scented; I recognized the incense smell. Odette insisted on placing it to my lips, on being the one to hold the lighter that I might have to touch her fingers to steady the flame. I inhaled. At least her ways were not subtle, and surely could not be so hard to fight once I had regained myself. But just then I felt a sudden rush of sensation in my head; I thought I must have spoken.

"No words," she said softly.

So we smoked. Soon I felt that there was an unspoken under-current of communication between us, all the stronger for its silence. I felt almost that I could read her heart. Longing, for peace, serenity, a haven from despair—what despair I did not know. I could feel her pulse beating against the blue veins of her delicate, almost translucent skin. Longing, for protection, understanding: longing for me.

And I knew with equal certainty that nothing I felt was hidden from her: desire, resistance, the urge to shelter her from all harm.

And the moon stared down, impassive.

I was almost delirious with my new knowledge, my certainty of my power. I moved closer, and closer still, and when she lay her head against my shoulder I felt I had never before known bliss.

The door slammed open behind us.

"That wind!" I heard a male voice exclaim. I experienced a moment of fury entirely outside my character. *Who were these people who would intrude on two hearts communing!*

"Take my hat," a woman's voice said, and I became aware of a discordance between their words and my understanding. They seemed to be speaking from far away, and their words were fragmented, as if being torn from their mouths by a sharp wind. There was a wind, but it was not the hurricane, surely, that it seemed so suddenly to me; in fact the air was warm and soft upon my neck.

And when I turned to see who spoke, I was utterly unprepared for what I saw: faces made grotesque by simple moonlight, grimacing skulls whose bones shone through the merest sheen of skin.

For a moment I doubted my own sanity. Would Odette appear so? I turned to her face, her beautiful body, and perceived rot and corruption there.

"Odette."

"Silly Edouard," she said, and she laughed with pleasure. "It is only your cigarette."

Then I remembered: the sick-sweet smell of incense. The seeming lifting of a veil over my consciousness. The lucidity of the opalescent moon.

"What is in those cigarettes?"

"The finest Egyptian tobacco," she said, and suddenly her smile was snakelike. "And opium, of course," she added lightly.

I threw mine to the floor and crushed it with my foot. There was nothing to resist. The image of Odette I had been so eager to test myself against existed only in her powers of seduction and in the drug, not in the woman herself. I saw now that her makeup was badly applied, and the kohl around her eyes was uneven; that the blush on her cheeks was garishly bright against her pallid skin; that her laugh was a shield and not an invitation.

"You should have told me," I said stiffly. Nothing but tinsel, this surging silver feeling. Gone was the delicious pull of mutual attraction. There was nothing but this drugged and pathetic woman in front of me.

"You don't like the way it makes you feel? As if you could float right up to the moon as if you were part of the sky. And it sweetens other things."

"No," I said flatly. "I don't like it. I like feeling what I feel, not what some inhalant makes me feel. I want all of my feelings to be true."

"Oh, Edouard, where is the fun in that? Anybody can feel. I prefer to open the doorways to experience. To go beyond mundane feeling and truly live."

"I am sorry, Odette, if I misled you." She laughed and laughed.

"I misled you, dear innocent Edouard. And yet, you would have been such a pleasure to corrupt!"

"I will take that as a compliment, but I must take my leave."

"You will remember, Edouard. I guarantee you will remember Odette and your missed opportunity."

"And I thank you for the memory," I said sincerely, and I kissed her cold hand and left her on the patio with the moon.

The party had lost its charm. The great oak I had wanted to climb had proven merely a bush with sweet-smelling, poisonous flowers, and I was no longer tempted by their fragrance.

I drifted back into the ballroom. No one was dancing, and all the guests seemed merely shadow puppets miming gaiety. I knew I was still affected by the opium I had ingested, and I was disgusted with myself. What a bumpkin I was indeed, out of my depth among the glistening falseness of the throng. But I had promised Natalie a full description of the ladies' dresses, so I walked about alone, making mental notes.

My attention was drawn to several young men discoursing in loud voices in the corner by a blazing fire. " . . . the finest play ever to have been written," I heard, and, "Nonsense! Everything he writes is scurrilous nonsense!"

I heard, and the first, quite distinctive voice: "He is the greatest artist of our time."

Three young men were talking intensely, two on a pale green

settee, and one lounging on the floor. *Literature,* I thought. *I can talk about literature.* I might not have lived, but I had read.

I grabbed a whisky off the tray offered me by a servant; I needed to steady my nerves. Certainly cerebral conversation with these young men would prove an antidote to opium, delirium, and Odette.

"May I join this learned discussion?" I asked, glass in hand.

"Of course you may join our discussion," the young man with the distinctive voice said with great force. He seemed to speak only with enthusiasm, which was just the antidote I needed. He was the one lounging on the floor.

A man of ideas, I thought, and realized that perhaps whisky was not the wisest choice of drink after opium.

The room tilted, once, and was still, but something must have shown on my face.

"Come," said another of the young men. "Sit. Have you had a visit from the Green Fairy?"

The first young man laughed: a pleasant bray. "There are fairies all about tonight. No, I can smell what you've been up to."

"I had no intention. She told me they were Egyptian cigarettes."

All the young men laughed heartily, but somehow I was unashamed.

"Oh, you must point her out to me. I am Theo, and I am pleased to make your acquaintance." I gave him my hand and my name; his grip was firm, his skin soft as a woman's. "I have no cure for Egyptian cigarettes. I myself would never seek such a cure, but I think that if you take a seat and talk quietly with us by the fire, you will feel more yourself presently."

"You can listen to Theo expound on one of his favorite topic his very favorite. What does he care for more?"

"Absinthe."

"Ah, gentlemen, gentlemen, you will frighten poor Edouard, and it is clear that he has already had a fright. Here, Edouard, finish your drink. It will make a man of you."

For some reason this struck Theo's cohorts as exceedingly comical; but I didn't mind. There was no malice in it. I thought of Odette and shuddered.

"Oh, look!" Theo exclaimed. "Someone is going to be mopping the floor tonight!" And I looked to where he pointed and saw a bright red trail of blood. I thought of the dead man I had photographed, I thought of Tabby. But this blood came not from death but from life.

"It is an honest accident," I said. "A woman cannot always control her flow."

"Are you one of those men who finds that a woman's menses adds a certain sweetness to the act of love?"

I blushed. But I held my head up. "I have not yet found my true love," I said. And thought of Augustine, her blue eyes clear, sparkling without glycerin, arresting without kohl. Augustine, who had no arsenal of feminine tricks and yet was the personification of all that is beautiful; Augustine, who had only looked into a mirror a half dozen times before she came to La Salpêtrière. I missed her passionately.

"You should tell her," Theo said to me seriously—so seriously that I did not at first realize that it was he who spoke.

I said, "I know," and Theo smiled at me, then turned to the young man next to him and said, "But you haven't read it!"

"Of course I have!"

"I meant that you haven't experienced it."

I noticed that Theo wore a dyed-green carnation in his lapel.

Oh my Lord, I thought, I have landed in Sodom! But somehow I was not disgusted. I was more inclined to laugh, for what could be funnier, after escaping the clutches of the siren, to land among a temptation so far from my nature as to seem of another planet? But I did not laugh. I liked what Theo had said to me far too much for me to wish to hurt him in any way. And what a man does who hurts no one is not any business of mine.

"He is a great writer," I said quietly, almost to myself.

Immediately Theo pounced. "And what do you think is the greatest of his works?"

"His cape," I said, laughing. Oscar Wilde, some of whose fans affected green carnations after Wilde appeared onstage in one. Some of his followers called themselves the Green Carnation Society.

"Give the gentleman another drink!" But I protested, and was not pressured. My head was beginning to ache. I did not want to think about what had passed between me and Odette. I did not even want to think about Augustine; I felt I had done her an injustice. Talking about Oscar Wilde with cultured young men of this ilk seemed a good tonic for now.

At this point I decided that the swirl of activity around us was making me lightheaded, and decided that after all another drink, as well as some tobacco, would best steady my nerves. That, and more talk.

"What do you really think is his most important work?"

"His cape!" I said again, and then, as Theo lit my cigar. "I know that Wilde is most famous for his plays, and indeed they are delightful. But the work I most respect is *The Picture of Dorian Gray*."

"Edouard!" We all turned at once, a dutiful audience. And Odette fulfilled her role: Her hair was in a pretty state of dishabille (it had been neater ten minutes ago), her eyes were sparkling, and her lip rouge made her look as if she had sprung from some fairy ring of violets.

She looked healthier than she had so shortly before, but I knew it was an artificial opium shine. The glimmer in her eyes was something she used as she used a brush to smudge the kohl about her eyes; and when the opium glimmer was gone her eyes would be dead again, as I had last seen them, naked and dead.

But I watched with amusement as Theo and the others became fools in the face of her beauty. I knew that these young men were not drawn to Odette as I had been. (I felt disgusted as I remembered how enamored I had been of that attraction, that temptation, more enamored of that than I had ever been of the actual woman, and how close I had been to losing my self-possession, my integrity, my very right to care for a girl as pure as Augustine.) No, Theo in particular was clearly awestruck by Odette's aura of danger, her obvious, experienced decadence. One need not desire her physically to be fascinated by her; I could see the effect she had on the women around her, who, while they stepped away from this obviously *bad* woman, stared at her covertly with hooded eyes and unconsciously open mouths, ready to drink in whatever it was that made Odette, Odette. She cast her net wide and without discrimination, and as I watched Theo rise to kiss her hand I felt a dart of worry for him: *He is in danger*, I thought.

"Edouard," Odette protested. "You should not have left me alone!" Never had there been a woman in less need of protection, but I rose and kissed her hand again and made my obsequies, feeling only amusement. Was this woman really the creature I had so lately found utterly hypnotic? Perhaps I had just wanted to lose my head, but not to Odette. No, not to Odette.

She continued to make pretty remonstrations for her audience's sake, but clearly she had lost interest in me. Theo, however, seemed to be proving satisfactory; although his interest was clearly not romantic in nature, it was intense, and his flattery genuine: He was mesmerized by her.

As I watched their gentle thrust and parry, I began to feel fatigued. I was not made for social excitement, I reflected; my nerves were overstimulated, and besides, I felt a headache coming on, likely the effect of Odette's "Egyptian" cigarettes.

I longed for home, for my desk near the fireplace. I wanted nothing more than to be seated there now, my little cat Goncourt purring in my lap as I composed a letter to Natalie. I rose to take my leave of Theo, only to find him gone, and Odette as well; and his friends had scattered to the trays of food and drink circulating about the grand room. I made my way to the door, pausing to find and thank my hostess, and doing my best to catalog in my memory the various dresses, fabrics, hairstyles, and diamonds I passed along the way. If I failed in my mission to bring every essence of this party to life for Natalie, my now-terrible headache would be for naught. I looked in vain for Richet but could not bring myself to go back to the patio, although I knew he loved a good smoke and might easily be found there.

As I stepped outside I felt I had never before appreciated a cool breeze. I decided to walk the three miles to my lodgings, hoping to clear my poor sick head while cementing all of the evening's important details in my memory.

But, I thought ruefully, there were certain experiences of this night that I would definitely not be sharing with my baby sister.

Chapter 41

From the Journal of Augustine Dechelette

"AUGUSTINE, YOU MUST keep our visits a secret." V and I were sitting, as we had during her first visit, on my pathetic bed. In a beige faille skirt decorated with lavender leaves, and a lavender jacket with half-moon-shaped ivory buttons, she was so finely dressed that I was astonished she did not even brush off the sheet before she settled herself onto the bed.

I had to smile. "But Madame Soulavie, the entire ward already knows by now! News travels as fast as thought in this place!"

"Not from the other patients," M. Soulavie said with his clipped politeness. "From any other visitor you might have. From your parents."

An expression crossed Mme. Soulavie's face as swiftly as the shadow of a hummingbird: contempt. And then she lay her hand gently on her husband's arm, and said, "Don't frighten her,

Charles," and her voice was loving, her face calm, and I knew I had misread her eyes. " It's just . . ." She turned to me. "It's just that we are well known in certain circles. I would not wish for people to think that our visiting you gives them the right to do what was so awful years ago: to tour the hospital to visit the pitiable insane. That is not why we are here, Augustine. But we travel in fashionable circles. And it is so easy for some simple thing one does to become fashionable to all the rest. There are those who would come and stare while telling themselves they are making a charitable gesture.

"And you do not need charity, Augustine. I did originally come for selfish reasons—you look so like my dear sister! But now that we have become friends—we are friends, aren't we, dear Augustine?" And suddenly she was at my feet, her little hands surrounding mine, her flower face imploring.

"Yes, Madame Soulavie," I stammered.

"V. You must call me simply V. I am just a girl like you."

I burst out laughing, and so did she.

"It's true!" she said, tugging at my hands in mock anger. "We are not so different, Augustine!"

"Oh, V!" I exclaimed, surprised at how easy it was to use her Christian name. "You are from a very different world. I am just a farm girl. Even now I sometimes fear I smell of dandelions and cow pies!"

V's lovely face became pensive. "I spent one summer in the countryside. I was at boarding school; I was ten. Usually my summers were spent traveling with my family. But this summer I spent with the other children from the school, those with no family to go home to, those whose families did not want them. We played every day out of doors in a great meadow filled with dandelions.

I love that smell to this day. It brings it all back: the sun, the freedom, the innocence." She paused. "I cannot say that I am familiar with the smell of cow pies, though."

She lightly squeezed my hands and jumped up; sometimes she really was like a little girl.

"Augustine, I have something for you." Her husband, who had been standing at a discreet distance, stepped forward and handed her a wrapped package from his coat pocket. He was regarding her as he always did, with indulgence and pride and a kind of secretive admiration, as if each time she surprised him again with her grace and kindness.

"For you," she said, handing me the parcel and sitting once again at my feet. She leaned her arm companionably on my thigh and said, "Open it!" Then, turning to M. Soulavie, she said, "Darling, would you be so kind as to wait outside? This can be of no interest to you. It is silly girls' business."

"Of course, my love," M. Soulavie replied. He bowed his head to me and left.

"He will go wait in the carriage," V assured me. "And he has his newspapers to read. You know, those things that are so fascinating to men and so utterly useless to women.

I felt a sharp pang of longing for my father, but I also found myself wanting to be the girl V thought I was. And I wanted to open my package, because I had known instantly what it was.

And it was more beautiful than I could ever have hoped for or imagined. I had opened it with its back to me, and it was fine bright silver, and the oval was bigger than my whole hand. It was etched from the bottom of the handle with raised vines that spread up and resolved themselves into a lilac tree that enveloped the entire back. I was afraid to turn it around. I was afraid to look into it.

"You are beautiful, Augustine. Do not be afraid."

But still I could not look. Surely my face would be as dark as any farm laborer's, to V's cool porcelain. My lips had probably lost what little color they had in this place, whereas hers were rose petals. My hair was coarse to the touch, hers a silken waterfall.

"I knew you would be this way, silly girl! So I have brought along some other things for you. And she brought out of her bag two small tin pots and a blue glass-stoppered bottle. "Green rice powder," she said. " It is what I use. And blush—I thought Cherry Blossom would be right for you. I use Ashes of Lavender myself. And hair oil with chamomile and honey."

"That is what my mother puts on my hair!"

"You have a wise mother. Now come, let us make you feel beautiful. It does not matter in the least that you already are. No woman is ever completely assured of her own beauty."

I picked up the tins one by one. The rouge was Bourjois, the finest brand in Paris; it had also been the first. I opened the top gingerly and almost gasped in delight at the lovely shade of pink that met my eye. I put it down reluctantly and opened the next. Green rice powder! That was for women with fair skin—surely V could not think me half so fair as she? But just as surely she would not have gotten me the wrong color powder. I started to stammer out my thanks but I was so moved as to be near tears.

V sat on the bed and patted the space next to her. "Now," she said in a practical voice. "Down to work. I suspect you have never applied makeup before."

I did not say that I had used Adelaide's blush; I felt somehow that it would disappoint her, and I found myself more willing to lie than to disappoint V, something I thought myself incapable of just a few months ago. "Heavens no!" I said. "Papa says that the application of makeup is simply the first step toward a woman's degreda—Oh! I'm so sorry!"

Her laugh was golden. "A girl should have a strict papa."

I thought again of Papa, and home, and V became serious. "We are here, Charles and I, to free you, Augustine. Charles has connections. You have already become dear to me. Now, don't cry! There is nothing I can do about red-rimmed eyes with only the small arsenal at our disposal! Have patience, you will see how much better things will get for you, and how soon. Come, let me show you how, Augustine."

Chapter 42

Edouard

THEY FOUND HIM sprawled in the gutter, his pockets turned out, his face horrible. I was not disposed to get up, to say the least, when Martin arrived at my apartment so early in the morning. My head was still full of smoke and pearls and whisky; I did not feel at all well, or at all intelligent. How anyone can smoke such stuff on a daily basis! I had Martin fetch me a coffee and some bread. I broke off half the loaf and gave it to him, for which he was silently grateful, and sent him on his way with four sous in his pocket.

As I readied myself I thought about the world I had entered last night, and I was profoundly grateful to be back in my own mundane reality. I was due at La Salpêtrière at nine and hoped to visit with Augustine after my work was through. I hurriedly boarded the bus, barely missing the mud kicked up by the horses that drew it, and stood in excruciating proximity to a woman loaded down by an impressive amount of garlic.

Capt. Bezier was waiting for me. "An easy case," he said without preamble as I approached. "But there was no identification found on the body. Obviously he was robbed, most likely by his own kind."

I expected to see the sort of gutter criminal one sometimes found, his clothing in tatters, beaten and robbed by fellow thieves. But this young man was exquisitely dressed, although his jacket was missing, as well as his tie. Matted blood about obscured the color or print of his vest or shirt, even the color of his hair. I leaned to look at his hands: They were perfectly manicured, although two of the nails on his right hand had been torn away, and his palms and fingers bore slashes on both hands. His face was turned away. I moved to his feet, which were shod in softest calfskin. This man had been a dandy, not some member of the criminal gang. I glanced up at the captain, who was regarding me with an indulgent expression.

"You haven't noticed the flower that lies near the body? A lovers' quarrel, I have no doubt."

A green flower, smashed but recognizable. Suddenly I found myself kneeling with my hand on his hair, brushing it back to reveal a pallid cheek, a closed eye.

"I know this man," I said quietly; my heart was not quiet. It was all I could do not to give way to tears.

"What? How on earth?"

"I met him at a party at Mme. Gaudet's house last night, just a block from here."

"A party? With this sort of man? Do you know what the green carnation signifies?"

"Yes. He was a very pleasant gentleman. His name is Theo.

Was. Theo DeManard, I think. Certainly he took pains to resemble Oscar Wilde—his cape is missing, you know. He was quite witty." I was moved to unbearable sorrow by the look on Theo's dead face. Rigor had not set in: His horror was genuine.

"A lovers' quarrel, as I said," Capt. Bezier continued. "That sort is not difficult to—"

Sadness turned instantly to anger. My head throbbed, I was back in Mme. Gaudet's lovely ballroom, there were beautifully dressed people and the smell of fresh-cut flowers and melting wax, and the candlelight set certain things aflame: a woman's elaborate hair, a man's bright cravat, the delicately patterned purple of Theo's vest.

"He was a human being, Captain Bezier! He has as much right to live as any of us. And he was so full of life. Why would I care in what manner he loved?"

"Ah, Edouard, I am sorry. I was unaware he was your friend, and of course I should have known that you would not possess the prejudices common to the ordinary man."

"I am nothing if not an ordinary man," I said wearily. "I am almost finished here. Is there more you would require of me?"

"Only your forgiveness, Edouard."

I looked up, surprised. I had never thought Capt. Bezier had even noticed me as a human being, really. I assumed he thought of me merely as another apparatus used in the investigation of crime; that I was nothing more to him than my camera and photographs.

"Of course I forgive you, Captain Bezier. I know that my thinking is unorthodox in some ways. I cannot help it."

"Nor should you," he said warmly, then seemed instantly ashamed at having shown so much. "Now run along," he said brusquely. "Get to La Salpêtrière. You are no longer needed here."

Chapter 43

From the Journal of Augustine Dechelette

THE MOST HIDEOUS thing has happened. Poor Adelaide! News travels oddly here. It is almost impossible to get our mute attendants to speak. I have written before of how they simply appear in the doorways like big white birds that have landed with silent feet. Sometimes I am so engrossed in my writing that I do not even hear the opening of the door. Of course they do not knock. Privacy is a luxury we do without in this place. And of course they do not speak, any more than birds speak. Oh, *Come*, they say, *It is time*, and other such short inanities, but these have no more real meaning than the sounds birds make. Certainly I have never been able to get any actual information out of one of them.

When something happens, though, the air begins to buzz. It is almost a feeling: I will look up from my book to hear faint, urgent noises down the hall. It is as if the heart of the hospital starts to beat faster, the very breathing of the walls quickens. Of course I cannot simply step out into the hall. I must wait to be taken to my next treatment, my next meal, where all the women are twittering like little birds in a bush.

When I am taken to the lunchroom, then, standing in line to have my bowl filled, I tilt my head back over my shoulder and say, "What?"

"Adelaide."

"Adelaide?"

"She went into the room where the photographers work."

Another voice, ahead of me, another head tilted back: "Has she been reprimanded?"

"No, worse than that."

Another: "Much worse."

"What, then?"

"She saw a head."

"Rosalie's head."

"What?"

"She went into the room dressed only in her shift."

"That girl has no shame." Other voices have joined, and they all seem to be speaking at once.

"She wanted to seduce the—"

"What do you mean," I broke in, "she saw Rosalie's head?" I cannot bear the things they say about Adelaide.

"Well, you remember that Rosalie died two days ago, don't you? Well, apparently the Great Doctor decided to examine the head."

"—always photograph the head in such a case."

"I hear your suitor was the one in charge of this particular."

"Edouard?" I had not thought of Edouard being in the hospital when he was not with me. Of Edouard walking the halls when I was unaware of it, going about his duties at the hospital; for me he existed only in my little room and at the Friday morning lectures. I felt a stab of something akin to jealousy, then something akin to shame. I was not the only reason he came to this place. Perhaps I was only a curiosity of his employment, and perhaps only one of many. He spoke to an insane girl, he photographed an insane woman's head. Different facets of the same job, the same quest to understand and categorize the mentally defective.

"—what these men do! It is monstrous."

"Poor Rosalie. She always thought herself so dignified."

"—you think they have done with her rosary?"

"Holy Mother, do you remember the way she was always praying?"

"Remember! Rattling those beads everywhere she went, mumbling her litanies to her plaster gods."

"—to blaspheme so! Are you not ashamed of yourself?"

"What happened to Adelaide?" I could not bear it; in the space of a moment I had lost Edouard as my friend, my confidant, my suitor; I was humiliated and afraid, and I had not yet found out what had happened to Adelaide.

"Oh, look at Augustine! Are you jealous that Adelaide went in her shift to see your suitor?"

"Oh, please tell me what happened to her!" Had I lost Adelaide too?

"Leave Augustine be, you know she and Adelaide were close as sisters."

"All right, all right. Well . . ." Now we had to speak softly and quickly because we had reached the servers.

"Adelaide went into the little room behind the Amphitheatre. The photographers were there, Monsieur Edouard and that other one, what is his name?"

"Monsieur Richet."

"Yes, Augustine would know the name."

I blushed red from my chest to my forehead. But I was no longer the same Augustine as I had been when I got here. Was Dr. Charcot in the room too? Anything to make them stop thinking about me and Edouard. There was no Augustine and Edouard. But I did not cry.

"Well, Adelaide went in and saw the head, and now she is insane."

"What? She has lost her reason?"

"She has."

"But Adelaide is sane as can be! She has more reason than Dr. Charcot! After all, he's the one having people's heads cut off and brought to his laboratory to be photographed! Where is Adelaide now?"

"Mademoiselle Dechelette? You are on the vegetarian diet, are you not?" asked one of the servers.

"What? Yes, yes. The soup and the fruit compote, please."

"The fruit compote is not an acceptable part of your diet, Mademoiselle Dechelette. The acidity of the fruit acts as an irritant on the nervous system. It says here"—and she checked her ledger—"that the plain pudding would be—"

"Oh, very well!" And then, to the air behind my shoulder, "Where is Adelaide now?"

"They took her for an electric treatment. I expect she is there now."

Adelaide. Strapped to a gurney, immobile and defenseless. Adelaide who always made fun of the idea that electricity could cure anything at all, Adelaide who danced in her room when no one was watching, Adelaide who was of all the residents of La

Salpêtrière, patients and staff alike, the most truly sane. Electric shock. I had heard the stories. I had seen the machines. And one time Adelaide had seen a treatment being administered to Rosalie, as fate would have it—and mimicked it for me so convincingly that I was afraid to sleep that night.

"Perhaps that is the best idea," I said as we sat at one of the long tables, not realizing I was speaking aloud. "Perhaps the shock will bring her back to her senses. and bring her back to us. Bring her back to me."

Their laughter was derisive, dismissive. "Why don't you ask Rosalie?" said one young woman. "You know that she was Dr. Charcot's pet before you got here. She was very good indeed at acting the hysteric for the camera." She had always been jealous of the attention Dr. Charcot had paid to Adelaide, and I knew that now she was jealous of me too.

"Adelaide already knows how to be insane!"

"She won't have to put on a show for the Great Doctor now!"

"At least now," I said softly, almost to myself, "she has something that cannot be taken away from her."

"I don't think you'll have any competition now, Augustine, in being the star of La Salpêtrière."

"I never wanted to take anything away from Adelaide. She is my friend."

"Adelaide was only out for Adelaide. She would have taken your young man from you in a flash, you silly girl."

"He is not 'my young man.' I would never begrudge anyone his friendship." Suddenly I could not even bear to look at my food. Adelaide stole my pudding, on the rare occasions they let me have any. It was a game we played: even as I uttered loud protestations I was slipping her spoonfuls; her pleasure in the simple sweet was as pure as the pleasure she took in everything else: good gossip, a good book, a handsome man, a fresh flower, a treasured memory. And friendship.

"But you do not know of how Adelaide spoke of your young man when you were not around, Augustine."

I knew. The same way she would speak about a meal she wanted to have when someday she and I were free. But not a meal she would steal.

"I do know. I wish you would just . . ." They had all become nothing but strange faces, every one of them. I stood up so suddenly I spilled both my soup and my pudding. That spilled pudding was too much for me: spilled pudding that Adelaide should be eating. I burst into tears and ran out of the cafeteria. I did not care that I would lose privileges for spilling food, not eating my lunch, and leaving a room without permission. I ran, and I was surprised not to hear the heavy footsteps of the attendants following me.

But as I stumbled up the stairs toward my room, I did hear steps behind me. Quiet steps, fast but even, with something familiar about them. As I reached the hall to my room I turned around, ready for one of the girls to have followed to taunt and torment me.

It was Lucille. She was breathing rapidly, but her face showed no more emotion than it ever had. Her hair, loosed from its bun, fell in pretty wisps about her face, and for a moment I could see the woman she might have been had Life not condemned her to madness.

"Lucille?"

She stood hesitant, then stepped toward me. I saw uncertainty in what I now could see were pretty eyes, eyes darker even than Adelaide's.

"Lucille?"

And I realized that for a fraction of a second her eyes had met mine, another thing that had never happened before, that I had never thought would happen. Then we stood in the hallway, Lucille looking intently at my shoes, for so long that I almost turned to go to my room. But I was deeply grateful. I had no idea her childish mind could comprehend my situation. No, I thought suddenly, not my situation. My pain.

And then Lucille stepped forward; she thrust out her hand. There was something. I smiled and reached to accept her offering: two crushed dandelion heads, almost unrecognizable but with their sunshine smell still intact. I took them from her damp hand and held them, as though they were something precious, up to my nose to breathe in their uncontaminated sweetness.

"Thank you," I said, heartily but softly. "Thank you, Lucille."

"Loo-cee-oo," she said. "Fang-koo."

I knew better than to touch her; many times I had seen her attack attendants simply for taking her arm.

I was crying. "Good night," I managed, and ran down the hall to my room.

Chapter 44

Edouard

My dearest Augustine,

Please forgive my tardiness in replying to your letter: It arrived before ten, but I did not return to my room until past the luncheon hour. I was engaged in business with Capt. Bezier, of the Prefecture of the Paris Police Force. I would very much like to tell you about our conversation. We are engaged in the investigation of a most intriguing series of murders.

But first let me say how delighted I was to arrive home to a missive from you. My feet were worn from walking, my mind worn from debate with my employer. I have told you I have two jobs, but I have never talked to you in detail about what I do when away from La Salpêtrière, simply because it has never before seemed necessary: Our time has been so full.

Oh, Augustine, I do not quite know how to say what I want

need to say. I have wanted to say it for a long time now, and perhaps I am a coward to write it to you instead of kneeling at your feet; could you possibly do me the kindness of thinking it more romantic to receive a declaration of love on paper? Because that is what this is: a declaration of love.

I love you, Augustine. I think I knew it from the moment our eyes first met in the Amphitheatre. Certainly I have known it for weeks, months even. But at first I thought you too delicate to receive the attentions of a young man in such a place as La Salpêtrière. Forgive me, my darling, for I did think you were ill. It was by no action of your own but merely the fact of your being in this place, and also that Dr. Charcot seemed to believe it. You never seemed in the least ill to me. Can you forgive me, Augustine? And will you forgive that I call you darling? I do not know if you realize how difficult it has been for me to refrain from endearments all this time. Please grant me the right to them now.

But I should be answering your most heartrending cry for help, Augustine. So I will put aside my feelings for the moment and tell you all I know of what transpired regarding your friend Adelaide. It is true that she came to a small room off the Amphitheatre where certain photographic documentations are done. And it is true that Dr. Charcot had asked me and Richet to photograph the head of a recently deceased patient, taking measurements first and recording them faithfully. It was a most unpleasant task. I remembered Rosalie, and although I must confess to being of so small a mind that I never properly pitied her, in death I found her piteous indeed and sorely wished that I had shown her more kindness in life.

Richet and I were taking measurements, as I said the

circumference of the head, the distance, on each side, from ear to nose, when Adelaide simply appeared. She looked disheveled; her hair was wet and her shift was not fully dry. These things I did not notice at the time, only that a patient was where a patient most decidedly should not be.

She smiled. She said my name. And then she saw what was left of Rosalie so coldly laid out on a metal table. And she started to scream. I went to her, Augustine, and I tried to console her, but I could not even keep her from breaking away from me and running toward the head. She would actually have succeeded in lifting it straight off the table had Richet not nearly tackled her. I am afraid she was somewhat roughly treated, but she was so strong! I had not realized a woman could be so strong. We did manage to restrain her until attendants appeared. It broke my heart to watch them fetter her in a straitjacket. She fought, and the attendants were much less gentle than Richet and I had tried to be.

I am being honest with you, Augustine—brutally honest because I do not want there to be any secrets between us. You asked what happened to Adelaide: I am telling you, because you are very strong and because it is the right thing to do. I can only hope that I have not hurt you too much. I can only hope that you can forgive my honesty and selfishness; because I am selfish in wanting you to give real consideration to what I have written concerning my feelings for you, at a time when it may be both inconsiderate and cruel to ask such a thing of you. I can only hope you can understand that I love you, Augustine.

Your Edouard

Chapter 45

Charles

WHEN V ASKED me to take a girl from one of the Big Numbers, I was surprised. The prostitutes who work at the Big Numbers are afforded a protection denied street girls and those that work the small houses. Taking a girl from one of the small establishments would not be difficult; but V insisted, precisely because of this difficulty.

I was familiar with the house V chose, although I did not tell her that. But I was grateful for it; I already knew the layout and the madam, which could make my job less difficult.

The night we were to kill again, V dressed with special care, as though she were not going to get blood all over her lovely clothes. She dressed entirely in white, from the froth of her petticoats to the satin choker around her slender neck, which featured a perfect white pearl. Her dress flaunted an abundance of delicate, expensive lace that cascaded down her sleeves, her breast, and her skirts. Her slippers were satin, and white, and unsuited to rough cobblestone. But we had our carriage, which that night I drove myself, so she would not have to walk far. The only variance in color came from her blood-red scarf, the one she so often chose to wear. It made her look bloodied; it made her look more fair.

We left the carriage around the corner from the establishment; of course I knew that V would refuse to sit in it and wait, but she certainly could not walk up to the door with me; nor could she simply loiter about in front of the house. But V had a graceful solution to any problem and proposed to wait across the street, where the door recesses were deep and dark. She parted from me at the corner, and I did not worry for her welfare, for all that she was a small, beautiful woman alone. I could not think of anything on earth that could get the better of V.

I was grateful that she did not hear me greet the madam with warmth, nor ask about various of the girls I had visited. I wasted no time in requesting the services of the girl who had always been my favorite, Monique. And I was surprised at how honestly happy I was to see her. She had always been sweet, and feigned innocence, and allowed me to do whatever I pleased without complaint. She was attired only in a violet silk dressing gown, low-cut and adorned with purple lace on the neck, sleeves, and hem. She was small, like V, but with a more rounded figure, curly red hair, and bee-stung lips. She greeted me with a smile and stood on tiptoe to plant two light kisses on my cheeks, and the madam motioned toward the stairs. But, "No," I said. "I would like to take Monique out with me."

The madam frowned. She was a well-fed creature of habit who had been a great beauty in her youth, which no doubt accounted for the fact that she would brook no opposition to any of her decisions. I leaned in close. "I would like to share Monique with my wife," I said quietly. "Well, you understand that I cannot have her simply walk up the door to your establishment!"

"If you want two girls, you know I have the best." Her frown had not shifted in the slightest.

I smiled, deprecatingly, I hoped. "This is my wife's own request, and I make it my practice to deny her nothing. She particularly asked for Monique." As I spoke I took my wallet from my pocket and started to sort through bills almost absentmindedly.

"Perhaps something can be worked out," said the madam. "There is a back door very few know about."

"Outside the bedroom," I said, "my wife is shy, and I know I could not bring her to mount your steps. No, we must have Monique, in our home, in our bed. I insist." I took several large bills out of my wallet as I spoke.

The madam eyed my money. She looked enquiringly at Monique, who smiled and nodded, as I'd known she would. And when she did not return, the madam would likely not even try to contact me. I knew that Monique was unhappy here. I knew she was a spitfire and had almost certainly made plain her dissatisfaction with her portion of the profits. So when she failed to return, the unpleasant business of contacting the police would be dispensed with, and Monique would become nothing but a memory. Even if she were identified at the Morgue, I need not be suspected. The ways of prostitutes are flighty and unpredictable, and even though I would claim to have offered her my carriage, she had simply refused it, having, as she said, a better offer. An easy story to stick to and difficult to disprove. Our apartments were set well back from the sidewalk and hidden by a profusion of roses; no one would notice whether, when my carriage alighted, one woman or two had gotten out.

If Monique got out at all.

I waited, as a gentleman should, and the madam, after the appropriate hesitation, turned back to me and smiled her assent. When I filled her palm with bills she waited, hand held out and still smiling, so I filled it more, smiling myself. And I held my arm out to Monique, who put a delicate hand upon it, and then laughed, saying, "Charles, I am not even dressed!" The madam arranged for a wrap to be brought. I was adamant that we not dress Monique and I placed it gently around her shoulders and took her out into the night.

"Pretend you do not know me," I told her as we crossed the darkened street. Monique smiled and nodded, and so met V smiling. V's own smile was deep and genuine; Monique's wrap did little to disguise her voluptuousness, and I could tell that V was well pleased.

"Charles!" she said with girlish simplicity. "Introduce me to your friend," and I knew that I had been a fool to think I had kept anything at all from her. I made introductions, and we made for the carriage; V took Monique's arm shyly and whispered, "I have not—I do not know how . . . you will help me, will you not? You are so very lovely." And Monique assured her that there was nothing to fear. And yet V feigned a very pretty trepidation even after they had gotten into the carriage. I lingered for a moment, eager to see how far V would carry the charade. But V said, "Do not worry about me, Charles. I am sure Monique does not bite!" I had to take my place high up on the driver's seat. But it was a fairly long ride, and it gave me ample opportunity to imagine what might be taking place below me.

When I stopped the carriage and opened its door, I experienced the utmost pleasure at the picture presented by the women: V was in a charming state of dishabille, and quite pink with embarrassment. How does a woman who blushes at nothing in the world blush at will?

When I stepped into the carriage instead of handing them out, Monique merely thought, and rightly, that I wished to take some pleasure even before we got into the house. And she obliged, kissing and caressing V gently and with what seemed real pleasure. It did not matter that I knew it was not; rather, it stoked my fire. I let the play continue for quite a long time, until V looked pleadingly at me and said, "Charles! We are getting cold. Be a gentleman!" And I slipped the knife from my pocket without Monique's seeing and leaned as if to kiss her: I did not kiss her. At some point V said urgently, "Give me the knife," but Monique did not utter a sound the entire time, and died with horror in her pretty eyes.

V said, "I know you wanted to bring her into our apartments," and I said, "I know you did."

"It would not have been prudent," she said, her white silk soaked with blood. "Did you notice," she continued, smoothing my cravat with bloody hands, "that she put up no fight at all?"

I had. Monique knew me. She knew there was no point.

"You chose well," was all V said, then, "Your clothing is dark, and so does not show the blood. I will retire and clean myself up while I await your return."

"Do not clean up," I said. "I want you just as you are." Already the corpse on the seat next to V had ceased to exist for us.

"Then I will not even wash my hands," she assured me, and leaned to kiss my bloody cheek. She licked her lips. I climbed back up onto the driver's seat, watched her float like a bloodied wraith into our home, satisfied that no one saw , and drove away, knowing that an almost immediate pleasure awaited me: I would undress the body and leave it by the Seine—and that an even greater pleasure awaited me at home.

Chapter 46

Edouard

"It is true that it is unlikely the killer is a woman acting alone, Edouard. I believe she must have an accomplice. But the young man found in the alley beyond the home of the Gaudets' . . . well, that is a long way from the slum where the previous bodies have been found. What makes you think his case is connected to the others? That was a very messy murder, clearly the work of an amateur. I see no reason not to assume that murder was committed by common thieves."

I was kneeling on the ground in that slum in which the other bodies had been found, photographing another beautiful young woman, another found without clothing or identification, soldier-straight, and still.

"Because of the lack of identification," I said as I took pictures. That this was becoming so ordinary was the perhaps the most disturbing thing about it.

"Theo's murder was sloppy, and it would seem to me . . ." Oh, how carefully I had to word my opinions! " . . . that there was more equality in strength between the victim and the murderer. Theo fought hard, and he almost escaped. Note that the wound that proved fatal was to the back."

"Yes, Edouard, you are proving my theory!"

"But all of his identification was taken. A young man of his station would surely have carried calling cards. Did your men find any such cards at his home?"

"Well, their primary interest was in finding out the young man's contacts."

"Have them go back. There will be calling cards, probably scented."

"Scented?"

"His handkerchief had been dipped in lavender water. Such a man might well have scented cards."

"Is that what you were doing, then, sniffing at his pockets? I thought you had gone quite mad!"

As we spoke I moved around the young woman's body, noting, to my astonishment, the quality of the surrounding light and the angles best suited to capture her injuries, which were many and brutal.

"Yes, Captain Bezier, that is what I was doing. And I smelled the scent of roses. At his home I am certain you will find his calling cards beneath a rose sachet.

"But the point is, anything that could identify Theo was removed from his body. Why would a common thief do that?" I was talking about the other cases for two reasons: They had to be talked about, and I could not bear to talk about this one. Not just yet, when I had seen this before and before and before and had been in all this time unable to help any of them at all.

Capt. Bezier pondered.

"The identity of the victim tells you the identity of the criminal that is still true more often than not, Edouard."

He used to say always, I thought tiredly.

"If it was in fact someone who knew him, would it not behoove that person to eliminate all identifying papers?"

"I thought you said it was a common thief."

"Your theory has shed new light on the subject."

"Oh, Captain Bezier, let us go on to the next case. Madame Odette Alexandrovna."

"I do not think her case is associated in any way with that of the others. You cannot convince me. She was killed by strangulation, by one thing!"

"But she knew Theo! I saw them together the night he died."

"Society parties bring together the most peculiar cross-section of classes, Edouard. This is not something you would know. Madame Alexandrovna was a countess. She was also a known habitué of a certain opium den well-known in police circles, did you know that?"

"No," I said. "But I am not surprised." Her smoky eyes appeared to me, I heard her throaty laugh.

"Clearly Madame Alexandrovna was invited to this party as a kind of curiosity. It is often done. I am told she was exotic."

The kohl that flowed too thickly beneath her fevered eyes, her tapered fingers with her Chinese nails. Suddenly I felt her hand upon my arm as I had on the patio, and it was all I could do not to cry out.

"Edouard, are you all right? Forgive me. I had forgotten that you knew the lady. I did not mean to disturb you."

For a moment I had felt her breath in my ear. "It is always disturbing when a human being is murdered," I said shortly. I had photographed Odette; I cannot write of it.

Capt. Bezier took a few moments to perform the ritual of packing and lighting his pipe, which was kind of him. After he was finished he took a long, satisfied drag of the tobacco and said, "Now, tell me what makes you think Madame Alexandrovna's murder is connected to the rest, other than the fact that she was acquainted with Monsieur Theo Moreau." The young woman in front of me had beautiful, luxuriant red hair. My photographer's eyes were noticing every detail of every shot, even as I spoke of other deaths than hers.

My mind was again clear, although I could still see Odette's eyes as if they were in fact in front of me. I imagined I might always see them, at least from time to time.

"Follow me here, Captain Bezier. The first two murders were executed with an almost professional precision. The murder of Monsieur Moreau, on the other hand, was executed by someone quite unaccustomed to killing, someone whose strength was not greater than that of the victim, someone who might in fact have been intoxicated by, say, opium."

"Did you smell that on Monsieur Moreau's body as well?"

What could I say? That yes, I had smelled opium, and that Odette would have had to get quite close to Theo, and stay close for some time, for the smell to have lingered, and that that could not have happened on the patio? If the smell had not lingered on me on short exposure, it certainly would not have lingered on Theo.

"Yes," I said to Capt. Bezier. "I am such a fool that I actually thought it was her perfume!"

He laughed heartily at that. "You really are an innocent, Edouard. But I did not notice such a thing. When you met Madame Alexandrovna, did you think perhaps that she had been smoking opium? That you thought you smelled it again because she had made a strong impression on you?"

I swear I blushed, and I a grown man!

"Edouard," Capt. Bezier said gently. "Madame Alexandrovna was an extraordinarily beautiful woman. But you must tell me. It is important to me. It is important to the investigation. Were you at any point intimate with Madame Alexandrovna? Not inappropriately, Edouard!" he cried, seeing my face. "If you were to tell me that you and she had had inappropriate contact, I would not even believe you! Certainly I know you, of all people, better than that!"

I thought of the prostitute I had kissed, and was obscurely proud. I must have smiled, because he said, "Edouard!" in a shocked tone.

"No, Captain Bezier, I assure you that Madame Alexandrovna and I had no inappropriate contact. You do know me better than that. But she did address me by my Christian name, and asked that I address her by hers. You see, I already knew Odette—I had met her at the Amphitheatre at La Salpêtrière."

"You did not tell me that," Capt. Bezier scolded. And I realized that Odette had been a delicious secret to me.

"I did not think it pertinent," I said stiffly.

"Edouard, I am not a fool. If anything, you think a great many more things pertinent to an investigation than actually are pertinent. So do not be impertinent."

He could not conceal smiling over his own cleverness; he made me smile, too.

"Beautiful as Madame Alexandrovna was, she was not the sort of woman that a man like I would feel comfortable boasting of knowing. I do her no injustice here," I added hastily. "I doubt she boasted of knowing someone like me."

"You mean that no one would believe that you had actually made the woman's acquaintance."

"Exactly." It was such a lie. Hadn't I boasted, over and over, to myself? I knelt again; the pavement was warm from the sun. The young woman's hair was lit as if on fire, spread out across the dirty cement.

"We spoke of nothing confidential," I went on, anxious to get away from myself. "Neither at the Amphitheatre nor at the party. She did not tell me where she lived, or what her habits were, although she evinced a keen interest in photography."

At this Capt. Bezier laughed aloud and slapped his knee. "Oh, Edouard, you really are hopeless. Madame Alexandrovna interested in photography?"

"She seemed quite well educated," I said lamely.

"Yes, educated in the weaknesses of men! But come, she must have given you some indication of her private life. Did she arrive alone at the party, do you know?"

"No. But the first time I saw her she was in the company of a very fine couple, the Soulavies. They were at the party as well; I supposed she came with them."

"Soulavie," M. Bezier wrote in his journal. "Well! That is something, certainly. And Edouard, it is just the sort of thing I would have expected you to come out with almost immediately. Why did you not?"

"Yes, it was an unlikely thing for me to forget. I can only say that I was overwhelmed with Odette. I hardly thought about her friends, either time I met them."

"And did she speak of them? Indicate in any way how close the relationship was? And were they Russian, or did that escape you as well?"

"Soulavie is a French name, Bezier. Do not make me out to be even more of a fool than I know myself to be, please. And yes, the wife was French as well."

"Edouard, there is not a man alive who has not at some point fallen under the spell of a woman who is either above him or beneath him."

"It was like a spell," I said, speaking more to myself than him. "There was something almost repulsive about her."

"She was a drug addict."

Had the woman before me been a drug addict? It was curious that neither I nor Captain Bezier was speaking of her at all; but there was no need really. There was no mystery in this death, at least not to me.

"Perhaps it was that. But she seemed always to be playing at some game known only to herself. As if everything I said or did either confirmed or denied certain assumptions she had formed of me. Almost as if she had to deem me worthy because she had already formed an idea of some future use she could make of me."

"By helping her to murder?"

"No. I spoke too quickly. I do not think so, no. I could not discern her motives, although I did try. You cannot think I did not wonder what such an exotic creature was doing wasting her time with me."

At this Capt. Bezier slapped his knee again. He laughed and laughed until he had tears in his eyes from laughing. "Oh, my. Oh, my, my. Did it occur to you, my dear foolish Edouard, that perhaps her aim was to have you fall in love with her that she might destroy you?"

"No." I thought for a moment. "Corrupt, perhaps, but not destroy."

"That is because she did not know you as I do. One must corrupt in order to destroy, and you are incorruptible, no matter that you blush and look alarmed. No, Madame Odette would not have succeeded with you. But, and I want you to think about this, you felt that she was in fact grooming you for something, is that true?"

"Perhaps attempting to ascertain whether I could be groomed." Suddenly I was as excited as I always am at a new puzzle to solve. "This woman here was a prostitute, wasn't she? Perhaps from one of the Big Numbers?"

"That is very likely, Edouard. She is far too clean for this area, too well groomed. But she is the right age, and certainly she is beautiful enough for one of the Big Numbers."

"What if there is a gang, for want of a better world—this has been my feeling all along, Captain, although it is you who has helped me to articulate it. You know I have never believed that the criminals were a prostitute and her protector, simply robbing, then disposing of witnesses. Were that the case, there would be no need to take all identifying papers.

"What if, Captain Bezier, this gang, or whatever you want to call it, is killing innocent people and stripping them of their IDs in order to have them sent to the public morgue?"

"Edouard, are you mad? Murder is one thing, but murder for . . ." He hesitated, unable to find the words.

"Art," I said simply. "Murder to create art." I snapped my last picture of this latest masterpiece.

"Edouard, you are mad! Doubly and triply mad. You almost had me believing that these four murders really were all connected".

"Five," I said, but I do not think he heard me. He had stood and started to refill his pipe; I knew it was only to calm his nerves.

"I will check out this couple, the Soulavies, whom you mentioned. But you have been wasting my time with nonsense, Edouard. The first two killings were simple robberies. The murder of Monsieur Theo, well, I have heard certain things about that young man's conduct and character that do not bear repeating. It is only a wonder he did not meet a bad end sooner. And Madame Odette was a drug addict, a very seductive drug addict with a fine title but nevertheless, a woman only a few steps from the streets herself."

"She was an artist," I said. "An artist of seduction. And I will continue to believe that her death was somehow related to the others. All the signs are here. The fact that we have not spoken of it makes it no less true. And yes, these five murders—and perhaps Lenore DuPrey's as well, although she was not posed in precisely the same way as the intentional victims of the original Artists of Death—are all part of a concatenation of events the object of which has been to stage a kind of performance at the Paris Morgue."

"Edouard, people are murdered every week on the streets of this city. Absolutely the only thing these murders have in common is that all the victims have been found without identification."

"Henri, aside from the way four of the victims—the intentional victims, if you will—I saw one of those victims leave a party with a woman who became a victim herself not three days later. Does that tell you nothing?"

"Certainly it does, Edouard," he said, not seeming to notice that it was the first time in our long acquaintance that I had used his Christian name. "But I am an officer of the law, not a fanciful young man whose vision has been clouded by infatuation and"— for the first time indicating the victim—"pathos. I have already told you that I am going to have this couple thoroughly investigated. But true police work does not rely on the intuition of young men. It relies on a thorough examination of all the facts, not just the ones you find convenient to fit your poetical notions of art."

"I did not claim to be right," I said wearily, beginning to gather my equipment to depart. "But these are not ordinary murders, I am convinced of it. These killings have not been driven by greed or passion, except possibly Odette's. But that could just as easily have been revenge. You say the identity of the victim gives the identity of the criminal every time. Odette was unstable, untrustworthy, scheming, and a drug addict. Not someone who could be trusted to do as she was told. Not someone who could be trusted to keep a secret. And I truly believe that all that woman needed was an excuse to kill. She was evil, Henri. I do not know if she can be held accountable for what she was, but she was evil. And the person who murdered her was even more evil. Certainly, it could all be coincidence, but coincidences happen far less often than is commonly believed. And if it was because of the bad company she kept, well, surely you would have heard something already, what with your connections in the underworld. You know this is true.

"But I bore you with my foolish conjectures. My things are ready." I turned to go, my heart breaking a little at my last glimpse of red fire.

"Now, Edouard, do not be this way. You know I value your—"

"I bore myself," I said sharply. " I am a fool so enamored of a darkness that it is not within my own nature that I let my imagination quite run away with me. I am never going to solve these murders, Captain Bezier; I am an ordinary man with morbid fantasies. I do not have a poet's soul. I am made of nothing but earth and wheat. Good evening, sir."

And I left, wishing, wishing, wishing it were true.

Chapter 47

From the Journal of Augustine Dechelette

I CAN HARDLY believe the events of the last twenty-four hours. I look around this room and it seems as if it all might have happened to somebody else.

But if I am to order my thoughts, I must start at the beginning.

I woke this morning as happy as if I were looking forward to a walk by the Seine with my young man. My young man! Oh, Edouard, what have I done? I will be with you soon, my darling, but will you be angry to find what I have done? I hardly know how it happened myself. I should not have consented to this. But, oh, V was so persuasive, so charmingly tearful, and I must admit I was intimidated by M. Soulavie.

Augustine, slow your pen. I woke up happy this morning, as I said, having received Edouard's letter yesterday afternoon. The day seemed full of promise: Edouard was to visit. I had been strug-

gling with myself over whether I should break my confidence with
V and tell him that she and M. Soulavie were planning to arrange
my release from the hospital. It was a great kindness on their part,
a great gift—why was I unsure? I could not understand why I
could not tell my dearest Edouard. But I trusted in V's assertions
that after I was free of the hospital she would contact Edouard
immediately.

I still trust her.

But I was entirely unprepared for V and her husband's visit
this morning. V had always, excepting the first visit, informed me
by letter when she would be visiting next, always taking care that
it would be at my best convenience. There have been so many sessions and treatments that it is a wonder I have had time for visitors
at all!

But I suppose that is all behind me now.

And I am so afraid

I was writing in my journal when one of the attendants knocked
on the door; I was daydreaming in ink. About Edouard, of course.
About a future that seemed, because of V's precious offer, as if it
might really come true. So of course when I was told that it was
V wishing to see me, I was elated. Almost before she was through
the door I had thrown myself at her feet like a child and hugged
her waist, and said, ``Oh, you do not know how happy I am that
you are here!"

And then I noticed M. Soulavie behind her. He had not accompanied her in some time, and I was immediately chagrined, and
leapt clumsily to my feet.

V took my elbows and turned my embarrassment into a pretty
embrace. What must it be like, I wondered, not for the first time,
to have your every movement be graceful?

"I'm sorry," I said, and V laughed.

"For what, you silly girl? Now, it is time to go. What have you to bring with you?"

I stood, astonished and unable to speak. I saw that M. Soulavie was holding a small traveling bag; V took it from him and laid it on the bed.

"Look what we have brought you!" And she removed a pair of men's brown pants, a white shirt, a brown jacket, and men's boots, workman's clothes, by the look of them, but new. "I packed as carefully as I could, but I fear I could not avoid a few wrinkles." She was talking brightly, as though we were discussing a trip to the shore. She turned to me and said, "You will need your journal, yes? And your brush and mirror, of course! Although there will be plenty of mirrors at home, and you will be free to admire your loveliness whenever you want!"

They had not gotten the requisite papers and permission to do what they were doing. How I knew this I cannot say. It was the first time I had doubted V. But she was looking at me so beseechingly. She came and took both my hands. "There is nothing to be afraid of, Augustine," she said, looking into my eyes. "I just want you out of this hideous place. You do not belong here." Her pretty lips trembled. "Don't you trust me, Augustine?"

"Of course I do," I said sincerely.

"She is shocked, V," said her husband. "We show up unannounced with men's clothing and tell her she is to leave immediately—that is too much for a young girl to take in all at once." He seemed nervous; he was always so detached that I found this almost frightening.

"But what we're doing is wrong!" I cried. "And what about Edouard?"

V laughed. "I promise you, once we have gotten you home, we will send for your young man. But I told you before, Monsieur Mas is far too upstanding a fellow to allow us to spirit you away like this. You know that is true."

"I don't want to wrong him," I said. I felt much more than that. I felt that I was betraying Edouard. He had pledged his love, and yet almost my very first action was to deceive and wrong him. I felt my eyes start with tears, and although I loved and was grateful to V I could not raise my face to hers.

Her fine satin petticoats rustled as she knelt before me. "Oh, my poor, sweet Augustine," she said, and she petted my hair with fairy hands. "Cry, darling, if that is what you need to do. Of course you are frightened, my love. Who would not be frightened? It is not to your shame; you are such a brave girl. You have already been put through so much. But remember, Augustine, under whose aegis your barbaric treatments have been carried out." Her voice, although soft, was firm, as though she were explaining something emotionally difficult to a cosseted baby sister. She smelled of lilac powder. "Look at me, Augustine." A sister she believed in. I knew I had to live up to that, to be the Augustine she saw in me; I wanted that every bit as much as I wanted to be the girl Edouard saw when he looked into my eyes.

"Dr. Charcot," I said like a dutiful student.

"Yes. Dr. Charcot. Do you tell your mother what really happens at the Friday afternoon shows?"

I noticed that she did not call them "lectures." I blushed my deepest red. I had thought often of that: *What if Maman were to see me posing?* How many times had I thanked the heavens that Papa never let magazines into the house!

"It is no coincidence, Augustine, that the doctor's hysterical patients strike lascivious poses. And make amorous noises."

Amorous noises. If it is possible, I blushed deeper.

"I will not stand by and continue to see you treated thusly. Charles will not have you treated thusly. I will not see you corrupted by that man."

"Charles?" I said, incredulous and forgetting he was in the room. "Charles cares?"

V took both my shaking hands into her own. "Of course he does! I know my husband has a hard exterior." At which I started, seeing him as if for the first time; he was staring at me intently, with an expression impossible to read. "I have even had my female friends confide that they find him frightening!" Charles, starting himself as he came from his reverie and saw that I was regarding him with an expression almost of horror, smiled easily at me. But his heart is warm, Augustine. It is just that he is a man, and men do not know how to show these things. No, Charles and I have had long talks about you, and he is the one who has made all the preparations. A carriage, these clothes, Charles would do anything I asked of him, but this is something he wants to do, for you. There is nothing to be afraid of."

I started to cry again: shame or relief. "You will notify Edouard?" I asked tearfully.

"I will bring him to you directly we are home, and safe." She squeezed my hands, then stood. "You must be strong, Augustine. For Edouard, and for yourself. Here, dry your tears. We do not have much time. We cannot remain at the hospital for longer than our usual visit. Now, let us see how you look in these clothes."

I felt no embarrassment at the thought of V helping me to dress. Maman often pulled my stays at home, but I was repelled and fascinated by the clothing laid out for me. "Monsieur Soulavie!" I exclaimed, but he was already disappearing through the door.

"Shh," V cautioned softly. I stared at the pieces of clothing and picked them up wonderingly, one by one: I had never thought I would ever in my whole life wear men's pants.

"Go ahead, Augustine, put them on." V was smiling her child's smile, as if this were a game of make-believe.

And in truth it felt like make-believe. I smiled back at her, a child myself. I let her help me into the strange male garments, stifling our laughter when I could not properly get my second leg into the pants. They turned out to be not so different from my pantaloons, but they were dreadfully scratchy against my thighs.

As soon as I was dressed, V touched my shoulder and said, "Augustine, now you must be brave: You must leave this room. The attendants have not been present during our visits—surely you must have noticed that." I had noticed, and I was grateful for it. It was so nice to laugh and be free in V's company without fearing the attendants watching us. I knew that as the star hysteric of La Salpêtrière I was being given special treatment.

"You will walk out of your room, Augustine, and down the hall, and right out the front door of the hospital. I will go out ahead of you to meet Charles, and we will drive our carriage around the corner to the left, outside the hospital grounds. You will wait ten minutes, precisely, before you follow.

"Augustine"—and she looked at me and the child was gone and her eyes were stern—"you can do this. You will do this. Now," she said, jumping up and kissing both my cheeks, "I will go." And her smile was as complicitous and innocent as it had been moments before.

I watched her go, waited ten minutes, and walked out the door.

I remember only vaguely walking down the hall and away from my room. I do not remember opening my door at all, I was so scared.

I walked down the hallways, somewhat surprised to find that I remembered the way to the front entrance. I looked neither right

nor left. I tried to walk like a man but gave that up almost immediately: Even an accomplished actress could not have acted that
part without practice.

But no one noticed me, because no one was about. The hospital
seemed empty; I did not even hear voices, or cries, or shouts, as I
usually did. But I did not relax my vigilance, and when I neared
the large, airy lobby I found the familiar globe rising in my throat.
Just a small distance, Augustine, I told myself, just a few minutes,
and you will be free.

As I rounded the corner into the lobby I saw Dr. Charcot talking to a group of young men. I stopped, terrified, but he seemed
not to notice me. "There is no such thing," he was saying, "as hysteria." It was all I could do to burst out laughing.

And I simply walked through the lobby and out the front doors.
The row of tall trees that led to La Salpêtrière seemed as long as in
a nightmare, but I walked with a resolution born of numbness and
determination both. If I did not know it was impossible, I would
swear I did not breathe at all the entire way.

And I turned the corner and the carriage was waiting for me. I
recognized it at once in all its opulence: V could possess nothing
less. There was a driver who did not even turn his head to take me
in. The entire carriage was gleaming, with not a single mud splash
or scratch on the paint. As I approached, the door opened and V's
proud smile greeted me, and I breathed again.

The interior was magnificent. Brushed gold leather seats, black
velvet curtains, even a tray affixed to one side that held various
glasses, a tall container of water with tiny brass spigots, and a
bottle whose label I recognized from advertisements. V slid her
arm around my waist, squeezed, and said, "Now you have done
the hard part, darling. Relax and enjoy the scenery."

It didn't feel real. All my senses were heightened, but what I noticed most were the dresses! It seemed a different color and fabric met my eyes every time I shifted my gaze. An ankle-length royal blue cape, opening to reveal a glimpse of a rose faille skirt with a cascade of white lace down the front; a short brown leather jacket riveted with brass grommets and edged by long gold tassels that covered a brown leather dress that moved, for all its heaviness, like slow water. The girl who wore it was arresting: short full hair no longer than her chin, chestnut-colored and curled in a perfect frame about her perfect face. I had never seen short hair on a woman before, outside of magazines. Her eyes were a confident brown, her bee-stung smile a confident red. I do not believe her lips were stained that color. It was too natural, too much a part of her whole demeanor, which was mischievous and sensual and excited and coolly sophisticated all at once. She was no older than I.

I think I will retain the image of that young woman for the whole of my life.

I felt more the country bumpkin than ever, no matter how fine the carriage, how exquisite my patroness. But I was only crestfallen a moment. "That hat!" I exclaimed.

"Which one, dearest?" V asked, and only then did I realize that I had spoken aloud.

"That one." Our carriage was amid a crush of traffic such as I had never before witnessed. I wished it wasn't stopped; surely a hat I admired would be of no interest to V. But at a glance she knew which hat I meant, and her delight seemed genuine.

"Satin," she said, "and garnet. Two of my favorites. And look how that lace falls!" Black, in a ripple around the sides of the face, and longer in the back, all the way to the shoulders. It swayed becomingly as its wearer walked the boulevard. A huge black ostrich feather completed what seemed, to me, perfection.

"I can have a hat like that one made for you," V said, "once we are settled."

Settled? I thought, and banished the thought. V was excited; we both were. I said, "I would love that," and was ashamed of my flash of doubt when I saw how genuinely happy V's smile was.

I was simply nervous. This was such a big step. Augustine's Great and Terrible Adventure! Then I saw another hat and forgot everything else but *I wish I could* wear that hat for Edouard.

"That one," I said to V.

"Close the curtains," M. Soulavie said suddenly. "I am tired of this chatter."

I started, frightened, and more so when I saw that V's smile went cold. "Of course, my love," she said, in the same endearing voice she had just used with me.

"V." I started. I wanted to ask, *What is happening?* But instead I said hesitantly, "V, do you really have a full-length mirror at home?"

V laughed and laughed while I tried not to cry. I thought about wearing the finest dress I had seen, the grandest hat. I thought about wearing rouge and kohl as though it were the war paint I had seen on pictures of African tribesmen.

"I want you to teach me to wear makeup!" I blurted.

V stopped laughing. She considered me; she said, "You are not so simple as I thought."

"Enough," said M. Soulavie. "I am tired of hearing her talk."

Good, I thought savagely, tears starting again in my eyes. I turned my head so that V could not see my face and stared where a moment ago the entire world had been going by, and I had been free.

And now I have no choice but to trust her.

Chapter 48

Edouard

I WAS NOT frightened, at first. I had gone to the hospital with a light heart and a lightheaded step. I had never before declared myself to a girl: I had never before been in love. I had been too in love with photography to busy myself with the girls in my hometown, and here in Paris all is impersonal although Richet has told me several times that young women have been making eyes at me, flirting at the fruit stand or the Opera, when I have not noticed it at all.

The halls were quiet except for the occasional echoing laugh or scream. There were, as usual, no attendants about. But I did not want to be seen going into Augustine's room, although I had no illusions about my visits being secret. I had learned, from Augustine herself, what it meant to be the most favored hysteric at the Saltpêtrière.

It felt like an eternity since I had seen her last.

When I reached her door I knocked, twice, as I always did, and waited for the soft footsteps I had not realized till that minute that I would recognize anywhere, on any flooring.

But they did not come. Augustine did not nap during the day; she had excellent health, and the regimen of cold baths and brisk walks had been good for her constitution, I suspected, even as it had done nothing to dispel symptoms of a disease with which she was not afflicted. Here was a girl, after all, used to the country life. As I gave her a few moments more to answer the door—perhaps she was brushing her hair, or pinching her cheeks to give herself a bloom she did not need, as I had seen Natalie do—I wondered if she would like Paris as much as she thought she would, would in fact love it as I did. I had just come to the conclusion that she most certainly would when I realized I had been standing far too long, and knocked again.

Again I waited; again I knocked. Finally I could stand it no more and simply turned the knob of the door, which came unexpectedly open beneath my hand.

The room was empty. I had never been in her room when it was empty, and all I did was ascertain with certainty that she was not ill in bed before I hurried out. In the hallway I began to call for the attendants. Surely she had an unscheduled visit with Dr. Charcot, I told myself. Surely, she had a surprise treatment to go to.

But even as I began to hurry down the hall toward the courtyard I knew these things were not true. I do not know why I chose that way; I was not thinking with my head but with my heart. *Adelaide will know,* I found myself thinking, and then, *But Adelaide is mad.* But somehow I was convinced that the answer to Augustine's disappearance would be found in the courtyard.

It was only later that I realized that from the first I thought of it as a disappearance.

On my way through the labyrinth of the hospital I passed the rooms where Augustine took her water treatments, and I paused to sprint into the outer room and enquire about her. The nurses there assured me she had no treatments scheduled, which I already knew, but as I said, I was thinking only with my heart: Augustine had never scheduled a meeting with me that would have conflicted with her rigid schedule. I ran out of the rooms with a thank-you thrown over my shoulder and almost collided with one of the burly attendants. I thought I recognized him, remembering with a pang how Augustine always laughed and claimed they were all the same young man, magically able to be in many places at once. I asked him if she had been summoned to Dr. Charcot's office and he said no, then immediately seemed to think better of having answered my question. I asked if he was aware that her room was empty, and he tried to disguise his surprise with no success, and in fact excused himself hurriedly and set off down the hall toward her room.

My heart was threatening to beat out of my chest. *She is in the courtyard,* I told myself sternly, but my heart's beating told me it was not true. And when I reached the courtyard she was not there.

Chapter 49

From the Journal of Augustine Dechelette

I AWAKE AND I do not awake. I am at La Salpêtrière, but this is not a familiar bed, that is certain. And what window is this? I start upward and realize that I am no longer wearing my man's disguise but a very light shift without even a chemise.

As I pull the thin covers up over my neck I hear the tinkle of laugher. I don't want to look at her, so I watch the way the patch of sky out the window changes moment to moment from gray to blue and back to gray. Suddenly I am horribly cold.

"The fire is dying," she says in the same sweet, melodic voice that she always used at the hospital. "Here, take my shawl." I cannot seem to move, cannot even imagine moving. As she comes close and gently drapes the soft rose shawl around my shoulders with easy familiarity, I notice that she smells as nice as ever, the orange-peel tartness mixed with lavender water and white, clean talc.

As I feel her gentle hands I start to speak, but all that comes out is an anguished cry, a cry not unlike Lucille's.

And for a moment I was in between worlds, smelling the grass, the dandelions of the hospital courtyard, and happy, happy because I am helping Lucille and because Edouard is with me.

And at the same instant in time I am entirely in this room, which is ugly and ill-lit and has no air. There is dust on the windowsill and ash on the hearth; the walls are cracked and in need of painting. The only clean thing, the only thing lovely, is her.

"Get away from me," I say.

She laughs again, the same pure flutelike laugh she used at La Salpêtrière. "The only one here who wants to get away is you." There was an edge, a shiny knife's edge, to her voice now that I had never heard before.

"You are vile," I said. "You are monstrous."

"And you are insane"—she smiled—"and not likely to be missed for too long. And here"—she reached to rearrange the shawl, which had fallen from one shoulder—"you will pose only for Charles and me. He is out getting absinthe right now."

I flinched away from her gentle fingers and burst out sobbing.

"Would it comfort you to have your journal? Because you will not be leaving us for a long while."

She held out my journal, the one she had given me in red Moroccan calf because, she said, red sat so well against my hair.

"No? Well, then, I'll just leave it here while I make you some tea. Oh, and you will drink this." She walked over to the mantelpiece and picked up a blue glass bottle. I knew what it was. Once my mother had given me a tablespoon of laudanum for a headache. It was garnet in the spoon, like port; it smelled acrid and tasted bitter. Maman had told me there was honey in it, along with wine and saffron and cinnamon, but the bitterness inherent to opium overwhelmed these gentler flavors.

"He already made me drink that," I said. I had an unreal and uncomfortable memory, more like a dream, of Charles forcing my head back by the chin. My body began to shake, my hands, my head, my breath staggered in my lungs.

"Take this," she said peremptorily, her voice iron now. "And then write. I will be going out for supplies."

I was a big-boned country girl. She was much slighter than I, but I was weak—weak in bone, body, and heart. I had been drugged, and she was going to drug me again. And I realized I was terrified of what she might do should I resist. *Supplies.* Who knew what other supplies were already on hand in this place besides laudanum? As I obediently allowed her to spoon the bitter liquid into my schoolgirl mouth, she said, "You cannot get out, and you can scream," she said gently, with a steel smile, "out the window or through the door, for hour upon hour, and no one who hears you will care. Augustine, listen to me." Already I felt as if my body were beginning to float up toward the beckoning evening sky. "They do not care. No one cares about you except Charles and I."

"Edouard," I managed faintly.

"No, Augustine, not Edouard. He knows about this. He has been playing with your childish heart the whole time. Oh, you didn't realize that? Poor girl. But you will see your dear Edouard again. He has promised to come in a few days to join us in our play."

I picked up the journal from where it lay beside me on the bed, looked down, and started to write.

Yes, I wrote, *Edouard will come. I don't know how or when, but my Edouard will come and rescue me.*

Augustine's Great and Terrible Adventure. One of the stray sheets I had written on when I first came to La Salpêtrière had fallen from the journal and lay face-up on the mattress next to me.

And suddenly I was laughing and crying at once, and for the first time truly felt myself insane.

Chapter 50

Edouard

I STOOD FOR a moment at the entrance to the courtyard; indeed Augustine was not there.

But Adelaide was, and I hurried over to where she sat in seeming meditation on the crumbling steps to the ancient door that led to nowhere. She was singing softly to herself, as was usual, I had been told: "The head is dead, the head is dead, I heard the words the dead head said . . ."

I said her name. She did not respond. I touched her shoulder. She screamed.

"Adelaide," I said her name again, softly, softly.

"No! No! The head! The head! Where is her body, Dr. Charcot? Where is her—Edouard!" Her eyes cleared, and she grabbed my sleeve. "Will it ever stop?" As though I knew the answer.

"Yes," I said. "It will." We sat in silence until her hand on my arm relaxed.

"She's gone," she said finally.

"I know."

"Do you love her?"

"Yes." I was in an agony to ask her if she knew anything of the manner and reason for Augustine's leaving; I waited.

Adelaide turned her big brown eyes to me. "Do you think you could love me, Edouard, now that Augustine is gone?"

"No," I said gently. "Although you are beautiful and charming, I can love no one but Augustine."

"Ah!" She smiled and pulled her knees toward her chest, as though protecting her heart.

"But she has left you."

"Has she? Is that why she went?"

Adelaide busied herself watching a ladybug walking across a dandelion leaf. It suddenly flew away.

"Do you think that is what Augustine did?" I asked, as the ladybug flew up and disappeared into the glare of the sun.

Adelaide said nothing for so long that I thought that she was lost to herself.

"Did she escape?" I asked gently.

"No." She had picked the leaf and was busy tearing it into tiny pieces. I picked a leaf myself and did the same; feelings of violent helplessness overtook my fingers, and I ripped at the innocent green.

"Did you kill Rosalie?" Adelaide asked.; I whipped my head around to see that her face was calm, her fingers not so ferocious as mine.

"No."

"Good. Do you know how to get her head attached to her body again?" Her fingers having briskly finished their destruction, she reached for another leaf.

"Rosalie is dead, Adelaide. She died of old age, that is all. Her soul is in heaven."

This made Adelaide laugh for so long that I began to worry that an attendant might come. But finally her laughter died away, and she sat impassive. Finally she said, "She didn't want to go. It was a fine suit, though."

"Suit?" I could not tell whether Adelaide was speaking truth or nonsense. Not nonsense: her truth. When she spoke again her voice was bitter.

"It is the talk of the hospital: Their star has gone missing. She put on a suit of men's clothing and walked out the door. I am not sure how this can be known; no one saw her. But everyone is quite certain." She picked up another leaf. "A fine thing it would be, to see a fine suit of men's clothing walking about without a head! I would like to know what the great Charcot would make of that, eh?"

"Augustine was wearing a suit of men's clothing?"

"A fine suit," Adelaide corrected me. Suddenly she asked, "Do you think I could be the star of La Saltpêtrière now, now that she is gone?"

"Perhaps."

"You think I am evil."

"I do not think you are evil."

"I loved her!" Adelaide cried suddenly, and she threw herself on my shoulder. This was not part of her madness; her love for her friend was genuine. "And I saw her. But I told no one. I was lurking outside my room. I saw a man coming down the hall and sent my clod-footed attendant into the room because, I told him, there were demons inside." She laughed, again for too long. "I always want to see a new man. I get so little chance to practice for the day I must find a husband. Or a poet."

I thought of Odette, the web-spinner, the man-eater. I looked at this lovely young girl and could have cried. I almost did.

"Help me, Adelaide. I want to bring her back to us."

"To you," she said angrily, shoving me as she moved away from my shoulder.

"I would free you from here if I could, Adelaide," I said, and I meant it. "But right now, you need to be here."

She regarded me, looking suddenly tired, and older. "I will always need to be here," she said without rancor. "Even before, I knew. I am going now." And she stood and kissed the top of my head, which startled me. But I thought to ask, "How did you know it was Augustine?"

"She had a head," Adelaide said reasonably. "I thought she was dressed for her next performance. I thought she was performing for them."

I waited for more. "Them?" I ventured.

"I don't think they love her," Adelaide said pensively. " I don't think they want her to be free."

"Why not?"

"Because if she were free, she would choose to be with you."

"Then why do you think they helped her leave?"

"I think," she said, "that they want her to perform for them."

"Who, Adelaide? Please. Who?"

"The fine lady and gentleman, of course."

"What fine lady and gentleman?"

"Are you jealous of him?" Her look was sly and hopeful.

"No. I just want to find Augustine."

Adelaide started to sing softly. "Rosalie, Rosalie, she lost her eyes and cannot see. She lost her mouth and cannot lie. She lost her head and cannot be, Mary Magdalene to thee."

I waited.

"The lady is very fair," she said at last. "Very fair. Her name is . . .'"

I waited.

"You will never love me?" she asked.

"Not in the way you wish, Adelaide. But you are dear to me."

Adelaide considered this. "I do not know her name. She is small and fair, and she gave Augustine a mirror. But you know that."

"I did not know that."

"She does not love you. She cannot: She has not told you everything."

"I don't care whether she loves me," I said fiercely. Nothing mattered but to bring her back. She was in danger. Adelaide was mad, but she was not lying, and the things she was telling me had nothing to do with her madness. " I just want her safe."

"Good. Then we want the same thing. Augustine with her head on. But I do not know the name. You must find out for yourself."

"You do know, Adelaide. You do. Please tell me."

"I will tell you for a kiss."

Why were women always asking me to kiss them? "I cannot," I said. " I respect you too much." This was a lie: I had respected the prostitute as well. But I could not kiss Augustine's friend. And, more to the point, I knew that kissing her would not get me what I needed but would only lead to more favors, more tokens of feelings I did not have.

"Please, Adelaide."

"I have forgotten." And then she did forget, suddenly I was not there any longer and she was singing again, singing nonsense and loss to the dandelions and the ladybugs.

And she was utterly lost to me, lost to herself, present only as a voice as light and tender as a will-o'-the-wisp's.

Had I made a mistake not to kiss Adelaide? No. I would ask the attendants who it was who came to see Augustine. I would ask Dr. Charcot. Why had Augustine not told me? I was suddenly colder than the afternoon warranted. Cold in my heart. I stood. I looked at Adelaide for a moment, then turned and walked away.

Chapter 51

Charles

"You are . . . going to . . . kill me."

"Yes. I am going to kill you. But not now. I have only just acquired you, Augustine. You are going to serve as a wife to me."

Seeing her distress—her acute, uncomprehending distress, which clearly the laudanum I had forced her to drink had done nothing to alleviate—was a potent aphrodisiac. Her eyes were wide and wild with dilated pupils. "You need a drink, my dear. I see you are frightened. There is no reason to be frightened, Augustine." I realized I was talking to her as V did, softly, as though she were a small furred animal that might start and leap away. I busied myself with her drink.

"I used considerably more sugar than I usually do, my pet. I thought you would like it better that way."

"It is vile. You are vile. My Edouard will come for me, you just wait and see. I know he will."

"Yes, he will come. Here, now, just drink this. I cannot get V to drink with me. It's the only thing she refuses me—" And I realized that I had not meant to say as much, and also that Augustine's distress was not quite so pleasurable as I had first thought. I saw Tabby's terrified eyes. I had wanted to kiss her. I had wanted those eyes to be full of desire, of pleasure. Now I longed for Augustine to look at me with the same frank lack of fear Tabby had at first evinced: before she found out what I was.

But Augustine had always known what I was.

I am not ashamed of what I am. Even before I murdered I had always reveled in gaining an innocent young girl's trust, and abusing that trust to get what I most desired: another conquest. And I had always liked best the reluctant conquest, the maiden who required gentle, or not so gentle, coercion. So what was different now? As I looked into Augustine's eyes, I realized that now that I had absolute power over life and death there were times when I would choose at least to delay it; perhaps not to exercise it at all. I wanted Augustine to trust me. I wanted her to desire me. I wanted to grant her all of her most romantic desires before I killed her.

"Come," I said more gently. "If you are a good girl I may not have to kill you. Drink with me."

She eyed me with repugnance and disdain. I hit her and she did not flinch. She did not raise her hand to her mouth to still the trickle of blood I had given her. And when she picked up her glass she did it in a manner that made it seem it was her own choice to do so.

She drank. This time she did not make a face as she had at the laudanum. But all the anger had gone out of me as quickly as it had risen. She had not been trying to provoke me. I disgusted her, and she had not the guile to hide that.

She surprised me by saying, "May I have a handkerchief? And a mirror? And then I will be happy to drink some more with you." I took a small sadistic pleasure in choosing, from the cedar chest V kept at the apartment to hold her delicates, her finest handkerchief, knowing blood would ruin it. I wondered what was happening to me. I wanted to take this girl, and take her with her will, before V knew. It would not happen, of course, but how could I even be thinking such a thing? I fetched the handkerchief, of softest cloth with intricate lace V had tatted herself, but when I reached for the sinuous odalisque —of the mirror, I hesitated. I knew now that Augustine would pretend no embarrassment at handling such an object, but I found myself wanting to give her something simple, something pure.

There was nothing pure in this place.

I brought her the items she had asked for, and she surprised me yet again by thanking me sweetly. I knew it was a lie, but what a convincing lie! She even let me daub the blood from her mouth and hold the mirror for her, and she accepted my blandishments about her beauty with grace, almost with aplomb. Where had this new woman come from? She had seemed, up until the moment I hit her, incapable of concealing one single thing she thought of me and of her situation. What had changed? Fear had not cowed her; quite the opposite.

Ah! It was the absinthe that was soothing her nerves, her mind, her soul. Perhaps I would receive my secret desires after all. Perhaps. But looking into her eyes, which now met mine with the guileless frankness I had longed for, I was not so sure.

At that moment the door opened, and V came in with a sweep of wild air that I could not imagine lasting up the four flights to the apartment. It was in her hair, it was part of her. She was carry-

ing a small bag that she revealed to me without so much as looking at Augustine, let alone asking about her. Not for the first time
I wondered what and how much V guessed about me when I was
not with her.

"More laudanum," she said with satisfaction, setting the cobalt
bottle on the mantelpiece. "Rope. Candles. I want to drip candle
wax onto her nipples. And look!" she said as though she were a
child showing her mother a freshly picked flower. "Isn't it perfect?" I was foolish and slow; I stared at the black silk scarf she
held. "A blindfold, Charles, you great goose." She was merry and
gay, and again I wondered what was the matter with me. Then she
surprised me by saying, "Let us go out and take the afternoon air,
Charles. Look," she said as she gestured over at where Augustine
had sunk asleep into the bed. "This girl will not wake for hours.
You look as though you need sustenance before we play. Let's go
to that café two blocks down, the one with the excellent fois gras."

"She was awake a moment ago," I said stupidly, though it was
likely the combination of laudanum and absinthe would knock
out a girl unaccustomed to such things.

V went over and shook her roughly. "She's not awake now,"
she said with satisfaction. "We could go to another place if you'd
rather." She turned away from what had apparently become for her
no more than a lifeless puppet for which she had no need as yet.

I went over and examined the girl for a moment. Her breath
was shallow but steady, and her arm limp when I lifted it. I felt a
delicious thrill at the way her arm simply fell when I let go of it.

"Yes," V said behind me. "She is ours to command. I know the
type—I told you that. Oh! I picked up some cocaine balls on the
way home, I almost forgot! I know a doctor." She laughed, taking
another bottle out of her purse. "Well, not really a doctor, he is

an old reprobate who ministered to . . . but that does not matter. What does matter is that I know precisely the correct dosage of cocaine and laudanum to keep our young lady compliant. Perhaps even amenable. You would like that, wouldn't you, Charles?"

I realized I had been staring at Augustine's face. So young. So very young, and innocent. Young, innocent, and ours to do with as we wished. Smiling I turned to V and said, "You pick the restaurant, darling."

Chapter 52

Edouard

DIRECTLY I LEFT the courtyard I headed toward Dr. Charcot's office. Normally I would never have dreamed of bursting in on such an important person. But right now, Augustine was the most important person in the world.

On the way to his office I found a surprising amount of attendants about, and suspected why, and I tried speaking to each of them. But it was as Augustine said: They might as well be deaf as well as mute. Five different young men completely ignored me as they stood in front of their appointed rooms, or walked down the hall, or turned from where two of them were speaking to a doctor. That doctor knew nothing either, seeming almost to think me as mad as his patients for asking such a thing as who would be visiting Augustine. From his demeanor one would not even know that Augustine was at that moment missing from La Salpêtrière.

So I made my way to Dr. Charcot's office, which I had never entered. I found that I had not knocked, and I was simply standing in his office, and he was looking at me from behind his desk with no surprise whatsoever.

"Where is she?" I demanded.

"You know I do not know, Monsieur Mas."

"Who were the people who were visiting her?"

"I am not at liberty to talk about anyone who visits with any of my patients."

Looking at the doctor's deep-set eyes, I could read nothing: concern, irritation, boredom? It did not help that the room was so dim.

"And that is all?"

"I have alerted the proper authorities." He seemed to think that was enough. He seemed not to be afraid of what could befall Augustine at all.

"Aren't you even worried about her?"

Dr. Charcot looked, for the first time, discomfited. He took a pipe and tobacco out of his vest pocket and began to busy himself with them.

"You knew," I said.

The doctor tapped tobacco into the pipe—an expensive brand, by the smell.

"You knew!"

"Monsieur Mas, keep your voice down."

I scarcely ever raise my voice, but I had just screamed at him.

"You let them do it," I said flatly.

"Whom? There is no record of anyone visiting Mademoiselle Dechelette, not even," he said pointedly, "you. And no one saw her leave the hospital. The most likely scenario is that she has secreted herself somewhere on the hospital grounds."

"That is nonsense, and you know it."

"She was deeply disturbed when her friend Mademoiselle Blanchot lost her reason. She has been unsettled since then. Surely you had noticed that?"

"It only happened two days ago," I said dryly. "And my duties here do not permit me to spend as much time with Augustine as I would wish. I am grateful to you for this job, Dr. Charcot. But Augustine did send me a letter about Adelaide, and I think my reply was a comfort to her. And I told her news that I am certain would prevent her from leaving or hiding."

"What news was that, Monsieur Mas?"

"Well," I said, my accursed blush staining my cheeks. "I revealed to her my true feelings. I so much as asked her to be my wife."

The doctor, who was in the process of lighting his pipe, laughed until his laughter turned to coughing. I moved to help him, but he held up his free hand.

When he could breathe again he was still smiling. "I wish you had informed me of your intentions first," he said finally.

"Whatever for?"

But he had already launched into his explanation: "—would have served to frighten a girl in her condition," he was saying. I despised pipe smoke, but he was in a cloud of it. "That is the reason she has hidden herself."

"She left the hospital," I said, as calmly as I could.

"No one saw her leave."

"Adelaide did."

"Adelaide? That girl has lost her reason. You know you cannot believe what she tells you, Monsieur Mas." He smiled again as he pulled on his pipe.

"Adelaide told me the truth. And I know Augustine would not hide at a declaration of love from me. I may not be a world-famous doctor, but Augustine is gone, and I believe I know that she was coerced in some way. And I know she was being visited by a very fine couple, another thing Adelaide told me. Augustine is fragile, and it is not difficult to gain her trust. She responds to kindness." My voice began to break. "Dr. Charcot, please help me. Please help Augustine."

The doctor puffed impassively on his pipe, staring past me at the black door.

"Never mind," I said bitterly. "I can see that you do not care enough to help. I suppose this couple who has been visiting Augustine has made generous contributions to your studies." I stood, turning to leave.

"Edouard."

I turned back from the now-open door, surprised at hearing my Christian name.

"Go do what you must, Edouard. And rest assured that your job will be waiting for you when you get back."

It took every ounce of restraint that I had not to slam the door on the way out.

Chapter 53

Charles

"Charles, there is something I never told you." We had not yet left the apartment; I had half undressed V and taken her instead, standing, and forcefully. Augustine still lay in a deathlike swoon, and we spoke as though she were not even there.

"A woman must keep some secrets," she said coquettishly.

"Tell me," I said, leaning forward. I suspected that I was about to hear a very good story.

"Would you like absinthe first?"

"You are a tease, V. No, I would not. I have a feeling that your story will more than suffice for enhancing my mood."

"In that you are right," she said with surprising solemnity. She busied herself for a moment with cutting the cap off a cigar for me, almost as though she were shy to start, she who was never shy.

"Do you know why I decided that we must put bodies in the Paris Morgue?"

"I thought you had long wanted to do that."

"No, no," she said seriously. "I have been enamored of death since I was a child. and I thought about the Empress's Children. "But I had never thought to create death."

"Go on, darling."

"Well, one morning I was staying at the apartment (this is before I met you). I was staying there alone." She placed a pleasant emphasis on that word. "And I woke early. I don't know why. You know how I love to linger in bed!" And we laughed together, and I stroked her thigh through her yellow dressing gown.

"I woke before dawn. Perhaps there was a noise, I do not know. But I felt compelled to go downstairs and outside. And there she was."

"Who?"

"Your cigar has gone out already."

"Damn my cigar, I have to hear this! Who was there?"

"A lovely blonde corpse. I think she had just been left there. She did not belong on these streets, Charles. There was something pure—in her expression, even in death. She was not a prostitute, nor a midinette. She lay in the courtyard with a certain dignity, and she had been posed; I think whoever had killed her had also loved her. I think she had been laid with reverence on that cold, dirty ground. And I fell in love with her."

I hardly knew what to say. It was the last statement, oddly enough, that I found most strange.

"Not like that!" V said, laughing again. "You men really are all the same." I felt a pinch of disappointment; I did not want in any way to be all men to her.

"Don't you see? I fell in love with the idea of purposeful death, Charles. Even as I was talking to you at the Morgue the first day

I was thinking of her. Even as I was looking at her, I wanted to create something beautiful. Something the world has never seen. And we did it! I could not have fallen in love with you, you know, if I had not seen something similar in you."

I thought about how I had wanted to see V displayed, dead, before all Paris, and she said, "And certainly I did not want to be your first experiment!"

"And yet you did not fight me."

"I knew we were destined to be together, just as surely as I knew that I would meet you on that bridge that night. So no, I was not afraid. You only confirmed my suspicions. My knowledge. She stroked my thigh, higher and higher.

"I think it is time for some green," I said. V's tinkling laugh echoed sweetly around the tiny apartment.

"Shh," I cautioned. "You will wake the girl."

"She will not wake," V said confidently. "Not until we wake her."

I liked the sound of that.

"But we are going out to dinner first, remember?" she called from the bidet.

"Then let me dress you," I said.

"Of course, Charles. You know I will never deny you anything."

"Nor I you, my love," I said, rising to mix my suddenly necessary poison while thinking how to dress V.

"Charles, could you make sure that what you choose for me to wear will go with the red scarf I was wearing the night we met on the bridge?"

"Of course, V," I said, but I wondered why, for she was never a sentimental woman.

"Would you like to know where I got that scarf?"

And suddenly I knew, but I wanted her to tell me.

"I took it from the corpse in the courtyard. It was so loosely tied about her hair. There was still blood on it that night?"

"Is there still blood on it now?"

"No, I am afraid there is not. You know I am attached to it, and the blood, once it had stiffened, would have ruined it."

"That is all right," I said cheerfully. "We can always find some more."

I WAS HESITANT to leave the girl, but it seemed important to V, who had not been privy to my conversation with Augustine. And yet, perhaps she did know, and that is why she insisted we go out to dine early, knowing that my appetite, already whetted, would be raging by the time we got home.

"Are you certain she will sleep?" I asked again. V assured me again, and she let me dress her. I chose a yellow frock of satin and faille with wide red sleeves that captured the arm below the elbow and a twist of red satin about the waist. I put around her neck the red silk scarf. I shod her feet in pale brown ankle-length boots with a French heel and fur inside and around the top; and I presented her with a golden velvet cape I had been saving for her birthday. She asked only to add a green hat I had bought her, of which she was particularly fond, and I was pleased to have her ask.

And we went out onto the disreputable boulevard.

"Do you feel like walking, my love?" she asked as we left the building; we had left by the secret stair, giddy in the light fog of the afternoon.

"I feel like having good fare for this dinner."

"And you will need it." She laughed. "I know I suggested the café two blocks down, but I know a much finer place, not too far but just far enough to give you time to dream."

We walked for a while, talking of ordinary things. I did not much bother about which way we walked; even after all this time I did not know much more about this neighborhood than that it was even more of a den of thieves than Belleville, and more dangerous. But we never feared a thing when we walked here. Knowing that you have committed murders gives one an impenetrable aura of danger in itself, and a certain imperviousness to any threat.

I was proud to have V by my side, proud of the covert glances and obvious stares she garnered from both envious women and lustful men, and prouder still to be walking with our secret between us, held tightly in our hands where they clasped one another in my pocket. Several times she reached her fingers to stroke me, and always she found me ready.

Eventually we stopped at a surprisingly posh establishment with deep booths and fine wine. We ordered extravagantly, oysters and duck and curried rice. We talked a great deal, but we did not talk about the girl passed out back at our apartment. It was unnecessary. She was a constant companion at our table, and good company. We formulated our individual plans in delicious silence, knowing that to speak, now, of what was to come would only weaken the drug. It was easy to talk about what sorts of dresses V ought to have for the coming season, knowing that we would confide our secrets to each other later, when the moment for it was real. It was easy to discuss where we wanted to winter: Greece, perhaps, or Sicily. Someplace warm where V would wear a wide-brimmed hat to preserve her perfect porcelain skin, and a delicate shawl for the same reason, while I would turn ruddy in our walks along the beach.

V drank wine without showing any effect at all. I drank absinthe but retained a clarity of mind that I knew came from an excess of adrenaline in my veins. But still the song that throbbed in my blood was sweet. I leaned across the table to kiss V; she reached again for me under the table and it tickled, quite inexplicably and for the first time, and we laughed and laughed. We were merry indeed.

When our meal was finished V insisted I take an extra two glasses of green; she could always gauge my moods, and even the extent of my inebriation, better than I could myself.

The walk home was translucent. I realized I had never truly thought, before, of our apartment as home. The newly risen full moon, full in the early-evening sky, kept us company, playing hide-and-seek among the shredded clouds. V s hand was in my pocket again, but quieter; and we were quieter. Our minds and souls did not need words to communicate now. All of my thoughts were images that transmitted themselves directly to my lover's mind, and I knew that some of the images were hers, sent to me as surely as mine were sent to her. Occasionally I squeezed her hand, that was all.

As we neared home I began to rise out of my beautiful lassitude and become energized. I walked faster; V laughed, and asked that I slow my pace. "What is waiting will be waiting still, no matter how slowly or quickly our steps." I knew she was right, and I slowed, relishing this delirium. The secret steps, when we entered them, seemed to move with the wind that had just kicked up, and seemed to be lit by the moon outside. There was a nimbus around V's hair as she led me up the stair, and her hair moved with the illusory breeze.

And I was happy. A man needs a task, work to do, to be truly happy, and I, who had thought I would forever be a dilettante, had found my life's work. And I had found, by the greatest good fortune, the muse to bring out the artist in me.

As we mounted the steps I was ready.

Chapter 54

From the Journal of Augustine Dechelette

I SHOULD NOT . . . write. But . . . Edouard will help me . . . when he sees what I have sent.

"What is your name?" I asked her that.

"Rose Bertin," she answered. "But you should not be here."

"But I . . ." I tried to sit up . . . I am lying now in a dirty bed, my words . . .

. . . scrawl across the page.

"Be quiet now, Miss, perhaps I can be of help, if only they don't return too soon." Clearly she was . . . afraid. Of V and M. Soulavie.

"No. No. Look, I will . . . give me paper, please." Because I could move even less then, my body could not obey me. "Just a . . . small piece . . . oh, my mind, it floats . . . yes, like that. Can you write, Rose?" . . . I should not write these words here, I should throw this in the fire, before she comes

. . . before she . . .

Chapter 55

Charles

HARDLY HAD WE got in the door when V went to where the girl lay on the bed, I assumed to rouse her. I was using the andirons to light the fire, which had gone out. The room was cold, and for our purposes we would have it warm. V said nothing, but I knew it would not be easy to wake the girl; we had, after all, drugged her heavily. But I imagined that if the girl could not be roused, V would loosen and undo her garments.

So I worked quickly to make the flames, and as I did I felt a delicious anticipation building in my loins and fingertips. I did not turn to watch V undress the girl, luscious as that would have been. At this point I preferred to dream. Augustine was not so lovely as V, but her skin looked soft, her muscles supple. Her eyes were bright morning cornflower to V's gray daytime sky, to Odette's moonlit midnight. And I had never before seen fear the likes of the fear in her eyes: Tabby had been ready to fight. This girl was innocent, a virgin. She was not ready to die, and I was ready to see if she had some fight in her.

"Charles!" V's voice had an urgency I had never heard before. For a moment I feared the girl dead.

But she lay undisturbed, breathing slowly but steadily. For some reason V was whispering. I stooped to hear her, my hand on her shoulder. She shook it off. Never had V shaken away my touch. I reared back in surprise.

"Look at this." V's hand was trembling a little. V's hands, no matter what they did, never trembled. She held out the journal the girl had left on the table. I scanned the page, saw only a scrawl. The girl had regularly shared her diary entries with V, but to my panicking eye there was only purple ink on a page.

"She has gotten help," V hissed. "We must stop it."

"What help?" I found myself whispering as well, although we could have been shouting for all it meant to the unconscious girl.

"Rose." The name was filth in V's mouth.

"What?" I said stupidly.

We had agreed not to call for Rose for as long as Augustine was in the apartment. Rose disgusted me. She was old and unclean. She had worked hard all her life. She was the face of misery. We used her to do our shopping for us, that we might have food at the ready. She took our laundry once a week. We did not even ask that she clean, as I disliked having her around, and once I became used to the filth here, I came to like it.

"Clearly she will be heading to La Salpêtrière, and Edouard. Go. Find her, kill her, and strip her naked."

"Naked? It is still daylight, and you know Rose has no identification on her, no wallet, no pocket journal. She is a washerwoman."

V's eyes were thunder. Once a woman's wrath is turned toward a man, there is no stemming that tide. I should have taken the blame. There was no point fighting the water, the wind. But I found myself angry: V was my wife. She should not have spoken to me so. I resisted the urge to say that it was not I who had left the girl with writing materials.

"Rose was not supposed to be here today."

"But she was. And now this."

"Rose will not have gone far. She hasn't the wits of a dog, anyway."

"Go," V hissed, and she turned away. I wanted to raise my voice. But the flood of rage in that one word stilled my tongue. *I will deal with you later,* I found myself thinking. There were things I had wanted to ask V to do to our young lady. Maybe I would not ask.

I turned and left without a word.

Chapter 56

Edouard

1:35 P.M.

Henri,

Augustine is missing. She left the hospital, I know not when, apparently in men's garb. I do not know where she got the clothing. I have been told that for some time Augustine has been receiving visitors of whom I have been unaware; I spoke to Dr. Charcot but he would tell me nothing. This makes me think that these visitors are moneyed enough to buy the Great Doctor's ignorance.

Forgive me, Henri. I am not myself. I want to run out the door and through the streets of Paris screaming her name. Please contact me as soon as you receive this letter; I will stay here at the hospital, impossible as that seems to me now. I cannot believe that my Augustine would leave the hospital— leave me—in such an irresponsible manner. I fear she has been coerced in some way. I fear she is in danger.

Please help me, Henri.

Chapter 57

Charles

IT WAS DARK but not yet late. I knew that I would catch up with Rose long before she reached her destination, which I was certain was La Salpêtrière. A young man like Augustine's photographer would surely, diligently, always work late. I walked as hurriedly as I could. V had expressly forbidden my using the carriage, and of course she was right, for how would it look to see a well-born gentleman wrestle an old serving woman into a carriage on the street at the dinner hour? People were beginning to flock to the cafés for an early appetizer or that first drink. I longed to stop, just for one quick absinthe. I saw a bar: Danton's Revenge. I had been there—it catered to a rough clientele. I wanted a rough crowd, dangerous men only, no women at all, not even whores.

I slipped into a doorway. I slid my flask out of my inner pocket, felt the reassuring cold outline of her torso, her flowing hair. Even sugared and watered my absinthe would be nothing like the real thing. Stripped of ritual, addiction loses its romance.

I drank. The liquid went instantly sour in my stomach. I gritted my teeth and drank again, and this time the liquor went down smooth. Damn Rose Bertin. Damn Augustine and her scheming. The thought of having to undress the old woman after I'd killed her soured my stomach more, almost to the point of vomiting. I resolutely drank once more and suddenly all was calm within my heart. This was the latest challenge; that was all.

I hurried my step. One bit of unpleasantness, then back to the apartment and its untold pleasures, for surely V would have prepared some vignette especially for me, some scene in which I was to play a most exciting part.

I saw her. She was hurrying through the crowd, and nobody but me would have noticed her at all. It was closer to twilight than I had realized, and yet Rose's agitation showed even before I grabbed her arm.

"You were at the apartment, Rose."

"Oh, no, sir, not today. The mistress told me not to come till she told me."

"You were there. You saw."

"Saw?" The whites of her eyes were whiter than her smock.

"V told me she saw you leaving the building not so long ago." A lie, but a convenient one.

"I was visiting with my friend Nanette. I often do, of an afternoon."

"Why did you go into the apartment?"

She smelt of fear and sweat and onions. The idea of touching her was nauseating; I released her arm so suddenly she stumbled, but she did not run. She did not even seem to realize she was free.

Because she knew me, and knew that she was not.

It was a quick and entirely unsatisfying chore.

And there she lay. I turned away, relieved. This was simply an unpleasant episode; in half an hour I would be back at the apartment.

But then I paused. *Find her, kill her, and strip her naked.* I was loath even to look at the old woman's body clothed, but V wanted that body naked, and I had never before disappointed V; I would not disappoint her now.

But as I leaned over the body, revulsion overcame me, and even my absinthe courage deserted me. I simply could not undress Rose. I could not even remove her apron. The alley was empty, and night was falling fast. There was no danger of being caught here. For a long time I did not even move. I settled, at last, for searching the body. As I gingerly touched and lifted the apron I could smell potatoes and laundry soap. I knew Rose would not have any identifying papers on her person, but I checked the pockets of her apron, I checked the pockets of her skirt: they contained lint particles and roses. I crushed the petals as I pulled them out, and felt the oddest stab of remorse. The petals had almost no color, but they retained a sweet smell, one that would cling to my fingers all the way back to the apartment.

I left her then. It would be the first time—the only time—that I had not done as V wished. She had been my willing slave on so many occasions but I had always been hers. I took a bitter drink from my flask and left the unwanted, anonymous body.

Chapter 58

Edouard

WHEN I WAS summoned to the phone I was ashamed to find myself a bit in awe of it, almost frightened. I had never had reason to use a telephone before. I felt shallow to be fearing such a thing while Augustine was missing, but at the time I was still telling myself that since she had walked out, and not been carried, that she must have wanted to go, no matter how much the thought cut my heart; no matter that it was impossible for me to believe it.

The call was from Henri. I spoke to him briefly: The fact that he sounded exactly the same through the peculiar mouthpiece was less strange to me than that I noticed it at all. After asking a few questions and assuring me that the police were doing all they could to find Augustine, he informed me that he had a murder victim he wanted me to photograph. My Augustine was missing, and I knew that she had not left of her own volition. But Henri was the one person I needed most right now; he had gone so far as to telephone me at La Salpêtrière when he got my note. So I gathered my equipment and was furnished with a carriage and driver—certainly a first— and made all haste to reach the destination provided. And I was grateful to him.

But my thoughts kept going back to Augustine. And the knowledge that she had been receiving visitors, apparently for weeks or months, yet not told me. I was ashamed. Why did she feel she could not confide in me? Augustine's heart was pure, and for her to keep something so vital from me there had to be a reason, and I suspected what it was. That Augustine had been encouraged and assisted in her escape I had no doubt, and I was certain this couple I had been told about was responsible, and equally certain that they had planned this in advance. Only the most favored of Dr. Charcot's hysterics received such mercies as visitors and journals. Surely she had been sworn to secrecy. Oh, that I could have protected her from such predatory people! Did they plan now to set up such shows as Dr. Charcot orchestrated? Or were their plans even more nefarious? Oh, that she had seen fit to confide in me! She was so fragile; at first I had thought her to be what Dr. Charcot said, and that she most certainly was not. This couple, these faceless people, had stolen her. Augustine had been hypnotized by Dr. Charcot; perhaps these people, or one of them, had a similar power of persuasion. From the description I had received, I suspected that it was the woman who had charmed my Augustine. She had been described to me as being exceedingly refined, elegant, and beautiful. Augustine would be bewitched by these things that she thought she could never possess. My beautiful Augustine, her loveliness unsullied by drawing-room manners and false vanity!

This made me think of Odette, and the fact that I had kept Odette a secret from Augustine. Ultimately my behavior with Odette had not exceeded the boundaries of gentlemanly behavior, although it had wandered far indeed into vain foolishness. Yes, Augustine's secret must have been the result of something of that same fascination, mine with what I lusted after but did not ultimately want, hers with what she desperately did want but in no way needed.

The woman described to me was small, blonde, and fine-boned. Suddenly I remembered something.

Mme. Soulavie. The couple who had accompanied Odette to the Tuesday lecture where I had made her acquaintance. Mme. Soulavie was lovely, like a china cup. And small, and blond, and fine-boned. And of great elegance and refinement. And her husband was handsome, sophisticated, and urbane, but even in that one meeting I had been struck by something wolfish about him.

They could have seen Augustine there, on another day. Perhaps I was half-mad with grief and terror, or perhaps I was thinking nonsense in a desperate effort to feel that I was doing something.

There was no record at all of any visits to Augustine at La Salpêtrière. That Dr. Charcot knew I had no doubt. How could he have allowed such a thing? I thought of Adelaide, clad only in her shift, and it still damp from her hydrotherapy session, clinging to her lovely and pathetic body. Augustine had been quite certain that Adelaide was not mad. Surely this girl was mad to come into that room, in that state but now suddenly I hated Charcot, and resolved to leave my position at La Salpêtrière as soon as I had found Augustine and made her my wife.

As I thought these things, the carriage stopped at an ordinary street in an ordinary poor neighborhood full of people on their way home or out to dinner. The weather was half-cloudy and raw. I noticed bits and pieces of things: a woman's pink, waist-length cape worn over a bright green dress; another's black hat with a huge garnet bow; a man's arm around a girl's shoulder; the bright flash of a silver watch being pulled from a pocket; badly dyed yellow feathers in dark hair. I looked for her, I looked for her. Was she still wearing men's clothing? Surely she would not be here anyway, but I could not stop myself. And as I left the carriage I noticed every small woman and every tall man walking by me on the street.

I was met by a uniformed policeman who pointed me toward an alleyway. *Of course,* I thought. *It is always an alleyway, isn't it?* Or a dirty courtyard. And I thought of the murder victim I was to photograph and was ashamed of myself.

Death had not seen fit to stop doing its business while Augustine was missing; I could not stop doing mine. As I turned into the alleyway I noticed a girl begging at the entrance. She was like any other beggar, but something about her stayed with me as I walked up to Henri and warmly shook his hand.

"I have half my force out looking for her now, Edouard," he said instead of hello. "We will find her, I promise you."

"Thank you for taking me seriously." I had not intended to say that.

Surprisingly, Henri laughed a little. "I am long past not taking you seriously, Edouard. Now, just do your work here. It will not take long, and it will do you good to have activity for your mind and hands."

The corpse was that of an old woman—definitely no art piece. She lay, legs akimbo, on her side with her back turned toward me. Her hands were gnarled from arthritis; she had led a hard life. As

I knelt I chanced to look back up the alleyway and saw that the beggar girl was staring intently at us and what we were doing, with more curiosity than the body of an old woman would be likely to draw in this neighborhood. I saw that Henri had noticed her at the same time. "Do not frighten her," I whispered, but still I was surprised when he simply turned away. I turned likewise for a few moments, busying myself with necessary arrangements for my work. I did not realize until I looked back up the alley that I had not been breathing.

The girl was still staring toward us with huge eyes and a terrified expression, but there was something else, too, something I had seen when sometimes I chanced to meet Henri's contacts among the criminal element: They were always aware that something must be in it for them, and they were always on the lookout for a deal. This girl, for all her youth, had that same hungry look. Who could blame her? I thought, and I smiled at her.

She ducked away, and for an instant I thought I'd lost her. But her head reappeared around the corner, her shoulders poised for running while her pinched face tried to smile back at me. Had I given her any money when I entered the alley? I might have, on another day, with more time or better spirits about me, and still I might have on the way out, distracted enough to see only a begging hand. I held my smile as I walked toward her, and for the first time truly looked at her.

She was perhaps twelve, and very pretty, as well as very dirty. She wore a brown cotton dress that did not cover her ankles, and she wore no shoes against the coming winter. Her hair was black, oily, and brushed back from her forehead, evidently with her fingers. Her eyes were also black, and pervaded with a sadness neither fear, nor greed, could displace. Her mouth might never have truly smiled. She had a russet woolen shawl over her shoulders, and she held, to my astonishment, a violin, seeming in good repair. As I approached her she astonished me still more by starting to play. It was a gay little ditty I knew from my youth in the country; here it was heartbreaking. I wanted to ask her to stop hurting me, but of course I did not. Augustine should have been with me, listening to the beggar girl play, and we would give her almost all our money, saving just enough for mocha, and go away happy.

The girl held my eyes as I walked up to her, and then she stopped playing and said, "He gave me a gold coin."

"What did he look like?"

She hesitated and looked down.

"I do not have a gold coin," I said, "but I will see that you are paid."

"It's not . . . it's not just that." She swallowed. "He was a very frightening gentleman, Monsieur."

"I'm sure he was. But I need to know."

"A tall man. Dark brown hair, not long. Short, like a businessman's." She took a breath, and I thought that the man must have been frightening indeed if just the memory of him had her in this state.

"It is all right," I said.

"I will move my corner," she said. "Brown eyes, but fevered. He had been drinking absinthe. I know the look." She glanced down again, and I could have cried for her and what she may have had to do in the evenings to survive. "A very handsome man, in a wolfish way. Very high cheekbones and a full mouth. He came from money. He would have liked to kill me." She had raised her eyes and stared at me straight, and I knew she told the truth.

"Henri!" I called. I turned to the girl. "Stay there, dear. I will come back with money for you."

She nodded and bit her lower lip and reminded me of Augustine, and I fled back down the alley.

"Have you checked for identification?" I asked, grabbing my camera like a drowning man a raft. The serving woman lay sprawled, as I said, quite unlike the other corpses we had found, but the knowledge that we had a witness lent urgency to my curiosity. That and the description of the man as tall and wolfish.

"The Soulavies," I told Henri the moment he could hear me. "They knew Odette. They were at Mme. Gaudet's party. They visited Augustine at the hospital. They are the ones who have Augustine, and they are the Artists of Death, as well."

"There is no reason to think that this woman would be one of your art pieces, Edouard," Henri said indulgently, but yes, I did check. Not that a woman of this class would have any identification anyway."

"She had roses," I said, almost to myself. Petals lay scattered across the pavement. I shook my head. "Sometimes, Henri, I wonder if I have ever actually known another human being in my life."

"She had onions, too, it looks like," he said, still unperturbed. "I know you want to be looking for your Augustine. But I assure you that I have many men on the case right now. I will transmit your latest information. We will scour all of Paris, Edouard. We will find her. For now, it is best for you to concentrate on your work."

He was right, of course. The pebbly leather of my camera soothed my heart a little, though it made me feel shallow to be so easily comforted; but suddenly I was crying as I started to photograph the old woman. I took my pictures instinctively, making all the right movements with my hands, my eyes, my equipment, and seeing nothing. And then I felt remorse—this dead woman deserved the dignity of my attention.

I knelt to photograph her head. Her bonnet was askew and hid her face. I adjusted it and something fell from the ribbon around the crown. A white piece of paper, paper I recognized instantly. Handwriting I recognized instantly.

"Henri!" I cried. "Augustine!"

"What?" He sounded quite as confused as he ought to have.

"It says 21 rue Mazarine. Oh my God, we have found her."

"Edouard, what are you—" I handed him the paper, already rising to pack my equipment.

"That is Augustine's handwriting. The old woman must have been bringing it to me at La Salpêtrière. Henri, it is Augustine, and I must go to her now."

He grabbed my arm. "Not without my help." He turned to one of the men who was at the scene. "Ariste, secure the scene. I must go. Give that girl all the money you've got." He indicated our violinist. " I will see you are repaid."

And bless his dear old crusty heart, he took my arm and hurried me away toward the carriage, toward the rue Mazarine, without even letting me gather up my photographic equipment.

Chapter 59

Charles

WHEN I GOT to the apartment she would ask me if I had gotten rid of the old woman. I did not want to talk. I just wanted my green, my flask being empty. And I wanted my ritual as well: the spoon, four sugar cubes, and a generous portion of water poured slowly, drip by drip, until the liquid reached a perfect louche.

Walking quickly, with fury and chagrin, I remembered that I had not told her all I had felt about Tabby. But she had not needed to ask. She had not needed spoken words, so keen had been all the ties that bound us, skin and muscle and nerve and bone, heart to heart and soul to soul.

I had never before been angry with V, but I was angry with her now. There was never any need to strip the old woman: That had merely been punishment. Would one glance tell her what I was unwilling to tell? She delighted in hearing me recite the details of our kills as we sat out on the boulevards at public cafés, or in the privacy of our elegant bedchamber and the dirty garret bed. At first this had been highly stimulating to me as well, knowing how it excited my lover.

But there had come a subtle change. V needed larger and larger quantities. Even Monique's had satisfied her for barely a day before she insisted we bring Augustine home. Perhaps after we had killed this girl I would recommend a change of scene. Anything can become a drug, and any drug weakens the system to the point where more and still more is required to achieve the requisite effect. If simply killing would satisfy V, I would kill every woman in Europe. But although we committed our kills together, we both knew they really belonged to her. I was more than V's accomplice: I was her willing puppet. Long before I got home I was too tired to think. V met me at the door, but she had not readied the objects she knew I would surely need for my green ritual. And then, as I walked by her to the wheeled glass table where my implements were kept, she said, "Make me a glass, Charles."

I was taken aback. The only time V had ever tasted of my poison was when I had given her an absinthe-dipped sugar cube the night she offered me her life. I glanced at her, but she was not looking at me, and for a moment I felt as invisible as a servant, and my temper flared.

And then she looked into my eyes and laughed her golden laugh.

"It has been a long day, Charles. Look how muddy you are! Come, I will mix your poison, and I will share it with you."

And for a time we spoke no more. She knelt and removed my boots as she always did, and she performed my ritual with her usual sensual grace and efficiency, and when she set our glasses out she did not drink of hers but watched me drink, with an eagerness in her cat's eyes.

"You are certain," she said as I finished my first drink, "that there is no identification on the body."

"Of course," I said. There were flowers under the table—V's hand was petals on my thigh.

"Certain," she repeated.

"I unclothed the old hag," I said cheerfully. I had not thought I would lie. I thought that perhaps my punishment had merely been to be given the distasteful task; perhaps I was right.

"Oh, Charles, that must have been ghastly!" For the first time she took a sip of her drink; her cat's tongue flicked to taste bittersweet green. "Tell me."

And I realized she knew.

"Oh, V," I said; the petals had become a silken rope that played and tugged and pulled me taut. "I do not want to speak of it now. Erase my memories of ancient flesh. You have erased them already, surely you can feel that."

"I thought perhaps that was for the old lady!" She laughed. She was a kitten now, only and always my V. Something had been troubling me on the way home . . . something . . . She finished her drink and said, "Charles! I think perhaps we are floating!" And as she stood she was floating indeed, diaphanous white billows of silk a cloud around her silken hair, her silken white body.

I had a moment's terror that she would bid me to go to Augustine. Instead, she said, "The girl is passed out again; she is most unattractive now." She indicated the bed that I had not dared look at. "Take me here on the flagstones in front of the fireplace, Charles. Show me why it is that you so love your Green Muse."

And I, her servant, her puppy, her lord, and her lover, was more than happy to oblige.

Chapter 60

Edouard

HENRI'S CARRIAGE TRUNDLED through the streets at a reckless speed; mud flew everywhere, and people ran. On the way, something about the address vexed and troubled me and as we pulled up I realized that we had stopped at the very place where I had photographed the murdered body of Lenore DuPrey.

Night was falling fast, and a fitful moon lit the same unsteady towers I had seen before. Still they seemed about to tumble down upon us, almost swaying in the night and the wind.

We flew from the carriage, to the front doorway. But there was a commotion I had at first been too distracted to notice, a gaggle of workmen and a very large, covered object they were attempting to carry up the interior staircase.

"Step aside," Henri said with authority. "Police business." At that moment one of the workmen flung aside what covered the large object: It was a piano. The moon abandoned a cloud to shine her full brightness through the doorway upon the ludicrous scene.

"We have to get in here!" I cried, and the foreman said matter-of-factly, "And we have to get this damn piano up four flights of stairs."

"This is urgent police business," Henri said in his most imperious voice, and as he spoke he tried to move around the piano to mount the staircase.

"We'll be out of your way in no time. We just have to deliver this piano to—" He checked his work order. "Odette Alexandrovna."

"Madame Alexandrovna?" and "Odette?" Henri and I cried at once.

"You know her? 'Cause nobody answered the door up there. But I'll be damned if I'm going to cart this damn thing all the way back to the docks at this damn time of night. So up it goes. Come on, you, what are you standing around for?" He gestured to one of his men. "Officer, go round back and guard the back stair."

The workmen were clearly not impressed with us, police or no. For a moment Henri and I simply stood, frozen by the dream-like scene of piano and moon and impervious workmen in dirty overalls. Then love and fear galvanized me. And I was off to find it before a word could be said. I could hear Henri's raised, frustrated voice behind me, could almost feel his impotence. *A piano! A slum, a murder, an abduction, a three-word ribbon of hope, a beautiful waif with a violin, and a piano, along with a romantic moon!*

But then all thought left me but for one word: Augustine. I ran as I had never run, an old image suddenly flashing into my mind: chasing our best milk cow with my sister Natalie one morning while even the delicious smell of morning sausages could not dissuade us from our unkind, enjoyable pursuit of the poor animal. And then it was gone, and I was racing around the back corner of the building where no one had seen anything of Lenore DuPrey, where fully half the residents could not even be confirmed to be whom they claimed to be.

There was a dirty door, and it was open. Not simply unlocked, but open. The officer lay in muck and blood. Jean-Beauclaire stood over him looking shattered and very young. *In the time it took him to be surprised,* I thought, and I ran up the stairs as fast as I could, hearing faint sounds in the background of angry voices and the creak of the front stairs under their heavy burden. I was too late; I could not be too late. If Augustine were dead I would be dead already myself, and that irrational thought was my hope and my impetus.

There was only one apartment on the fourth floor. I threw myself against the door and almost fell headlong into a filthy gray room. The door was unlocked, and so old that it had hardly taken a shove to split its hinges, to in fact bust the wood to wild, flying pulp.

"Augustine!" I cried. "Augustine!" with my soul in my mouth.

And there she was. She lay on sheets so old as to have almost no color, and she was barely conscious, with an open laudanum bottle spilling its contents out onto the floor next to the bed. But her eyes, when their blue beam met my own, unremarkable eyes, were clear.

"Edouard," she said softly. "I knew you would come. They lied to me. They said . . . they said you were one of them." And I saw that her blue belied her condition—she was obviously drugged.

"Augustine," I said. "Are you all right?" As preposterous a question as the piano I could hear coming up the stairs.

"No," she said. "They made me drink absinthe. They made me drink laudanum. I feel awful."

"Where are they?"

"You didn't catch them?"

"No," I said regretfully, acutely aware of how badly I had failed her.

"You won't," she said. "They are . . . hardly human, Edouard. Oh, will you ever forgive me?" And she was crying, partly, I knew, from the drugs, and partly from her good heart.

"Yes. They tricked you, didn't they?"

"She seemed so . . . oh, Edouard, she was so lovely! So loving. He was . . . like a wolf. He always frightened me. But I thought . . . I thought that because he loved her, he must be kind, that only his exterior was hard. Edouard, I kept their visits from you, their plans! They said that they would send for you after they had me released from the hospital, but then they said . . . they said—" And her eyes began to close, her voice to fade.

I had been kneeling at the floor next to the bed; I rose and sat next to her and cradled her in my arms, and she felt like every good dream I had ever had.

"Augustine, Augustine, there is nothing to forgive," I said to her now-sleeping form. "When I look at you, I see the world."

Suddenly the racket outside intensified, and Henri burst into the room as if shot from a cannon.

"How's the piano?" I asked equably; at this moment nothing could distress me.

"Where are they?"

"They have gone."

Augustine's eyes opened again, and we realized that the perpetrators had gotten away. But still I had the presence of mind to ask Augustine, "Do you brew a good pot of coffee, my love?"

Chapter 61

Charles

"CHARLES, WE MUST go. I hear a noise downstairs."

"They could not have found us, V."

"You did not strip the body, did you? It is likely the girl gave Rose Bertin something by which to find us." She spoke without rancor, moving about the room, gathering. My hat, my coat, her cape, her red scarf.

"Go."

"V."

"They already know it's us," she said reasonably. "Let us see what fools the police are, shall we?"

There were sounds at the street floor, a strange, deep knocking and voices.

"Come along now," V said lightly, slipping my coat onto my shoulders and standing on tiptoe to set my hat on my head. "We are not done with each other."

"But—"

"The secret stair. We will not be caught. Here, take your knife," as she handed it to me.

"But she—"

"Oh, go, Charles," she hissed, and shoved me toward the stair with the clucking noise a wife saves for a foolish husband.

Chapter 62

From the Journal of Augustine Dechelette

I REMEMBER VERY little of what transpired in Charles and V's apartment, and I am grateful for that. I do remember waking to Edouard's concerned eyes; I will never forget it. And there was a Capt. Bezier there, who fluttered about like a wingless bird in his concern. It was very endearing. And other policemen, and questions for which I was not ready.

I do not know if I will ever be ready.

But Edouard assures me there is time for questions, and that the priority right now is that I rest and get well. And he does not mean well in the sense of recovering from green disease! Dr. Charcot has apparently agreed that my fortitude and resourcefulness (his own words) prove that I am not in fact suffering from green disease and that, indeed, I never was. That would make me angry if it did not make me so happy!

Maman and Papa have been told of what happened, and told also, by Edouard, that he wishes to make me his wife. Dr. Charcot has given his hearty approval, and a nice recommendation of Edouard as well, and that seems to be good enough for my parents. They are to arrive within days, and I fear my heart will burst. Although I have had to reassure him, I know that they will love and respect Edouard as I do.

I am to stay at the hospital until I am strong, but without water therapies and dreadful menus that include only salad. Then, after we are married (married!), Edouard and I will be living in his bachelor apartment. He says it is not good enough, but that the bedroom will hold a bigger bed . . . well, he could not really say that, not in so many words, and his cheeks went crimson for the longest time! I find that my own blushing is now entirely a thing of the past. At least I was cured of something at the Hôpital Salpêtrière.

This makes me think of Adelaide. I have not yet seen her, but Edouard assures me that we will see her as soon as I am stronger. I am no longer lodged with the hysterics but in an apparently ever-so-secret wing reserved for well-to-do society women who need a rest from the rigors of everyday life. But I want to see her desperately, and I will visit her regularly for as long as it takes her to get well. I believe in Adelaide, and I always will.

But now I will lay down my pen, because for once I really am tired when I am supposed to be, and because Edouard is due to arrive soon, and I will not have his future wife looking haggard, or tired, or anything at all like a mental patient!

Chapter 63

Charles

I HAD ALWAYS known what my fate was to be. Ever since V had given me her life, in that dimly lit room that had seemed strewn with red roses, I had known. She had given me her life to do with as I pleased. I could have had what, since boyhood, had been my deepest dream: I could have had my love displayed naked, covered only by a sheet, in front of all Paris. To everyone—*to anyone*—any vagrant who walked in off the street could have had his fill of her nakedness.

I let her live. And in turn I knew the price I was to pay for that. If our activities were discovered, I was to go to the bank of the Seine, to the same quay where I had met V in the rain not so long ago. I was to undress myself completely, having previously taken care to destroy any identifying papers and discarding my wallet and watch in the flowing water, and use my knife to die by my

360 JESSIE PRICHARD HUNTER

own hand. As V had once used the knife with which she had just pared an apple.

But there are people, now, who know my name, know my face. V never told me what she would do after the event of my death. If I were not to appear in the Morgue. And of course I had not asked. She would follow me, I knew. And I cannot have that.

There is weeping in my heart. I listen to the soft old voice reciting familiar words as I write. I pause to thank the waiter, who has just brought over glass and clinking ice, the familiar glint of silver spoons on a crystal tray; the poet pulls himself out of his verse to say, "Thank you kindly, Charles," and reaches for his poison. We are silent as each prepares the green in his own way.

"Like the rain falling on the city." Paul finishes reciting his work, drinks. "V, you have hardly said a word."

I can still feel the soft rain against my forehead, feel it turn to the silk of V's petticoats against my cheek. The world is good; the world is as it should be.

She does not answer him. She turns to me as I stir my clouded drink. "Charles, you know how it is to be."

Epilogue

THIS MORNING I was called upon to perform a familiar service. I had just finished my cup of coffee, thinking with pleasure of how Augustine has assured me that she makes the finest cup of coffee in Paris. Though, in fact, my darling girl has never actually made a cup of coffee in Paris.

I took care to give Martin several sous that were neither Argentine nor Spanish, pleased that he has gotten beyond the habit of biting them to assure their authenticity. I had my camera ready, my slides, and my enthusiasm, if not a satisfactory bellyful of coffee. For I seem to float, these days, on a quiet joy that grows with every letter I receive, with each visit I make to a small provincial village where the clocks do not yet run on Paris time.

I like to imagine Augustine moving through her day. I could almost blush at the photographs I have taken of her, because the poses indicative of hysteria are so indelicate, and even though I know that the Augustine I saw was not the Augustine I am going to take to wife, that she had taken on a role as an actress recites her lines and moves about the stage, still the pictures disturb me. That they were the finest pictures of hysteria that I had ever seen or taken I do not doubt, and that irony is not lost on me. I prefer to think of Augustine in her garden, or baking, which she tells me she loves, or going through the fine linens and silks of her hope chest with her mother.

Dr. Charcot had decided to harbor no ill will toward me. Augustine no longer hates him, although she tells me she considered confessing that all her posing was a sham, but she was afraid he might think her mad! "I played the good girl," she said, and for a moment I was confused.

"You are a good girl, " I protested, and oh how she laughed! And how I loved all that I do not yet know about this girl it seems I know everything of. She is, after all, an actress!

We plan, after our marriage, on visiting Adelaide often, for she shows no signs of recovering from her own ordeal. And of course we will see Lucille as well: Augustine feels toward her something like love, and Lucille returns her warmth with the occasional word or glance into our eyes.

I was thinking of Augustine as I rode the omnibus to the location I had been given, down by the Seine, which sparkled intimately in the newly sown spring sun.

But almost instantly it was as though the sky had gone cold and dark. Death is always sobering, but it was more than that.

For as soon as I saw the body I thought about the Artists of Death. The way they had posed their murder victims: the calm of the clasped hands, the elegance of a false surrender. And myself on my knees, my hand running lightly down the pebbled leather, sighting the body in the camera's lens, gauging the light. Was there so much difference between us? No, I did not murder; I was not like them. But when I photographed their work, was I not doing their final bidding? Was I not complicit in completing the artistic process?

How Henri would laugh at that! Henri values me, and I value him—if not his insights, then his trust, his ability to listen to an artist. He still laughs at what he calls my "poetic soul," but he is inordinately pleased about my engagement to Augustine, and he has given me a raise in pay. And although I know that I will continue in my work at La Salpêtrière, I now know where my heart truly lies. Not with the dead, although it is the dead from which I create my own art. No, it is and always has been the causes of death that truly interest me, that absorb my mind and heart both inside my darkroom and out. So I will continue to let the dead speak to me, to tell me their stories and, sometimes, to solve the mysteries of their deaths.

It is all I can do.

On the edge of the Seine all was quiet and still; even the water seemed to have gone silent. Henri had never seen him, but I knew him immediately: He lay naked and soldier-straight, his hands crossed on his chest and his feet pointing toward heaven. And a great gash across his neck, which he could not possibly have made himself.

And I knelt, and ran my hand down the pebble-grain leather of my camera, and breathed in the damp, the decay, the dawn, and began my work.

Acknowledgments

I WOULD LIKE to thank my agent, Jeff Gerecke, for his diligence and tenacity; my editor, Marguerite Weisman, for her vision; Leah and Joshua Bayer, just for being; and David Bayer, for every little thing.

About the Author

JESSIE PRICHARD HUNTER is the author of the psychological thriller *Blood Music*, forthcoming from Witness Impulse. She currently resides in New York's Hudson Valley with her husband and two children.

www.witnessimpulse.com

Discover great authors, exclusive offers, and more at hc.com.

If you loved THE GREEN MUSE, check out these
other Witness titles. Read on for excerpts from

Prince

by Rory Clements
and

Cambridge Blue

by Alison Bruce

Prince

Chapter 1

FOUR MEN STARED down at the body of Christopher Marlowe. A last trickle of bright gore oozed from the deep wound over his right eye. His face and hair and upper torso were all thick with blood. One of the four men, Ingram Frizer, held the dripping dagger in his hand.

Frizer looked across at Robert Poley and grinned foolishly. 'He came at me.'

'Boar's balls, Mr Frizer, give me the dagger,' Poley said angrily.

Frizer held out the dagger. All the living eyes in the room followed the tentative movement of the blood-red blade. A sliver of brain hung like a grey-pink rat's tail from its tip. Poley took the weapon and wiped it on the dead poet's white hose. Suddenly, he struck out with the hilt and caught Frizer a hard blow on the side of his head. Frizer lurched backwards. Poley pushed him to the floor and jumped on him, knees on chest, hitting his head again, harder, pounding him until Nick Skeres tried to pull him away.

Poley stood back, shook off Skeres's hands and brushed down his doublet with sharp irritation. He was not a tall man, but he was strongly built and the veins in his muscled forearms and temples bulged out and pulsed. He kicked Frizer in the ribs. 'You were only supposed to gag him and apply the fingerscrew, you dung-witted dawcock. Not kill him.'

The afternoon sunlight of late May slanted in through the single, west-facing window. The presence of the men and the body made the room feel smaller than it really was. It was cleanly furnished; a well-turned settle made of fine-grained elm, a day bed where the body now lay, a table of polished walnut with benches either side and half-drunk jugs of ale atop it. The dusty floorboards were scuffed by the men's shoes; there was, too, a lot of blood and a few splashes of ale on the wood between the table and the day bed.

'And you ...' Poley turned to Skeres. 'You were supposed to hold him. He was out of his mind with drink and you couldn't keep a grip.'

Ingram Frizer pulled himself painfully to his feet. He was doubled over, clutching his side where Poley's boot had connected.

Poley handed him the dagger. 'Here, take it. And listen well: it was *his* dagger – Marlowe's dagger. He came at you, pummelled your head with it. You fought back. In the struggle, the blade pierced his eye. You were defending yourself – it was an accident.'

Frizer took the dagger. He was slender with a lopsided face, the left eye half an inch higher than the right. The skin had been cut from the side of his head by Poley's beating. There was a livid gash, almost to the bone. His head and ribs throbbed, but he understood Poley's plan well enough. 'I liked this dagger,' he said, turning the weapon over in his hands and examining the ornate hilt and narrow, sharp-pointed blade. 'Cost me half a mark.' He tried to laugh.

'Well, it'll be Crown property now. Marlowe was always fighting. He was going to kill you. It's a simple story; remember it.' Poley turned to the third man, Skeres. 'And you, Mr Skeres.'

Skeres nodded. His bulbous face was sweating heavily. He mopped a kerchief across his brow. His gaze kept flicking towards the body, and then across to the fourth man, who stood close by the door. So far he had said nothing.

'No, let's change that,' Poley said, shaking his head slowly. 'Someone might recall that dagger. Say it was yours, Mr Frizer, but Marlowe snatched it off you, then you wrenched it away from him as he battered you. You struck backwards wildly, didn't know what you had done. Got that? And the knife didn't cost you half a mark, it cost you a shilling. The rest of the story holds.' Poley suddenly slammed his fist down on the table. 'Where's the screw?'

Ingram Frizer pointed to the floor beneath the window, to where a five-inch by four-inch vice of iron lay. It was designed to crush the fingers of a hand, slowly and painfully.

'Do I have to think for both of you? Pick it up!'

Frizer scurried across the room and brought the device back to Poley, who thrust it inside his doublet.

At last the fourth man spoke. He was heavy-set with a wispy beard. 'I'm going now. Wait two hours, drink some ale, then call the constable and the coroner. None of this comes back to me or my master. I was never here.'

'No,' Poley agreed. He understood well enough. There must only ever have been four men in this room, not five.

The man took one last look around the room and met the eyes

of Poley, Skeres and Frizer. 'Not one word.' He lifted the latch and silently left the room.

The other three watched him go. A seagull landed on the sill of the open window, defecated, then flew off. 'There's a problem,' Skeres said, shaking the sweat out of his eyes.

'The only problem,' Poley said, 'is *you*. You're a flaccid prick of a man, Skeres.'

'We've got to say what they were fighting about, haven't we?'

'It was the bill, of course. The reckoning. Frizer said Marlowe had drunk more so should pay more. Mr Marlowe wanted to quarter the bill evenly.'

'The coroner will never believe it.'

Poley laughed. 'Pour the ale, Mr Skeres, then light me a pipe. How has a coney like you ever lived this long? Hear that, Mr Frizer? Mr Skeres says the coroner will never believe it.' Poley laughed again, louder this time, and Frizer and Skeres laughed nervously with him.

Cambridge Blue

Chapter 1

ROLFE STREET WAS only a short walk from the heart of Cambridge, but it was a perpetual backwater, seeing no accidental visitors and few daytime inhabitants.

A lone man stood on the pavement waiting to speak to Lorna Spence: the same woman who was spying on him from her first-floor window. So far he'd knocked twice, but she had no intention of letting him know she was at home.

She stood behind a carefully placed ruck in the curtains. She knew he couldn't see her but, even so, she kept perfectly still in case he glanced up and caught the flicker of her shadow.

Lorna Spence had gone to bed wearing nothing but yesterday's knickers, and that was all she wore now as she studied the top of his head.

He took a few short steps towards the door, and then a few

towards the street. Again he ran his hand in an impatient foray through his hair, completing the gesture by clasping it across the back of his neck. He drew closer to the door, leaning in towards it and listening. His hand, still on his neck, massaged the rigid muscles which locked the top of his spine.

He was obviously stressed.

She imagined him swearing under his breath. He took a step back and his gaze shot up to her window, boring into the gap between the curtains. He seemed to stare straight into her face, but she didn't blink.

A tingling feeling sprang across her bare skin, racing in waves across her shoulders and trickling across her small, freckled breasts. Only her chest moved, rising and falling ever quicker; trying to keep pace with her heartbeat.

Lorna waited for him to knock again, but instead he stepped away and out of sight of her little spyhole. She moved closer to the gap and crept around until she had a view of the closed end of the cul-de-sac. She soon located him again. He stood on the edge of the kerb with his hands on his hips.

'Go away. Go on, get in your car and drive away,' she whispered down to him.

His attention had settled on the rows of parked vehicles flanking each side of the road. She knew he wouldn't recognize any of them.

Then he left, walking briskly towards his own car at the end of the street. He'd accepted what she already knew: that he had no reason to believe she was at home.

She waited. He started the engine and let the postman pass without cross-examination. Then he pulled away and drove out of sight. But she still waited, watching the road until she'd counted to one hundred and was sure he wouldn't return.

And then she exhaled with a long puff. Her heartbeat gradually slowed and her pulse steadied.

The letterbox creaked as it opened and there was an echoing snap as it shut. The junk mail made a heavy thud as it hit the hallway's tiled floor. She leant over the handrail and checked, in case an unexpected letter looked tempting enough for a dash downstairs.

A large holiday brochure lay face down, obscuring any other post that may have been underneath. A photo of a caravan park and the words 'Family Entertainment' jumped out at her through the clear plastic envelope.

'Why me?' she groaned. Last week the mail had been sit-in baths and stair-lifts. What a waste of time.

Her dressing table was a wide antique pine chest of drawers with a reproduction pine mirror on top. She only owned the mirror and the battery clock next to it. It was 8.35 a.m. and she was going to be late for work.

In the circumstances, late would be a good thing. But not too late, she couldn't afford trouble at the office as well. She padded into the bathroom, pulled off her knickers and threw them into the corner with the rest of the week's laundry. She ran the hot tap until the water flowed warm, and meanwhile damped down her short, ash-blonde hair, working her fingers through the feathered strands at the back so they lay close to the nape of the neck.

She dressed quickly and chose Warm Mocha lipstick. She ran it back and forth across her lips, then dabbed it on to her cheekbones, rubbing it in to give the approximation of blusher. That would do.

She checked her reflection, aware that the skim of freckles across each cheek and a lucky gap between her two front teeth gave her face more character than any layer of make-up.

She grabbed her bag and hurried downstairs. As she reached the bottom stair, she could see other letters buried under the brochure.

Five pairs of her shoes were lined up beside the door; in two-inch heels she made five foot five. Just.

She reached for the post, slipping her feet into her highest shoes as she turned the envelopes over. There were four. She flicked through them. Mobile phone bill, bank statement, credit card bill. Then the fourth. White, A5, and emblazoned with an advert for a bank loan. But it was the addressee's name which caught her eye. Miss H. Sellars.

Lorna frowned. A chill tickled her scalp, then vanished. How strange, she thought. She shook her head and smiled. What an amazing coincidence. She suddenly wondered whether the holiday brochure was similarly addressed. She slid it from under the other post.

The black print on the white label jumped out at her. Instant fear washed the smile from her lips. She recoiled and the post scattered, tumbling from her fingers on to the floor. The corner of the clear envelope hit the mat, bounced and landed, slapping down flat on its face.

She opened the front door and hurried away down the street. Behind her, the hall tiles stayed cold, rebuffing the unanswered ring of the telephone upstairs.